PRINCESS OF REALMS

BOOK TWO OF THE FIRST WITCH SERIES

EMBER EAST

Cover Design by Muhammad Kaleem

To my wonderful Discord family,
Between the Pages,
Thanks for everything

Also to a younger Ember,
just look at how far we've come

Trigger Warnings

Abuse

Alcohol

Animal sacrifice

Blood

Demons

Fire

Kidnapping

Murder

Occult

PTSD

Sexual Assult

Sexually Explicit Scenes

Stalking

Torture

War

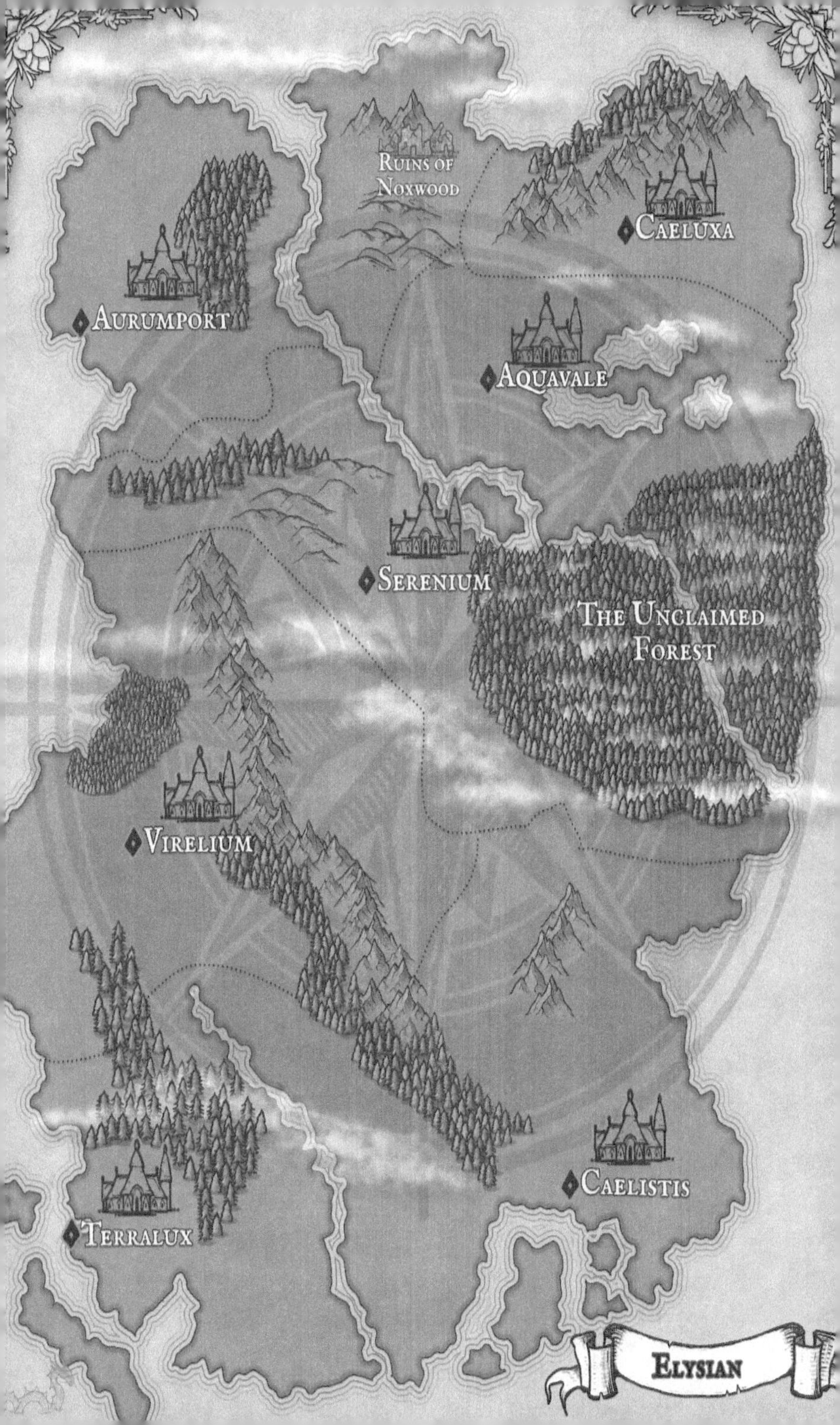

Ruins of Noxwood
Caeluxa
Aurumport
Aquavale
Serenium
The Unclaimed Forest
Virelium
Caelistis
Terralux
Elysian

Contents

Chapter One

The night draped its dark veil over the city as I moved on silent feet down the desolate back alley. The moon, barely a crescent, struggled to pierce through the thick canopy of clouds, leaving me to navigate the uneven path by the feeble glow of distant streetlights. My long silver hair flowed behind me like a ghostly banner.

I reached a rusted iron door, its surface corroded by the passage of time. I rapped my knuckles on it, the sound echoing in the dark stillness of the night. With a slow, protesting creak, the door cracked open revealing a wiry, greasy man on the other side. Suspicion carved deep lines into his sallow face as he peered out at me. "Vale," he hissed, his voice dripping with bitterness. "Get out of here, you've brought us enough trouble."

He moved to slam the door shut, but my arm shot out with unnatural speed, stopping it. I locked eyes with him, my lips curving into a wry smile. "Now, now, Simon," I cooed, my voice all velvety charm. "Is that any way to treat an old friend?"

"You're no friend of mine," he snapped, his eyes narrowing into thin slits. "And Jaks says you aren't to be allowed in here anymore. Not after your friend's last visit."

Wren, my best friend, had paid Jaks a visit about a month ago after the half-demon had sold out information on my whereabouts. That encounter had not been a friendly one, and Wren had ended up roughing up both Jaks and Simon.

"Oh?" I raised an eyebrow, feigning ignorance. "Whatever do you mean?"

"You know damn well what I mean." Simon crossed his arms in defiance. "You've got some nerve showing up here again. Get lost."

My fingers closed around his neck before he could even blink and I tightened my grip on his windpipe, cutting off his air supply. He made a strangled noise and his eyes widened in shock.

"Listen, Simon," I said, my tone laced with a dangerous edge. "I've got no time for your shit. I just want a few minutes to talk to Jaks. I'll be gone before you know it. Now, let me in."

His fingers frantically clawed at mine as he choked. I maintained the pressure, unyielding until the fight began to ebb from his eyes. Finally, he nodded weakly and I released my grip. He stumbled and bent over, his hands on his knees as he sucked in great gulps of air.

"Out of my way." I stepped inside, not waiting for his invitation. I strode into the dim interior, my keen eyes adjusting to the shadows. I had been here with Wren more times than I could count, and I'd memorized every inch of this dump.

The seedy bar lay hidden within the heart of the city's underbelly, a sanctuary for those who thrived in the shadows and reveled in the murkiness of their dealings. It was a place where the damp scent of old wood, aged liquor, and decades of secrets mingled in the air. The bar exuded an atmosphere of grime and desperation, as though it had absorbed the sorrows of countless patrons over the years.

The bar's interior was a labyrinth of worn, wooden beams and low-hanging ceilings, giving the illusion that the place had been carved directly into the bowels of the city. The walls, once a faded crimson, now sported dark stains that whispered of past brawls and spilled drinks. Each booth offered a semblance of privacy, an illusion of escape from the harsh realities outside, where patrons could huddle together in whispered conversations.

The bar itself was a long, scarred slab of wood, pockmarked by the imprints of countless elbows and the remnants of long-forgotten confrontations. Behind it, rows of dusty bottles stood like silent sentinels, their labels faded and illegible from years of use. The bartender, a grizzled figure with a face that bore the stories of a hundred bar fights, moved with a slow, deliberate grace as he mixed drinks and passed them to the few patrons brave enough to venture out on this desolate night.

The clientele was a motley crew of lost souls, Otherworlders nursing their own private demons as they sought refuge in the dimly lit corners. Shadowy figures huddled at worn, sticky tables, their whispered conversations blending with the melancholic strains of a forgotten jazz tune playing softly from a crackling jukebox in the corner.

Jaks was seated in his corner booth, his head bent over a table. A woman leaned over him, her mouth moving close to his ear, her hands massaging his shoulders. Another girl sat on the bench opposite him, her skirt riding high on her thighs.

As I walked towards Jaks's table, I noticed several people giving me suspicious looks. They recognized me and had good reason to be wary. I wasn't a regular in this den, but my reputation preceded me. They knew what I was now and they knew better than to fuck with me. Word spreads fast among the Otherworlders of this realm and they had heard about my recent exploits in Erebus, the demon realm. Of course, I supposed that might give some reckless people a reason to pick a fight anyway.

I maintained a steely composure as I continued my approach. They watched me like predators sizing up potential prey, yet they hesitated to engage, their caution born of fear. I was something different, something new while also something ancient. Witch.

"Jaks," I spoke his name with familiarity as I stood in front of his booth.

At the sound of my voice, Jaks and the two girls seated with him at the table all turned their heads in my direction. Jakslocked his beady coal-black eyes onto mine and his expression hardened. He rose slowly from his seat and the two girls stood up with him. A hushed exchange of words passed between Jaks and the brunette on his right, prompting her to scurry away.

The remaining girl sidled up to Jaks, her gaze sweeping over me as if I were an inconvenience. I shot her a cold look. "Why don't you give us a minute, sweetheart?"

She scoffed and tossed her hair over her shoulder. "Excuse me? Who do you think—"

Jaks interrupted her abruptly, his voice gruff and commanding, "Do as she says, Kari."

Kari's expression hardened further and she opened her mouth to protest, but Jaks's grip on her shoulder tightened, his fingers digging into her skin. "We'll pick up where we left off later, now go."

A flash of annoyance crossed her face and I could tell she was burning with the desire to give me a piece of her mind. Instead, she shot Jaks a venomous look and, with a sharp turn on her heel, stomped away.

"What the hell are you doing here, witch?" Jaks growled, his eyes narrowing into slits. "You're not welcome here. And after what happened last time—"

"Save it," I snapped back at him, my patience running thin. I had no intention of indulging Jaks's whining or dwelling on the past. I had come here for a reason and that was the only thing on my mind.

I took a seat at his table, casually putting my feet up as if I owned the place. The audacity of my actions seemed to fuel Jaks's anger even further. "Just give me a bounty contract and I'll be on my way."

"Are you crazy?" he hissed, his voice rising a notch. "I'm not giving you a bounty. After what your friend did—"

"Don't make me do something I don't want to do, Jaks," I interrupted him again, my voice a low, menacing whisper. I held his gaze, watching for the flicker of fear that I knew was there, fueled by the rumors of my recent confrontation with the demon lord Zephyrian. "Give me a bounty, or things are going to get messy real quick."

"Fuck off," Jaks spat, his eyes glittering with anger, but beneath it, a lingering hint of worry remained.

I leaned in closer, my elbows on the table, narrowing the distance between us. "What's it going to be, Jaks? Should I torch this place, or should I torch you?" I smiled at him, my eyes burning with the same fire I threatened him with.

His lips thinned and he stared at me, his gaze hard, but the underlying unease simmered beneath the surface. For a tense moment, Jaks held his silence, his eyes locked onto mine. The dimly lit bar had gone quiet, anticipation swirling around us like a suffocating fog. The patrons watched Jaks and me with unabashed curiosity. Then, with a muttered curse, he snapped his fingers at a half-demon guard standing close by. The thug brought over a worn leather folio and Jaks reached in and extracted a stack of papers, slamming them down onto the table in front of me with a smack.

"Fine, take a damn bounty, then get the fuck out of here," he growled, his frustration boiling over as he shoved the files toward me.

I offered a self-satisfied smirk in response to his begrudging compliance. "Thank you," I replied, my tone dripping with condescension.

Jaks's eyes flashed with resentment and suppressed anger, his jaw tightly clenched.

I leisurely began to shuffle through the files, each one representing a dangerous demon with a price on its head. My fingers danced over the papers until I found the dossier of the biggest, most notorious demon among them all. I plucked it from the stack, holding it up with a wicked gleam in my eyes. "I'll be taking this one," I declared, my voice filled with a perverse sense of anticipation. "He looks fun."

Jaks's pallor drained of color as he stared at the chosen file, disbelief creeping into his expression. "Have you gone insane?" he snapped.

I feigned innocence, raising an eyebrow. "What do you mean?" I asked, my tone infuriatingly nonchalant.

"Don't play stupid with me," Jaks hissed, his patience wearing thin. "You know exactly what I'm talking about."

With a sly smile, I leaned closer, my eyes locking onto his. "Well, enlighten me," I taunted, my boredom thinly veiling the danger lurking beneath the surface.

"I know why you're really here," Jaks snarled, his gaze burning into me.

I frowned. What was he getting at?

"I'm not a fool." He jabbed his finger on the paper, his eyes blazing. "You can't be serious. You want to hunt this bastard down?"

I stared at him. "What are you talking about?"

"Don't pretend you don't know." He sneered. "There's no way you could take down this monster. You'll end up dead."

"Well, then you'll finally be rid of me," I said, smiling.

"Are you suicidal? He'll tear you apart," Jaks scoffed. "If you're determined to kill yourself, why don't you just go jump off a building? It'll be much quicker."

"Thanks for the tip," I said, still grinning. "But I'm good."

Jaks's face turned to stone, his features hardening with a chill that matched his harsh words. "I always knew you were a cold-hearted bitch, but I never thought you were insane."

I regarded him with a cool detachment, my smile fading. "Careful, Jaks," I whispered softly, my voice carrying a hint of dangerous allure. "You don't want to piss me off."

His eyes flared with a volatile mixture of anger and pride. "Do you think I'm afraid of you? Just because you can use some magic doesn't make you better than the rest of us."

A sinister glint danced in my amber eyes as I leaned in closer. "Doesn't it?" I hissed, my voice laced with a venomous promise. "I could kill you myself, right now, without using a speck of magic."

"Get the hell out," Jaks snarled, his voice cracking with barely contained rage.

I didn't flinch, my eyes stayed locked onto his, a silent challenge. He glared back at me, unwilling to yield.

With a subtle smile, I finally rose from my seat and turned to leave, my every step echoing in the quiet bar. As I headed for the door, Jaks's angry words sliced through the air behind me. "This is the last time I ever do business with you, Vale. Stay the hell away from me and my establishment."

I couldn't help but chuckle under my breath.

When I reached the exit, the worn door creaked open and Simon stepped back to allow me to pass. His eyes were wary as if he half-expected me to turn back and stir up more trouble.

A wry, self-assured smirk played on my lips as I passed by him. "Don't worry," I assured him. "I'm just leaving."

"Good," Simon grunted, his tone curt. "And don't come back."

Stepping outside, I was met with a gust of cool night air, which carried the faint scent of distant rain. The city's dimly lit streets stretched out before me, a labyrinth of secrets and shadows.

I took a deep, cleansing breath, savoring the freedom that came with being outside that grim establishment. I had a new target now, a purpose that burned within me like a relentless fire. The demon's days were numbered and the anticipation of the hunt surged through my veins, invigorating me.

A shiver ran down my spine, but it wasn't from the chilly night air; it was the thrill of the chase that consumed me. The demon, the one whose actions were etched in the dossier I held, had a date with destiny and I would be the instrument of his reckoning.

Chapter Two

The dark night held no secrets from me, not with my keen supernatural eyesight. The world took on an eerie, silver hue as I ventured deeper into the heart of the run-down part of the city. My hair shimmered in the moonlight as I moved with silent grace, navigating the twisted streets that had long since fallen into disrepair.

My destination loomed ahead – a decrepit, ominous structure that had once been a grand hotel. Its glory days were buried beneath layers of grime and decay, visible only in the faded elegance of its ornate façade. Time had not been kind to this place and now it stood as a sinister relic of forgotten luxury.

I pushed open the creaking double doors, their paint peeling and revealing the skeletal wood beneath. The lobby was a haunting scene frozen in time. A broken chandelier hung precariously from the ceiling, casting long, ghostly shadows across the cracked marble floor. Tattered remnants of velvet curtains billowed like mournful spirits in the cold breeze that swept through the broken windows.

"Are you sure this is a good idea, daughter?" The First Witch, Rowena, spoke in my head. She was always with me now thanks to a ritual I had performed that merged our souls. The ramifications of which had still not completely come to light.

"Oh, come on. This is an excellent idea." I said to her, smirking.

The atmosphere was thick with an unsettling stillness as if the very air held its breath in fear. The demon I sought had been lurking within these forsaken walls for some time now, preying on squatters who had sought refuge in this grim sanctuary. Murmurs of its vileness had reached my ears. Tales of grotesque murders that had gone unpunished, for none had been brave or reckless enough to confront the monster.

But that was precisely the kind of dangerous situation I yearned for now. The thrill of the hunt, the rush of danger – they were the flames that burned within me. Flames I stoked to burn brighter than the emotions I had been trying to avoid for weeks now.

I had been born into this world of shadows and magic and I had embraced it wholeheartedly. Tonight, I would face more than just one demon and justice would be served.

The hotel's haunted corridors beckoned and with each step, I ventured deeper into the heart of darkness, where the murderous demon's dark presence awaited.

Every floor of the abandoned hotel was a twisted maze, a nightmare of dilapidated hallways and doors leading to rooms that held nothing but the shroud of dust and cobwebs that clung to their desolate interiors. The once-elegant establishment had crumbled into a macabre parody of its former glory, the grandeur of bygone days now replaced by decay and despair.

"I think you should stop this foolish quest and turn back now," Rowena said.

"Your unease is noted and I'll take it under advisement," I told her coolly.

As I ascended to an upper level, I sensed a subtle change in the air. A cold, tingling sensation crept over my skin, raising the fine hairs on the back of my neck. The atmosphere grew heavy, like a thick blanket that threatened to smother me.

I knew I was getting close.

My blackened fingers reached toward my hip and closed around the hilt of my axe, its cold steel a reassuring presence in my hand. It was a familiar weight, a weapon that had seen countless battles and had never failed me.

Turning a corner, I found myself in a long, dimly lit hallway lined with doors on both sides. At the far end of the corridor, a large archway beckoned, opening into a spacious chamber. I approached cautiously, alert for any signs of movement or danger.

As I drew closer, the unmistakable stench of death assaulted my nose, the putrid odor so pungent that it threatened to make me gag. My pulse quickened, the anticipation of the hunt sending a surge of adrenaline coursing through my veins. The thrill of the chase, the impending confrontation with the evil presence that had terrorized this place—it was what I had lived for this past month.

My eyes gradually adjusted to the gloom, revealing the chamber's grim contents. Broken furniture and debris cluttered the space, their shattered remains scattered haphazardly across the floor. It was as if the very essence of this forsaken hotel had been tainted by the venom that dwelled within its walls, turning it into a nightmarish realm.

And, there, huddled in a corner amongst countless decaying bones, was a lone figure. The demon.

It had lurked from the depths of Erubus with its sickeningly putrid smell of rotting flesh. Its nightmarish form was draped in tattered rags and its twisted limbs ended in sharp talons that threatened to tear apart everything in its path.

Its head was contorted into an unspeakable evil. It had two black pits for eyes and a gaping maw filled with sharp teeth ready to rend apart anything within reach. The demon rose to its feet, towering above me menacingly.

I didn't hesitate.

I pressed the attack, hacking and slashing at the demon's body, the scent of its decaying flesh filling the air.

The demon staggered, wounded, but it hadn't even started. With a bellow of rage, it lashed out, its claws raking across my leg, tearing through my clothes and skin.

I cried out in pain but didn't falter. I was fueled by my rage and a thirst for revenge, this demon had been responsible for the deaths of several innocents and I would not let it escape justice.

I ducked under another attack and struck out with my axe, slicing deep into the demon's side. It shrieked in agony and swiped at me again, its claws catching my shoulder and tearing a bloody gash across my flesh.

The pain was intense but I forced myself to ignore it, pushing through the haze of agony. I had come too far and had been hurt too deeply to stop now. I would see this through until the end, no matter what the cost.

The battle continued, the sound of our fierce engagement echoing through the chamber. The demon's movements weren't hindered at all by its wounds. If anything, they seemed to fuel its rage, pushing it to fight harder and faster.

The fight was intense, both of us giving it our all. The demon was strong and its attacks vicious, but I was driven by a determination that surpassed its fury. I fought with a savage desperation, refusing to yield.

The axe bit into the demon's flesh and its howls of anguish filled the air. Enraged, it swiped at me before I got the chance to pull my axe back.

The force of the blow knocked the air out of me and sent me crashing against the wall. My back collided with the rough concrete, the impact jarring my bones. I slid to the ground, momentarily stunned.

The demon loomed over me, its fetid breath hot on my face. Its claws raked against my chest, drawing blood.

I gritted my teeth against the pain, refusing to yield.

Then, almost as if on cue, the shadows around us coalesced, and out stepped a dark-haired figure, his sword flashing in the darkness. Kaelan, my demonic ex, was here to save the day, just like I knew he would be.

Kaelan attacked the demon, his blade slashing through its foul flesh. The demon roared in fury, whirling to face its new opponent. The two adversaries battled fiercely, their clash a blur of motion and violence. I staggered to my feet, the pain in my chest sharp.

The battle raged on, but I could see that Kaelan was gaining the upper hand. I summoned my magic and flames began dancing around my black upturned hand. With a fierce cry, I hurled the fiery projectile at the demon.

It struck the beast's head, engulfing it in flames. The demon howled in agony, reeling backward. Kaelan didn't waste the opportunity. He charged forward, plunging his sword into the demon's chest. The blade sank deep and the demon shrieked, its body convulsing. Then, with a final shudder, it collapsed and disintegrated into a pile of ash.

Kaelan's sword slipped free, slick with blood and viscera. I stared at him, breathing hard, the pain in my chest and leg still throbbing. The silence in the room echoed mercilessly, broken only by the faintest echoes of my labored breaths.

"Well, what a pleasant surprise," I quipped, finally cutting the tension.

"Vale," he replied, his eyes burning into mine. "Are you okay?"

"Never better," I said with a grimace, my voice laden with sarcasm.

"You're hurt," he replied, his expression inscrutable, a mask he'd mastered over the years I was sure.

"Nothing I can't handle." I took a moment to regain my composure, pushing past the throbbing pain of my wounds to focus on the matter at hand. "I've been looking for you," I told him coldly.

"Looking for me? Vale, what the hell do you think you're doing going after a demon like that by yourself? Why didn't you think to use your magic from the beginning?" he yelled, his eyes flashing with anger and frustration.

"You know why," I replied, my voice like ice.

"What? Why?" he asked, confused.

"Because you're an asshole, that's why," I shot back, glaring at him with a defiance that matched his fiery anger.

"That's not an answer to anything I asked," he retorted, his irritation now clear as day.

"I know," I admitted as I maintained my grip on my stubborn pride. "I just wanted a reason to call you an asshole," I added, grimacing against a throb of pain that pulsed through my battered body.

"You don't need a reason," he muttered, his words laced with resignation.

"True, but it's always satisfying," I replied, smirking in response.

His eyes, intense and probing, bore into mine. "Why have you been looking for me, Vale?" he asked, his tone cautious as if he was worried about what I was about to say next.

"We need to talk," I told him, my voice taking on a serious note.

"About what?" he pressed, his expression growing more guarded.

"You know damn well what," I snapped, my anger flaring within me like a wildfire. "I know you've been out there, lurking in the shadows, following me."

He hesitated for a moment, then admitted, "I was keeping an eye on you."

I glared at him, the fury simmering just beneath the surface. "I don't need anyone watching after me, especially not you."

"Obviously, you do," he countered, his voice holding an undercurrent of exasperation. "You just went running off into the night after a higher-level demon and got your ass handed to you."

"I could have killed that demon without a second thought if I had wanted to," I retorted, my irritation mounting with each passing word.

"I saw the whole thing. You were struggling the entire time. There was no way you were going to be able to beat that thing without using your magic. What were you trying to prove, Vale? That you're too stupid to use the power you have at your disposal?" His words cut through the air like a blade.

"I wasn't trying to prove anything. I was luring you out of the shadows," I retorted, my voice sharp and unwavering.

He looked taken aback, his eyes narrowing in confusion. "Luring me?"

"Yes," I hissed, thoroughly irritated. "And here you are, so I guess it worked."

"You could have been killed," he said, his eyes darkening.

"I had it completely under control, especially since I knew you would step out of the darkness at any moment. You'd be incapable of sitting on the sidelines while I was being hurt." I sneered at him, my voice bitter.

"So you let that thing hurt you on purpose? To get to me?" His disbelief was evident in his tone. "You've always been so reckless, but this is ridiculous, Vale." He ran his hands through his hair in frustration, clearly struggling to comprehend my actions.

"Brilliant plan, wasn't it?" I said, my voice dripping with sarcasm once again.

Kaelan, still trying to make sense of my actions, said nothing for a moment. Then, in a burst of exasperation, he threw his hands up in the air. "You've gone insane," he declared.

"Oh, come on," I scoffed, my tone defiant. "If I had wanted to kill the demon, I could have."

His expression twisted with incredulity. "No, instead you let it claw the shit out of you," he said, pointing to my bleeding chest.

"Exactly," I said, "it was the perfect way to draw you out."

"So, what, you did this to punish me for following you around?" Kaelan asked, frustration evident in his tone.

"Punish you? No, I want my library back," I retorted.

He scowled, thoroughly baffled. "What?"

"My library. In your house," I clarified slowly as if he were a half-wit.

"You want a book?" he asked, his eyebrows shooting up in surprise.

"Several, actually," I replied with a cool determination that seemed to catch him off guard.

"You were attacked by a demon and nearly killed, and now you're standing here talking to me about some books?" he said, disbelief clouding his expression.

"Yes, as a matter of fact, I am," I said without hesitation. "It's high time I took them back."

"Fine. Take the books, take anything you want," he growled. "But if you think for one second that I'm going to leave you alone, you're dead wrong. You can't stop me from protecting you."

"Protecting me? Is that what you call stalking me all over town?" I demanded.

"Someone has to keep an eye on you, especially since Wren is so busy with his pack," he countered, unwilling to yield.

"I can take care of myself," I said through clenched teeth.

"I know you can," he conceded, his expression softening slightly. "But that doesn't mean you shouldn't have backup."

"I don't need backup," I argued defiantly.

"Yes, you do," he insisted, his eyes filled with a genuine concern that cut through my defenses. "You're powerful, but you're still vulnerable. You can't do everything on your own."

"Says who?" I demanded, my pride refusing to yield an inch.

"Says me," he shot back, his voice cold. "Vale, you can't keep going around taking unnecessary risks. One of these days, you're going to get yourself killed."

I shook my head. "I won't stop taking risks. It's who I am. Besides, you're one to talk. You're even more reckless than I am."

"I can handle it. You, on the other hand, need someone to watch your back," he said, his voice firm.

"And that someone has to be you, right?" I retorted, completely annoyed.

"Yes," he simply said.

"You're an arrogant son of a bitch," I seethed, glaring at him.

"Perhaps," he conceded with a hint of a wry smile. "But you're just as arrogant. We're perfect for each other."

"That's the biggest load of bullshit I've ever heard," I scoffed, shaking my head in disbelief. "Perfect for each other? Yeah, right."

"Admit it, Vale," he said, his tone turning serious, his words sincere. "You know we're meant for each other. The connection we share is undeniable."

"Yeah, the connection you orchestrated when you had us share blood," I snapped, my bitterness seeping into my words.

"That's not all there is to it, and you know it," he countered, his eyes flashing darkly. "I felt the connection before that. So did you."

"You're wrong," I said, my voice cold and hard, a wall of denial that I refused to let crumble.

"I'm not," he said, his voice softening as he took another step closer. "And you're lying. You can't deny the pull between us. It's stronger than anything either of us has ever felt."

"Fine, I'm not denying it," I said, my resolve wavering as he closed the distance between us. "But that doesn't mean I have to give in to it. It doesn't mean we're meant to be together. Not in any real way."

"Why are you so hell-bent on fighting this?" he asked, as he tried to bridge the gap between us.

"I can never trust you again, Kaelan, and not just because of the blood bond. Everything you've done, you did while knowing you were betraying me."

His shoulders slumped slightly, and he spoke with a hint of desperation. "Vale, I never wanted to hurt you."

"And yet you did, and that's all I can think about," I replied.

"I fought back as much as I could," he pleaded, his gaze searching mine. "Zephyrian, he pried everything out of me. I was powerless then."

"You were a coward," I accused, my words seemed to have struck a chord within him. He stared at me for a moment, pain evident in his eyes, as the weight of my accusation hung heavily between us.

"I was a coward," he agreed, hanging his head.

"You should have trusted me and told me the truth," I said, my voice firm yet tinged with a deep hurt.

"I know, and I regret it every single day," he confessed.

"It still doesn't change the fact that you lied to me and betrayed me," I said, my heart twisting painfully in my chest, the wounds of the past still fresh.

"I know," he repeated, his voice heavy with the weight of his transgressions and his eyes reflecting the depths of his regret.

"I can't forgive you," I whispered, my voice breaking as I confronted the reality of our fractured trust. "I can't forget."

"I know," he said once more, his expression anguished.

"And the worst part is, I still care about you," I said, the words tumbling from my lips before I could stop them.

His eyes widened, hope sparking in their depths.

"You do?"

"I can't help it," I admitted softly.

"Vale, I…"

"Don't," I interrupted. "Just don't."

"Let me try to make things right," he said, taking another step toward me.

"It's too late for that," I said, my voice hollow.

"Please," he pleaded, closing the distance between us.

"Don't touch me," I said, my voice sharp and harsh.

"Vale…"

"Leave me alone," I said, my tone leaving no room for argument. Kaelan's shoulders slumped and he stepped away from me.

"If that's what you want," he said, resignation lacing his voice.

"It is," I replied, my own voice heavy with the bitterness of the lie that I fed him.

"You can come and go within the library any time you please, you know that, right?" He asked, a strained note in his voice as he grasped at the last threads of our connection.

"No, I'm going to anchor it to a different point," I declared, my words cold and final. "After that, I won't have to see you again."

He flinched and I despised myself for the pain my words inflicted on him. Unable to bear the sight of the anguish in his eyes, I turned away, my heart heavy with the knowledge of what had to be done.

"Vale..." His voice reached out to me, a desperate plea.

"Go home, Kaelan," I said, my gaze still averted. "I'll get the books later."

I didn't hear him walk away, but when I finally mustered the courage to turn around, the room was empty and the hollowness of the silence echoed my own conflicted emotions.

I stood there for a long, agonizing moment, fighting the overwhelming urge to run after him, to take back everything I'd said and to mend what was broken.

But I couldn't. As much as I wanted him, as much as my heart ached for him, I couldn't forgive him. I had to let him go.

It was the only way to protect myself.

CHAPTER THREE

The chilly fall night enveloped me as I made my way back to my apartment. The late-night air was crisp, carrying the faint scent of fallen leaves and damp earth. Each step I took echoed softly in the silence of the deserted streets, the faint hum of the city reduced to a distant whisper.

My familiar, Nyxen, a fox-like lower shadowkin demon, followed close behind me, playfully chasing after my shadow. His presence was a comfort in the lonely night and I was grateful he was with me.

A chill crept through me as I pulled my jacket tighter around my body, the cool breeze ruffling my hair and sending a cascade of silver strands tumbling over my shoulders. The faint glow of streetlights cast long, eerie shadows that seemed to dance in the corners of my vision, creating an atmosphere of haunting beauty.

But there was something more than just the autumn chill that sent a shiver through me; a nagging feeling gnawed at the back of my mind, a sense of being watched. Despite the harsh words I had exchanged with Kaelan, I couldn't shake the unsettling suspicion that it was him trailing me through the darkened streets.

I quickened my pace, the echoes of my footsteps growing louder as my heart pounded in my chest. My senses were on high alert, every rustle of leaves, every distant car passing by, amplified my unease. Nyxen seemed to catch on to my wariness and walked closer, staying within the confines of my shadow.

The city felt like a labyrinth of shadows and I couldn't escape the sensation that someone was lurking just out of sight, concealed within the darkness.

I reached the entrance to the old button factory I called home and fumbled for my keys, the metallic jangle breaking the silence. As I hurried inside, Nyxen trailing behind, I couldn't help but glance back one last time into the obsidian night, searching for any sign of the one I had just sent away.

The empty street stared back at me, offering no solace, no confirmation of my suspicions. With a heavy sigh, I closed the door behind me, locking it with a sense of finality that didn't quite manage to quell the lingering unease in my heart.

Whatever the future held, whatever dangers might await me, I would have to face them alone. For now, at least. I turned away from the door and headed up the narrow staircase, each step echoing in the stillness of the building. The familiar embrace of home awaited and it was the one place where I could truly find comfort.

As I pushed open the door to my apartment, the smell of dust and old books enveloped me, a comforting scent that never failed to bring a sense of peace. The room was bathed in the soft glow of a few scattered lamps, casting warm pools of light against the dark wooden bookshelves.

Despite the familiarity of my surroundings and my familiar bounding around the space, a pervasive sense of loneliness crept over me, the silence of the empty room pressing down like a heavy blanket. Wren spent all his nights with the pack now and I missed having him home. I shook off the feeling, unwilling to let it consume me.

Crossing the room, I reached for the light switch and bathed the space in a brighter, more inviting illumination. The shadows that had clung to the corners were dispelled and the room felt more welcoming, less desolate.

My old cat, the one we had never given a name, lazily crossed over to me from where he'd been lying on the leather couch and wound his way between my legs, purring affectionately. He gave Nyxen a wide birth as he passed, still not knowing what to make of the strange creature. I scratched him under the chin and he accepted the affection before batting at my hand playfully.

My gaze fell upon the desk where I had been working earlier that night, the remnants of my failed homebrewed potion still scattered about. My mission had ended in disappointment, but there was a small sense of accomplishment in how close I had come to success.

I approached the desk, my fingers tracing over the smooth glass vials that held the meticulously labeled ingredients. At this point, I knew the potion by heart, its intricate steps and precise measurements etched into my memory, but I couldn't resist reading through the list again. There was a strange comfort in the familiarity of the process, a reminder that even in the face of adversity, there were things I could still control.

But as my gaze drifted over the neatly written words on the potion recipe, something struck me as odd. Something I had missed before, too engrossed in the intricacies of the concoction itself. It wasn't one of the ingredients that seemed out of place; it was the list itself.

It was short. Too short.

The realization hit me like a punch to the gut. There had been one ingredient missing from the potion, one crucial component, without which the entire concoction was rendered useless. And I had been so certain that I had everything I needed.

The answer to the riddle was painfully clear.

Without Kaelan's blood, the potion would never have worked. Without that vital ingredient, the blood bond between us could never have been broken. I knew he would never willingly offer his blood to me to sever the bond, not when he still clung to the hope that we could reconcile our differences.

A surge of frustration and regret welled up inside me. I thought I had been so close to freeing myself from the tangled web of emotions that bound me to him. And now, I was back at square one, my escape from his influence slipping through my fingers like grains of sand.

I sank into the chair, the realization pressing down on me like a physical force. The room around me seemed to close in. I had been so certain that the potion was the answer, the solution that would finally free me from the blood bond and the suffocating hold Kaelan had over me. But now, I was left with the crushing knowledge that there was no escaping the connection we shared.

It was a connection that I had chosen, however unknowingly. The thought of being eternally tethered to him, to his emotions and his will, was stifling.

Even as I thought the words, a tiny spark of hope flickered to life in the back of my mind. Maybe, just maybe, there was another way. Another option. A way to sever the blood bond without breaking it entirely. There had to be.

The idea was absurd, reckless, and potentially dangerous. But it was also a chance. A chance to regain my independence, my autonomy. A chance to be free.

I pushed myself out of the chair, determination coursing through my veins like wildfire, banishing the hopelessness and despair that had threatened to consume me. I couldn't give up. I wouldn't give up.

I would find a way. I had to. If not, I would be bound to Kaelan forever, a fate I refused to accept.

With a weary sigh, I shuffled into the bathroom, the dim light casting long shadows on the cold, tiled floor. I crouched down and rummaged under the cabinets, my fingers brushing against various forgotten items until they finally closed around the familiar shape of the first aid kit. As I sat down on the edge of the old porcelain tub, I winced at the pain radiating from the claw marks that marred my body. I knew I had to clean and disinfect them, even though it would hurt like a bitch.

With deliberate care, I removed my pants and shirt, revealing the crisscross of angry red gashes that marred my skin. The coldness of the bathroom tiles beneath me only intensified the discomfort, but I pushed aside the pain, knowing that tending to my wounds was a necessity.

The sting of antiseptic met my senses as I began to clean the claw marks and I bit my lip to stifle a hiss of pain. I tried to focus solely on the physical task at hand, but it was impossible not to let my thoughts drift back to the implications of my recent conversation with Kaelan.

I had anticipated a far fiercer resistance from him, a desperate fight to win me back at any cost. Instead, he had accepted defeat far too easily. A part of me felt relieved, a relief mixed with a tinge of disappointment.

I had assumed that the depth of his feelings for me would drive him to do whatever it took to reclaim my trust and love. Yet, he had seemingly given up, relinquishing his claim on me without a fight.

I couldn't decide whether this outcome was better or worse. On one hand, it made it easier for me to move on without the constant struggle of resisting his advances. On the other, it raised doubts about whether he had ever truly cared for me at all.

I finished bandaging the wounds, the stark reality of the situation settling over me like a heavy shroud. I tidied up the first aid kit and returned it to its place beneath the bathroom sink, still lost in thought.

The shrill ring of my phone snapped me out of my reverie and I fumbled to retrieve it from the pocket of my discarded jeans. Half-expecting to see Kaelan's name on the caller ID, I was surprised to find Harker's name flashing on the screen.

"Vale, did you find Kaelan? Will we be getting the library back now?" Harker's voice crackled with excitement on the other end of the line. She was a centuries-old vampire with an insatiable thirst for knowledge and the loss of access to my magical library full of arcane texts had nearly driven her to madness a month ago.

"Yeah, I found him," I replied, my voice carrying a hint of weariness from the night's events.

"Well, are we getting the library back or not?" Harker's tone was insistent, her impatience flaring to life.

"Yes," I confirmed, though I couldn't help but find some amusement in her eagerness.

"Thank the Gods, because the waiting is killing me," she said, her excitement practically radiating through the phone.

"I'm sure you can wait another day," I teased, unable to suppress a smile at her enthusiasm.

"Are you kidding me? I need to get my hands on those books. I've got a lot of research to do and not enough time," she insisted.

"Harker, you've had a lot of time," I pointed out, my amusement growing.

"Not enough," she repeated.

"Alright, fine," I relented, knowing that arguing with her about it would be futile.

"So when do I get to have the library back?" she pressed.

"I'll figure it out and let you know," I promised, though I had no concrete plan in mind.

"Okay, well sooner rather than later would be good. Talk soon," she said, ending the call.

I sighed and tossed the phone on top of my ruined jeans, a mix of emotions swirling within me. I was relieved that Harker's obsession with the library had kept her from asking questions about my encounter with Kaelan. I wasn't sure I was ready to answer those questions, to confront the complex and painful truth of my feelings for him.

But as I lay back against the tub on the cool bathroom tiles, the events of the night and my choices replaying in my head, I knew that sooner or later I would have to face the consequences of my actions and confront the tangled mess of emotions that had ensnared me.

I shook my head, attempting to clear the thoughts that had consumed me, and headed into the dimly lit kitchen. The flickering overhead light cast eerie shadows on the worn-out linoleum floor.

As I opened the fridge and grabbed a bottle of water, my thoughts stubbornly returned to Kaelan, like a relentless undercurrent in the depths of my mind. Why had he given up so easily? The question gnawed at me, a puzzle with pieces that refused to fit together.

With a sigh, I twisted open the bottle and took a long, refreshing drink. The cold water soothed my parched throat, but it did little to quench the fire of confusion burning within me.

I couldn't deny the lingering feelings I felt for him. Nor could I ignore the fact that a part of me had secretly hoped he would fight harder for me, to prove that he was willing to go to any lengths to win me back. It was a dangerous thought, one that threatened to undermine my willpower.

But the rational part of my mind argued that it was better this way, simpler, less emotionally messy. It would be easier to move forward without the constant struggle and tumultuous history of our past.

Yet, even as I tried to convince myself, the nagging doubts persisted, like a shadow that refused to be dispelled. Why had he given up so easily? Did it mean that he didn't care as much as I had believed? Or was there something else at play, hidden beneath the surface of his actions?

I leaned against the worn kitchen counter, the questions swirling in my mind like a relentless storm. In the solitude of my dimly lit apartment, I had no answers, only the disconcerting sense that I had opened a door tonight that I couldn't close.

I was still no closer to answering those questions when the sun began its slow ascent, painting the sky in delicate hues of gold and pink. The soft, early morning light filtered through the gaps in the blinds, casting dancing patterns on the walls of my apartment.

I crossed the room and entered my bedroom, readying for bed. Nyxen crawled underneath it to lay down in the shadows there, my faithful guardian through the night. Exhaustion weighed heavily on me, both physical and emotional, yet sleep remained elusive. My mind was a whirlwind of thoughts, doubts, and regrets that refused to let me rest. I tossed and turned in my bed, the sheets tangling around my limbs.

I knew one thing with certainty— I couldn't continue running from my past. The decisions I had made, the choices that had led me to this point, could no longer be ignored or evaded. It was time to face the truth, no matter how painful or difficult it might be.

Only by confronting the past head-on could I hope to move forward and find some semblance of peace. The uncertainty of what lay ahead was daunting, but the path of avoidance was no longer an option.

With a deep sigh, I rose from my bed and shuffled over to the window and closed the blinds, shutting out the increasingly bright morning light. I crossed back to the bed and climbed back under the covers, resigned to the fact that I would be no closer to reaching any kind of decision today.

In the dimness of my room, I closed my eyes, allowing exhaustion to overcome me. Sleep finally came, but it was fitful, plagued by haunting dreams that carried the echoes of Kaelan's words.

"Let me try to make things right."

The words lingered in my mind, a haunting refrain. But as I drifted deeper into sleep, the unanswered questions remained. Would his efforts be enough to bridge the chasm between us? Could we ever rebuild the shattered trust that had once held us together?

Only time, that relentless and unforgiving force, would reveal the answers.

Chapter Four

I gradually emerged from the depths of slumber, my room still enshrouded in the comforting embrace of darkness, thanks to the thick curtains that defied the late afternoon sunlight. A gentle movement at my side made me look over at the cat napping contently on the bed. Its rhythmic purring served as a soothing backdrop to the sleepy haze that enveloped me.

With a heavy sigh, I reluctantly pushed myself up into a sitting position. My movements were slow and lethargic, still tired from the night's events. Tousled hair cascaded around my face as I yawned, stretching my arms to dispel the lingering remnants of exhaustion. Nyxen was nowhere to be seen, but that wasn't uncommon. He preferred to stay in the demon realm, presumably romping around with the other shadowkin there.

I got up and reached for my clothes, which were strewn about haphazardly on the floor, my fingers moving with practiced ease. I dressed in silence, the process second nature despite my bleary-eyed state.

My phone had been set to silent mode during my restless slumber, a brief respite from the storm of thoughts that had plagued me in my dreams. I picked it up from the bedside table, the screen revealing a missed call from Wren. Slightly worried, I dialed his number and the phone rang a few times before he answered.

"Hey, Vale," he greeted me.

I couldn't suppress another yawn. "Wren, what time is it?" I mumbled, the words slurred by sleep.

"Four o'clock in the afternoon," he replied, a hint of amusement in his voice. "You've finally decided to join the land of the living?"

I stretched and blinked away the last remnants of sleep. "Yeah, well, you know me. Night owl and all that."

"Yeah, I know," Wren replied, a warm chuckle escaping his lips. The sound was a welcome break from the somber thoughts that had haunted my recent days.

I settled back down against my soft pillows, their plushness offering a small comfort as I cradled the phone to my ear. "So, what's up?" I asked.

Wren's concerned tone was clear in his voice as he probed, "I'm just calling to check in on you. How are you doing?"

I sighed softly, appreciating his genuine care. "I'm fine, Wren," I assured him.

"Really?" He pressed further, his concern refusing to wane.

"Yes, really," I reiterated. "Stop worrying about me."

"Okay," he conceded, though a hint of doubt lingered in his voice. "But if you need anything, don't hesitate to ask."

The offer touched me and I couldn't help but smile. "I appreciate that, but I'm all good," I repeated.

"Well, alright, if you say so," he relented, though his voice was skeptical. "Anyway, I won't keep you. I've got alpha business to attend to and all that. Come by the camp soon, okay?"

"I will. Thanks, Wren," I replied, genuinely grateful for his unwavering support.

"Anytime," he said before ending the call.

I tossed the phone onto the bed, where it landed with a soft thud. The cat, roused by the motion, blinked slowly at me with its orange eyes.

"Don't look at me like that," I muttered, running a hand through my tousled hair. It seemed even the cat could sense the inner turmoil that still gnawed at me, despite my reassurances to Wren.

The cat responded with a low rumble as if offended by my comment.

"Look, I'm sorry, okay? It's been a long night."

The cat, seemingly appeased by my apology, responded with a less hostile purr. Its feline pride was on full display as it stretched languidly.

I sighed once more, feeling a kinship with the animal. "You're right," I admitted, the words whispered more to myself than to the cat. "It's not an excuse."

With a nod from the cat, or perhaps just a random twist of its head, I decided it was time for us both to get moving. "Come on," I suggested, the weariness of the night's contemplations still hanging around me like a shroud. "Let's go get something to eat."

The cat followed, its agile form moving with grace as it trotted beside me, its tail held high in a display of contentment or superiority, it was hard to tell.

In the kitchen, the cat jumped onto the counter and I couldn't help but smile at its boldness. It watched with keen interest as I set about preparing a quick meal, its feline eyes never leaving the tantalizing aroma of the food.

The simple act of cooking was a welcome distraction from the weighty thoughts that plagued me during the night. As I finished the meal and cleared the dishes, I found myself absentmindedly glancing out of the window.

The sky beyond was a brilliant shade of blue, a stark contrast to the darkness that had enveloped my thoughts for so long. Only a few wisps of clouds drifted lazily across the horizon and the sight filled me with a strange sense of hope. "It's a beautiful day," I remarked aloud, my voice hushed in the quiet of the kitchen. Outside, a flock of birds wheeled and danced in the warm air, their freedom and carelessness a stark contrast to the turmoil within my own heart.

The cat, however, was less interested in the view and more concerned with the passage of time as it made its demands known with a loud meow.

"All right, all right," I laughed, reaching out to scratch behind its ears. "You're such a demanding little creature, you know that?"

I turned to retrieve the cat's bowl, the worn linoleum cold beneath my feet. In the dim light of the kitchen, I filled it with fresh food. Setting it down on the floor, the cat wasted no time in approaching and devouring its meal, purring loudly between bites.

I watched it with amusement and affection, leaning against the counter. Despite the gruff exterior and its disapproving stares, the old cat had become an important part of my life. I couldn't imagine my home without its quiet presence.

After all, it had been a stray, much like me. And sometimes, I felt like the two of us had a lot in common. We were both survivors, doing whatever it took to make our way in a world that often seemed determined to see us fail.

A small, nostalgic smile tugged at the corners of my lips as I thought about the journey that had led me to this point. The people I'd met, the places I'd been, and the choices I'd made. The cat continued to eat, blissfully unaware of the direction my thoughts had turned.

"At least one of us is enjoying themselves," I murmured to the animal.

As the cat finished eating, I cleaned its bowl with a sense of routine, the sound of the running water a soothing backdrop to my thoughts. Returning it to its usual place, I glanced around the cozy, quiet kitchen.

From there, I wandered into the living room and sank down on the couch, a sigh escaping my lips as I felt the tension in my shoulders begin to ebb away. The room was bathed in soft sunlight, the warm glow washing over the furniture and knick-knacks that adorned the shelves.

My eyes were drawn to the familiar bookcase, crammed full of books and mementos from my past. Each item held a story, a memory, a piece of my history. It was strange, but I had always found comfort in objects that had once belonged to other people. They held a certain kind of magic, a connection to a time and place that was no longer.

A pang of loneliness echoed in my chest as I reached out and traced my fingertips over the worn spines of the books. Each one was a portal to another world, another life. I had spent countless hours lost in their pages, seeking solace and escape from the challenges of my own reality.

"Maybe it's time to start making new memories," I whispered to myself, the words barely audible in the quiet room. The cat, always attuned to my moods, joined me on the couch. It curled up next to me, purring contentedly as it closed its eyes.

As I absentmindedly petted its soft fur, a determined idea began to form in my mind. It was time to make a decision. I couldn't keep running, hiding from my past and the choices I had made. It was time to face it all.

I stood from the couch and began to gather my belongings, my movements purposeful and efficient. It was time to confront the demons of my past, literally. To make amends and build a future free from the shadows that had haunted me for so long.

I didn't know what the future would hold, but I was ready to find out. The cat watched me with its wise, orange eyes as if silently offering its support and approval.

I stepped out into the evening air, the fading sunlight casting long shadows on the ground. I had chosen a daunting path, but I was determined to walk it. I was ready to take back what was rightfully mine, to face whatever challenges lay ahead.

And nothing, not even the ghosts of my past, was going to stand in my way.

CHAPTER FIVE

I stood in the heart of the ancient library, surrounded by towering shelves that held countless tomes of arcane knowledge. Harker stood by my side. She was practically giddy with excitement, her gaze darting around the room as if each bookshelf held a long-lost friend. Nyxen was off sniffing the shelves curiously.

"Let's get this over and done with," I muttered impatiently. Time was of the essence and I wanted to reclaim my magical library as quickly as possible.

I opened the book in my hand, its pages brittle with age, and turned to a page I had marked previously. The text was written in an elegant, archaic script and I quickly scanned the instructions.

"It says to erase the anchor point, I need to anoint the door with my blood around the doorknob, say the incantation, and then pull the door open," I explained to Harker, who seemed barely interested, her attention still wandering among the books.

I sighed, realizing that I was going to have to repeat myself. "Harker, pay attention. We need to do this right."

She finally tore her eyes away from the shelves and focused on me. "Right, right, blood, incantation, door. Got it."

I couldn't help but roll my eyes at her nonchalant attitude. "Good. Let's do this."

I held out my hand and made a small cut on my wrist with a small silver dagger I carried for such rituals. Blood welled up and I quickly anointed the area around the doorknob as instructed in the book. The air seemed to tingle with magic as I did so.

With my blood in place, I took a step back and cleared my throat. "Now, the incantation." I began to recite the ancient words, my voice resonating with power.

> *"By mystic forces, I now beseech,*
> *To erase this door, its presence breach.*
> *With whispered words and gestures fine,*
> *Vanish it from the threads of time."*

The words seemed to come alive, dancing in the air as I spoke. Harker watched me with a newfound curiosity, her eyes fixed on my every movement.

Taking a deep breath, I gripped the doorknob and turned it slowly. The door creaked open and I felt a surge of energy rush through me. The anchor point was breaking and the library was once again mine to access.

As the door swung open completely, revealing the empty wall behind it, I couldn't help but feel a sense of triumph. The library was back in my grasp and I was one step closer to severing the blood bond that had haunted me for so long. The door vanished completely under my grasp.

"Well, that was easier than I thought," Harker said, her voice breaking the silence that had settled over the library. She walked closer to me, her eyes filled with curiosity as she looked to where to door had been.

I nodded in agreement, still feeling the residual energy from the ritual coursing through my veins. "Yes, it was," I replied, feeling the rush of magic fade.

"So what are you going to do with the library now?" Harker's question brought me back to the present. I knew I had to act quickly to secure it once more.

"I've got nowhere else to anchor it besides my apartment," I explained, my voice thoughtful. "I've fortified the wards around the factory and I'll place more wards around the door after I anchor it. It's not the best alternative, but it's the only one I've got."

Harker nodded in understanding. "Better than losing it altogether," she pointed out, her fingers lightly tracing the spines of the books on the nearby shelf.

"That's true," I conceded. "Now, let's create the new door," I said, refocusing on the task at hand. I turned to Harker, my expression expectant. "Did you grab the chalk?"

Harker blinked in confusion for a moment before her eyes widened in realization. "Oh! The chalk," She hurried to the cabinets that held the supplies left by the witches who had created this place centuries ago. Moments later, she returned with a box of chalk in hand, clearly annoyed with herself for not bringing it upfront.

"Here," I said, taking the box from her and opening it. "Now, let's create the new door."

I knelt down on the cold stone floor, chalk in hand, and began to carefully draw the outlines of the new door. I focused on my memories of my apartment, imbuing the magic with a new anchor point.

As the lines were drawn, I placed a few drops of blood inside the outline. The door began to glow, its form materializing in front of us.

The magical energy crackled in the air and I could feel the connection between the library and my apartment being established.

With a final flourish, I completed the drawing, knocked three times and the door stood before us, a shimmering portal to the world of knowledge and magic that I had surprisingly missed so dearly.

"Wow," Harker whispered, her eyes wide with wonder as she stared at the shimmering door. "I'm starting to think that there are some things I'll never get used to."

I couldn't help but smile at her reaction. "You and me both," I muttered, taking a step closer to the door and grasping the ornate doorknob.

With a turn of the knob, the door swung open, revealing a familiar view of my bedroom. My heart soared with relief; it had worked. The library was now anchored to my apartment.

"Thank the Gods," I murmured, stepping through the doorway and into my room.

Harker followed me inside, her gaze scanning the surroundings. "It looks the same," she remarked.

"It'll be safe here as long as the wards hold," I assured her, my eyes flicking to the intricate patterns etched into the walls of the room.

"Well, let's hope they do, for both our sakes," Harker replied, her expression still somewhat grim.

I couldn't help but chuckle at her concern. "We'll be fine. Come on, let's go see the others."

I closed the door to the library behind us, sealing it with a few whispered words. The magical lock would keep unwanted visitors out until I had a chance to place stronger wards. I'd need some of Harker's blood to make sure she could go through them. But that could wait for now.

"Well, that's that," Harker mused, her fingers trailing along the edge of the doorframe. "Hopefully, the rest will be just as easy."

I shook my head, knowing that the challenges ahead wouldn't be simple. "I wouldn't count on it," I replied, leading the way toward the living room. "Nothing ever is."

"Nyxen?" I called out into the dimly lit room. My familiar stirred forth from the depths of the shadows behind the couch. He responded with a questioning chirp, his glowing yellow eyes fixed on me, awaiting my command.

"Can you shift us to the camp?" I asked, knowing that Nyxen's unique ability to shadow-shift us would be particularly useful in getting us to the werewolf camp that Wren, my best friend, was currently alpha of.

Nyxen emitted an affirmative chirp, his consciousness briefly nudging mine. He padded over to me, his shadowy form shifting like mist. Harker, standing nearby, took a step closer and the shadows began to swirl around us, enveloping us in their dark embrace.

With a gentle but swift pull, we were swallowed by the darkness, leaving my apartment and its library behind. The sensation of being transported through the shadows was disorienting, even for me, and I could tell that Harker was feeling a bit queasy from the rapid trip.

As the shadows released us, we emerged in the heart of the camp, standing near the central bonfire. A few Otherworlders who happened to be nearby gave startled jumps at our sudden appearance. Some were aware of my powers, but few had actually witnessed them in action.

"We really need to get you a better mode of transportation," Harker quipped, her tone carrying a hint of mild discomfort.

"Hey, it gets the job done," I retorted, a smirk tugging at the corner of my mouth as I watched her recover from the shift.

"If you say so," she replied with a frown, clearly unimpressed by the mode of travel.

As Harker and I approached the bonfire, its flickering flames casting a warm and mesmerizing glow, the scent of woodsmoke filled the night air, reminding me of Kaelan. Shadows danced and played in the corners of the camp, creating an eerie yet comforting atmosphere.

Wren and Venna, his beta, sat together on a log, their voices low as they engaged in what seemed to be an earnest discussion. The campfire's light played across their faces, accentuating their strong features.

"Wren," I called out, my voice carrying across the crackling fire. Wren's head turned in my direction and his forest-green eyes met mine. He offered a nod of acknowledgment, his dark skin illuminated by the firelight.

"Vale," he greeted me with a soft smile. His attention then shifted to Harker, who stood beside me. "And Harker. Glad you two could be here."

Harker, never one for lengthy greetings, chimed in, her tone laced with a hint of sarcasm. "Wouldn't miss it for the world."

I took a seat on a log close to the fire, feeling the warmth against my skin. Nyxen appeared from the shadows and began romping around the fire. The familiar sounds of the camp filled the air—the quiet murmurs of conversations, the occasional rustling of leaves, and the distant howl of a wolf in the night.

"How are things going?" I asked Wren, genuinely curious about his progress. I knew that taking over as alpha hadn't been an easy feat, especially considering the friction within the pack during the transition.

Wren shifted his position, leaning back against the log behind him. Venna sat nearby, her attentive gaze alternating between Wren and Nyxen. "Pretty good," Wren replied, a note of relief evident in his voice. "The pack has accepted me as the new alpha, and things are starting to settle down."

A genuine smile tugged at my lips at the news. "That's good to hear," I said, the weight of worry lifting from my shoulders. It was crucial for Wren to establish himself as a capable leader, not just for his pack's sake but for the stability of the rest of the Otherworlders that now called the camp home.

"So, how are you settling into your new role as leader of the pack?" I asked as I saw Nyxen leap headfirst into a shadow playfully and disappear.

Wren's expression turned pensive for a moment, a flicker of uncertainty crossing his features. "It's a challenge," he admitted. "There's a lot to learn and a lot to do. But I'm up for it."

I couldn't resist a teasing remark. "Well, you've got the support of the witches."

Wren chuckled, his green eyes dancing with amusement. "Seeing as how you are the only witch in all the realms, that doesn't mean as much as you think it does."

I couldn't help but playfully protest, my voice filled with mock indignation. "Ouch, Wren. You wound me."

He just grinned in response, clearly enjoying the banter.

I leaned back on the log, my thoughts drifting to a more pressing matter. "So, how is it going with the other pack?" I asked, referring to the rival group of wolves who had formed their own pack after being banished when Wren had become alpha. They had shown no inclination toward cooperation with Wren's pack and tension had been simmering between the two groups.

Wren's eyes softened with a hint of sympathy as he spoke. "They're holding their own, for now," he said, his voice carrying a note of understanding. "But I think it's only a matter of time before they come back to the fold. After all, they're just trying to survive."

Venna didn't share the same sentiment. Her gaze remained cold and unyielding as she added her perspective. "They've had their chance," she chimed in, her voice firm. "They chose to leave the pack. They're on their own."

I couldn't help but feel torn. On one hand, I understood the importance of unity and survival within a pack, but on the other, it was difficult to ignore the desperation of those who had been cast out.

"They're not a threat, are they?" I asked.

Wren shook his head, reassuring me. "Not at the moment. But it's always good to keep an eye on them. Better to be prepared than caught off guard."

I nodded in agreement, trusting Wren's judgment. After all, he had far more experience with the complexities of the werewolves and their politics than I did.

Curiosity spurred my next question. "So, what's the next step for the pack?"

Wren's grin widened and he leaned forward, clearly enthusiastic about their future plans. "Well, now that we've established ourselves here, we're going to start building a more permanent settlement. We can't keep living in tents forever."

Harker, with her straightforward nature, couldn't resist commenting. "I can't believe you've managed to stay in tents for this long," she remarked, her tone laced with amusement. "Isn't that a little... primitive?" Harker raised a valid point.

"It's not like we had a choice," Venna pointed out. "Where else would we have housed all these people?"

My thoughts turned to the safety of the camp and its inhabitants, particularly concerning the potential threat posed by the demons. "What about defenses?" I inquired, my concern evident.

Wren leaned forward, his expression serious as he addressed the issue. "We've got a decent wall built and we're working on a gate. It's not impenetrable, but it'll help keep us safe."

"I'll work on warding the camp too," I offered. "Though I'm not sure how easy it'll be to protect a place this big."

Wren's gratitude was clear as he responded, "Anything you can do would be greatly appreciated."

Harker, always one to interject with a touch of humor, chimed in with a smirk. "Well, if the demons try anything, I'll kick their asses."

Venna couldn't resist making a sly comment. "You'd probably do better than most," she said. "For a vampire."

Harker's eyes narrowed at the remark, her response laced with cool confidence. "I can hold my own," she retorted, clearly not one to back down from a challenge.

Before Wren could address the conversation further, a sudden commotion near the camp's entrance grabbed everyone's attention. His demeanor shifted instantly, the authority in his voice surfacing. "What's going on?" he demanded, his gaze turning toward the disturbance.

"Intruders!" one of the sentries called out urgently. "Demons!"

Wren's attention snapped to the sentry, his eyes narrowing in response to the alarm. "How many?" he inquired, already pushing himself up from his seated position.

The sentry's voice trembled as he replied, "A dozen or so. They're attacking the perimeter!"

Without hesitation, Wren emitted a low, menacing growl. "Let's go," he said, his voice now a low primal sound. His transformation into his wolf form was swift and purposeful.

"Looks like you'll get a chance to prove yourself, Harker," Venna said before shifting into her wolf form as well and running after Wren.

Harker stood ready for action, a gleaming knife firmly gripped in her hand. The werewolves who had previously encircled us revealed themselves as part of Wren's personal retinue as they took off after him.

Harker turned to me. "Come on," she urged, determination in her eyes. "Let's kick some demon ass."

I followed Harker, Wren, and Venna as they sprinted toward the brewing battle, my heart racing and adrenaline coursing through my veins.

The camp had erupted into chaos, with wolves and demons locked in furious combat. Wren and his loyal followers lunged headfirst into the turmoil, their claws and teeth ripping through the demonic invaders. Harker moved with calculated precision, her fangs a deadly flash in the flickering light of the fire as she engaged a nearby demon.

I joined the fray, summoning my fiery magic to unleash a torrent of flames upon the encroaching demons, incinerating them where they stood. Together, our combined efforts made quick work of the demonic attackers, leaving nothing behind but piles of ash as grim testaments to their failed assault.

As the last echoes of the battle subsided, I scanned the immediate vicinity, checking for any signs of injuries among the wolves.

"Is everyone alright?" I asked, my breath coming in short pants as I scanned our immediate surroundings.

"A few injuries it looks like, but nothing serious," Wren responded after his wolfish features morphed back into his human form.

Relief washed over me. "Good," I muttered, grateful that the battle hadn't exacted a heavy toll on our group.

Wren's expression darkened as he considered the recent skirmish. "I'm guessing that was just the vanguard," he said, his voice carrying a grim undertone.

I furrowed my brow, confusion etching my features. "What do you mean?" I asked, urging him to clarify.

"That attack was merely a small group of demons," he elaborated. "There are likely more on their way."

"More?" I echoed, my shock evident.

Wren nodded solemnly. "This was a test," he continued. "They're assessing our strength and resolve. They'll be back."

"And when they return, we'll be waiting for them." Venna chimed in, a steely determination in her eyes.

Wren's voice was steady as he said, "We'll show them that this pack isn't going anywhere."

Harker, her loyalty to our cause solidifying with each passing day, chimed in, "Damn straight." Her fierce expression mirrored the determination in her words.

As I glanced around at the faces of the assembled werewolves, I could see the unwavering resolve etched in each of their expressions. They were a formidable force, determined to protect their home at any cost.

"We'll be ready," I declared, my voice carrying with it the same resolve that had filled Wren's words moments earlier. It was a promise, not just to Wren and Venna, but to the entire pack.

The battle we had just faced was merely a prelude, a warning of what was to come. This was just the beginning of a new chapter in our lives, one fraught with challenges and threats from the Otherworld.

But we were united, determined, and prepared to defend our home and each other. Together, we would face whatever the future held and emerge victorious.

CHAPTER SIX

The night was thick with unease as Harker and I shifted back to my apartment. The adrenaline from the demon attack at the werewolf camp still coursed through my veins and the memory of the battle was fresh in my mind. We needed a break, a moment of respite before we faced whatever might come next.

My apartment was a welcome sight as we materialized in my dimly lit living room. Nyxen brushed up against me, his form passing slightly through my leg before he padded off to his favorite corner full of shadows. Exhaustion weighed on me, but there was one task left to do. With a sigh, I led Harker into my bedroom, where the entrance to the magical library awaited.

Unlocking the library door required a special incantation and I murmured the words under my breath. The door's ancient wood creaked and groaned as it swung open, revealing the library's familiar interior. Books upon books lined the shelves, each containing a wealth of knowledge and secrets.

Harker practically skipped into the room, her excitement infectious. It had been weeks since she last had access to these arcane texts and she was eager to dive back into her research.

But as she stepped further into the room, a sudden and unexpected voice shattered the silence. "Where in the seven realms have you people been?" it screeched. "You left me all alone with nobody but that sulking demon for company and he is dreadfully depressing these days."

I turned to see Elara, the library's resident ghost, floating before us. Her ethereal form glowed with a faint, otherworldly light, and her translucent eyes bore into us with annoyance.

Harker raised an eyebrow, clearly taken aback by Elara's outburst. "Well, hello to you too," she quipped.

I sighed, pinching the bridge of my nose. "We didn't exactly have access to the library for a while."

Elara's ghostly form wavered slightly as if considering my words. "Next time, try to inform me when you'll be gone for so long. I do get rather lonely in here."

I nodded, feeling a pang of guilt. "I promise we'll be more considerate next time."

Elara seemed to accept my apology, "Good. Now, if you'll excuse me, I have some overdue conversations with the books to catch up on." Her translucent form floated back toward the shelves.

Harker chuckled and began pulling books from the shelves with glee, already lost in her world of research. As I watched her, I couldn't help but feel a sense of normalcy returning, despite the circumstances.

We might be dealing with demons and supernatural threats, but in this library, with its eccentric ghost and endless knowledge, there was a comforting familiarity that grounded me. It was a reminder that even in the face of the unknown, we had our own unique sanctuary.

The night enveloped the library in a soothing darkness, the soft glow of magical lamplight illuminating the pages of the books spread across the room. The world outside seemed distant and unimportant compared to the knowledge contained within these ancient tomes. Harker and I were fully immersed in our research, flipping through pages filled with spells, incantations, and arcane wisdom.

The scent of old parchment and ink hung in the air, comforting and familiar. The rustling of pages and the occasional murmur of incantations were the only sounds that filled the room. With her intense focus, Harker had lost track of time entirely, absorbed in deciphering cryptic texts and diagrams.

As for me, each word I read was like a puzzle piece, slowly fitting together to form a bigger picture. The stress and worries of the day began to recede, replaced by a sense of purpose and determination. We may not have had a concrete plan to defeat the demons yet, but being surrounded by these ancient tomes and having my friend by my side filled me with quiet confidence.

The library was another sanctuary, a place where the supernatural met the tangible, where the impossible became a puzzle to be solved. I knew that with time and effort, we would find a way to confront the looming threat of the demons. The answers were here, hidden within these pages, waiting to be uncovered.

The hours passed, marked only by the turning of pages and the slow progression of candle wax from the magical lanterns around the library. We delved deeper into our research, chasing down leads and exploring every avenue of magical knowledge. The sense of unity and purpose between Harker and me, and the presence of the ever-watchful Elara, made this night feel like a beacon of hope in a world filled with uncertainty.

As the night wore on, I stole a glance at Harker, who was still engrossed in her reading. Her dedication and unwavering support were a source of strength and I felt grateful for her friendship. Together, we were determined to find a way to protect the camp from the demonic threat.

With the first light of dawn creeping through the curtains, I finally closed the book I had been studying. The weight of the knowledge I had gained settled within me, along with the realization that our journey was far from over. But for now, I could rest, knowing that we had taken another step towards confronting the darkness that loomed on the horizon.

I stretched, feeling the tension in my shoulders release and then turned to Harker. "I think it's time I got some rest," I said softly, my voice breaking the silence. "Not all of us are restless, nocturnal vampires."

She looked up from her book. "Okay, I'll be here for a few more hours. Can I stay in Wren's room for the time being?"

"Yeah, that shouldn't be a problem," I told her. I carefully closed my books, returning them to their rightful places on the shelves. Elara floated nearby, serene and content. As I prepared for a well-deserved rest, I couldn't help but reflect on the night's progress.

We might not have all the answers yet, but we had each other, the wisdom of the library, and the unyielding determination to face whatever challenges lay ahead. The night had given us strength, and as I settled into sleep, I held onto the hope that the next day would bring us one step closer to victory.

The bookshop, nestled on a charming corner of the street, was a haven of knowledge and stories, a place where the past and the future coexisted among the shelves. It had always been a refuge for those seeking the magic of literature and the solace of the written word. The warm, earthy aroma of old books permeated the air, creating an atmosphere of comfort and nostalgia.

The shop itself was a cozy space with well-worn wooden floors that creaked softly underfoot. Tall bookshelves lined every wall, reaching up to the ceiling and filled to the brim with books of all shapes and sizes. The shelves were organized meticulously, a testament to Juniper's dedication and love for the written word.

Juniper had died from a demon attack in this very bookshop not too long ago and the wound was still fresh and raw. But I was slowly learning to live with the grief. The herbs in the sunroom were dreadfully neglected though.

Sunlight streamed through the windows, casting dappled patterns on the floor as if the books themselves were sharing secrets with the sun. The windows were adorned with lace curtains that filtered the light and added a touch of elegance to the space.

As I moved about, dusting the shelves and straightening the books, memories of Juniper flooded my mind. She had been the heart and soul of this place, her warmth and passion for literature drawing in customers from all walks of life. Her absence was still painfully obvious here, a reminder of the void left by her untimely death.

The bookshop had been closed to the public since that fateful day, a period of mourning and reflection. But today, as I bustled about, I couldn't help but feel that it was time to reopen these doors. It was what Juniper would have wanted, for her legacy to live on and for the bookshop to continue to serve as a retreat for those seeking the magic of stories.

I carefully wiped down the countertops, polished the display cases, and tidied up the reading nook in the corner, where Juniper had often sat, lost in the pages of a book.

The bookshop had been my home not so far away from home for so many years and it was a place that held a special place in my heart.

With each passing minute, the space became more alive, filled with the familiar sights and smells that I had come to associate with the bookshop. I could almost hear Juniper's voice as I straightened the chairs, her cheerful greeting and gentle smile welcoming me back.

I stepped back, admiring the bookshop's newly polished interior. It was time.

Unlocking the front door felt like unlocking the door to a world of endless possibilities. With a simple flip of the sign, I welcomed the world back into this sacred space, a space that had offered solace and inspiration to countless souls over the years.

The first customers who entered did so with a sense of reverence as if they were stepping into a sacred sanctuary of words and stories. They meandered through the aisles, their fingers lightly tracing the spines of books, their eyes alight with curiosity.

As the day unfolded, more and more people ventured in, the book-shop buzzing with the energy of renewed life. The stories whispered from the pages seemed to resonate with those who sought them, of-fering an escape from the worries of the outside world.

With each book that found a new home, I couldn't help but feel a deep sense of fulfillment. The bookshop had been revitalized and it was once again fulfilling its role as a sanctuary for the curious, the dreamers, and the seekers of solace in the written word.

As the sun dipped below the horizon, casting a warm, orange glow through the windows, I knew that this was just the beginning. The bookshop's legacy would continue to thrive and its stories would weave themselves into the hearts and minds of those who passed through its doors.

Just as I was beginning to prepare for the day's end, the tiny bell above the door chimed merrily, announcing the arrival of another customer. I glanced up from my task, ready to offer a warm greeting, as I had done countless times before. But what I saw sent a jolt of alarm coursing through my veins.

Six formidable fae males strode into the bookshop, their presence immediately sending my guard up. Two of them were unmistakable—Thalion and Aerion, the very fae who had abducted from this very bookshop me not so long ago. I swore under my breath. The fucking nerve of them to show up here again.

My heart pounded as memories of my harrowing escape from their clutches flooded back. I had managed to slip away from them by the skin of my teeth and the encounter had left me shaken and wary of the fae. Now, they stood before me, their powerful forms a stark contrast to the cozy, book-filled surroundings.

My magic responded to the threat, flames flickering to life in my blackened outstretched hands. The fire danced and crackled, a warning that I was not to be trifled with. I didn't want to send the bookshop up in flames, but I would do what I had to if it meant I wouldn't be taken again. Nyxen, sensing my distress, bounded from the shadows behind the counter and emitted a low growl, watching the fae with glowing yellow eyes.

Thalion and Aerion exchanged a glance. They knew I wouldn't go down without a fight. The flickering flames in my hands were a vivid testament to my readiness to defend myself.

The other fae, unfamiliar to me but equally imposing, regarded me with a mixture of curiosity and wariness. It was clear they hadn't anticipated such a strong reaction from me.

My heart raced, and I steeled myself for whatever might come next. The bookshop, once a sanctuary, now felt like a battleground and I was prepared to defend it with every ounce of strength I possessed. Nyxen stood steadfast beside me, prepared to help in any way he could.

The air seemed charged with tense energy, the delicate balance between aggression and negotiation hanging by a thread. I couldn't afford to let my guard down, not with Thalion, Aerion, and their intimidating companions in my space.

Thalion's voice was an unexpected contrast to his intimidating presence, carrying a low and almost soothing quality. "Easy, princess," he implored, his words barely louder than a whisper. "We mean you no harm. We only wish to talk."

My eyes remained narrowed, the fiery manifestation in my hands responding to the tension in the room. "Then why the full show of force, fae?" I spat the last word like an insult.

Aerion, the one I had struggled to escape from before, took a step forward. His voice, like Thalion's, was a stark contrast to the danger they represented, smooth and honeyed. "We had no choice. You've made it clear that we cannot trust you. The only way to ensure your cooperation is with an equal show of strength."

My grip on my magic remained tight, though Aerion's words did give me a moment of pause. "I don't know whether I should be flattered you think so highly of my strength as to bring along four other of your thugs, or enraged that you're back here again claiming you can't trust me after it was *you* two who abducted *me*."

Aerion chuckled, his amusement not reaching his eyes. "Perhaps a little bit of both. But know this, princess, we have no intention of harming you. Quite the opposite, in fact."

His cryptic words left me even more wary, my flames flickering slightly. "What is that supposed to mean?"

"It means," Aerion continued, his voice laced with intrigue, "that we are here to offer you an alliance."

The shock of his words reverberated through the room, and for a moment, I couldn't find my voice. An alliance with the fae was something I had never anticipated, and it left me teetering on the precipice of a decision that could change the course of my life forever.

Chapter Seven

The silence enveloped the room like a dense fog. My eyes locked onto Thalion and Aerion as they revealed their unexpected proposition. An improbable alliance with the Fae—sworn enemies turned potential allies.

"An alliance?" I repeated incredulously, skepticism heavy in my voice.

"Yes, princess," Thalion replied, his earnest expression contrasting with the tension in the room. "An alliance between you and the Fae of my court. We need your help."

My scoff echoed through the space. "You have to be joking."

"We are deadly serious," Aerion said firmly. "We need your power, your strength if we are to face the danger looming over your realm."

The cryptic mention of danger only deepened my unease. "Danger? What kind of danger?"

Thalion and Aerion exchanged a knowing glance. The collective disquiet was unmistakable, a sentiment mirrored by the other Fae in the room. "Is this the best place we can talk, or can we go somewhere less public?" Thalion inquired.

I maintained my stern posture, the flames still licking across my hands. "This is as good as you're going to get, princeling. Now talk."

With a resigned nod, Thalion began. "There is a threat to your realm, princess. A threat far greater than anything you've faced before. There is a king among the Fae, one of the seven Fae kings, who is beginning to garner support to launch an assault on the mortal realm and you with it."

"Me?" The word escaped my lips involuntarily, the concept almost too preposterous to comprehend.

Thalion nodded solemnly. "Yes, princess. You, the First Witch come again."

Silence stretched between us as I digested their words, my mind a whirlwind of disbelief and cautious consideration. Could I believe them? Or was this an elaborate ruse born from Fae trickery?

"How can I trust you?" I questioned, my skepticism unabated.

Aerion stepped closer, his grey eyes flashing with an intensity that was impossible to ignore. "You can't. But you have to. Your realm is in grave danger and our realm with it. The chaos that ensues would surely destroy both of us."

I was acutely aware of the gravity behind his words and I found myself at a crossroads, facing an alliance that could potentially alter the fate of both our realms.

Thalion's agreement was a solemn nod, his eyes locked onto mine as if trying to convey the urgency of the situation without words. "We need your help, princess. The mortal realm is no match for the power of the Fae kings. We must join forces if we are to stand a chance against such a threat."

"And why would you two care about the mortal realm?" I asked.

The question seemed to catch Thalion off guard, but Aerion was quick to respond.

A hint of emotion flickered across his features. "I know what it's like to have a home torn from you," he said, his voice soft but strained.

Their words echoed, filling the room long after they were spoken. I couldn't fully trust them, but their desperation was impossible to ignore. If their claims were true, the mortal realm was indeed in grave danger.

"Fine," I finally relented, allowing the flames in my hands to subside. "But don't think I trust you. Tell me more about all of this."

Aerion's smirk, laced with the peculiar charm that seemed to be characteristic of the Fae, conveyed his understanding. "We wouldn't expect anything less, princess."

With a degree of tension now eased, the Fae in the room visibly relaxed, though their demeanor remained guarded. I couldn't help but notice the subtle shifts in their posture and expressions, betraying the deeper currents of their emotions.

"You should have a seat," Thalion suggested, gesturing towards the cozy reading nook nearby.

I obliged, taking a seat and watching them cautiously. Thalion and Aerion followed suit, their movements as fluid and graceful as ever. They looked ridiculous sitting in the bean bag chairs we had in the nook. The other Fae lingered nearby, their gazes betraying no hint of emotion.

Thalion and Aerion wasted no time delving into the dire situation at hand.

"There are seven Fae kings," Thalion began, "Each with their own court. For centuries, they've focused their attention on each other, warring for territory within Elysian, the Fae realm. After the witches, their power remained unchecked, but they turned on each other before they had a chance to venture into the mortal realm. However, with the Fae king, Haldir, is now trying to gather multiple courts under his banner. There's a very real chance he'll succeed."

"But why now? After all these centuries?" I couldn't help but ask.

Thalion's eyes locked onto mine as he answered, "Because you are rising in power, princess. And where your power grows, the resurgence of the witches isn't far behind. Haldir knows this and is aware that his window of opportunity is closing rapidly. We have strong suspicions that he's planning to send someone to eliminate you."

The revelation shook me to my core. "But how could I reestablish the witches if they have to be born, not made?" I asked incredulously.

Thalion and Aerion exchanged a meaningful glance. "You mean, you don't know that you have the power to create new witches?" Aerion asked.

His words struck me like a bolt of lightning. Create new witches? The prospect of forming a community of witches, of not being alone in this perilous journey, was exhilarating. "I have never heard anything about the ability to create new witches, nor have I ever read about it in the library," I admitted.

Thalion leaned in closer. "I read about it long ago in an ancient text, one that currently resides in my family's personal library. There can be no mistake, you indeed possess this power," he confirmed.

"I can't be sure that this power is real, or something you're simply using to try to manipulate me into your service," I stated firmly, doubting them entirely.

Thalion's gaze was unwaveringly sincere. "Why would we make something like that up?"

I didn't relent, my skepticism still lingering. "I have no idea. I don't trust you, Thalion. Nor do I have any reason to, after the way you and the other Fae have treated the witches throughout the centuries."

Aerion couldn't hide his exasperation, rolling his eyes. "I could show you the text if that would ease your mind, but you'd have to come with us to the Fae realm. However, we're running out of time. The threat grows greater by the day. Will you at least consider working with us?"

Their words echoed in the silence as I remained deep in thought, wrestling with the implications of their proposition. The responsibility was immense and I couldn't afford to make a hasty decision.

"I'll need time to think this over," I finally replied, my voice sure.

Thalion nodded understandingly, rising from his seat. "Of course. But please, do not take too long. We'll be back in three days' time for your answer."

"Three days," I repeated quietly.

"Three days," Aerion affirmed, his expression earnest.

They turned to leave and I followed them to the door. As they filed out, I couldn't help but feel the magnitude of the decision looming before me. Could I trust them? The fate of two realms now rested in my hands and I had to choose wisely.

My decision was a heavy weight on my shoulders as I pondered whether I could trust these Fae. The thought of working alongside the very beings that had once held me captive made me uneasy, a bitter reminder of the past.

With a burdened spirit, I turned away from the door, my thoughts mired in uncertainty. I locked the door with deliberate care, the metallic click of the lock sliding into place reverberating through the bookshop like a final verdict.

The dimly lit bookshop had always been a refuge for me, a place of solace and knowledge. But tonight, it felt more like a prison of my own making, my doubts and fears keeping me confined within its walls.

With a sigh I began climbing the stairs to my apartment, my exhaustion hitting me in full force.

As I climbed into bed, thoughts of today's events still swirling in my head, I knew that sleep would be a luxury I couldn't afford. The room was bathed in the soft glow of moonlight seeping through the curtains, casting long shadows that danced on the walls like spectral apparitions.

I couldn't escape the doubts that plagued me. My mind was a tempest of conflicting emotions, a battleground where trust and suspicion clashed with the fate of two realms hanging in the balance.

My thoughts drifted to the other six Fae kings, mysterious and powerful beings whose intentions remained shrouded in uncertainty. The threat they posed loomed ominously, like a dark cloud on the horizon, and I couldn't shake the feeling that things were about to get a whole lot more complicated and dangerous.

With a sigh, I closed my eyes, hoping that sleep would offer some respite from the turmoil within me. In the stillness of the night, I wrestled with my decision, knowing that in the morning, the sun would rise on a new day and a new path—one that held both promise and peril.

The next morning, I made my way to the werewolf camp, feeling a pressing urgency within me. As I approached, I spotted Wren near the central bonfire, his expression serious as he spoke with Venna. The camp was bustling with activity, but I knew I needed to talk to Wren about the Fae situation.

"Wren," I called out as I approached, drawing his attention away from his conversation. He nodded in greeting and I could tell he was curious about the reason for my visit.

I took a deep breath, aware of the profound implications of the situation. "I need to tell you about something that happened last night," I began. "I had an unexpected visit from some Fae, including the ones who kidnapped me a month ago."

Wren's brow furrowed with concern. "What? What happened?"

"They claim there's a Fae king named Haldir who's amassing power and planning an attack on both the Fae and mortal realms," I explained. "They say he's a major threat and they want to form an alliance with me to stop him."

Wren's expression was one of serious confusion. "Let's talk more in my tent, come on." He said, leading me to his large tent.

Inside, I sat down on the worn couch as he busied himself with making coffee. We didn't continue the conversation until be placed a steaming mug in my hand.

"Start from the beginning," he said, sitting down beside me.

I explained to him everything they had told me about Haldir and his plans. How I could possibly create more witches, and how I was quickly becoming a threat to him.

Wren's expression darkened as he listened. "I don't know about all this, Vale. These Fae have already tried to kidnap you once and very nearly succeeded. What if this is just another ploy to get their hands on you?"

I could understand Wren's skepticism, it was a valid concern. "Believe me," I replied, "I've thought about it. But they could have easily overpowered me last night with those friends of theirs and taken me then if that was their true intention."

Wren still didn't look entirely convinced and I couldn't blame him. The Fae were known for their cunning and deceitful ways. This alliance was a risky proposition and the fate of both realms hung in the balance.

"We need to be cautious," Wren finally said, his voice low. "I don't trust these Fae, but if what you're saying is true, we can't afford to ignore the threat. We'll need to gather more information and consider our options carefully."

I nodded in agreement, relieved that Wren was at least willing to consider the possibility. This was just the beginning of a complex and perilous journey and I couldn't predict where it would lead us. But one thing was certain: we couldn't face this threat alone, and the Fae might be our only chance at stopping it.

"Whatever happens," Wren said, "you can count on me. I'll stand by you no matter what."

I met his gaze, gratitude welling up inside me. His unwavering loyalty was a source of strength that I couldn't underestimate. I believed in the path we were considering, but it wouldn't be easy, and knowing Wren was with me bolstered my resolve.

"Thank you," I said softly.

"You're welcome," Wren replied, his words echoing with a sense of commitment.

Setting the coffee cup aside, I rose from my seat. There was work to be done, preparations to make, and allies to consult. "We'll talk again tomorrow," I said, looking at Wren. "I've got to prepare the protections for the camp. Harker's been researching the right wards for the job and I'm sure she's come up with something by now."

Wren stood, his eyes locking onto mine. "Good luck. Keep me updated on everything, Vale. You can always come to me, you know that."

I nodded, my heart warmed by his words and the knowledge that I had a true friend by my side. "I do."

With a final nod, we parted ways for the time being, each of us carrying our own heavy burdens and responsibilities in the face of an uncertain future.

Chapter Eight

The shadows parted as I stepped into my apartment, a familiar sense of homecoming washing over me. I had spent countless hours within these walls, finding solace and purpose in the tomes that lined my bookshelves.

As I made my way to the library, I could already hear the telltale signs of an argument in progress. Harker's assertive voice was unmistakable and it seemed she had found herself in yet another dispute with Elara. I sighed, knowing that this was a battle neither of them would ever truly win.

Pushing the library door open, I found Harker and Elara amid their heated discussion. Books lay scattered on tables and the floor\ and it was clear that this particular debate had disrupted the usual order of the library.

"We need some kind of system in here, Elara," Harker was saying, frustrated. "You can't just throw books in wherever you please. It's chaos in here."

Elara, her ethereal form shimmering with annoyance, shot back, "This system has worked for over two hundred years and I'm not changing it now."

Harker rolled her eyes and crossed her arms. "That was back when there was nobody but your ghostly ass in the library."

I couldn't help but smirk at their ongoing banter, though I knew it was a lost cause. Elara was fiercely protective of her library and no amount of arguing would change that.

With a long-suffering sigh, Harker turned to me, her exasperation still evident in her expression. "When I'm a ghost, I'm coming back to haunt Elara."

I chuckled at her threat. The library was a place of refuge for me, and the quirks of its supernatural inhabitants only added to its charm. In the grand scheme of things, a little disorder in the library was a small price to pay for the knowledge it contained.

"Maybe we can find a compromise someday," I suggested, though I doubted that would ever happen.

Harker gave me a wry smile and shook her head. "Don't hold your breath, Vale. It's ghosts versus vampires in here, and the ghost has home-field advantage."

I nodded in agreement, a sense of contentment washing over me as I settled into the familiar surroundings of the library. Whatever arguments and chaos awaited me, it was good to be home.

"So, what's up?" Harker asked.

I filled her in on the fae's visit and their request for an alliance. She listened intently, her expression growing more serious as I described the threat of Haldir and his plans.

When I finished, Harker was silent for a moment, clearly processing the information. "This is big, Vale. Really big. And if it's true, it could mean trouble for all of us."

I nodded, fully aware of the situation's importance. "I know. That's why I need your help, Harker. If I'm going to decide what to do, I need to know more about the Fae and this threat."

Harker's eyes lit up, a rare look of excitement passing over her face. "I'll start looking through my books at home. There has to be something in there that can give us more information."

I smiled, knowing that if anyone could uncover the answers we were seeking, it was Harker. Her dedication and passion for research were unmatched and I was grateful to have her on my side.

"Did you ever find any useful wards for the werewolf camp?" I asked her, remembering why I'd visited in the first place.

"Not yet, but I'm still looking. Don't worry, I'll have something before the end of the day."

With that, we got to work combing through the library's vast collection of books and scrolls in search of the answers we needed. The hours passed by in a blur as we delved deeper into the realm of protective magic.

The ancient magical library was sentient. You could ask it for what you needed and it would spit it out, quite literally, for you. But the answers weren't always straightforward and you got to go looking for clues more often than not.

The air in the room was still as we concentrated on our task and the soft glow of lamplight illuminated our faces as we pored over ancient texts. The sound of turning pages and the scratch of pen on paper filled the room as we diligently recorded our findings.

By the end of the day, I was exhausted, my mind and eyes weary from hours of intense research. However, our efforts had not been in vain. We'd managed to find several promising wards for the werewolf camp, each with its own unique strengths and requirements.

"Well, that's one hell of a spell," Harker breathed, her voice low, as she read aloud from a particularly potent incantation. "An animal sacrifice to bind the ward. Are you sure this is the best option?"

I frowned, contemplating the grim requirement. "It's powerful, which is what we need. And if we can spare the goat, I think it's worth the risk. The alternative is just not as strong."

Harker sighed, her gaze shifting between the text and my face, concern etched in her features. "I know, you're right. Just, be careful, okay? Animal sacrifice is not something to play around with."

I smiled, grateful for her understanding and support. "I will. Don't worry, I've gotten good at this whole witch thing, remember?"

She rolled her eyes in a mock display of exasperation, but there was warmth in her gaze. "Alright, fine. Just don't make me regret letting you do this without me."

With the promise to keep her updated, I carefully closed the tome, its ancient binding creaking as it settled. I had a plan and though it carried risks, it was the best chance I had to protect the werewolf camp.

I'd have to call Wren about the goat, though. Surely someone at the camp knew where to get one by tomorrow night.

"So, about that Fae alliance," Harker began, her tone serious. Her sharp gaze bore into mine, searching for answers.

I sighed, my fingers absently pinching the bridge of my nose as I leaned back in my chair. "I don't know. It's a huge risk, but if they're telling the truth, we could really use their help. I'm just not sure we can trust them."

Harker nodded, her expression thoughtful. She leaned forward, resting her elbows on her knees. "It's a tough call, Vale, but it's not like we have a lot of options. I don't think we can afford to ignore the possibility."

I ran a hand through my hair, feeling the burden of responsibility on my shoulders. The past had taught me that trust could be a dangerous thing, especially when dealing with beings from other realms. I couldn't help but remember the last time I had trusted such a being like this. It had ended in betrayal.

The room held a sense of intimacy, illuminated by a single lamp that cast a warm, inviting glow. The soft murmur of the city outside seemed distant, leaving only the hushed tones of our conversation to fill the space. Harker's words hung in the air, her encouragement grounding me.

"I just don't want to get blindsided by these Fae. They're tricky," I admitted, my voice tinged with a hint of concern.

Harker, always pragmatic, simply shrugged. "I have no doubt, but we're tricky too. Don't underestimate yourself, Vale."

Her words were a balm to my unease, a reminder that I had faced formidable challenges before and emerged stronger for it. I nodded in acknowledgment, the impact of our discussion still lingered with me.

"I won't," I assured her.

With a sigh, I rose from my chair, preparing to leave her to her research in the library. The night was young, but I knew there would be no sleep for me, not with the weight of this monumental decision hanging over my head. The clock was ticking, and soon, the Fae would return, expecting an answer.

As I made my way out of the library, couldn't ignore the profound seriousness of the situation. The fate of our realm rested on my shoulders and every choice I made had the potential to change the course of our world. So just another Tuesday then.

I decided to take a walk in the brisk night air, hoping that the solitude and the cool breeze would help clear my mind. The city streets were quiet and the moon hung low in the sky, casting long shadows across the pavement. Each step I took felt like a step into the unknown and I couldn't shake the feeling that my life was on the verge of a profound transformation.

Only time would tell what the future held and I could only hope that I would make the right choices.

The city streets stretched out before me, the night air cool against my skin as I continued to wander aimlessly, my thoughts in disarray. How was I supposed to make a decision of this magnitude? Could I truly trust these Fae, beings known for their cunning and tricks?

Lost in my contemplation, I turned a corner without paying much attention, and there, almost at a collision course, I nearly ran into Kaelan. His presence was unexpected, and I could see the stormy emotions churning in his eyes.

"Vale," he murmured, his voice a low, tense growl.

I couldn't hide the frustration that surged within me, my nerves frayed from the weight of my decision. "Oh, what is it now?" I snapped, my patience worn thin. I was in no mood to deal with Kaelan's presence, to confront the feelings I had been suppressing.

Kaelan, never one to back down, stood his ground, his jaw clenched with barely contained irritation. His eyes blazed with emotion and his voice was a low rumble when he spoke.

"I'm not going to let you just dismiss me like that. Not anymore."

His words were a challenge and I could feel the tension between us already rising. I knew he was right and yet I couldn't bring myself to acknowledge it.

"Look," he said, his voice still laced with frustration. "I get it. You're scared. You're scared that I'll hurt you again. But you can't run away from this, Vale. We're bonded, you can feel it, I know you can."

My heart hammered in my chest as I struggled to respond. I was caught between the urge to run and the need to stay. I *could* feel it, that small thread that pulled me towards him, but I was terrified.

I swallowed, the emotions swirling within me, threatening to overwhelm me.

"I can't," I finally whispered, my voice hoarse with pain. "I can't do this, Kaelan."

"Well maybe I'm too much of a demon now to care," he growled. "Because I don't give a fuck."

And then his hands were on me, pulling me closer, and his lips were on mine, hard and demanding. And despite my fear and uncertainty, I could feel the pull between us strengthening, the bond that refused to be ignored.

I pulled back quickly and smacked him across the face hard. Which resulted in a low growl from his throat. I turned to walk away when he reached out and grabbed me by the throat, spinning me around and pulling me into a side alley.

I gasped as he pressed me against the wall, his eyes flashing dangerously.

"You don't get to just walk away from me, little witch," he purred low in his chest. "We're bonded, whether you like it or not."

I could feel the heat radiating off his body and I knew that this wasn't the time to argue. He was a fully unbound demon now and there was no telling what he was capable of. I remained as still as possible as if cornered by a wild animal.

I stared up at him defiantly, trying to ignore the way his touch sent sparks of electricity through my body.

"Then prove it," I challenged, my voice barely more than a whisper.

Kaelan's eyes flashed and before I could react, he was kissing me, his lips hot and forceful against mine.

I gasped as his tongue slid into my mouth and I could feel the fire building between us, the bond pulling us together like magnets. I tried to push him away, but he was too strong, his arms holding me in place. And as much as I hated to admit it, part of me didn't want him to stop.

He broke the kiss suddenly, his breathing ragged, his eyes blazing with desire. "Vale," he rasped against my throat, his voice thick with emotion. "I'm not going to let you push me away."

And then his lips were on mine again and all thoughts of resistance fled my mind.

I gave in, letting him claim me with his kiss, the bond between us burning with renewed intensity.

My body responded to his touch and I could feel my own desire building, the fire within me raging out of control.

I knew that I should stop this, that I should walk away, but I couldn't. Not when every fiber of my being was begging for him.

So I surrendered, giving in to the pull of the bond, letting it consume me.

Kaelan's hands roamed over my body and I gasped out a small moan as he cupped my breasts. Summoning a shred of resistance, I roughly shoved his hands away, breaking the kiss. He quickly grabbed both my wrists in his hand, pulling them above my head and holding them there with one hand.

"Kaelan, what are you—" he cut me off with another kiss, his hand curling around my throat while the other still pinned my hands above my hand.

"You're mine, Vale," he growled, his voice low and dangerous.

His words sent a shiver of desire through my body, and the energy between us seemed to amplify.

I tried to free myself, but his grip was like iron.

"Let me go, Kaelan," I gasped, my body betraying me as I arched against him, desperate for his touch.

"Not a chance," he whispered in my ear, his free hand slipping beneath the hem of my shirt, his fingers brushing against my skin.

I let out a soft sigh as his lips trailed kisses down my neck, the heat within me rising to a fever pitch.

I knew I should stop this, that I should put a stop to his advances, but my body was no longer under my control. I was his, and we both knew it.

His hand moved lower, slipping beneath the waistband of my pants and I cried out softly as his fingers found the aching heat between my legs.

"That's it," he murmured, his voice a low rumble. "Give in to me."

I was helpless to resist as his fingers teased me, circling my clit, sending waves of pleasure crashing through my body.

"Kaelan," I gasped, his name a breathless plea on my lips.

He finally let go of my wrists and I dropped my arms, wrapping them around his neck, and fisting my hands in his hair roughly, enough to hurt.

He kissed me again, his lips claiming mine as his fingers slid inside me.

I could already feel the pleasure building within me just from the sheer ferocity of the moment and I knew that there was no turning back.

Suddenly, he pulled his fingers out of me and roughly turned me around, pressing me up against the cold brick wall.

"What are you doing?" I panted, my heart hammering in my chest.

"Showing you who you belong to," he growled, his hands shoving my pants around my ankles.

The cool night air sent a shiver through me and I gasped as I felt his hardness pressed against me, teasing me.

I moaned as he thrust inside me with no warning, filling me completely, and I surrendered to the pleasure of his touch, his body moving in a frenzied rhythm.

He was everywhere, surrounding me, claiming me, touching me, and I could feel the bond between us burning brighter than ever. His shadows pressed around us, caressing my skin like a cold mist, keeping out any prying eyes.

I cried out as his fingers dug into my hips, his cock thrusting deeper, sending shockwaves of pleasure through my body. My blackened fingertips dug into the brick beneath my hands.

I was lost in a haze of lust and desire and I could feel the pressure building within me, threatening to overwhelm me.

And then, just as I was about to fall over the edge, he pulled out, leaving me gasping and desperate.

"Not yet," he growled, his breath hot against my neck.

He flipped me around, his hands gripping my hips as he lifted me, pushing me up against the wall. I wrapped my legs around his waist as he plunged into me again, his movements frantic and hungry.

I gripped his shoulders, my nails digging into his skin and leaving angry red marks, as he sent me hurtling toward the edge.

I threw my head back, crying out his name as the orgasm hit me, waves of ecstasy washing over me, stealing my breath away.

Kaelan growled, his thrusts becoming more erratic as he chased his own release. I clung to him, the pleasure threatening to tear me apart.

"Vale," he breathed, his voice rough and ragged. "Fuck, I've missed you"

And then he came, his body shuddering as he spilled himself inside me, his breath hot against my skin.

We stayed like that for a moment, our bodies intertwined, our breath coming out in ragged gasps.

Finally, Kaelan pulled back, his gaze intense as he stared down at me.

"I love you."

I went stock still as soon as the words left his lips, my eyes wide. It was like my mind had snapped awake from a trance. Kaelan's expression was shocked as I pushed him away roughly.

"You can't say that," I growled, anger surging through me. I had just been a victim of his seduction, and I hated myself for it. "This was a mistake," I hissed, pulling up my pants and refusing to meet his gaze.

Kaelan grabbed me by the arm, his expression pained. "It's not a mistake," he insisted, his voice desperate.

"Yes, it is!" I snapped, pulling my arm away from his grip.

"I don't expect you to forget," he replied, his voice rough. "But I'm not going to give up, Vale. Not when I know how you feel about me."

I glared at him, my fists clenched at my sides. "How I feel doesn't matter. Not anymore. You lost the right to be a part of my life when you chose to betray me. So don't expect anything from me, Kaelan. You're wasting your time."

With that, I turned and stalked off, my heart hammering in my chest, the memory of his touch still lingering on my skin.

Kaelan called after me, but I ignored him, disappearing into the darkness of the city streets. I had made my choice and no matter how much it hurt, I knew it was the right one.

My footsteps echoed down the empty street, the air thick with the scent of impending rain. The storm was coming, and I could feel it in the very depths of my soul.

Chapter Nine

The werewolf camp was nestled on the outskirts of a dense forest, where tall, centuries-old trees formed a protective canopy overhead. The moon, radiant in the night sky, filtered through the leaves, casting dappled patterns of silver light across the camp. The camp itself was a collection of tents and makeshift huts, arranged in neat rows.

As I stood within the camp, I couldn't help but feel a sense of awe. It was a reminder of the profound connection between the werewolves and the natural world around them. The gentle, but eerie howling of wolves in the distance added to the serenity of the moment.

Beside me, Wren stood with an air of authority. Venna was a formidable presence at his side, her sharp eyes always scanning for any potential problems. They were the embodiment of strength and loyalty and I was grateful to have them by my side tonight.

I turned to Wren. "Did you manage to get the goat we needed?" I asked.

Wren nodded, an amused smile playing on his lips. "Of course. We've got everything ready for you. Just point us in the right direction."

I felt a surge of appreciation for his support. "We need to gather in the very center of the camp."

"That would be the largest bonfire near my tent. Let's go." Wren led the way as Venna and I trailed behind him. We came upon what was indeed an impressively large bonfire, the camp was full of them.

"I'll need to set up beside the bonfire, you two can stand off to the side," I told them. "And I'll need that goat now."

Wren signaled to a couple of wolves nearby and they hurried off to retrieve the goat. As we waited for their return, I couldn't help but marvel at the camp's beauty. It was a place that was quickly becoming like a second home to me, a testament to the resilience and strength of the pack.

I set about preparing the space for the ritual and soon, the wolves returned with the goat. I took a deep breath, ready to start the ritual. The forest seemed to come alive with the magic of the moment as I got ready to safeguard the camp from any coming threats.

With a focused and steady hand, I began the intricate process of preparing the warding ritual. The dirt yielded beneath my finger, forming a perfect circle in the hard-packed earth. Each stroke was precise, connecting seamlessly to create a continuous barrier around me. I carefully placed eight small black candles, representing the lunar phases, at equal intervals along the circle's edge.

As Wren and Venne watched from the side, their eyes filled with anticipation, I waved for the black goat to be brought forward. Wren brought it to me himself and it stepped gingerly into the circle, unaware of its looming fate. The small wooden plate I placed down, adorned with a moonstone crystal at its center, held a delicate balance of various herbs — rosemary for protection, rue for warding off negative energy, and sage for purification. Beside the plate, a silver chalice gleamed, its presence pivotal for the upcoming ritual.

With a deep breath, I ignited the candles one at a time using the flames from my own hands. I smiled up at Wren as I did so and he rolled his eyes and chuckled at my attempt to show off. The candle flames danced in harmony with the whispered words that spilled from my lips, like an ancient song.

"Obscuritas prohibere, lumen custodire, custodem fidel," I chanted softly, the words humming with power. Each repetition carried a sense of purpose, a connection to the very essence of the protective magic I sought to invoke.

I dropped the moonstone into the silver chalice, watching as it shimmered in the moon's light. The fragrant herbs followed suit before I poured in the contents of a small glass vile from my pocket. I had made the potion earlier that day, the horrible smell had permeated my small apartment horribly. The goat bleated nervously but stayed within the circle.

The air around me hummed with magic as I continued the chant, my focus unwavering. More and more werewolves had stopped and stood staring at me, watching my progress with curious eyes. The world beyond the circle faded into obscurity, leaving only the moonlight, the candles, and the soft words leaving my lips in a pulsing cadence.

I continued the ritual, each step deliberate and filled with an ancient, almost primal energy. With a quick and precise motion, I made a small cut on my forearm, a few drops of crimson blood dripping into the chalice, mixing with the other ingredients. My blood, offered willingly, would give more power to the ritual. It was a symbol of my commitment to the protection of the camp.

But there was another vial, one filled with deep red liquid, that I retrieved from my pocket. It contained Wren's blood, collected earlier when we had discussed the ritual's requirements. Pouring the contents into the chalice, it mingled with my own, an unspoken oath that bound the wards to Wren. As long as he remained within the camp's boundaries, the wards would hold steadfast.

My chanting continued, a low, melodic murmur that mingled with the gathering magic. The candles flickered in response, casting eerie shadows that danced along the edge of the circle.

The camp was cloaked in an eerie silence, a stark contrast to the turbulence coursing through my veins. The chalice, gleaming with an otherworldly light, rested upon a crude altar fashioned from fallen branches. The incantation, ancient and resonant, flowed steadily from my lips, words passed down through generations of guardians.

My focus remained unbroken, but my heart ached with empathy for the creature before me. The goat's dark eyes, wide with terror, mirrored the despair in my own. It struggled against the rope that bound it, its efforts futile, the coarse fibers digging into its neck. It had been chosen as the sacrifice, a grim necessity to safeguard the camp and its inhabitants.

I briefly noticed a flicker of darkness out of the corner of my eye outside the circle. Nyxen had shown up without me calling him, drawn here by my flowing magic. His presence seemed to heighten the crackling energy in the air.

Continuing the incantation under my breath, I took measured steps toward the quivering goat. My silver knife, cool and gleaming, felt weighty in my hand as I approached. The creature's breath came in ragged gasps, and I couldn't help but share its anxiety.

Gently but firmly, I grasped one of the goat's sturdy horns, my fingers trembling. It stared up at me, innocence and fear mingling in its gaze. As I uttered the next words of the chant, my voice rang out with unwavering resolve, *"Custodi hunclocum, accipe munus!"* The moonlight seemed to intensify, casting an ethereal glow upon the altar.

In one swift, decisive motion, the silver blade descended. The blade met flesh, severing the goat's life with merciful swiftness. The chalice eagerly received the warm torrent of blood, and an otherworldly reaction ensued. The mixture sizzled and smoked, as though the life essence itself was a conduit of power.

My heart ached for the sacrifice, but I knew its purpose was noble, to guard the camp and those who called it home. As the moonlight danced upon the glistening chalice, I couldn't help but wonder if Nyxen's presence was a sign of approval or a silent witness to the dark necessity of our world.

Nyxen growled outside the circle, the sound filled with a strange mix of reverence and excitement. The goat slumped to the ground, its eyes staring lifelessly. I closed my eyes and murmured a brief prayer to the Gods for the animal's soul, thanking it for its sacrifice.

With the chalice in hand, I watched as the moonlight bathed the liquid within, casting a silver glow upon the mixture of blood and herbs. A swirling mist began streaming from within and the air was permeated with the potent scent of the herbs inside.

The assembled wolves stood still, their eyes locked on the ritual's climax. The forest itself seemed to hold its breath as if awaiting the final words that would unleash the gathered magic. *"Custodi aperire, et protegat omnes hic,"* I intoned loudly for all to hear.

As I spoke the last words, the ancient language flowing effortlessly from my lips, a surge of energy burst from the chalice. It erupted into the night sky, twisting and twirling like a celestial dance. The magic sought the camp's perimeter, which had been marked with a circle of salt, weaving itself into an invisible shield that would guard the werewolves against danger.

I closed my eyes and exhaled, feeling the energy settle. Silence descended, the air crackling with residual power. I opened my eyes and saw the wolves gazing at me, their expressions filled with a mixture of awe and respect. It was then I realized I was standing within a ring of flickering light, a faint barrier shimmering around the outer edge.

As the light faded, so did the spell. The wards had taken root, securing the camp in their protective embrace. The effort left me breathless, but a profound sense of accomplishment settled over me. The wolves surrounding the circle erupted into cheers, their voices ringing out into the night. Wren and Venna joined in.

Wren walked over to me as I began smothering the candle flames and placed a strong hand on my shoulder, gratitude reflecting in his eyes. "Thank you," he said sincerely. "The people here will surely never forget this."

"I'm just glad everyone will be safe now," I told him.

Venna gave me a rare smile. "That was some impressive work," she remarked. I grinned back at her, feeling a wave of satisfaction wash over me.

"Now," Wren declared, his tone shifting to one of celebration, "let's celebrate with some food and drink!"

The wolves' cheers grew louder at the prospect of a good meal and I couldn't help but smile. The seriousness of the ritual had lifted and it was time to revel in the victory I had accomplished here tonight.

After cleaning up after the ritual, the wolves began celebrating in the aftermath of the success, their jubilant voices echoing through the camp. The fear of uncertainty and impending danger had been replaced with a sense of security and triumph. I could only hope and trust that the magic I used here tonight was strong enough. The last time my wards had failed me, Juniper had died. I roughly pushed that thought out of my mind.

As the night continued to unfold the atmosphere grew increasingly festive. I found myself drawn into the heart of the celebration, a surprising warmth radiating from the wolves. They approached me with gratitude and admiration, their initial reservations seemingly forgotten in the wake of my accomplishment. It was as if I had earned my place among them, my actions proving my dedication to their cause.

I stayed among the pack, relishing the camaraderie and sense of unity that filled the air. It was a stark reminder of the importance of our mission, a testament to the bonds that held this community together. Laughter and stories flowed freely, carrying with them hope and strength. Nyxen, never one to miss a party, bounded from my shadow and ran over to a group of laughing children, their screams of delight at the strange creature brought a smile to my face.

I approached Wren as he was sitting next to the large bonfire, listening as a man told the story of a wolf who had swallowed the moon. The tale held me in its enchanting grip as I settled beside Wren, the crackling fire casting dancing shadows across his rugged features. The storyteller's voice was like a soothing melody, weaving a tapestry of myth and wonder that transported us to a world far removed from the pressing concerns of the present.

I glanced at Wren and saw his eyes were glued to the storyteller, a look of wonder and fascination playing across his face. It was a rare moment to witness the pack leader so captivated, the weight of his responsibilities momentarily forgotten.

Wren turned his attention from the storyteller to me, his eyes gleaming in the flickering firelight. "Vale," he said with a smile, "thank you again. You've done more than you know for these people. The pack will always owe you a debt." His voice was filled with sincerity and his words struck a cord deep within me.

I chuckled softly, brushing off his thanks with a wave of my hand. "Oh please, you know I'd do anything for you, no questions asked," I replied, a warm smile gracing my lips.

Wren and I shared a history that ran deep. We had grown up together in the same orphanage, our shared childhood marked by the trials of life without parents. From there, at age nine, we had both been tossed into the lower ranks of the Academy, an institution known for its ruthless training methods, where we were groomed to become the future enforcers of the Otherworld.

Our paths had seldom crossed within the confines of the Academy, where competition and isolation were the norm. It wasn't until that fateful night when we were abruptly roused from our bed, an unsettlingly common occurrence at the Academy, and thrust into the wilderness surrounding the institute. Left to fend for ourselves in the biting cold of winter, we faced the harsh reality of survival.

I had been shivering near my feeble campfire, huddling down, desperately needing the warmth when a group of merciless boys had descended upon me. The encounter had quickly turned brutal and I found myself outnumbered and overwhelmed. I was on the ground, my arms wrapped around my head protectively as they beat and kicked at me when Wren appeared. He had been a force of nature in his wolven form, tearing through the group with a primal fury to reach me.

He had shielded me from harm and in that pivotal moment, our friendship was sealed in blood and fire. It was a bond formed in the crucible of adversity and it had endured through all the trials that had come our way. We were both misfits at the Academy, with my strange ways, always trying to hide the truth of what I was, and Wren, who was bisexual, something that was never tolerated inside the Academy walls and among the law keepers.

We had run away from the Academy together at the ages of eighteen one fateful night, unable to continue living the lie of what was demanded of us. The system was built on lies, on suppressing anything that didn't conform to its rigid ideals. And we had had enough when we had been tasked with ending the lives of some unfortunate Otherworlders who had just been trying to get by.

We had soon found the bustling city full of Otherworlders in the state of Washington and built a life for ourselves. Using funds earned from bounty hunting, we bought the abandoned button factory and transformed part of the space into a bookshop.

We had been both proud and strong and had no need for any sort of family except each other. The times had certainly changed, Wren with his own pack and I with my band of unlikely allies.

I was brought back to the present as Wren spoke again. "Have you thought about this alliance with the Fae anymore?"

As the fire crackled beside us, I considered Wren's question of the Fae. It was a choice I had wrestled with, a decision that felt final like it would shape the course of my journey in unimaginable ways. But responsibility pressed on me, urging me to make the right call.

"I have and I think the best choice would be to go ahead with the alliance," I confessed, even though my voice was uncertain. "I can't trust the Fae, not completely, but I also can't afford to ignore the danger they spoke of."

Wren considered my words and then finally nodded thoughtfully, understanding the complexity of the situation. "It's a difficult decision but I trust your judgment. Just promise me you'll be careful in Elysian."

I gave him a wry smile. "You know me, Wren. I'm always careful." I said, my eyes dancing with amusement.

He chuckled, knowing that was the opposite of the truth. "I'll miss having you around the camp."

"Hey, I'll be back whenever I can," I assured him. "Which reminds me that I need to ask Ava to start looking after the bookshop. I think she'll be a good fit for it. Maybe she'll find someone else to help her."

"You want to go visit the Otherworlders now? It's been a while since I've checked on them." Wren asked, standing up.

"Yes, it's been a while since I've seen them too. Let's go."

I said a few quick goodbyes to the wolves who were gathered nearby and we headed over to the corner of the camp reserved for the mixed group of Otherworlders. Wren and I had housed them at the factory after the demon attacks had begun to rise before they had finally ended up here, safely within the confines of the camp.

The Otherworlder's portion of the camp had transformed into a small haven within the larger wolf community. Tents and shelters were scattered around, but despite the makeshift living arrangements, there was an air of resilience and unity among them.

As the festivities continued around us, I couldn't help by feel relieved. It was moments like these, where I saw the harmony between different races and beings, that reminded me why we fought so hard to protect this world.

A group of children ran past us, chasing after each other and giggling. They were a mix of species, with some displaying the slightly pointed ears of the Fae, while others had the tell-tell signs of demons in them. It was a heartwarming sight, a testament to the hope that could flourish in even the darkest of times.

As we approached, several members of the group greeted us with warm smiles and friendly waves. Jason, the unofficial leader of the group, spotted us and came over.

"It's good to see you two. It's been a while." He greeted the both of us.

"Sorry about that," I apologized. "We've been so busy with everything going on. I'm glad to see everyone doing so well," I said to him as I watched the children play.

"How is everyone here?" Wren asked curiously.

"We're doing well, thanks to you two. Things have been pretty quiet lately," Jason said, looking around at the happy group.

"The pack members haven't been giving you any problems, have they?" Wren asked, some of the pack had voiced their dissent in offering refuge to the Otherworlders.

Jason shook his head. "No, nothing like that. Everyone has been very welcoming. We appreciate all that you're doing for us."

"Good. That's really good to hear." Wren responded.

"Jason, do you know where Ava is?" I asked him, remembering the reason why I had needed to come over here.

"I think she's over with the musicians." He said, gesturing towards a group of people seated around the fire, playing various instruments softly.

Jason's directions led us to the heart of the musical celebration, where Ava was fully immersed in the joyous atmosphere. Her voice, clear and melodious, harmonized beautifully with the others.

As we approached, I couldn't help but be drawn into the music and joyous atmosphere. The people around the fire clapped and swayed to the rhythm, their laughter and cheers punctuating the music. It was a stark contrast to the harsh realities we often faced in our world.

For a moment, I allowed myself to forget about the Fae, the impending threat, and the heavy responsibilities that weighed on me. I simply stood there, absorbing the warmth and happiness that surrounded us.

Eventually, Ava noticed us and made her way over, her smile radiating warmth and affection.

"I haven't seen you guys in a while, where have you been hiding?" she asked, her voice playful.

"We've been pretty busy lately," I replied, smiling at her. "How are you?"

Ava's smile brightened and she glanced around at the joyful gathering. "Everything's wonderful."

"That's great, Ava. I was actually wondering if you could help me out with something, though," I said, shifting the conversation to the reason for our visit.

Ava's eyes widened and she nodded her head, waiting for what I would ask.

"I have to leave the city for a bit and was wondering if you could look after the bookshop. I was planning on reopening it permanently and you would be the perfect person to run it. Maybe someone else here could help you?" As I spoke her grin widened.

"Are you serious? That would be amazing! Of course, I'll do it, I would love to!" Ava replied, her enthusiasm infectious.

"Thank you so much. I really appreciate it. You can start as soon as tomorrow if you'd like." I said, feeling a weight lift from my shoulders. She gave me a quick hug before returning to her friends, the smile never leaving her face.

Wren and I stood watching the celebration for a while, feeling a sense of pride and accomplishment. The Otherworldershad found a home here, a place where they could live freely without fear. It was a victory, albeit a small one, but one that gave us hope.

After a while, Wren and I said our goodbyes to the others and returned to his large tent.

"You should go home and get some sleep, I know you've been keeping long hours recently," Wren said, looking concerned.

"I will, I promise. Thank you for the support, Wren," I said, my heart swelling.

"Anytime." He said, the corners of his mouth twitching upward.

"I'll see you soon."

I stepped outside, the night air cool against my skin. I walked across the camp, Nyxen at my side, my heart lighter than it had been in a while.

"Take me home, Nyxen," I told my familiar affectionately. Nyxen's consciousness brushed up against mine in response.

"Vale." A voice in my head rang out, and in pure shock, I looked down at the shadowkin. He looked back at me with gleaming yellow eyes, intelligence shining through. I knew the connection between us was ever-growing, but I had not imagined this would happen. Without wasting another minute, his shadows enveloped me, a sense of safety washing over me as they did, and we shifted into the night.

Chapter Ten

The following day was a whirlwind of preparations. I had placed enhanced wards around the library, ensuring that they would remain protected in my absence. The new wards would not only deter any demons but also alert me if anyone attempted to breach them.

One critical task involved mixing Harker's blood into the ritual that powered the wards. It was a precaution to allow her to bypass the defenses and access the library. Harker had been slightly apprehensive about it, but she understood the importance of being able to access the library.

As night settled over the city, casting long shadows through the windows, I sat in my bedroom, surrounded by a jumble of clothes and essentials strewn across my bed. Packing for a journey into the unknown was never easy and this time was no different.

The door to the library was ajar and I could see Harker inside, engrossed in one of the books. She probably knew more about magic than I did at this point. She had always been diligent in studying the books found in there and it was no different now, even with the looming threat from the Fae.

As I shoved clothes into my pack, Harker eventually emerged from the library, a determined look in her eyes. She approached me with a small leather-bound notebook in her hands.

"Vale," she began, her voice soft but earnest, "I've been working on this for a while now. It's a sort of grimoire, filled with spells, rituals, and notes that I think might be useful to you during your time with the Fae."

I accepted the notebook, running my fingers over the smooth leather cover. The significance of her gift was not lost on me.

"Thank you, this is amazing," I said, my voice filled with gratitude. "This means a lot to me."

She smiled, a rare expression of warmth on her usually reserved face. "You're welcome. Just promise me you'll be careful out there."

I nodded, appreciating the significance of Harker's gesture. It wasn't often that she opened up or expressed herself in such a way. Her life had been solitary and mysterious, spent delving into the arcane mysteries of ancient texts and social interactions had never come easily to her, despite her confident outward appearance. The fact that she had presented me with this grimoire spoke volumes about the bond that had quietly developed between us over time.

With a sense of reverence, I carefully placed the notebook in my pack, ensuring it was well-protected for the journey ahead. Harker's notes, spells, and rituals could prove to be invaluable in the unpredictable world of the Fae.

As I continued to pack, I remembered one more important detail. I glanced over to where the black and white cat was peacefully snoozing on the windowsill, completely oblivious to our conversation.

"Oh, by the way," I said, diverting Harker's attention to the feline, "since you're staying here, can you please take care of the cat?"

Harker's gaze shifted to the cat and I couldn't help but notice the wariness in her eyes as she regarded the seemingly contented creature.

"Sure, I can do that," she replied hesitantly, her tone uncertain. "How hard can it be?"

I couldn't help but chuckle at her apprehension, fully aware that Harker had no prior experience with animals, let alone cats. It was an unexpected request from me and I could see the skepticism in her expression.

"Just make sure he has food and water and that the litterbox is clean," I advised with a reassuring smile. "He shouldn't be any trouble; he's a good cat."

Harker nodded, though her wariness remained. Taking care of a cat was a far cry from her usual solitary pursuits and I could tell she was silently contemplating the challenges that might come with the responsibility.

"I took some time to do research on the Fae back at my house," she said. Her expression had turned slightly grim as she began to speak. She shifted uncomfortably on her feet, her eyes dating towards the dusty volumes lining the library's shelves, clearly ready to get back to reading.

I leaned forward, curiosity piqued by her words. "Yeah? Anything particularly interesting or concerning?"

Harker's brow furrowed as she continued. "Kind of," she began, her words measured. "Though the information is limited, as most of it was passed down orally. From what I read, the Fae have been around since the beginning of time. They were here when the realms were brand new and many believe that they are the most powerful beings in existence, created by the Gods."

Her words echoed with a sense of awe and reverence as if she couldn't help but acknowledge the immense power that the Fae were said to possess.

"Their magic is different than yours," she continued, her eyes meeting mine, "more elemental, tied to nature. The Fae are said to be mysterious, inscrutable, and notoriously untrustworthy. But if there's anything the lore can agree on, it's that the Fae are a force to be reckoned with."

A warning glinted in her eyes as she emphasized the last sentence, trying to convey the monumental importance of our impending encounter.

I swallowed hard, my unease growing as the implications of her words settled in. "I guess we'll find out the truth of it soon enough."

Harker nodded solemnly, clearly sharing my apprehension. "There are a lot of warnings and cautions and tales of Faetrickery, especially if you end up bargaining with them."

I ran a hand through my hair. Our limited options here were frustrating. "Well, I don't have much of a choice at the moment."

Her voice took on a protective tone as she continued her briefing. Her gaze was steady and unwavering, which was particularly chilling coming from the ice-blue eyes of the vampire. "And this Haldir character, I couldn't find too much on him— just a small scrap describing the seven current Fae kings. Apparently, Haldir was always known as the most cunning among them. If there's a silver lining in all of this, I guess it's that you're not dealing with a complete unknown."

I managed a weak smile, appreciating Harker's attempt to provide some semblance of reassurance, however slight it might be. "I guess. It doesn't make the situation any less terrifying, though."

There was genuine concern in Harker's eyes are she stared at me. "That's true, but it's better than nothing. At least we know he's dangerous, which means you should be on your guard the entire time you're in their realm. And remember, the Fae have a reputation for being devious and manipulative. Whatever you do, don't make any deals with them. You can't trust anything they say and everything is open to interpretation. They can twist the truth and turn your words against you."

"Thanks, I'll try to remember that." With that, Harker turned and went back into the comforting embrace of the library.

As the evening grew later, the anxiety I felt grew with each passing minute. I was leaving my life behind, traveling into the unknown, with only a vague sense of the dangers that awaited me.

Midnight had crept up on me and my room was awash in a dim, silver glow cast by the crescent moon outside. I had meticulously packed the essentials for my journey to the Fae realm, ensuring that I had everything I needed. The sense of impending departure sat heavily on my shoulders and I couldn't shake the lingering unease that had taken root in the pit of my stomach.

But just as I was beginning to find a fleeting semblance of peace amidst the chaos of my preparations, a familiar sensation disrupted the silence. It was as if an invisible string, tethered to the core of my being, had been abruptly pulled. A surge of alarm coursed through me, and I knew that something or someone was attempting to breach the newly erected wards guarding the apartment.

I moved with swift, practiced grace, driven by a sense of urgency. The leather straps of my weapons sheaths dug into my skin as I threw open the window, my eyes scanning the dimly lit streets below. In the pallid glow of a nearby streetlight, I saw him. Kaelan's presence was all too familiar, reminding me vividly of the first time he had shown up at my apartment in the middle of the night.

The memories threatened the flood my mind— of that night, of his touch, of the stolen kiss that had left an indelible mark on my heart. But I pushed them away, focusing instead on the fact he was here now.

"What are you doing here?" I hissed into the night air, my voice laced with irritation.

Kaelan's eyes, like twin pools of darkness, bore into mine, even from a distance. He spoke calmly, knowing that my keen Otherworlder hearing could pick up every word. "I just want to talk."

I clenched my jaw, my patience waning with every passing second. My instincts urged me to tell him to go away, to scream at him to leave me alone. But for now, I merely huffed, my gaze locked onto his unwelcome form in the street below, my fingers tightly gripping the windowsill.

He stood there out on the darkened street, unmoving, his eyes never leaving mine. A myriad of emotions swelled in my chest, threatening to overwhelm me. There was anger, pain, and an aching longing that had lingered ever since the night we had met. If there was one good thing that would come out of leaving tomorrow, it was that I would finally get the distance I needed right now from Kaelan.

Turning away, I broke our connection and slammed the window shut, muttering curses under my breath. I didn't want to confront him now, not among the chaos and uncertainty that lay ahead. Yet, as if guided by an invisible force, my feet betrayed my intent and led me down the apartment stairs to the factory's main floor. Exhaling an irritated sigh, I opened the back entrance, peering into the moonlit night. Kaelan had vanished into the shadows, nowhere to be seen.

I took a tentative step outside, looking around curiously. It was then that he emerged from the shadows, materializing before me like a ghost. My patience had already worn thin, and I couldn't help but snap at his eerie tactics.

"Could you not act all dark and spooky right now?" I muttered irritably. "I don't have the time for this. What do you want?"

Kaelan responded with a casual shrug, an infuriating calmness radiating from him. His demeanor grated on my nerves, kindling the fiery frustration within me.

"I told you, I just want to talk," he stated calmly, his lips twitching with a hint of a smirk.

"Than talk," I retorted, my impatience evident. "Say what you have to say and leave. I have things to do."

His smirk persisted, only adding to my irritation. He met my gaze with an unyielding intensity, his voice steady as he continued.

"I know you're leaving," he began, locking his eyes onto mine, "and I don't think you should go."

My annoyance flared, fueled by his predictably protective stance. "Of course you don't. You think I'm being reckless, again," I snapped, our familiar argument rearing its head. "You think I'm going to fall into a trap and get myself killed. Well, save it, 'cause I've heard it before."

He shook his head slowly, his expression serious. "It's not that, and you know it. This is different, and you know that too."

His unanticipated words lingered between us, urging me to reflect on their significance. I couldn't deny the perilousnessof the situation and his concern, while exasperating, held a grain of truth.

"Look, I know this is the last thing you want to hear, but you're putting yourself at risk," he continued, his tone almost pleading. "You don't know what the Fae are capable of and you're walking straight into their world without a second thought. Don't do this."

I narrowed my eyes, torn between my determination and the worry gnawing at the edges of my resolve. It was all so frustratingly familiar, this clash of wills between us.

"I'm not going to sit here and argue with you," I retorted, my voice firm. "I've made up my mind and I'm not changing it now."

Kaelan's jaw tightened and I could tell there was a whirlwind of emotions brewing beneath the surface. He ran his hands through his hair in frustration, a gesture that had become all too familiar.

"Vale, you're making a mistake," he implored, his voice urgent.

I held his gaze, though turmoil brewed within me. We were stuck in this relentless cycle of disagreement. "And you're wasting your time," I shot back, unwilling to yield. "If that's all you wanted to say, then you can leave."

"I can't protect you if you're not here," he confessed, frustration coloring his words.

"I don't need your protection," I scoffed, my bravado a thin veneer over the complicated emotions that churned within me.

"Damn it, Vale!" Kaelan's voice sliced through the tense air like a blade, his shout echoing in the dimly lit street. It was a stark departure from his usual calm demeanor and his composure was slipping as anger and frustration boiled to the surface.

My own temper flared in response and I felt the heat of indignation rush to my cheeks. My fists clenched at my sides as I fought the urge to lash out physically. I wouldn't give him the satisfaction of seeing me lose control, not again.

"Don't you dare yell at me," I seethed, my voice carrying a venomous edge. "I've had enough of this and I'm done listening to you. Now if you'll excuse me, I have more important things to do than argue with you."

As I turned away, intending to retreat back to the safety of my apartment, his fingers closed around my wrist like a vice. The grip was tight and unyielding and I could feel the pressure of his desperation seeping through.

"On no, you don't," he growled, his voice low but firm. "What did I say before about how you don't get to walk away anymore."

I tried to wrench my arm free, frustration and rage coursing through me. The air around us crackled and I could practically taste his anger in the night air. I realized with a start that I could taste it. I could feel his damned emotions. They were faint but it was unmistakable. Surely this was a part of the blood bond growing and changing.

"This isn't a game, Vale," he implored, his tone shifting from anger to urgency once again. "The Fae are ruthless and unpredictable and they won't hesitate to kill you if they think you're a threat. You can't just barge into their world without a plan and hope for the best. It's too dangerous."

"I'm not a child, Kaelan," I shot back, my voice dripping with defiance. With a final determined pull, I managed to break free from his grasp. "And I'm not going to let the Fae intimidate me into backing down. This is bigger than just me and if that means walking into their world without a plan, so be it."

My breath came out fast and heavy, anger and frustration warring within me. I had made my decision and I wasn't turning back now.

Kaelan stood before me, his expression dark and stormy. His eyes, usually so steady and composed, were filled with turmoil that mirrored the storm of my own feelings.

"You're making a mistake," he finally said again, his voice a hushed murmur. "You're playing right into their hands."

I met his gaze squarely, my own determination clashing with the worry that was etched into his expression. It was a painful recognition of the truth in his words, but I couldn't afford to waver now.

"Maybe," I conceded, my voice resolute, "but that's what you said about the First Witch, too, and that turned out just fine. Maybe you should start trusting my judgment instead of wasting so much energy fighting me every step of the way."

With those words, I turned away from him, the weight of his concerns bearing down on me. It was a heavy burden to carry, knowing that he was right in some ways, but I couldn't allow myself to dwell on it. There was a path before me, one that I had chosen, and I had to follow it to its end, regardless of the consequences.

The cool night air surrounded me as I retreated back into the factory, leaving Kaelan behind in the darkness where he belonged. My heart ached at the unspoken words that lingered between us, but I knew that this separation was necessary, even if it tore at my soul.

I climbed the stairs to my apartment with a heavy heart. The exhaustion of the past few days weighed on my every step as I crossed into my bedroom. The bed welcomed me and I crawled beneath the covers, seeking refuge in the embrace of sleep.

As I lay there in the darkness, my thoughts were a chaotic whirlwind of emotions and doubts. The future was uncertain and I had embarked on a perilous journey into the unknown. But there was no turning back now; my path was set.

"Rowena?" I called out into the stillness of my room.

"Yes, child?"

Her voice echoed in the confines of my mind.

"Do you think I'm doing the right thing? By going with the Fae?"

"That is not for me to say. Only you can answer that question."

I sighed, her words settling upon me like a cloak of doubt. "Was this maybe part of those trials you saw me facing?" I pressed, my voice trembling slightly.

Rowena remained silent, a clear indication that she wouldn't divulge more.

"Please, Rowena, tell me," I pleaded, desperate for guidance.

"Perhaps, but the future is ever-changing. The choices you make tonight could change the course of your destiny. Only time will tell where it will lead."

Her words did little to ease my troubled mind. Despite her cryptic response, the weight of her words was not lost on me. My fate hung in the balance and the decision I made tonight would have far-reaching consequences.

I rolled over in bed and stared up at the ceiling, trying to silence the doubts and fears that echoed in my mind. Tomorrow would bring with it a new day and a new set of challenges. But despite the uncertainty, I was determined to face them head-on.

Chapter Eleven

The next afternoon was awash with anticipation and anxiety as I waited for the arrival of the Fae. Wren and Harker had come to see me off, their presence both comforting and bittersweet. I had let down the wards temporarily, not knowing if they would keep the Fae out or not, they were set to go back up once I had left. We had been waiting for what felt like hours, the minutes ticking away slowly as anxiety gnawed at my stomach.

Wren's expression was concerned as he looked at me, his eyes searching mine for any signs of doubt. "Are you sure about this, Vale?" he asked, his voice filled with genuine worry.

I nodded, even though the nagging anxiety still lingered deep within me. "Yes, I'm sure. I have to do this."

"It's not too late to change your mind," Wren urged, his eyes pleading. "We can find another way."

I shook my head. "There is no other way and we both know it."

Harker stood silently by, her gaze pensive as she watched the exchange. She knew there was no use trying to dissuade me once I had made up my mind.

We waited in tense silence until finally, a presence entered the bookshop, one that I had been both dreading and waiting for. Aerion stepped gracefully into the room, his striking appearance as captivating as ever. He was towering, taller than even Wren. He had a lethal grace that contrasted with his large muscular frame and his piercing grey eyes held a depth that hinted at the mysteries of the Fae.

Upon seeing the pack I carried, he made a confident assumption. "I see you've made your decision," he remarked, his tone as smooth as silk.

I met his gaze, my anxiety momentarily eclipsed by determination. "Yes, I'm going with you."

Aerion's response was brisk, a sense of urgency underlying his words. "Then hurry up and say your goodbyes. The sooner we leave, the better."

Turning towards Wren and Harker I began to bid them goodbye, the words catching in my throat as emotions swelled within me. It was a difficult moment, knowing that I was about to leave on a journey filled with uncertainties and I couldn't help but feel a sense of melancholy.

However, before I could talk, Kaelan appeared in the doorway, his presence disrupting the already charged atmosphere. His eyes bore into mine, frustration and concern etched across his features.

"It seems we have a guest." As Aerion's voice broke the momentary silence, I turned my glare toward Kaelan, frustration and irritation simmering beneath the surface. His continued refusal to accept my decision was testing my patience. Aerion's presence added to the tension and I could feel the collective curiosity of those around us as they watched the exchange unfold.

"You shouldn't have come here," I scolded Kaelan, my voice edged with annoyance.

Kaelan paid no heed to my words; instead, he continued to move closer to me, his gaze locked onto mine. Each step he took felt purposeful as if he was trying to bridge the emotional chasm that had formed between us. His desperation and fear for my safety were evident, and despite my resolve, I couldn't help but feel a pang of sympathy.

He stopped in front of me and his voice was soft as he implored, "Please don't do this."

His plea caught me off guard, but it wasn't enough to sway my decision. "You know I have to," I replied, my voice steady despite the confusion of emotions in me.

Kaelan's expression darkened and he closed the distance between us, his words taking on a low, urgent whisper. "Please, Vale. Let me help you, let me protect you. Just stay here, with me."

His words made me hesitate, the intensity of his emotions almost overwhelming. I stepped back, creating both physical and emotional space between us. "I can't."

"This is madness. It's too dangerous. Let me protect you," he pleaded once more, his voice desperate.

Aerion's unexpected interjection startled me, his voice cutting through the tension like a knife. "The girl said no, demon. What about that do you not understand?" he challenged.

Kaelan's anger surged and he growled in response. "Stay out of this."

Aerious, however, remained stoic. "No, I will not. If the girl does not wish for your assistance, then you have no right to interfere."

"I have every right!" Kaelan retorted sharply. "She's in danger and you are taking her into the heart of it. How can you expect me to stand by and watch her walk away to her death?"

Aerion's response dripped with disdain, his distaste for Kaelan clear. "Your concern is misplaced. If you truly care for her, then you should respect her decisions."

Kaelan's eyes flashed and he didn't mince words. "Don't try to fool yourself, Fae. Your kind has a long history of manipulating others for their own selfish gain."

The animosity hung heavily between them, the tension escalating with every word exchanged. I knew I had to step in before things got out of hand.

"Enough," I interjected firmly, my voice carrying a hint of warning.

Both Kaelan and Aerion turned their attention toward me, their faces reflecting a myriad of emotions.

"This isn't helping anyone," I said, trying to diffuse the situation. "Kaelan, like I've said before, I've made up my mind."

"Vale—" he started, his eyes pleading.

"No, don't," I cut him off, holding up a hand. "I've heard it all before and I'm not changing my mind. Aerion, let's go."

I turned away, ignoring Kaelan's protests. I had made my decision, and I was determined to see it through, no matter the cost.

Kaelan's fingers wrapped around my arm, his grim firm and unyielding, just as he had done the night before. This time, however, the presence of Aerion and Wren added a layer of tension to the situation.

Aerion's eyes narrowed, a clear display of his displeasure. "Unhand her, demon," he hissed, his voice edged with warning. Wren, on the other hand, took a deliberate step forward, a low growl rumbling in his throat.

"Take your hands off her," Wren demanded, his voice low and menacing.

Kaelan's grip only tightened, heedless of the two imposing figures confronting him. "I won't let you go," he muttered, his determination burning bright.

The standoff escalated, the air crackling with hostility. I could sense the impending violence.

"I said, take your fucking hands off her," Wren reiterated, his words laced with the promise of a threat.

Aerion moved closer to us, his expression dark and threatening. "The wolf is right. Release her. I won't ask again."

Still, Kaelan clung to me, his hold unrelenting, a stubborn defiance in his eyes.

"Damn it, Kaelan," I shouted, my voice filled with frustration as I wrenched my arm free, retreating a few steps. "I'm going, and that's final."

Kaelan's face contorted with a mixture of anguish and anger, his frustration palpable. "To hell with this nonsense. You're coming with me."

Before anyone could react, Kaelan grabbed me and shifted, whisking me away in a sudden burst of motion. We reappeared in his house, leaving behind a cloud of chaos and confusion. I stumbled, disoriented by the abrupt shift in surroundings, struggling to regain my balance.

I whirled on Kaelan, my anger burning hot within me. "What's the end game here, Kaelan? You can't just kidnap me and hold me hostage. I can leave anytime I want."

He crossed his arms and met my furious gaze with defiance. "Try it. See what happens."

"Are you serious?" I fumed, my incredulity mounting.

"Dead serious," he replied firmly, his obstinance unwavering.

Fury raged inside of me and I shot him a fiery glare. "You can't stop me from leaving," I insisted. "I'll just shift out of here with Nyxen and be on my way."

"Go ahead and try it. You won't get very far." he retorted without hesitation.

"You can't keep me here," I said, shocked that he would resort to this.

"Watch me," he countered.

Just then, a tremendous boom reverberated through the house as the front door was violently torn from its hinges. Aerionstrode into the room, his eyes filled with a dangerous rage, Wren followed closely behind him.

"I think that's quite enough, demon," Aerion growled, his voice a low and ominous growl.

Wren positioned himself next to Aerion, his body tense and prepared for action. The room crackled with tension as the three of them stood there, a volatile confrontation ready to erupt at any moment.

"No," Kaelan replied, his unyielding gaze still locked onto mine. "She's not going anywhere."

As Aerion and Wren advanced on Kaelan, their intentions clear, I desperately held up my hands, trying to halt the impending fight.

"Wait, don't-"

But my plea was abruptly silenced by a blur of movement. Kaelan sprang forward, his fists connecting with Wren's jaw with a resounding thud, sending him tumbling backward. Wren, however, recovered swiftly, his body contorting and bones cracking. In a matter of seconds, a russet-colored wolf stood before Kaelan, snarling menacingly with bared teeth and fiery eyes.

Aerion wasted no time in joining the melee, his own features shifting into something otherworldly and terrifying.

The room descended into chaos, a cacophony of growls and shouts filled the air as the three supernatural beings clashed in a whirlwind of violence. I was fed up with their stubbornness and the escalating situation. Flames crackled around my outstretched hands as I shouted, "Stop it now, or I'll burn this whole place down with all of us inside!"

Kaelan looked at me, his eyes flashing, and the others froze in their tracks.

"That's better," I said, my voice calm despite my fury. "Now, I'm going with Aerion, and no one is going to stop me. Is that clear?"

"Vale, this is foolish," Kaelan pleaded, his voice strained. "You'll be killed."

"I'm done indulging you," I retorted, my anger and frustration fueling my determination. "How dare you take me against my will! How dare you try and control me!"

I felt the power building within me and I threw up a protective shield around myself, one that would keep even Kaelanout.

"You will not stop me, no matter how hard you try." Turning to Aerion, I nodded firmly. "I'm ready."

"Good, because we've wasted enough time."

"We're taking Wren back first and then we're gone."

I fixed Kaelan with a steely gaze. "Don't come after us. Don't interfere."

With those words, I called Nyxen to me and we shifted away, leaving behind a bewildered and frustrated Kaelan, the world around us dissolving into the unknown.

We were back at the bookshop and Harker had stayed put. She almost jumped out of her skin as we stepped out of the shadows.

"You're back. What happened?" she asked, her eyes filled with curiosity as Nyxen bounded over to her, allowing her to pass her hand through his insubstantial form.

"Just a lot of alpha male bullshit," I replied, my voice laced with frustration, still seething from everything that had transpired.

Aerion smirked. "Quite."

Harker frowned. "Well, I'm glad you're okay. What's the plan now?"

"We go. We don't have time to waste," Aerion declared firmly.

I nodded, my resolve renewed. "Agreed."

Harker stepped forward and embraced me, her eyes sad. "Be careful, Vale," she murmured, her voice thick with concern. "We'll be here when you get back."

I hugged her tightly, feeling the depth of her words sinking in. "I'll do my best," I promised her.

Wren stepped forward next, his usually tough exterior giving way to worry. "Listen, Vale," he began, his voice gruff but filled with genuine concern. "Don't do anything stupid."

Despite the tension in the room, I couldn't help but laugh. "No promises."

He pulled me into a bear hug, his enormous body enveloping mine. "Just take care of yourself. We'll be here when you're ready."

I nodded, fighting back tears that threatened to escape. "Thank you," I managed to say, my voice slightly shaky.

I turned to face Aerion, regarding him curiously as the strange pull of his gaze made me uncomfortable.

"Ready to go?" he asked, his voice a caress that sent a shiver down my spine.

"As ready as I'll ever be," I replied, my voice tinged with a hint of nervousness that I tried to hide.

Aerion held out his hand, his eyes challenging me.

I hesitated for a moment before placing my hand in his, the touch of his skin sending a jolt of energy through me, making my heart race.

"So, how does it work, your shifting?" I asked him, attempting to distract myself from the mounting anxiety.

"Where your familiar can move you through the shadows, I bend reality to fold the planes of existence around me, allowing me to hop from one place to the next. I can not shift between realms though," he explained patiently, as though he were used to explaining this concept to others.

"That sounds complicated."

"Not as much as you'd think," he reassured me. "Come on, it's time."

His grip tightened on my hand and suddenly the world spun around me, colors blurring together, and the ground falling away as we shifted into the unknown.

Chapter Twelve

As Aerion and I shifted through the void, I felt a sense of unease. The world around us swirled with a chaotic dance of colors and sensations, marking my stomach churn. It was a disorienting experience, one that was so different than shadow-shifting that I wasn't sure if I could get used to it.

Finally, we landed on solid ground and I took a deep breath, relieved to be back in the physical realm. We stood in a dense forest, the trees towering overhead, their branches creating a canopy that filtered the dappled sunlight.

"These portals always seem to be in the woods, away from the city," I remarked, glancing around at our surroundings.

Aerion nodded in agreement. "Yes, it's by design. Portals that once existed within city limits would have most likely moved once the city was built. The Fae and demon realms are bound by their own set of rules and they do not conform to human urban planning."

I shook my head in wonder and bemusement. "I don't even want to begin to understand how that works."

Aerion chuckled softly and it surprised me. He seemed like the strong, quiet, gruff type. When I had first met him he was downright insufferable. His expression turned serious. "Vale, when we enter Elysian things will happen quickly. As soon as we arrive, I'll transport us directly to Thalion's castle, into his room. We don't want anyone outside of our court to know you're there until we officially present you to the other courts. It's for your own safety."

I nodded, trying to grasp the gravity of the situation. The Fae realm was a world apart from everything I knew and the stakes were high. I couldn't afford to make a mistake. "I understand," I replied.

Aerion's faint smile held a trace of reassurance. "Good. I will keep you safe, I promise. But you have to trust me and do exactly as I say."

His words worried me slightly, but I was resolved to see this through. I met his gaze, determination glinting in my eyes. "I'm ready."

He took my hand and a wave of warmth washed over me. The sensation was strange, but at least at this moment, I trusted Aerion's guidance. "Let's go."

We stepped through the portal simultaneously and for a brief moment, it felt like being plunged into icy water. Then, just as suddenly, we emerged on the other side. Aerion's hand was still firmly clasped in mine as he wasted no time transporting us out of the woods of the Fae realm and into a large luxuriously furnished room.

Before us lay a magnificent bed with intricately embroidered sheets and a canopy that draped down like a curtain of stars. The room was decorated with elegant furniture adorned in shades of silver and lavender and a large window framed in opulent drapes was open to a balcony.

I couldn't help but gasp at the breathtaking view that lay beyond. Outside, a vast and magnificent city sprawled beneath us, its streets winding through an architectural marvel of buildings that seemed to blend seamlessly with the natural surroundings. In the distance, towering mountains rose, their peaks kissed by the pristine white of snow.

My senses were overwhelmed by the sheer beauty and grandeur of it all. The room itself was a testament to the opulence of the Fae realm and for a moment, I forgot the perilous journey that had brought me here.

"Welcome to Virelium, princess," Aerion said, his voice hushed, almost reverent.

"It's beautiful," I breathed, feeling awed by the sights unfolding before me.

Aerion released my hand and I turned to face him. His eyes held a strange expression as he observed me as if searching for something deeper within.

"What?" I asked, feeling self-conscious under his intense scrutiny.

"I feel an echo to you, almost like you're more than just one soul," he mused aloud, his eyes never leaving mine. His words were a bit too close to the truth and I wondered if he could somehow sense the fragment of the First Witch's soul that was merged with mine.

"It's complicated," I admitted, "but what's important is that I'm here and I'm ready to do whatever needs to be done."

Aerion regarded me for a moment longer, his gaze thoughtful. "Indeed."

I was about to inquire further when I realized that Thalion, the one we had come to meet, was conspicuously absent. I had assumed he would be here, considering this was his room.

"Where is Thalion?" I asked, my curiosity getting the better of me.

"He was supposed to be waiting here," Aerion explained, "but due to our unforeseen delay, I'm sure he got called away for a moment on some business. I'll go and find him. You stay here and try not to get into any trouble."

I was slightly offended by his implication that I might cause trouble so quickly, but I didn't voice my irritation. Aerionturned and left the room, closing the door softly behind him.

Alone in the lavish surroundings, I took in the room's grandeur. It was spacious and fit for a king, adorned with tapestries that depicted scenes from the Fae realm. The plush carpet underfoot added to the room's luxurious feel, making it clear that I had entered a world unlike any I had ever known.

A fireplace sat in the corner, its flames dancing merrily, casting a warm and flickering glow across the space. But I couldn't resist the allure of the balcony. With each step, the plush carpet cushioned my feet, making me feel as though I were walking on clouds. The door to the balcony swung open easily and I stepped out into the cool, crisp air of the Faerealm.

The breathtaking view before me stole my breath away. The city sprawled out below, a magnificent tapestry of elegance and enchantment. Towering spires and graceful domes reached towards the heavens, their architecture unlike anything I had ever seen in the mortal world. The buildings seemed to meld seamlessly with the natural world as if the city had grown organically from the landscape.

In the distance, the imposing mountains stood proudly, their snow-capped peaks glistening in the gentle light. They were a reminder of the untamed beauty and wildness of the Fae realm, a place where nature and magic were inextricably intertwined.

Leaning against the intricately wrought railing, I couldn't help but feel overwhelmed by the enormity of the situation. I was here, in the Fae realm, a world steeped in mystery and danger. It was a surreal experience, one that I had never imagined would be possible, let alone thrust upon me. Yet, here I stood, with the fate of the mortal world hanging in the balance.

As I stared out at the sprawling landscape, my thoughts whirled with uncertainty. I wondered what the future would hold, and what challenges and trials awaited me in this mysterious realm. But one thing was clear— I had to be prepared for whatever lay ahead, for the sake of both worlds.

The sound of approaching footsteps pulled my attention back to the present. I turned, my gaze falling upon Aerion as he entered the room, followed closely by another Fae male, Thalion.

Thalion's presence was striking. Tall and slender, he exuded an air of regal elegance. His hair, a cascade of silvery-blond, flowed in straight lines down to just past his shoulders. His almond-shaped eyes, an enchanting shade of violet, were arresting, their depths seeming to hold untold secrets. His features were sharp and angular, giving him an otherworldly beauty that was both captivating and intimidating. He was dressed in a tunic and breeches of deep, forest green, a silver belt cinched around his waist, adding a touch of splendor to his attire.

Thalion's gaze, like a gentle caress, fell upon me and his lips curved into a faint smile that seemed to light up his entire face. His voice, when he spoke, was smooth and lyrical, carrying an air of formality.

"Princess Vale," he said, his words filled with a subtle reverence. "It is good to finally see you in Elysian, where you belong."

I offered a wry smile in response to his formality. "Thank you. I'm glad to be here, though I wish it were under different circumstances."

"Indeed," He agreed, his expression shifting to one of seriousness. "Much is at stake, but I believe with your strength and power, we can overcome any obstacles that may lie ahead."

His words, though reassuring, only served to remind me of the weight of responsibility I now carried. "I hope you're right."

Thalion continued, his gaze unwavering. "We'll do everything in our power to make sure you're safe while you're here. Aerion has graciously agreed to be your personal guard."

The mention of a guard caught me by surprise, and I couldn't help but express my astonishment. "I'm to be guarded?"

"It's for your own protection," Thalion explained patiently. "The other courts aren't aware that you're here and we want to keep it that way, at least for the time being. It will be easier to control the flow of information and the situation itself if it remains within the confines of my castle."

Understanding the gravity of the situation, I nodded solemnly. "I see."

Thalion stepped closer, his violet eyes locking with mine. "We will do whatever it takes to keep you safe, princess."

"You keep calling me princes, just because the woman whom you claim to be my mother was one doesn't mean I am," I told him. Thalion's amusement danced in his eyes at my remark.

"Your bloodline, while mixed with demon, speaks otherwise. You are a Fae princess, whether you like it or not." Aerionsaid, his impatience evident in his tone.

"Yes," Thalion confirmed, his expression serious. "And your presence here could ignite tensions among the courts, which is why we need to keep it under wraps for now. Only a few select people within my castle know that you're here and who you are."

Understanding the delicate nature of the situation, I nodded in agreement. "Alright," I turned my attention to Thalion, feeling somewhat overwhelmed by the circumstances. "So, where do we start?"

Thalion considered for a moment before responding. "Well, we will get you settled into a room and then Aerion can show you around the castle if that is what you wish."

Thalion approached a nearby door, which was adjacent to his bed, and swung it open to reveal another set of rooms beyond. "We've put you in my adjoining suite as a precaution. Anyone who sees you will automatically assume you to be a lover I moved into the castle."

I couldn't help but raise an eyebrow at the arrangement. "Well, it seems like you've got everything thought out."

Thalion chuckled, his violet eyes dancing with amusement. "I like to be prepared for all contingencies."

With a nod, I followed Thalion into the adjoining suite, my mind still reeling from the revelations and the responsibilities that came with them. It was clear that my time in the Fae realm would be anything but ordinary.

The grandeur of the castle continued to awe me as the day unfolded. Aerion directed my attention to a massive wardrobe and explained that clothes had been prepared for me. He advised me to change so I wouldn't stick out in this realm. He eyed my worn leather jacket as he spoke. I had quickly changed into a pair of breeches and a purple tunic.

After being shown to my room, which boasted exquisite tapestries and a bed fit for a monarch, Aerion took me on an extensive tour of the castle. The architecture was breathtaking, with soaring ceilings and intricate detailing in every nook and cranny. Each room seemed to outshine the last in its opulence and beauty.

Throughout the day, I was introduced to several key members of the court, including Thalion's advisors and his personal guard. Their curious yet cautious gazes followed me wherever I went, reminding me of the significance of my presence in their realm.

Amid the whirlwind of activity, Aerion had remained my constant companion, offering me guidance and reassurance. By the time evening approached, I was physically and mentally drained. I sat on the edge of the massive four-poster bed in my room, taking a deep breath in an attempt to steady my racing thoughts.

"I still can't believe I'm really here," I murmured, shaking my head in wonder at the surreal turn my life had taken.

Aerion's eyes met mine, his expression inscrutable. "I know it's overwhelming, but you are safe here. Thalion and I are committed to protecting you."

I offered what I hoped was a reassuring smile. "I appreciate that, truly."

Exhaustion began to weigh me down and I let out a weary sigh, running a hand through my hair. "I just wish I knew what to expect, how to prepare myself for whatever comes next."

Aerion's features softened, his gaze filled with empathy. "We will keep you informed and do our best to prepare you for what lies ahead. But for now, you should rest. It has been a long day."

As if on cue, a yawn overcame me and I found myself nodding in agreement. "That sounds like a good idea," I admitted, stifling another yawn.

Aerion stood from where he had been sitting nearby. "I'll leave you to get some rest, then. If you need anything, do not hesitate to ask."

With that, he quietly left my room and I settled under the soft covers of the luxurious bed, letting my eyelids drift shut.

My dreams were tumultuous, haunted by vivid visions of the realms burning and darkness engulfing everything in its path. I awoke in a cold sweat, the nightmarish images still vivid in my mind. Sitting up in bed, I took a deep, shaky breath, trying to dispel the lingering sense of dread that clung to me.

"Just a dream," I whispered to myself, my voice barely audible in the dimly lit room. I ran a trembling hand through my disheveled hair, attempting to soothe my frayed nerves.

My gaze wandered to the ornate clock on the wall and it confirmed what I had already suspected — it was the middle of the night. As the fog of sleep gradually lifted, I became aware of a faint sound emanating from outside my bedroom door. A hushed murmur, barely audible, drifted into my room, piquing my curiosity and unsettling my already anxious state.

Quietly, I slipped out of bed and padded towards the door, straining my ears to hear what was going on, but they remained too soft for me to make out the words. My heart quickened its pace as I cautiously rested my hand on the doorknob, turning it with the utmost care.

Peering into the dimly lit hallway, I could discern the silhouettes of two figures. Their voices were hushed and they seemed deeply engrossed in a discussion. One was unmistakably Aerion, his tall frame and distinctive presence apparent even in the dim light. The other figure was Thalion, his features less distinct but identifiable by his stature and bearing.

Though their words were barely audible, I strained to catch snippets of their conversation.

"...can't trust her..." Aerion's voice was a low murmur, and I had to strain my senses to glean the fragments of his speech.

"...must give her a chance..." Thalion's response was equally quiet.

A surge of unease coursed through me as I realized that they were talking about me. My pulse quickened and a chill settled in the pit of my stomach. It appeared that Aerion was harboring doubts about my trustworthiness, casting a shadow of suspicion over my intentions.

The revelation stung, and my initial reaction was defensiveness. I had agreed to this plan to assist, to play my part in preventing the impending darkness from consuming everything. Yet, the conversation I had overheard implied that there were reservations about my motives.

I listened intently, trying to catch more of their conversation, but the two males had moved further down the hallway and their voices had become too faint to hear. I withdrew from the doorway, closed the door silently, and returned to my bed. The unsettling conversation echoed in my mind as I lay there, my thoughts racing, wondering how I would prove myself.

The rest of the night was spent staring at the ceiling, my mind racing with thoughts of what the next day would bring.

Chapter Thirteen

After finally falling asleep, I was roused from a fitful slumber by a gentle knocking at my door. The remnants of my restless night clung to me like a heavy shroud as I struggled to shake off the remainder of my disturbing dreams. Nyxenlay at the end of the bed, curled up in the shadows there. He came last night, as if called by my inner turmoil, and kept me company until the sun kissed the tops of the mountains in the distance.

"Come in," I called out, stifling a yawn.

Aerion entered, his presence immediately drawing my attention. His expression, as usual, was a veil of inscrutability, revealing nothing of his thoughts or emotions. He moved with the grace and fluidity that were characteristic of his kind, his footsteps barely making a sound as he crossed my room.

"Good morning," he greeted me, his voice soft and devoid of its usual edge.

"Morning," I replied, my tone subdued as I rubbed the echoes of sleep from my tired eyes. I attempted a faint smile, but it felt forced, inadequate to conceal the unrest that had plagued my night.

His eyes, cool and assessing, lingered on me for a moment before he spoke again. "I hope you slept well."

I offered a noncommittal shrug, my attempt to appear nonchalant was betrayed by the shadows that clung to my eyes. "It was alright."

Aerion's next question sliced through the air, his tone laced with an accusatory edge. "Did you glean anything useful from the conversation you eavesdropped on last night?"

I froze, my heart skipping a beat at his direct accusation. How had he known? Panic surged within me, followed by the struggle to formulate a response. I certainly hadn't meant to eavesdrop and I needed to convey my innocence.

"I didn't mean to eavesdrop," I protested, my voice tinged with defensiveness. "I just woke up and heard voices."

Aerion's penetrating gaze bore into me, his eyes unyielding as they searched my face for any signs of deception. "What did you hear?"

My heart pounded in my chest as I recounted the fragments of their conversation. "I only heard bits and pieces, but it sounded like you were arguing about whether you could trust me."

Aerion's response was swift and unrelenting, his words sharpened by suspicion. "And what would you have me say, princess? That it is easy for me to trust a half-breed who may well have a hidden agenda? Your mother may have been Fae, but the blood of the demon world runs through your veins."

His words lingered between us, casting a shadow over the room. A tense silence ensued and I felt compelled to break the silence that hung heavy in the room between us. My voice was strained and tinged with bitterness as I spoke.

"I'm not my father and I didn't ask to be brought here," I stated, irritated that I had come all this way only to be met with suspicion.

Aerion's response was composed, his expression remaining neutral as if he had heard similar protests before. "I am not the only one you need to convince."

I held his gaze, determined to make my point. "But it would help if I did, right?"

Aerion didn't back down, his challenge delivered in a low, dangerous tone. "Then earn my trust."

My heart sank at his response, realizing that proving myself to him and any others was going to be an uphill battle. "And how do I do that?"

"Show me that you are not a threat," he replied, his words leaving no room for negotiation.

I clenched my fists, frustration welling up within me. "You are asking a lot when I know very little about this place."

Aerion's resolve remained unwavering. "It is the only way."

His ultimatum hung in the air, a stark reminder of the challenges I would face in gaining their trust. Taking a deep breath to steady my emotions, I acknowledged the reality before us. "I guess we'll just have to take things one step at a time," I replied, the words escaping my lips in a shaky exhale.

"Indeed," Aerion agreed, his gaze still piercing as if assessing my commitment.

The silence stretched between us, the burden of our unspoken understanding bearing down on us. Finally, Aerion's voice broke the stillness, his words measured and deliberate.

"I have been tasked with training you in combat, while Thalion will train you in the use of your powers. You must learn to harness your abilities and hone them into a weapon."

A wave of defensiveness surged through me. "I'm well aware of how to use my powers and I can easily hold my own in combat."

Aerion's response was steady, his tone firm and commanding. "That may be the case, but we must ensure that you are at the peak of your abilities."

I couldn't argue with his logic, though my frustration lingered just beneath the surface. "Fine," I sighed.

For the first time since his arrival, a small smile tugged at the corner of Aerion's lips, a glimmer of emotion in his otherwise stoic demeanor. "Excellent. We shall begin at once. I'll wait for you outside while you get dressed into something appropriate."

Before he could leave the room, I halted him with a question that had been gnawing at me. "Wait."

Aerion turned back to face me, his gaze attentive. "Yes?"

"How did you know I was listening?" I inquired, genuine curiosity in my voice.

His response was a candid admission. "I didn't. You confirmed it, though."

I couldn't help but shake my head, my irritation clear. "So, you're testing me from the start?"

Aerion's response was pragmatic. "It's only natural. We cannot afford any mishaps, not when the fate of our world is at stake."

Taking a deep breath to temper my rising frustration, I agreed, my tone forcedly calm. "Okay, I get it. But do me a favor and don't surprise me like that again."

Aerion inclined his head in acknowledgment, his inscrutable expression unchanged. "Very well, then. I shall see you soon." With that, he turned and departed from the room, leaving me alone with my thoughts.

I walked over to the massive wardrobe, its ornate doors revealing an array of gowns, tunics, and garments in various shades and fabrics. My fingers trailed over the delicate dresses as I contemplated what to wear. I eventually settled on a pale blue tunic and black leather pants, choosing a blend of comfort and practicality. I dressed quickly, the fabric cool against my skin as I fastened the tunic's intricate clasps.

Exiting the dressing area, I stepped into the adjacent bathing room and glanced at my reflection in the gilded mirror. My reflection showed a girl who appeared tired, the burden of her newfound responsibilities and the challenges ahead etched in the lines of her face. Yet, despite the weariness, there was a steely resolve in my gaze, a determination that refused to waver. I brushed a strand of hair away from my face and took a deep breath, mentally fortifying myself for the day's trials.

After brushing my hair and my teeth with the supplies I had brought from the mortal realm I left the main chamber of the suite and found Aerion waiting for me in the hallway, his posture patient and unwavering. "Ready?" he asked.

I nodded, my voice momentarily failing me.

"Let's go, then," Aerion stated, his words carrying an air of authority.

Together, we proceeded through the intricate hallways of the castle, an unspoken understanding and an uneasy alliance forming between us. I tried my best to memorize every turn we made but soon gave up. I was horrible with directions and would surely never learn the layout of this place.

The morning sun was high in the sky as we reached the expansive training grounds, a sprawling space dedicated to honing the skills of Fae warriors. Aerion led me through a series of rigorous exercises that tested my physical prowess and magical abilities. The morning passed quickly in a blur of exertion and concentration. By the time we paused for a quick lunch, the training grounds buzzed with activity.

Aerion's intense gaze lingered on me, his eyes scanning me meticulously from head to toe as if searching for any hidden flaws or potential. His face remained a mask of neutrality, leaving me unsure of what to expect from his evaluation.

"Not bad," he remarked, his voice as cool and collected as ever, devoid of any discernible emotion.

I took a moment to catch my breath, wiping the beads of sweat from my brow with the back of my hand. "Thanks," I replied, panting slightly.

Aerion's observation continued, his unwavering gaze still locked on mine. "You're holding back."

My defensiveness prickled and I straightened, meeting his penetrating stare with determination. "No, I'm not."

He didn't waver, his gaze drilling into mine. "Your powers are far stronger than this. You must learn to fully access them."

The truth in his words stung and I couldn't deny that I had been holding back, the fear of my own destructive potential making me cautious. I glanced down at my blackened fingers, the memories of the last time I unleashed the full force of my powers still fresh in my mind, the hellfire casting shadows across my soul.

"It's not that easy," I protested, my voice tinged with frustration. "The magic I possess is dangerous and it has the potential to destroy everything in its path."

Aerion didn't falter in his stance, his resolve unyielding. "You must learn to control it, princess. Even at its most volatile." And with that we broke for lunch, eating in silence seated several feet away from each other.

The silence continued to stretch between us as Aerion and I continued our training. My mind, however, was far from the physical exertion. I mulled over the revelations about Aerion's past. Thalion had called my mother Aerion's princess, and it had become clear that Aerion's court had suffered a great tragedy.

Something nagged at me, an itch of curiosity I couldn't ignore. I needed to know more, to understand the story behind Aerion's history. With a deep breath, I mustered the courage to press him for further information, hoping it might offer some insight.

"My mother, Lyra, was she really your princess?" I ventured, my gaze focused on Aerion, trying to gauge his reaction.

Aerion's face darkened, his voice somber as he nodded. "She was."

My curiosity wouldn't be sated with just that answer and so I probed further, still struggling to grasp the complexities of Fae royalty. "Does that mean you were related? You're a prince, right?"

Aerion shook his head, a touch of regret in his tone. "Not by blood. Lyra was the daughter of King Cael, my adoptive father. I was taken in at a very young age, found by the king wandering the woods one day. Lyra was already grown by then. However, I have very little memory of that time."

As he continued, the weight of the tragedy that had befallen his court became painfully evident. "Haldir was the one who destroyed our court, turning it into his dark Unseelie court. The bloodshed was insurmountable, and in the end, King Caelsacrificed himself to stop it."

I couldn't hide the shock and sympathy that welled up within me. Aerion's past was marred by violence and loss, and it was clear he had suffered greatly. My earlier resentment toward him began to wane as I heard his story, replaced by a deep sense of sorrow.

"I'm sorry," I finally managed to say, though the words felt wholly inadequate.

Aerion's gaze turned hard, the fleeting glimpse of emotion that had surfaced vanishing once more behind the mask of indifference he wore so well. "Don't be. We cannot change the past. Now, let's continue."

With that, he strode back towards the training grounds, leaving me with no choice but to follow, my thoughts clouded by the enormity of what I had learned.

The sun had dipped below the horizon, casting long shadows across the training grounds as the day's grueling exercises finally came to a close. I could hardly summon the energy to stand upright, my muscles aching and my mind foggy from the relentless training.

"That will be all for today," Aerion's voice cut through my exhaustion.

I could hardly contain my relief and a muttered expression of gratitude slipped from my lips as I offered a weak smile. "Thank the gods."

Aerion, however, was quick to douse my hopes. "Don't get too comfortable, princess. We will resume first thing in the morning."

A groan escaped me as I contemplated the prospect of another day of rigorous training. The fatigue settled in my bones, but I understood there was no room for complacency. If I were to play a role in saving the realms, I needed to be at my absolute best.

We made our way back to my chambers, each step feeling heavier than the last. Aerion's watchful gaze bore into me, a curious blend of concern and something else I couldn't quite decipher. His voice broke the silence, the praise in his tone catching me off guard. "You did well today."

"Thanks," I replied, feeling a flush of embarrassment at the unexpected compliment.

As we reached the entrance to my chambers, Aerion mentioned the practical matters of the evening. "I'll have someone bring some food up for you. After that, I suggest you take a bath." He said casually, as if the thought of me naked and wet didn't affect him at all.

I nodded in acknowledgment. "I will."

He lingered for a moment, his eyes traveling over me once more. It was a look that gave me chills, a mixture of intense scrutiny and something deeper, though I couldn't quite discern what it was. Then, without another word, he turned and walked away, his figure receding into the dimly lit corridor, leaving me alone with my thoughts. The intensity of his stare lingered with me and I couldn't help but wonder what he was thinking as I watched him disappear from sight.

The promised servant arrived with a tray of food and my growling stomach welcomed the sight. A colorful mixture of roasted bell peppers, zucchini, cherry tomatoes, and asparagus had been lightly drizzled with a fragrant olive oil infused with herbs. Despite the simplicity of the meal, every bite was a delight, the flavors dancing on my tongue in harmonious perfection. I ate with a level of eagerness born of the day's exhausting training, each mouthful bringing a sense of replenishment and comfort. The dishes were whisked away as I savored the last bites, looking forward to the promised bath.

I was pleasantly surprised to find that the Fae realm had plumbing. The thought of a hot bath was a tantalizing prospect. As the water filled the bathtub, I smiled at the idea of soothing my aching muscles. The steam rose, enveloping the room in a comforting warmth and I took a moment to relish the anticipation.

Stepping into the tub, I lowered myself into the steaming water with a contented sigh. The heat seeped into my tired muscles and I felt like I could melt into the soothing warmth. The room was filled with the scent of lavender, making it feel like a sanctuary of relaxation.

As I lay in the tub, my thoughts drifted to the two Fae princes I had encountered. Thalion, with his kindness and patience, seemed like someone I could trust. On the other hand, Aerion exuded an air of brooding intensity, with darkness lurking beneath the surface. It was as if a storm raged within him, a tempest he was desperately trying to suppress.

My brows furrowed as I contemplated Aerion. I knew I had to tread carefully around him. His emotions appeared unpredictable, like a volatile mixture waiting to ignite, and I had no desire to set him off. His puzzling nature left me with a sense of unease and intrigue.

I closed my eyes, letting the warm water envelop me. My mind began to drift, and I couldn't help but wonder what the next day would bring. Thoughts of my mission and the challenges that lay ahead swirled in my head, a constant reminder of the weight of my responsibilities.

Suddenly, my peaceful soak turned into a nightmare as a thin wire cord encircled my neck with a deadly grip. Panic surged through me as I choked, the assailant's grip mercilessly tight against my throat. The room was filled with the horrifying sound of my strangled scream before it was abruptly silenced by the constricting wire.

My face reddened as I fought for breath, my lungs burning with desperation. My trembling hands clawed at the wire, blood oozing from the cuts it left behind. Every instinct screamed for survival as I refused to relent, determined to break free from this deadly grip. My heart pounded fiercely, the edges of my vision dimming as oxygen deprivation took its toll.

Amid this life-or-death struggle, panic gave way to a surge of primal adrenaline, urging me to fight with every fiber of my being.

I stopped clawing at my throat and reached behind me, desperately trying to get my hands on the mysterious assassin. My magic surged within me, my body's automatic reaction to the danger present. My hand collided with his face, flames jumping to my fingers. My assailant screamed as he was burned and the pressure on my neck receded. I hurriedly climbed out of the tub and whirled, turning to see my attacker. He recovered quickly and came after me again, his arms outstretched. "You little half-breed bitch," he spat. I noticed the angry red handprints on his face with grim satisfaction.

"Who are you?" I demanded, the flames on my hands dancing in anticipation.

"The last face you'll ever see," he snarled.

"I don't fucking think so," I growled back at him.

He rushed forward and with a cry of rage, I released the magic building within me. A blast of flame erupted from my hands, enveloping him. His screams echoed through the room as he burned alive, his flesh melting from his bones.

The smell of charred flesh filled the air, making me gag. As his lifeless body fell to the floor, the flames slowly dissipated.

I took a moment to catch my breath, my heart still racing. Just then the doors to the bathing chamber were thrown open and Thalion and Aerion stormed in, looking around wildly before their eyes fell on the blackened body before me.

"Are you alright, princess?" Thalion asked, his eyes full of concern as he took me in from head to toe. I realized only then that I was still naked.

I nodded, still shaken by the sudden attack.

"Who is this?" Aerion asked, his gaze fixed on the charred remains.

"I don't know. He tried to kill me." I explained, my voice trembling. I reached my hand up to my throat and felt the blood dripping there from the cut. Aerion grabbed a towel and walked over to me, wrapping it around me securely.

"You're hurt," Aerion said softly, his eyes locked onto mine, a hint of concern softening his usually stoic demeanor.

"I'll heal," I whispered, unable to look away from his intense gaze.

Thalion continued to inspect the lifeless body, his expression clouded with disappointment. "Well, he's definitely dead," Thalion announced, his voice heavy with frustration. "We will never know who sent him."

"It doesn't matter. They're going to regret this night," Aerion growled, his eyes flashing dangerously. The anger radiating from him was unmistakable, giving me chills.

Thalion approached me, his touch gentle as he put his hand on my arm. "Come, let's get you cleaned up and then we can talk about what happened," he said in a soothing tone, his presence providing some semblance of comfort amid chaos.

I nodded, feeling overwhelmed by the whirlwind of emotions and danger that had engulfed me. Aerion watched us as Thalion escorted me out of the room, his eyes revealing nothing as he looked at me.

Once back in the main chambers, I hastily dressed, acutely aware of Thalion's lingering gaze on me. It was as though he was seeing me in a new light and the realization made me slightly self-conscious.

Thalion called for a healer and they worked deftly to clean and bandage the shallow cut across my neck. I sat there and let them work, the cut already starting to heal itself.

"Whoever sent the assassin wants you dead," Thalion said grimly, his voice cutting through the tension that hung in the air. His words were a stark reminder of the peril I now faced in this unfamiliar world.

"Clearly," I replied, my voice tinged with sarcasm. The events of the night had left me on edge and I struggled to hide my irritation.

"Surely it was Haldir. I'd love to find out how he knew you were here; only the most trusted among my court were informed," Thalion mused, shaking his head in frustration.

"You don't think anyone else here could have a problem with her?" Aerion interjected pointedly, his eyes locked on Thalion.

"I don't know," Thalion admitted with a sigh, clearly torn by the possibilities.

"We will have to increase the number of guards. Until we know for certain, she should not be left unattended," Aeriondeclared, his voice resolute.

"Agreed," Thalion concurred, the weight of responsibility evident in his expression.

Their attention then turned to me, their concern clear in their expressions. I felt a mixture of gratitude and frustration at their anxiety.

"I can take care of myself," I said forcefully.

"You shouldn't have to. This is our fault. We should have better protected you," Thalion said, his voice tinged with shame.

"It's not your fault," I replied, my tone softening. "Besides, I killed him easily enough."

"And almost died in the process," Aerion added darkly, his gaze intense.

I sighed, growing weary of their overprotectiveness. "I'm fine, really. And now that we know Haldir knows I'm here, we can be more careful. But don't treat me like I'm fragile. I'm a lot stronger than I look."

"That may be, but until we can be sure, we must err on the side of caution," Thalion reasoned, his gaze unwavering.

"I don't know what else I can say to convince you both," I admitted, frustration creeping into my voice.

"Perhaps nothing," Aerion replied, his expression inscrutable.

Thalion observed the interaction between us with a small, knowing smile playing on his lips as if he saw something that we did not.

"What is it?" I asked, curiosity piqued by the contemplative look on Aerion's face.

"I see so much of your mother in you," he replied, his words carrying a hint of nostalgia, though I suspected his true thoughts ran deeper and more complex.

"She was stubborn, too," Aerion remarked, a faint smile tugging at the corners of his lips.

"Yes, well, we can't all be perfect," I quipped, rolling my eyes, relieved by the brief moment of levity amid the tense situation. "Tell me about her," I asked Aerion, curiosity getting the better of me.

Thalion shifted his weight, a subtle tension creeping into his shoulders. I sensed that the conversation was one that neither found easy to navigate.

Aerion looked at me, considering the request I had just made. The creases on his forehead deepened as if the gravity of what I was asking weighed on him like an invisible burden. I felt the intensity of his gaze settle on me, a complex mesh of emotions twinkling behind his eyes as if he sensed that I was asking him to unveil a chapter of himself that he rarely allowed others to read.

He cleared his throat and began to speak, his voice resonant but tinged with a subtle emotion he couldn't completely mask. "She looked just like you, for starters." The gentleness of his words, punctuated by a deep and abiding love, surprised me.

I was riveted, unable to look away, as he continued to fill the room with the sound of his voice. "She was a healer, which was rare at the time, and is even rarer now." He paused as though sifting through a treasury of memories. "She had an affinity for the forest. Knew it like the back of her hand. Every tree, every leafy shrub, every scampering animal—she could name them all. She could tell you the name of each flower and explain their medicinal or mystical uses. She was like a guardian spirit, harmonious with the natural world in a way few could understand."

He looked down for a moment, gathering his thoughts. "But it wasn't just her knowledge that set her apart; it was her kindness. Her heart was a well of compassion, always putting others before herself. Yet, don't mistake her gentleness for weakness. She had a will of steel, an indomitable spirit that could bend even the most stubborn of souls to her cause."

As he spoke, the sincerity and depth of his feelings washed over me, a tide of unspoken emotions that had perhaps been locked away for too long. I sat there, transfixed, feeling as though I had been granted access to a sacred part of him that few had ever seen. And in that moment, I understood not just the woman he described, but also a little more of the complex man before me.

"I think that's enough for tonight," Thalion interjected.

"Fine," I relented, feeling my exhaustion catch up to me. The adrenaline of the attack was wearing off, leaving me mentally and physically drained.

"Get some rest. We'll double your guard tonight and we will speak more tomorrow," Thalion advised.

As Thalion and Aerion took their leave, I was finally alone with my thoughts. The events of the day had taken a toll on me and as I lay in bed, sleep remained elusive. Instead, my mind raced with questions.

Who had sent the assassin, and what were their motives? Was it truly Haldir, or could there be someone else involved, lurking in the shadows? The uncertainty gnawed at me, fueling my restlessness.

With a weary sigh, I rolled over in the grand bed, my thoughts still churning. The only thing I knew for certain was that the coming days in the Fae realm promised to be anything but boring and I would need every ounce of strength and determination to navigate the treacherous path ahead.

Chapter Fourteen

I awoke early the next morning, the faint light of dawn filtering through the grand window of my chamber, casting a soft glow across the room. The restless and anxious thoughts that had plagued me throughout the night still clung to my mind like a shadow, refusing to relent.

With a determined sigh, I swung my legs over the edge of the plush four-poster bed, the coolness of the polished marble floor meeting the soles of my bare feet. The events of the previous night had left me unsettled and I felt an urgent need to regain some semblance of control over the situation.

As I dressed quickly, the luxurious fabrics of the fae attire gliding smoothly over my skin, I couldn't help but glance at my reflection in the ornate mirror. My own eyes stared back with determination and uncertainty, mirroring the internal conflict that raged within.

Breakfast arrived promptly and I settled down at the elegantly set table, my appetite diminished by the lingering unease that clung to me. The fare was both decadent and exotic, a testament to the culinary prowess of the fae. I picked at my meal, eager to start the day but unable to fully shake off the lingering remnants of fear.

A soft, polite knock on the adjoining door to Thalion's chambers drew my attention away from the half-eaten plate before me.

"Come in," I called out.

Thalion entered the room, his long silvery hair tied back in a low bun at the nape of his neck, a testament to the timeless beauty of his kind. He wore an expression that was both friendly and concerned, his violet eyes reflecting the genuine worry he felt.

"Good morning," he greeted, his voice a warm and reassuring presence in the room.

"Morning," I replied, my response carrying a hint of the tension that still lingered within me.

He settled into the chair opposite mine. "How are you feeling today?" he inquired, his gaze moving to the line across my neck that was already healing.

"I'm fine, just a little shaken up, that's all," I replied, my attempt at nonchalance thinly veiling the turmoil beneath.

"Understandable, considering what you went through last night," Thalion acknowledged, his understanding tone offering a glimmer of solace.

I nodded in agreement, my fingers curling around the crystal goblet filled with fruit juice. The tangy sweetness danced across my taste buds as I took a sip, a momentary distraction from the pressing concerns that filled my thoughts.

"Have you had any luck figuring out how that assassin got in?" I asked, my curiosity and the lingering sense of vulnerability driving me to seek answers.

His frustration was evident in the furrowed lines on his forehead and though his words offered some reassurance, the apprehension that had taken root in me continued to fester.

"No, but I have doubled the guard and increased security measures. You should be safe," Thalion replied, his voice carrying an undertone of resolve as if he could singlehandedly safeguard me from any threat.

I nodded, grateful for his efforts even as I couldn't shake the unease that had settled within me. "That's a relief."

"In the meantime, we will continue with your training," Thalion announced, his tone unwavering, a reminder that strength and preparation were our best defenses.

"I'd like that," I replied, my voice tinged with anticipation. My eagerness, however, was tempered by the knowledge that training with Aerion would be anything but a leisurely endeavor.

"Oh, before I forget, I wanted to mention that tomorrow night the fae courts will be coming together for the Aeloranthia celebration," Thalion continued and I couldn't help but raise an eyebrow, my curiosity piqued.

"The what celebration?" I asked, genuinely intrigued by this fae tradition.

"Aeloranthia is a celebration of the autumn season," Thalion explained with a hint of nostalgia. "It's a time when we all come together to honor the bounty of the harvest. There will be a grand feast tomorrow evening and during it, we will introduce you as a member of our court."

"But, I'm not," I reminded him, a note of uncertainty in my voice as I couldn't fathom how the fae would accept a half-demon into their ranks.

"You're the daughter of Lyra," Thalion replied, his gaze unwavering and resolute. "And so, you are as much a part of the fae realm as any other. It's also the best way to offer you protection while you are here. Any crime committed against you will be a crime committed against my court. It's not something many courts will take a risk on."

I contemplated his words, understanding the practicality of the situation even as I remained wary of the fae politics that seemed to govern their world.

"But one will, right? Haldir's court," I ventured, a hint of suspicion lacing my words.

"Possibly," Thalion conceded, his expression grim. "Though none would dare admit it openly."

I couldn't help but raise an eyebrow, my skepticism growing with each revelation. His demeanor remained unruffled, giving no hint of the gravity of the situation.

"What's the worst that can happen?" I asked, a trace of incredulity in my voice.

"They could declare war on us," Thalion replied matter-of-factly, his words causing a ball of ice to form in my stomach.

I let out an exasperated sigh, struggling to wrap my head around the intricacies of fae politics. "So, basically, you're telling me that the other courts are a bunch of self-centered assholes who only care about themselves?" I quipped, my frustration evident.

Thalion chuckled softly as if my observation was astute. "You could say that, yes. Fae politics are a complicated affair, and the different courts are always jockeying for power and influence. The Aeloranthia celebration is a time for the different courts to show their strength and unity. By introducing you to the court, we will show our strength and willingness to fight for your safety. We hope that by doing so, the other courts will think twice about harming you."

I shook my head in disbelief, amazed at the level of pettiness and intrigue the fae were capable of. "Sounds like a lot of bullshit politics to me."

"It can be, but it's a necessary evil," Thalion replied, his tone reflecting a resigned acceptance of their world's complexities.

I sighed, realizing that I had little choice but to navigate this tangled web of fae customs. "So, what happens during the Aeloranthia celebration?"

"Well, the different courts will gather and share a feast. There will be music and dancing and the overall mood is one of celebration and goodwill," Thalion explained, a hint of nostalgia in his voice. "Throughout the festival, we will introduce you to the various courts. Then the festivities will continue long into the night."

I couldn't help but feel excitement and trepidation at the prospect of attending such an event. "Will I be expected to dance?" I asked, my mind racing with all the possibilities.

"If you want to. Have you ever heard fae music, princess?" Thalion inquired, his eyes sparkling with a glimmer of mischief.

"Not really, why?" I responded, a sense of curiosity piqued by his question.

"Fae music is said to have the power to enchant. If you hear it, you will feel compelled to dance, whether you want to or not."

"Oh, boy," I mumbled, realizing that the Aeloranthia celebration held more surprises than I had initially anticipated. I wondered what other surprises were in store for me.

"I'm sure it will be an...interesting experience," Thalion remarked, a hint of amusement coloring his voice.

"Interesting is one word for it," I replied wryly, "How does this whole thing work, exactly? Who will I be expected to interact with?"

Thalion leaned forward, his expression thoughtful as he explained, "Everyone, essentially. As a guest of honor, you will be expected to make the rounds and meet with each of the fae kings and the important fae of their court."

"Great," I muttered, the burden of the impending social interactions pressing down on me.

"I know it seems overwhelming," Thalion acknowledged, his tone empathetic, "but I promise, the majority of them will be polite and courteous."

"And the others?" I couldn't help but ask, my skepticism resurfacing.

Thalion's eyes held a steely resolve as he replied, "The others will not dare to disrespect you openly. They may try to undermine you, but I will be by your side the entire night."

I nodded, taking solace in his assurance that I wouldn't be navigating this unfamiliar world alone.

"There is one other thing," Thalion added, a mischievous glint dancing in his eyes.

I leaned in, curious and slightly apprehensive. "What is it?"

"Some of the fae will not wear clothing," he said casually, as if discussing the weather.

My eyes widened, and I sputtered, "Wait, what?"

Thalion chuckled, clearly enjoying my reaction. "It is traditional for the fae to go without clothes during the Aeloranthia celebration, after the feast that is. Most uphold this tradition."

I cleared my throat, my face flushing as I asked, "Do you uphold that tradition?"

He smirked and winked at me. "I guess you will have to wait and see, princess." The way he said princess, like a caress, gave me a subtle chill.

I couldn't help but feel curious about the prospect. Fae customs were indeed different from what I was used to.

"Come, we should begin your training. Aerion will be expecting you," Thalion said, steering the conversation back to the present before I could ask more.

I followed Thalion to the courtyard, where Aerion stood waiting, his expression as inscrutable as ever.

"Are you ready to begin?" Aerion's voice was low and serious as he stood there, awaiting my response.

I nodded, a determined look in my eyes. "Sure, let's get started."

As I walked past him to begin the training, I could feel his eyes on me, or at least, I thought I did. It was hard to tell with Aerion; his emotions were always well-hidden.

The training session with Aerion proved to be one of the most demanding experiences of my life. He was an unrelenting taskmaster, pushing me to my limits both physically and mentally. There were moments when I felt like I couldn't go on, but I refused to give in. I pushed through the exhaustion and the pain, determined to prove myself.

By the end of the day, I was covered in sweat, dirt, and bruises, but there was also a sense of accomplishment. I had survived another grueling training session with Aerion.

"Well done," Aerion finally acknowledged, his expression as inscrutable as ever.

"Thanks," I replied, my breath coming in ragged pants as I tried to regain my composure.

He stared at me for a long moment while I caught my breath, his grey eyes darkening like storm clouds for a second before he looked away. He probably still didn't trust me.

"I'll walk you back to your rooms," he said gruffly. "Hopefully you can bathe in peace tonight." There was an edge to his voice, likely stemming from lingering irritation over the previous night's attack, I accepted without hesitation.

As we strolled back toward the palace, the crisp autumn air seemed to have a rejuvenating effect on my tired muscles. It was a stark contrast to the sweat-soaked and exhausting training session with Aerion.

"How are you feeling?" he asked, his voice holding a hint of concern.

I let out a weary sigh. "Honestly, like shit."

Aerion's response was a simple nod as if he had expected nothing less.

"Will it always be this brutal?" I couldn't help but ask, seeking some insight into what I had gotten myself into.

"For you, yes," Aerion replied matter-of-factly. "If you want to become a true warrior, you need to be able to handle the most difficult challenges."

I couldn't help but chuckle softly at his response. "I think I prefer the library."

Aerion's lip quirked into what might have been a smile. "The library may have its merits, but it won't prepare you for what's to come. You have the potential to be a formidable force, but you must be willing to endure."

We walked in a heavy silence that seemed to stretch between us. Eventually, we reached the doors to my rooms and Aerion paused, his gaze intent on my face. "May I ask you what happened to your hands?" His unexpected question caught me off guard.

"This is what happens when you mess with dark magic," I replied, holding my hands up, the blackened fingertips a testament to the sacrifices I had made.

"What would be important enough to compel you to do that to yourself?" He asked curiously.

"Saving the people I care about," I responded without hesitation.

Aerion regarded me for a moment, his eyes searching mine as if trying to decipher a complex puzzle. "They are worth such sacrifice?" he asked softly.

"Yes," I affirmed, my conviction unwavering.

Aerion continued to study me and for a fleeting moment, I thought I saw a glimmer of something in his eyes, a hint of understanding or maybe even respect.

"You are not what I expected, princess," he said in a hushed tone as if speaking his thoughts aloud.

I couldn't help but be curious. "What did you expect?"

His response was blunt and unvarnished. "A spoiled brat."

I couldn't help but chuckle at his candor. "Gee, thanks," I replied with a touch of sarcasm.

Aerion's features softened slightly and he offered a brief apology. "My apologies, but your mother had a reputation for being...difficult."

Aerion turned and swung the door open, striding into the room with a sense of purpose. I followed him inside, curiosity piqued as I watched him move. He began to prowl around the room, his steps calculated and deliberate.

"What are you doing?" I inquired, confused.

"I'm checking your room for intruders," he replied. "Wouldn't want anything else to mar that pretty neck of yours."

His unexpected compliment caught me off guard and my hand instinctively rose to touch the thin line on my neck where the assassin had attacked me. "Thank you," I murmured, my response hesitant, as I watched him continue his search. He moved seamlessly into the bathroom, inspecting it as well.

After finishing his examination, he turned to face me, his intense gaze once again raking over my form. "Take a bath and get some rest. Tomorrow will be a long day."

I let out a weary sigh, my exhaustion catching up with me. "Don't remind me," I muttered.

Aerion responded with a rare and crooked smile, a hint of his fangs showing. "And, princess," he paused, glancing back over his shoulder as he headed toward the door, "Try not to get yourself killed."

With that he exited the room, leaving me to my thoughts. I sank onto the bed, feeling exhaustion and confusion wash over me. Aerion remained a puzzle I couldn't seem to solve. His behavior swung between cold and aloof to teasing and complimentary, leaving me to wonder what was truly going on in his head.

I shook my head, trying to clear the thoughts away. There was no point in dwelling on it. Aerion was a mystery and one that I didn't have time to solve right now.

I rose from the bed, my muscles still aching from the grueling training earlier. My body yearned for the comforting embrace of a hot bath, a satisfying meal, and the promise of a restful night's sleep. With determination in my step, I made my way toward the bathroom.

Before entering the inviting steaming tub, I meticulously inspected every nook and cranny of the bathroom, taking no chances after the harrowing encounter with the assassin the previous night.

As I luxuriated in the soothing waters, the fatigue of the day seemed to wash away. I combed out my hair at the vanity, each stroke a gentle caress that untangled the knots and stresses from my body.

Then, as if on cue, there came a soft, polite knock on the door. I called out for the person to enter, curiosity piqued. In walked three women, the first among them a stern yet kindly-looking lady with greying hair and the distinctive pointed ears of the fae. The other two, considerably younger, had their eyes respectfully downcast.

"My lady, my name is Amris," the elder woman began, "and these two are Kelli and Joeline. We're to be your lady's maids and assist you in dressing for tomorrow's celebration if it pleases you. We thought it best to introduce ourselves now."

"It's nice to meet you, but please call me Vale," I replied, offering a warm smile, hoping it would be disarming. Amris reciprocated my gesture with a pleasant smile of her own, an indication that I might indeed like her.

"Thank you, my lady, Vale," Amris acknowledged graciously.

Curiosity compelled me to ask, "What are you here to do, exactly?"

Amris answered, "Anything you need, my lady. We are here to serve you."

The notion of having personal maids made me slightly uncomfortable, but I chose not to argue. They were merely fulfilling their roles and duties.

"Okay, well, thank you," I replied, accepting their assistance with a gracious nod.

Amris's smile conveyed a sense of pride as she introduced the two newer maids, their fresh faces tinged with bashfulness, a testament to their youth and inexperience. The court's training was no doubt rigorous and I was sure they were still learning.

"These two are the newest maids," Armis explained, "they have recently graduated from their studies and are still learning the ways of the court, I'm afraid. But they will grow as skilled as me in due time."

Kelli and Joeline exchanged demure glances, their expressions indicating a natural shyness that came with their novice status.

"It's very nice to meet you both," I greeted them warmly, hoping to put them at ease.

"You as well, my lady," Joeline replied with a soft smile.

Kelli asked, "Shall we prepare you a bath?"

I politely declined, saying, "No, thank you. I've already taken a bath, but if you could help me brush out my hair and maybe put a braid or two in it, that would be lovely."

Kelli nodded and picked up a brush, while Joeline busied herself lighting a few candles and arranging a plate of delectable fruits on the nearby table. Amris, on the other hand, appeared to be organizing items in my closet, her movements efficient and precise. I welcomed the idea of a few moments of relaxation while the maids took care of me.

As Kelli and Joeline worked their deft hands through my hair, I indulged in the juicy fruit and sipped more of the sweet juice that had been brought to me earlier. With each bite, my energy gradually returned. When the two maids were satisfied with their efforts, they stepped back to admire their work.

"You look beautiful, my lady," Kelli commented, her eyes reflecting a sincere admiration.

"Thank you," I replied, genuinely touched by their efforts.

"It's our pleasure, my lady," Joeline chimed in. "Now, we will have dinner brought to you. Please, call on us if you need anything."

"I will, thank you," I acknowledged with a grateful smile.

With the maids' departure, I found myself once again alone with my thoughts. Despite the efforts of those around me, the impending anxiety about the upcoming celebration continued to gnaw at me, growing more intense with each passing moment.

I wasn't sure I was ready to meet the other fae courts, and even more unsure of how they would react to me. Would they accept me? Would they try to hurt me? Only time would tell and I could only hope that Thalion and Aerion would help shield me from whatever came my way.

CHAPTER FIFTEEN

WREN

As the first rays of the morning sun shown down on the werewolf camp, Wren emerged from his sturdy tent, his eyes adjusting to the newfound brightness. The camp was alive with bustling activity, a chorus of sounds and motions that spoke of a thriving community.

Around him, members of his pack went about their daily routines, each task contributing to the well-being of their close-knit group. Some individuals chopped firewood for the nightly bonfires, their strong arms wielding axes with practiced ease, while others tended to the sizzling breakfasts over open flames, filling the air with the tantalizing scent of cooking meat. A few industrious souls were already tidying their temporary homes, keeping their spaces clean and organized.

Laughter and the gleeful shouts of children filled the air as youngsters raced among the tents and patches of morning sunlight, their youthful cheer a reminder of the resilience and hope that thrived within the camp.

Wren's sharp gaze scanned the camp, his eyes settling on Venna who was engaged in a conversation with a group of fellow wolves. Her presence was a reassuring sight amidst the morning bustle and he knew he could count on her for support.

Approaching her with purposeful strides, Venna ended her conversation with the others, sending them off to carry out their assigned tasks. Her leadership was a testament to her abilities and she held the respect of their pack.

Venna's keen eyes met his as he drew nearer and she smiled, acknowledging him with a nod. Breaking away from the group, she walked toward Wren, her expression a blend of determination and readiness.

"Wren," she greeted him, her voice cheerful.

"Venna," he replied, returning her smile.

As they stood amidst the morning activities, Venna proceeded to update Wren on the camp's developments. Her words were measured and her gaze unwavering as she informed him about the construction of the large community building that had been planned for some time.

"Our wolves with construction experience have begun organizing for the project," she explained, her confidence in their abilities evident. "I've taken the liberty of recommending Teris to lead the construction team. He has the most experience in this area and has garnered the trust of the others."

Wren considered her recommendation, his trust in Venna's judgment unwavering. Teris had proven himself time and again and if Venna believed in his leadership, Wren did not doubt the choice.

"Good," Wren replied, nodding. "Let Teris know he has my support and I trust he'll lead the team effectively."

Venna acknowledged his decision with a nod of her own, her gaze reflecting her loyalty to him and their shared commitment to the pack.

As Wren moved to speak, a small, slender figure emerged from the crowd, a determined expression etched on her face. Wren recognized the newcomer as Kyla, a recent addition to the pack, her youthfulness and inexperience were a source of concern.

"Wren," Kyla said, addressing him with nervousness and formality. "I have something I need to talk to you about."

Her words carried an urgency that piqued his interest. "What is it, Kyla?"

"I've heard some whisperings among the pack I thought you might need to know about," she started. "Some of the members are growing uneasy about the Otherworlder's presence among us. They think our resources are being stretched too thin while taking care of them. I'm worried that this unrest will lead to disloyalty. Some may start to question your leadership."

Kyla's words echoed Wren's deepest concerns and he could not fault her for her concerns.

"Your fears are valid, Kyla," he said. "The pack's welfare is my utmost priority, and I understand the pressures we've been facing. Thank you for bringing this to my attention, I can deal with it from here."

Kyla's expression relaxed at his words, her relief evident. Wren's gaze swept across the camp, his mind whirring with possibilities. He had hoped that their acceptance of the Otherworlders would ease the tension, but it seemed the problems were far from over.

"Kyla, please continue to keep me updated on any further developments," Wren added. "I want to make sure the pack stays strong and united. Our bonds are what make us a formidable force."

"Of course," she said, her voice soft. "Thank you, alpha."

With those words, Kyla turned and departed, her graceful form weaving its way through the bustling crowd of wolves. Wren watched her leave, his green eyes reflecting his deep concern. His mind was already at work, considering ways to alleviate the growing concerns within the pack.

As Venna stood beside him, her presence a comforting and steady one. Wren made a silent vow, that he would do everything in his power to ensure the stability of his people. Their welfare was paramount and he would not allow anything to threaten their livelihood.

Suddenly, Wren's sharp hearing picked up a commotion among the nearby crowd. He turned his attention to the source of the noise. There, he caught sight of a group of his wolves, engaged in a heated argument. Their postures were tense, their expressions strained.

A young male appeared to be the instigator, his words laced with malice and discontent. As the dispute grew more intense, the others joined in, their voices rising in anger.

"That's enough!" Wren boomed, his voice cutting through the din like a clap of thunder.

His authority immediately halted the quarrel. The group turned their attention to him, their eyes reflecting shame and fear. Wren stalked toward them, his steps deliberate and his gaze sharp. His pack knew that his disapproval was not easily earned, and his presence alone commanded respect, even though he was still a fairly new alpha.

"This behavior is unacceptable," he growled, his displeasure evident in the deep furrow of his brow and the low rumble in his chest. "I will not tolerate infighting. This is not how we solve our problems. If you have an issue, bring it to me and we will resolve it together." His words rang out among the camp, his message clear.

"Now, apologize to each other and make amends. We are a family and we will not let petty arguments divide us." Wren's command resonated through the clearing. The atmosphere, once charged with anger and tension, began to shift. The wolves immediately obeyed, their contrition apparent in the way their heads lowered.

"I'm sorry," the young male said, his voice filled with humility, his eyes downcast as he met the gaze of the wolf he had argued with.

"Apology accepted," the other responded, their tone warmer, the hard edges of their anger giving way to understanding.

As the tension eased, Wren felt a surge of relief that the situation had been resolved without further conflict. His gaze swept across the group, his voice unwavering and filled with the burden of his responsibility.

"Remember, we are all in this together," he reminded them. "We must be unified if we are to succeed. Now, get back to work."

The group dispersed, each wolf returning to their duties, the incident already fading into the background. The rest of the pack continued about their business, their spirits lifted as the harmony was restored. The scent of the pine trees and the sounds of the morning filled the air once more.

Wren watched them go, his thoughts churning. The recent disagreement was a sobering reminder of the challenges that lay ahead. Despite his best efforts, there were still pockets of dissent within the pack, and the stress of the situation was clearly wearing on some members.

He could feel the profound weight of his obligation pressing down upon him, like a mantle of duty that he could never set aside. But he would not shirk his responsibility, for he had pledged to protect and guide his people and he would stand by his promise.

Wren and Venna walked through the camp, stopping to talk to various members as they went. The morning's routines were a comforting ritual and it warmed Wren's heart to see his people thriving, working together toward a common goal.

The sun had climbed high overhead as they completed their rounds. Just as they were about to make their way back to Wren's tent, a sudden disturbance near the camp's edge drew their attention.

A sentry approached Wren, his expression fraught with concern. "Wren," he said in a hushed tone, "there's a group of Otherworlders asking for you. They look like Academy enforcers."

Wren's heart raced at the mention of the Academy. After five years of carefully hiding, could he and Vale have finally been exposed? He exchanged a quick, knowing glance with Venna, who stood by his side, her eyes reflecting the same unease.

Without delay, Wren and Venna approached the camp's front gate, where the sentry led them to a small group of people. The newcomers were dressed in a manner that identified them unmistakably as representatives of the Academy. Their grey uniforms were all neat and free of dirt.

"Can I help you?" Wren asked, his voice cautious but composed.

"We're here on behalf of the Academy," the man at the forefront of the group said, his posture rigid and his expression unreadable. "We're looking for two individuals we believe are hiding among your people. Vale and Wren."

Wren's pulse quickened with anxiety. How had the Academy managed to track them down? "There's no one here by those names," Wren replied firmly.

"We have reason to believe that's not true," the man continued, his voice cold and resolute.

"Look," the woman next to him added, her gaze somewhat more sympathetic, "we're not here to cause trouble. We just want to talk to them."

Wren exchanged a wary look with Venna, their thoughts unspoken but clear. The arrival of the Academy's representatives had thrust them into a precarious situation, one that jeopardized the safety of their pack.

"We can't help you," Wren said, his voice resolute, his stance unwavering.

"That's unfortunate," the man replied, his gaze hardening into a steely resolve. "We were hoping to avoid any… unpleasantness."

Venna, her eyes narrowed and her body coiled with tension, stepped forward, her posture defensive. "And what would that entail?" she demanded, her voice sharp with challenge.

"If we have to," the man replied, his tone dripping with a threatening undertone, "we will use force."

Wren's muscles tensed, his senses sharp and alert. His gaze never wavered from the man's, a silent message of determination. "Do you really think, with the size of my pack, that you would get very far?"

"These wolves are under the jurisdiction of the Academy," the man declared, his voice brooking no argument, "and therefore you will submit to the Academy's authority."

Wren's hackles rose, and his growl rumbled low in his throat. "The only authority this pack submits to is my own," he declared, his stance challenging and defiant.

The standoff between the two groups crackled with tension and Wren could sense the restlessness among the other wolves gathered. Their loyalty to their alpha was unwavering and they were eager for a fight. He knew he would have to act swiftly to avoid the looming threat of bloodshed.

"Let's not be hasty," the woman interjected, her voice a weak attempt at conciliation. "We don't want to cause any trouble."

"Then leave," Wren snapped, his patience running thin. "Before we make you."

"We can't do that," the man said, his tone unyielding. "We're here on official Academy business. You can either hand over Vale and Wren, or we'll be back to take them by force."

Wren clenched his fists, his jaw locked in frustration. He had no illusions about the Academy's resolve. The thought of his pack coming to harm was utterly unacceptable and he knew that he had to find a way to protect them without resorting to violence.

"I'm not going to warn you again. You are not welcome here." Wren said defiantly.

"This isn't the last you've seen of us," the man warned, his gaze unyielding, his threat hanging heavy in the air. "We'll be back, and next time, we won't be so accommodating."

Wren watched as the group slowly turned, their collective resolve unbroken. His jaw tightened, a storm of emotions swirling within him. The Academy representatives were leaving for now, but the specter of their return loomed ominously.

He could sense the uneasiness rippling through his pack, their concerns etched upon their faces and their gazes fixed on him for guidance.

"We can't let them make good on those threats," Venna murmured, her voice low but filled with determination.

"No, we can't," Wren agreed, his tone heavy with worry as he watched the retreating figures of the Academy enforcers.

"What are we going to do?" Venna asked, her eyes searching his for answers.

Wren's mind raced, a whirlwind of thoughts and plans taking shape. He knew the safety of his pack depended on his next moves. "I'm not sure yet," he admitted, his voice laced with urgency. "But we'll figure something out. We have to." The enormity of his responsibility was not lost on him, but he was determined to protect his pack at any cost.

CHAPTER SIXTEEN

I sat in my room, savoring a quiet moment of solitude as I enjoyed my breakfast. The morning sunlight filtered through the curtains, casting a warm, golden glow in the room. My thoughts drifted to the upcoming Aeloranthia celebration, wondering what it would be like.

Just as I was lost in contemplation, there was a soft knock on the door. As I told them to enter, the door to my chambers opened, and Amris, Kelli, and Joeline walked in. They would be a recurring presence in my life now I supposed.

Amris approached the bed, carefully placing a sizable box upon its surface. She looked at me with a glint of excitement in her eyes, which immediately piqued my curiosity. "My lady, Prince Thalion had a special dress made for you for tonight's celebration," she informed me, her voice tinged with a hint of reverence. "All the Fae of the court will be dressed in their finest attire tonight."

I set my breakfast aside, my interest fully captured. "Do you know where the celebration will be held?" I asked, eager to learn more about the event.

Amris nodded, a hint of a smile playing on her lips. "Each court will have its own celebration, but the most esteemed Faefrom every court will convene at King Galdimir's court in the city of Caeluxa for the grand feast and the ensuing celebration."

The ensuing celebration was a romp through the street naked, I assumed. I still couldn't quite wrap my head around that concept. It seemed the Fae were far less reserved than the Otherworlders in the mortal realm.

I stood up from the table and followed the three maids as they opened the box. Inside lay a breathtaking gossamer gown, the colors of autumn woven into its very fabric. Hues of oranges, reds, and yellows blended seamlessly, reminiscent of the vibrant foliage of the season. It was a masterpiece of craftsmanship and I couldn't help but admire the artistry that had gone into its creation.

Amris carefully inspected the gown with a discerning eye, her fingers tracing the intricate details of the fabric. "Prince Thalion truly spared no expense," she mused, her eyes shining with approval. "He wanted nothing but the best for you."

I couldn't help but feel a sense of gratitude towards Thalion for his generous gesture. The gown was a work of art and its beauty left me momentarily speechless. As the three servants helped me put it on, I marveled at how it fit me perfectly, accentuating my curves in all the right places.

"I feel like another person," I breathed, a smile playing on my lips as I examined my reflection in the mirror.

"You look beautiful, my lady," Joeline said, her voice filled with admiration.

Blushing at her compliment, I replied, "Thank you, Joeline." It was a humbling experience to be pampered and attended to in this manner, but I couldn't deny the warmth it brought me.

Kelli and Joeline moved behind me, their skilled fingers weaving my hair into intricate braids that sat elegantly atop my head. The rest of my hair cascaded down my back, adding a touch of wildness to the otherwise refined look. I told them that it looked marvelous, and the two girls blushed and thanked me, even curtsying, though I wished they wouldn't.

Turning to face the mirror once more, I couldn't help but admire the transformation before me. For the first time in my life, I could see the Fae in myself. The gown, the braids, and the aura of the upcoming celebration all combined to create an almost otherworldly vision.

My eyes widened as I took in the sight before me. "I look…," I couldn't quite find the words.

"Stunning," Amris finished for me smiling, her expression full of pride. "Prince Thalion will be quite pleased when he sees you."

As I stood there, adorned in the beautiful gown, I couldn't help but feel excitement for the Aeloranthia celebration ahead despite the horrors of introductions awaiting me there.

The women excused themselves and left, leaving me alone with my thoughts. I sighed, feeling nervous about the night's upcoming festivities. The grandeur of the celebration, the beauty of the dress, and the enchanting surroundings all added to the surreal feeling that this was just a dream.

I walked away from the mirror, drawn to the open balcony, where a gentle breeze carried the fragrant scent of flowers from the palace gardens below. The view was breathtaking, with the bustling city stretching out before me, its streets filled with Fae preparing for the night's revelry.

"You must not forget to be on your guard during the celebration tonight. Do not underestimate the dangers you may face there." Rowena's voice echoed through my mind. Her words were a sobering reality

check, grounding me in my true purpose here — to stop Haldir from unleashing chaos upon the mortal realm.

Despite my growing excitement for the celebration, I couldn't let myself forget my true mission. "You're right," I responded. "I'll remember to stay vigilant."

"See that you do, daughter."

Before I could dwell further on the impending challenges, a soft knock on the door between my room and Thalion'sinterrupted my thoughts. I called for them to enter and in walked Thalion and Aerion.

They both paused in their tracks as they saw me standing there, dressed in the stunning Fae gown. Their expression betrayed a look of awe, their eyes locked onto me as if they couldn't look away.

As I stood there under their intense scrutiny, a sudden wave of shyness washed over me. The extravagant gown they had prepared for me made me feel like a completely different person and I wasn't entirely comfortable with the attention.

"How do I look?" I asked my voice barely a whisper, my hands fiddling with the fabric of the gown.

Thalion, always composed and regal, was the first to find his voice. "Beautiful. You are a vision, Vale," he breathed, his words filled with genuine reverence.

"The gown is perfect, thank you," I replied, my gratitude heartfelt.

"I'm glad you approve," Thalion responded, a hint of a pleased smile dancing on his lips.

Aerion finally broke his silence, his voice tinged with a touch of awe. "She's definitely going to be noticed tonight. She looks like her mother come back to us."

Thalion agreed, a playful smirk crossing his face as he continued to scrutinize my appearance. "Yes, they'll go absolutely crazy over her. I'll have to make sure she has a guard."

"I will personally keep her safe," Aerion declared, his gaze unapologetically roaming over my body, which caused a blush to creep up my cheeks. His boldness was undeniable.

"Thank you, Aerion, but is that really necessary?" I inquired, genuine concern now etched on my face.

"You can never be too careful and your safety is important," Thalion responded, his expression turning serious. "Aerionwill stay by your side all night and keep a close eye on you."

I glanced at Thalion, arching an eyebrow, my curiosity piqued. "And what about you, Thalion?"

"I will be there most of the night too," he assured me, "but there may be instances where I will have to leave you."

Feeling a touch reassured, I nodded. "Well then, I will be fine with Aerion."

I couldn't help but notice the subtle shift in his demeanor at my words. His jaw tensed and his eyes hardened ever so slightly, as if he was displeased by the prospect of Aerion and I being alone.

As I tried to decipher Thalion's reaction, a whirlwind of thoughts and questions swirled through my mind. Was he jealous? The idea seemed absurd, as he had given no indication of having any romantic feelings for me. Or had he?

"So when do we leave?" I asked, eager to shift the focus away from my own thoughts.

"Later this afternoon, so you have some time before then to do as you please," Thalion replied, his expression returning to its usual neutral demeanor.

"I'm not sure what there is to do around here," I admitted, realizing that my time at the Fae court thus far had been almost entirely consumed by training.

Thalion pondered for a moment before offering some suggestions. "You could take a leisurely walk around the gardens and there is also our renowned library."

"The library?" I exclaimed, a bit too eagerly perhaps.

"Yes, our royal library is the largest and most comprehensive collection of books and scrolls in the entire city of Virelium," Thalion explained, a hint of amusement touching his lips. "Feel free to peruse it. I am sure it will contain something that will capture your interest."

"I'll do that," I responded, my excitement growing at the prospect of exploring the vast literary treasures that awaited me.

Thalion's face brightened with a warm smile. "Good. We will meet you in the entrance hall when it's time to depart."

With that, both Thalion and Aerion excused themselves, leaving me alone with my thoughts once again. I took one final look at my reflection in the mirror and let out a sigh, silently hoping that I could navigate the intricacies of the upcoming Fae celebration without causing an international incident.

I found the library without too much incident with the help of some servants passing by. I soon found myself in front of two huge double doors intricately carved with pictures of fantastical creatures. I pushed them open excitedly, surprised by how light the heavy-looking doors actually were.

The library's grandeur truly took my breath away as I stepped through those ornate double doors. The vastness of the room was awe-inspiring, with its towering shelves that seemed to stretch endlessly into the heavens. The artwork on the ceiling, depicting epic Fae battles and mythical creatures, added an air of enchantment to the already impressive space.

My footsteps echoed softly on the polished marble floor as I ventured deeper into the library, my fingers lightly brushing against the spines of countless books and scrolls. The scent of ancient parchment and leather bindings filled the air, making me feel as though I had stepped into another world entirely.

As I continued to explore, I noticed the layout of the library. Long wooden tables were positioned in the center, inviting readers to delve into their chosen tomes. Smaller, round tables dotted the periphery, offering more secluded reading nooks. A corner of the room was adorned with plush cushions on the floor, where a few Fae reclined comfortably, lost in their own worlds of written wonders.

My eyes wandered, scanning the shelves for something that might catch my interest. And then, there it was—an ancient-looking book that seemed to beckon to me. The spine was so worn that I feared the book might disintegrate in my hands. Gently, almost reverently, I plucked it from the shelf, handling it with care.

The pages within were yellowed with age and the ink had faded to a faint sepia hue. I squinted at the archaic script, my curiosity getting the best of me.

I nearly dropped the worn volume when a voice suddenly said from behind me, "May I help you?" The voice that had interrupted my concentration belonged to a tall, dark-haired Fae with an air of sophistication about him. His eyes, the color of deep emeralds, bore a slight hint of impatience as if he had been hoping for solitude in the library.

I blinked, momentarily taken aback by his presence. "Sorry, yes, can you tell me what this is about?" I asked, extending the book toward him.

He acccpted the tome, his fingers brushing lightly against its weathered cover as he examined it. "It's a history book about the wars between the Fae courts," he responded, his voice carrying a hint of disdain. "It's an interesting read, but there are better ones about the wars."

I furrowed my brow, intrigued. "Like what?"

With a curt nod, he turned and beckoned for me to follow him. I obliged, trailing closely behind him as we ventured deeper into the labyrinthine library. The shelves seemed to stretch endlessly in all directions, making me grateful for his guidance.

After a few turns and twists, he halted before a massive bookshelf that held an array of formidable tomes. His slender fingers moved deftly along the spines, caressing each one as he searched for the right volume. It was clear he knew this library intimately.

Finally, he retrieved a hefty tome and handed it to me with a flourish. "This is the definitive history of the wars," he explained. "It's more comprehensive than the others and has a lot of information that isn't in the other books."

"Thank you," I said, accepting the book with gratitude. "I appreciate your help."

A charming smile graced his lips. "Of course, it's my pleasure," he replied, his emerald eyes sparkling.

As I flipped through the pages of the newfound book, a sense of tranquility washed over me. The scent of ancient pages filled the air and I was surrounded by the comforting presence of knowledge and the countless stories it held. Lost in the narrative of Fae history, I remained ensconced in the world of words until the servants came to find me, gently pulling me from my literary reverie as the day began to wane.

As I left the library, my mind reluctantly shifted from the world of books and knowledge to the impending celebration. The fluttering in my stomach intensified at the thought, the festival having momentarily slipped my mind during my deep immersion in reading. With the servants as my guides, I made my way to the entrance hall, where Thalion and Aerionawaited.

The two Fae men were a striking sight, dressed in attire that exuded elegance and refinement. Thalion's ensemble consisted of a deep forest-green velvet tunic adorned with intricate golden embroidery. His silver-blonde hair, typically loose and flowing, was partially tied back, emphasizing his sharp features and striking violet eyes.

Aerion, on the other hand, wore a charcoal-gray coat with silver buttons, perfectly tailored to accentuate his broad shoulders and lean physique. His short brown hair, usually tousled, was slicked back, giving him a more polished appearance. His black trousers were neatly creased, leading to polished black shoes that gleamed in the soft light.

They both looked impeccable, the contrast between Thalion's earthy, regal elegance and Aerion's more contemporary refinement only adding to their allure. I couldn't help but admire them both, though my admiration was tinged with a touch of self-consciousness.

"Ready?" Thalion asked, his gaze sweeping over me.

I took a deep breath, determined to face the evening with confidence. "Yes," I replied, my voice steadier than I felt.

Thalion offered me a reassuring smile and extended his arm. I accepted the gesture, wrapping my hand around his forearm. He led the way, Aerion falling into step behind us.

As we made our way outside, I couldn't help but be curious about our mode of transportation. "How are we getting there?" I asked.

"Most Fae arrive at such celebrations days in advance, given the considerable length of their journeys," Thalionexplained. "Our court's Fae arrived there two days ago. Fortunately, thanks to Aerion, we have a more efficient method. We will be transported directly to King Galdimir's castle."

Aerion stepped forward, his posture composed and his tone matter-of-fact. "If you would hold on to me, we can depart."

Without hesitation, I moved closer to Aerion, placing my hand on his offered arm. I stood in between the two Fae princes as their arms wrapped around me at the same time.

As the three of us stood there a powerful surge of energy coursed through our bodies. In the blink of an eye, the world around us dissolved into a dazzling display of light and colors. Suddenly, the opulent surroundings of the palace were replaced by an awe-inspiring grand courtyard.

The air was alive with the sounds of laughter and animated conversation, interwoven with the enchanting melodies of string instruments playing in the background. The vibrant atmosphere was electric, a stark contrast to the quiet and regal ambiance of Thalion's palace.

Thalion and Aerion released me from their grasp and I couldn't help but notice the collective gasps and hushed whispers that rippled through the Fae around us. It was clear that my presence was already causing quite a stir and the weight of their curious gazes bore down on me. I glanced at Thalion and Aerion, who seemed unfazed by the attention, and took a moment to appreciate the breathtaking scene that surrounded us.

"The Aeloranthia Festival is said to be the most magical celebration of the year," Thalion whispered to me, his voice barely audible over the festive cacophony. "It's a time of revelry and excitement, a time when Fae from every court come together to celebrate the harvest."

The courtyard itself was a masterpiece of enchantment. A myriad of colorful flowers adorned the space, their vibrant hues creating a vivid tapestry against the backdrop of the Fae architecture. Brightly colored streamers hung from trees and floated on the breeze, creating a kaleidoscope of color that seemed to stretch endlessly.

With Thalion leading the way, I followed him through the lively throngs of Fae. Aerion remained a steadfast presence at my side, his silent support providing comfort as we weaved through the mesmerizing crowd.

As we gracefully glided through the animated crowd, the gentle hum of their conversations surrounded us. Whispers rippled through the Fae like a gentle breeze, their hushed tones betraying a mix of astonishment, wonder, and apprehension.

"Is that a half-breed?" one of the Fae voices inquired, laden with awe and an underlying sense of trepidation.

"It appears to be," came the reply from another, her voice skeptical.

My heart pounded in my chest as their words reached my ears, serving as a stark reminder of the extraordinary circumstances I found myself in. I had ventured into a world where I was an anomaly, a half-breed surrounded by beings of magic and myth.

As we continued navigating the bustling courtyard, the curious gazes of the Fae intensified, each glance akin to a probing examination. I felt like a specimen under a magnifying glass, as if the entire Fae court had converged to witness my presence.

Aerion's comforting words brushed against my ear like a soothing balm. "It's alright, they're just curious. They haven't seen a half-Fae here in centuries."

I offered a silent nod in response, trying to remind myself how powerful I was even though I felt incredibly small under all these curious eyes. Thalion skillfully guided us toward a majestic castle entrance, a grandeur of stone steps leading the way.

It was time to venture into the heart of it all, and I couldn't be any less prepared for what awaited me.

Chapter Seventeen

The grand stone steps rose beneath our feet, carrying us toward the imposing castle entrance. The whispers of their hushed conversations surrounded us and curiosity permeated the very air.

As we reached the top of the steps, the voices of the Fae grew more pronounced, and the weight of their inquisitive gazes bore down upon us like an unseen pressure. It was as if we were the central spectacle of the evening, our presence an enigma that had stirred the fae's collective curiosity.

A female Fae with an air of reverence approached us, her voice tinged with awe. "Prince Thalion and Prince Aerion! Welcome," she greeted, her words dripping with deference. "We are honored by your presence."

"The honor is ours," Thalion replied with a measured formality.

She inclined her head in a respectful bow and stepped aside, allowing us to cross the threshold of the castle. The moment we entered, we were enveloped in a whirlwind of activity. Fae milled about in the grand entryway, their animated voices reverberating off the high-vaulted ceilings.

"Come, let's grab some refreshments and find a suitable place for you," Thalion suggested, his hand gently resting against my back as he guided me.

As we wove our way through the throng, I could still feel the collective gaze of the Fae fixed upon us. Their expressions bore a blend of fascination and caution, their eyes never leaving us for long. It was a scrutiny that weighed upon me, a constant reminder of the centuries-old conflict between witches and the Fae, though none here but the two Fae males beside me knew what I truly was. I took a deep breath, attempting to steady my nerves.

Aerion, who had been keeping a protective watch over me, leaned in close and whispered, "Just ignore them. In time, they will grow accustomed to your presence."

I nodded, my voice hushed as I replied, "I'm trying, but it's not easy." The strain of the situation was evident in my whispered words.

As we weaved our way through the palace and into a grand ballroom, the reactions of the Fae were unmistakable. Surprise and awe painted their faces and it was evident that they had not anticipated the presence of a half-Fae among them. Their responses ranged from unabashed curiosity to subtle apprehension, making it clear that my appearance was an unexpected turn of events in their celebration.

Yet, the fae's whispers and lingering stares were not the only details I discerned. Among the intrigued crowd, there were male Fae whose gazes held unmistakable desire, their eyes lingering on me with a hunger that made my skin tingle. It was a little unnerving, but beneath the unease, there was a thrill that coursed through me—a sense of allure and fascination.

Aerion, keenly observant, must have noticed the shift in the atmosphere around us. He moved closer, his hand finding its way to the small of my back, guiding me toward a table laden with drinks and pastries.

"They seem quite taken by your beauty," he whispered, his voice a soft caress against my ear.

His words sent a chill through me. He was so close that my stomach fluttered. I couldn't help but become acutely aware of his presence.

"Is that necessarily a bad thing?" I whispered back, my cheeks tinged with a faint flush.

Aerion's breath was hot against my neck. "Not at all. In fact, it might work to our advantage," he murmured, his voice dipping into a seductive undertone.

His words carried a clear implication—my newfound appeal to the Fae could serve as leverage of sorts. As we reached the drink table, Aerion drew nearer, his body brushing gently against mine. His proximity was magnetic, leaving me to wonder what it would be like to be even closer. It struck me suddenly that I hadn't thought of Kaelan once since arriving in Elysian.

Thalion handed me a goblet filled with wine and I accepted it with a grateful smile. The atmosphere of the celebration was infectious, yet I couldn't shake the underlying sense of unease that had taken root within me.

His gentle smile was reassuring and I welcomed the opportunity to speak with someone familiar in this sea of unfamiliar faces. "How are you faring so far?" he inquired, his voice carrying genuine concern.

"I'm doing okay," I replied, trying to sound more confident than I actually felt. "It's just... a little overwhelming."

"I can imagine," Thalion replied, his gaze momentarily drifting across the exuberant scene around us. The music grew louder, and my eyes followed his to the Fae who danced and reveled in the center of the grand room. There was an undeniable energy in the air, an intoxicating blend of excitement and anticipation that swept through the crowd.

The music that filled the grand room was not just sound but an enchanting tapestry of melodies that seemed woven with threads of magic. Each note echoed in the air, as if given life, beckoning the listener into a world of wonder and reverie. It was as though the very atmosphere had been charmed and the music stirred something deep within all who heard it—a primal, celestial joy that was both bewildering and utterly captivating. It was no mere tune but an ethereal spell, inviting all present to abandon their inhibitions and embrace the spellbinding allure of the evening.

Elysian was extraordinary, a realm of endless fascination and hidden depths. And while part of me was apprehensive about navigating its complex social undercurrents, another part of me was excited by the challenges and opportunities that lay ahead, waiting to be uncovered.

"So, what's next?" I asked.

Thalion's thoughtful expression lightened as he considered my question. "Well, we should go meet the king and queen, then we can enjoy the festivities," he suggested, taking a casual sip from his goblet.

"That sounds good," I agreed, though a surge of anxiety washed over me at the prospect.

Sensing my unease, Thalion offered me a reassuring smile. "It will be alright, Vale. You are a guest of honor tonight and I have no doubt they will be mesmerized by you."

I couldn't help but chuckle softly at his words, though my anxiety persisted. "That doesn't exactly make me feel any better."

Thalion's response was a warm, understanding look as he guided me toward our next destination amidst the lively celebration.

I took a small sip of the Fae wine, hoping its enchanting effects would help quell the fluttering nerves that had taken residence in my stomach. The liquid's warmth coursed through me as it slid down my throat, creating a pleasant buzz that soothed my frayed nerves a little.

As we continued to move through the vibrant and curious crowd, I couldn't help but notice the unceasing stares and hushed whispers that followed us. The fae's fascination with my presence was evident and their unabashed curiosity made it increasingly difficult to ignore their attention.

Grateful for Thalion and Aerion's unwavering presence by my side, I found solace in their protective demeanor. They were my anchors amidst the sea of unfamiliar faces.

At the edge of the crowd, Thalion told a regally dressed Fae of our arrival and they scurried off to inform the king and queen. He turned to me with a serious expression, his eyes holding mine. "The king and queen are waiting for us. Are you ready?"

I swallowed hard and nodded, attempting to mask the trembling in my voice. "I am."

"Remember," Thalion reassured me, his grip gentle as he took my hand in his, "you are an honored guest. There is nothing to fear so long as you stay with at least one of us."

With his assurance, I drew strength as he led me through a pair of colossal doors, their ornate design and grandeur a stark contrast to the festive courtyard outside. The throne room stretched out before us in all its opulence.

The walls were adorned with intricate tapestries, each telling a story of the fae's rich history. Enormous crystal chandeliers hung from the high-vaulted ceiling, casting a dazzling array of colors upon the polished marble floors. The thrones were awe-inspiring creations, and atop them sat the king and queen.

As we approached the imposing thrones, my heart quickened its pace. The Fae nobility seated there regarded us with a mixture of regal authority and keen interest.

"Your Majesty," Thalion greeted, his voice taking on a formal and respectful tone.

"Prince Thalion, welcome," the king replied, his voice resonating through the room, commanding the attention of all present.

"May I present Lady Vale of the Mortal Realm," Thalion continued, his voice carrying a weight of formality and respect as he gestured toward me.

"Lady Vale, we are pleased to have you join us for the celebration," the king acknowledged, his words laced with a subtle undercurrent of amusement.

I curtsied low, determined to maintain my composure. "Thank you, Your Majesty. I am honored to be here."

The queen, her presence commanding and regal, leaned forward slightly, her piercing gaze scrutinizing me with interest. "It has been quite some time since I have seen a half-breed Fae. You are a fascinating creature."

"I am very grateful for the opportunity to visit Elysian," I replied, a touch of uncertainty in my voice as I navigated the unfamiliar waters of their curiosity.

"I am sure you will find the festival to be a most enlightening experience," the queen continued, her mysterious smile hinting at hidden depths of meaning.

Their words left an indelible impression on me and it was evident that their interest went beyond simple curiosity. I exchanged a quick glance with Thalion, but his expression remained inscrutable, his features revealing nothing of his thoughts.

"I am sure it will be," I responded carefully, sensing the need to tread lightly in this unfamiliar territory.

"We would love to hear more about your journey here," the king suggested, a curious expression crossing his face. "We met in the mortal realm, Your Majesty," he interjected, his voice smooth and diplomatic. "And I could not resist the chance to show her the wonders of the Fae realm."

"A wise decision," the king replied, his tone implying that Thalion's reasoning had not gone unnoticed.

The queen leaned forward, her piercing gaze fixed upon me. "You have quite the intriguing aura," she observed, her voice laced with intrigue. "It is quite unusual for a half-breed Fae."

I was not sure how to respond to her observation, uncertain if I had inadvertently stepped into a dangerous territory. I hesitated, unsure of how to navigate such unfamiliar waters.

The queen's knowing gaze shifted to Thalion, then Aerion, who was standing protectively by my side.

"Perhaps your companions have something to do with your unique aura," she surmised, her tone carrying a hint of implication.

The king, noting the subtle implication, raised an eyebrow and nodded, his interest clearly piqued.

"Perhaps," I replied, attempting to keep my voice steady and even. I could feel my heart racing, but I was determined to maintain my composure.

Aerion, noticing my growing anxiety, placed a reassuring hand on my back. The contact was warm and comforting, his touch sending feelings through me that were both foreign and exhilarating.

The king, noting the interaction, exchanged a curious glance with his wife, before turning his attention back to Thalion. "We will allow you to return to the festivities. But know that your guest is welcome here and we look forward to furthering our acquaintance."

"Thank you, Your Majesty," Thalion replied, bowing his head in acknowledgment. "We are grateful for your hospitality."

With that, the king and queen returned their attention to the other nobles gathered in the throne room, and we were dismissed.

As we left the opulent throne room, I couldn't help but release a sigh of relief. The encounter had been short and I had navigated it without incident.

"You did well," Thalion commended, a genuine smile gracing his lips.

I couldn't help but feel a swell of pride at his words. "Yeah, it wasn't so bad."

"Let's see how you fare for the rest of the night," he replied.

I couldn't help but flush slightly under his approving gaze. I took another sip of the Fae wine in my hand, trying to steady my nerves. Aerion's cautionary words drew my attention. "Do not drink too much, the wine will have stronger effects on you than it does on the Fae," he warned, his tone low and protective.

"I'm going to need it if I have to keep meeting royal Fae who look at me like they want to eat me whole all night."

Aerion's gaze remained fixed on mine, there was an undeniable pull between us now. It was as if he were studying me, his eyes tracing over the curves of my form, making my heart race.

"Shall we dance?" Thalion's interruption came just in time, his question breaking the charged moment.

Dancing was not my forte and I watched the other Fae with apprehension. "I'm not much of a dancer," I admitted, not liking the idea of dancing in front of these Fae one bit, even with the seductive allure of the music swirling around me.

Thalion, ever the gentleman, was undeterred. "Don't worry, I will lead you."

I smiled reluctantly at him and relented. "If you insist." I handed my drink to Aerion who accepted it without a word.

Taking his hand, I allowed Thalion to guide me to the center of the room, where the vibrant dance of the Fae was in full swing.

Thalion took my hand in his, his other wrapping around my lower back. His touch was warm and gentle and I relaxed a little in his embrace.

"Just follow my lead," he whispered, his breath hot on my neck. The music changed to a slower, more seductive rhythm and I felt my heart skip a beat. "You can do this, just move with the music," Thalion said, his lips brushing against my ear.

As we began to dance, I allowed myself to let go and feel the music, to sway and move to its alluring beat. I felt the tension and anxiety leave my body as we danced. Thalion held me close, his hands moving with purpose across my body.

As we danced, I caught sight of Aerion watching us from the edge of the dance floor, a glass of wine in hand, his eyes dark with emotion. His gaze sent a thrill through me, leaving me to wonder if I was imagining his reaction or if his interest in me had become a reality.

I tried to ignore the pull of the music, the alluring atmosphere, and the desire that seemed to flow through my veins. I had come to Elysian for answers, and now was not the time to become distracted by the seductive charms of the Fae realm.

Still, as Thalion pulled me close, the intoxicating music wrapping around us, I couldn't help but surrender to the moment.

"You are doing well," he whispered, his eyes fixed on mine.

I couldn't help but admire his handsome features, the way his eyes seemed to see right through me. The music was pulsing and I was completely caught up in the hauntingly beautiful melody.

"You are a natural," Thalion said, his voice laced with admiration. I flushed, unable to find the words to respond. Suddenly, Thalion pulled me close, our bodies pressed together.

"Relax," he whispered, his voice low. "I won't bite unless you ask me to."

I swallowed hard, the feel of his body against mine making heat curl low in my stomach.

Thalion's hand on my lower back seemed to burn through the fabric of my dress. His other hand gripped mine tightly, the sensation of his skin against mine consuming my every thought.

The music continued, the tempo changing. Thalion spun me around, my skirt flaring out as we moved. The air was heavy with magic and I could feel it swirling around us.

My heart was pounding in my chest, my breath coming in short, quick gasps. The music seemed to pulse through my body, the seductive notes swirling around us.

Thalion leaned down, his lips brushing against my ear, his voice a low growl.

"I think you might like it if I bit you," he breathed, his tone dipping into a suggestive undertone. "Wouldn't you?"

I was surprised by his words. It was unexpected and yet, I found myself intrigued. The heat in his eyes left no doubt as to his intentions. I shook my head slightly, I was sure the music was getting to my head.

The music stopped, and the dance ended. The Fae around us clapped and I could hear the sounds of their whispers. I was panting slightly, my body still thrumming with the magic of the music and desire. Thalion looked at me, his eyes dark and filled with lust.

"You are quite the dancer," he breathed, his lips inches from mine. I swallowed hard, his proximity, combined with the music's enchantment made it difficult to think.

"And you are quite the dangerous Fae," I replied, my voice barely above a whisper.

Thalion's gaze intensified and for a moment, I thought he was going to kiss me. But then, he released me, a smirk on his face. "Perhaps," he said. "Or perhaps, you are the dangerous one."

"Me?" I asked incredulously.

Thalion's eyes glittered with mischief. "Yes, you. You have no idea the effect you have on Fae, do you?"

I blinked, caught off guard by his words.

He smiled, a wicked gleam in his eye.

"The Fae are very sexual creatures, as I'm sure you know," he purred. "And you are a rare and exotic beauty, with an aura that is irresistible to them. You are like a siren, calling to them, tempting them."

I felt a flush creep across my cheeks. "I didn't realize," I stammered.

Thalion chuckled. "Of course not.

"So, you're saying the Fae want to...what? Eat me alive?"

Thalion's smile grew wicked. "More or less. They're drawn to you, your presence, your aura. They want to possess you, to taste you, to make you theirs. And it's not just the males, either. The females want you, too."

I felt a rush of heat, my body responding to the seductive tone of his voice, the intensity of his gaze. "That's...a lot to take in," I murmured.

Thalion leaned in, his lips brushing against my ear. "The question is, what are you going to do about it?"

I stood there, unsure how to respond. My body was buzzing, and the music had a hypnotic quality. Thalion grabbed me by the hand and turned, heading back toward Aerion.

"Maybe a quick break from everything would be good," Aerion suggested, his voice like a soothing balm amid the Faerevelry.

"Of course," Thalion replied, his gaze remaining steadfast on me. "What do you suggest?"

"Perhaps a walk in the gardens?" Aerion suggested.

"You two go, I have duties to attend to, important Fae to talk to, and so on. I'll catch up later."

With a nod from Thalion, Aerion and I watched him depart, his duties calling him away.

"Would you like to go for a walk, Vale?" Aerion inquired, holding out his hand.

"Yes," I answered, my eagerness perhaps a little too apparent. I took his proffered hand and he skillfully led me through the bustling crowd, guiding us away from the prying eyes of the Fae.

The magic in the air was tangible, its intoxicating presence heightened by the Fae wine and the lingering sensations from our earlier dance. The moonlight bathed the garden in a soft, silver glow, casting enchanting shadows over the vibrant flowers and carefully trimmed hedges lining the pathways. The sweet scent of night-blooming jasmine filled the air, further enhancing the magical atmosphere.

Aerion led me to a secluded alcove, tucked away from the boisterous celebration, where the sounds of revelry were hushed.

"This is a beautiful garden," I remarked, my gaze drifting around as I admired the interplay of moonlight through the leaves.

"I thought you would appreciate it," Aerion replied, his eyes intently fixed on me, his expression unreadable in the dim light.

Watching him, I was drawn in by his steel-grey eyes. My heart raced as I contemplated the inexplicable circumstances that had led me to this moment.

"You know, it's kind of ironic. I've always thought Fae were dangerous yet here I am, in their realm, willingly," I mused.

Aerion's lips curled into a knowing smile, his gaze never wavering from my face. "Don't be fooled, all Fae are dangerous," he replied, his tone playfully teasing. It was a side of him I had never seen before.

I couldn't help but smile back, though my heart still pounded with uncertainty. "I hope not, for my sake," I responded.

Aerion took a step closer, the gap between us narrowing until his body was almost touching mine. The air seemed charged with unspoken desires.

"There are many Fae who are intrigued by you," he confessed, his voice laced with a hint of desire.

"Intrigued?" I asked, my voice barely above a whisper, my own curiosity growing.

"They find you beautiful and fascinating. Many have already sought me out, asking about you, while you danced," Aerion explained, trailing his finger along my neck.

"Oh," was all I could manage in response, my mind struggling to process the implications of his words.

"You are a mystery to them and that makes you all the more desirable," he continued, he sounded as if he spoke from experience.

"I never imagined this is how it would be. When I first came here, I was afraid. Now, I'm not so sure," I admitted, my voice filled with wonder and vulnerability.

"I can't blame them for their curiosity. You are unique, even among the Fae," Aerion said. His fingers moved with a feather-light touch to cup my face, his thumb tracing my lower lip as he leaned in closer. A chill coursed through me in the face of his captivating allure.

"Are you saying I'm special?" I couldn't help but tease.

Aerion's gaze darkened, his hand moving to the back of my neck with a confident, possessive hold. His lips hovered dangerously close to mine and I held my breath.

"You have no idea," he whispered, his voice a velvet caress that sent a shiver of anticipation surging through my body.

A charged silence enveloped us as Aerion's breath, warm and tantalizing, danced across my skin. Every nerve in my body seemed to be on high alert, my senses heightened by his proximity. I couldn't deny the electric pull I felt toward him, nor the stirring desire that coursed through my veins.

My heart, a wild, erratic drumbeat, echoed the tempo of my racing thoughts. Which he could surely hear. I was caught in a whirlwind of emotions, a potent blend of exhilaration and longing that left me breathless and uncertain. "Aerion," I said breathlessly, "What are you doing?"

Aerion smirked, his gaze holding a challenge. "Showing you what it means to be desired by a Fae," he answered.

I couldn't help but laugh, a nervous, giddy sound. "Oh? And is that something I should fear?"

Aerion smirked, his fangs flashing in the dim light of the moon. "Completely," he said, his voice laced with an alluring, sensual quality that made me melt. His eyes, so piercing in their intensity, remained locked onto mine. "I can sense the magic in you, even though you have yet to fully come into your power."

His words, like a revelation, hung in the air between us, leaving me with a sense of profound intrigue and a lingering question of why.

"That's why you agreed to teach me?" I asked, my voice quivering slightly, my curiosity seeking answers.

"It is part of the reason," Aerion replied, his hand still cupping my face.

My heart pounded harder, anticipation thickening the air around us. "And what is the other part?" I whispered, my breath hitching in my throat.

He didn't say anything. Instead, he silenced my question with a hungry, demanding kiss. His lips, tender yet insistent, captured mine in a fiery embrace. It was a kiss that spoke of longing, of unspoken desires, and ignited a passion that seemed to have been simmering beneath the surface.

I was helpless to resist, my body responding eagerly as he pulled me closer.

The magic in the air seemed to crackle and spark and I could feel the power emanating from him. He pulled away, his eyes wild with passion.

"I have wanted to do that since the moment you managed to slip away from me a month ago," he confessed, his voice ragged. "Do you understand how hard it is to escape my grasp? No man or woman has ever managed it. I found I quite liked it when you ran away from me." His last words were a seductive purr and I shivered against him.

I was breathless, my heart hammering in my chest. I couldn't believe what was happening, but I knew I didn't want it to stop.

He stepped away from me suddenly, releasing his grip on my waist. I was confused until a moment later when Thalionturned a corner and appeared.

"Thalion," Aerion greeted, his tone nonchalant.

"I'm not interrupting anything, am I?" he asked, his gaze flickering between Aerion and myself.

"No, not at all," Aerion said, his voice light and casual. I flushed, feeling embarrassed at being caught here together.

"Well, if you don't mind, I'd like to steal Vale for a moment," Thalion said, a small smile playing on his lips.

"Of course, by all means," Aerion said, inclining his head.

Chapter Eighteen

Thalion took my hand and led me away from the alcove, his gaze fixed on me. My mind was reeling from the encounter with Aerion, my body still tingling with desire. I couldn't help but think of his lips on mine, his touch sending sparks along my skin. I could tell from Thalion's demeanor that he was aware of what had happened between Aerion and me, but he didn't seem upset or angry. Instead, he seemed amused, his expression playful.

"You have quite the talent for capturing the attention of the Fae, it seems." Thalion's teasing remark made me feel both flustered and oddly pleased. His easy confidence and charming demeanor were starting to put me at ease, I was sure the Fae wine helped as well.

"Yes, it seems that I do," I replied.

"Everyone is talking about you, wondering who the mysterious half-breed Fae is." Thalion said to me with an air of secrecy, leaning in slightly as if sharing a hidden truth.

I blinked. "Still?" I asked, my eyes widening.

Thalion's reassuring smile helped quell my unease. "Yes, still," he confirmed. "It's nothing to worry about, though. Everyone is simply curious."

"I'm not used to being the center of attention," I admitted.

Thalion chuckled softly, his smile broadening. "I can tell," he said, his warm gaze never wavering.

There was something about the way he looked at me, a mixture of understanding and playfulness, that made my heart flutter. It was a feeling I couldn't quite explain but didn't want to analyze too closely.

"Maybe I need more time to adjust to everything," I said.

Thalion offered words of comfort, his tone gentle and reassuring. "Don't worry I promise no one will try to eat you as long as I'm here."

I chuckled at his words. "Thanks, I appreciate it."

As Thalion led me back into the grand hall, my senses were once again inundated with the sights and sounds of the Fae celebration. The group of Fae he approached turned their attention to us, their hushed conversation coming to a halt as we neared. Thalion, ever the graceful diplomat, greeted them warmly before turning to introduce me.

"May I present Lady Vale, our special guest," Thalion announced with a touch of pride in his voice. "Vale, this is King Therodrin and his wife Queen Lesta."

I felt a slight flutter of nervousness as the royal couple turned their attention toward me. Unsure of the protocol, I curtsied as I had for King Galdimir and his wife. "Your Majesties."

King Therodrin, an imposing figure with an air of curiosity about him, broke the silence. "So, you're the one causing a stir," he remarked, his tone filled with intrigue.

I shifted uncomfortably, feeling self-conscious under the scrutiny. "Not of my own volition, I assure you," I replied.

Queen Lesta, a figure of elegance and grace, observed me closely, her gaze unwavering. "Nonsense, we are all merely curious about the half-breed Fae," she remarked, her voice carrying a hint of assessment.

"I'm sure there are many things about Elysian that you will find strange or unfamiliar," the king added, a touch of amusement in his eyes.

I nodded, still unsure how to navigate this unfamiliar social territory. "Yes, there are," I admitted.

Queen Lesta's scrutinizing gaze seemed to pierce through me and I felt she was attempting to delve into my very soul.

"Don't worry, she won't hurt you, will you, dear?" King Therodrin interjected, noticing his wife's questioning gaze, his tone playful.

Queen Lesta's response was cold and measured. "No, I have no intention of hurting her."

King Therodrin chuckled heartily, seemingly amused by the exchange. "Good, because that would be a terrible diplomatic incident," he said.

I glanced at Thalion, who wore a subtle expression of amusement, his eyes twinkling with mirth. It was clear that the Fae had their own ways of engaging in conversation and their unique sense of humor was lost on me.

"Tell me, my dear, are sure you are half mortal?" The queen asked me, narrowing her eyes.

The queen's question hung in the air, causing a tense silence to settle over us. Her narrowed eyes bore into me, demanding an answer.

I glanced briefly at Thalion, my shock evident in my expression. This revelation had clearly taken me by surprise and I wasn't sure how to respond.

King Therodrin, ever the diplomat, decided to break the silence. "You are among friends and there are no secrets here," he assured me. "You can answer the question truthfully."

I took a deep breath as I replied, "Yes, I'm half-human." These Fae couldn't find out what I was just yet.

The king mused, "Ah, just as we thought. We must take care not to harm you, then. Mortals are so fragile, right, Lesta?"

Queen Lesta regarded me with suspicion, her eyes studying me as if assessing my worthiness to be in their presence. Her disdain was evident as she replied, "Yes, mortals are quite delicate."

Feeling increasingly uncomfortable under their scrutiny, I turned to Thalion, silently imploring him to intervene and change the subject.

Thalion spoke up. "Lady Vale has had quite the night, Your Majesties. If you don't mind, I was going to show her around some more before the feast begins"

"Of course," Queen Lesta said, her eyes still fixed on me. "Enjoy the rest of your evening."

"Thank you," I replied, dipping into another curtsey before quickly turning to Thalion, who grabbed another glass of wine from a servant.

"Here, this will help," he said, his voice reassuring as he handed me the glass.

"Thanks," I said, my voice steady as I took a long drink. The bubbly wine slid down my throat with ease and heat rose in my chest.

"Come, there is one more king you should meet tonight," Thalion urged, his voice gentle and reassuring.

As we walked away, my legs felt a bit shaky, surely the Fae wine finally catching up to me. Thalion's hand enveloped mine, his fingers stroking the back of my hand in a comforting gesture.

Approaching a group of Fae engaged in lively conversation, Thalion introduced me to them, including Queen Aria and King Oren.

"Ah, yes, the half-breed Fae. You certainly are an interesting sight," King Oren remarked, his tone dismissive and his eyes appraising me with a hint of condescension.

"Oren, be nice," Queen Aria chided him gently, her demeanor warm and welcoming.

"Nice? To a half-breed?" King Oren scoffed, showing little regard for his own queen's reprimand.

Queen Aria offered a kind smile, seemingly unaffected by her husband's rudeness. "I'm sure she is a lovely girl," she said, her gaze warm and friendly as she looked at me.

I returned her smile gratefully, feeling a bit more at ease in her presence. "Thank you," I said, offering a curtsey out of respect.

"You are welcome, child," Queen Aria replied kindly. Then, with a playful wink at Thalion, she added, "Now, Thalion, don't keep her all to yourself."

Thalion chuckled, his eyes crinkling at the corners. "I wouldn't dream of it, Your Majesty."

With Thalion guiding me away from the group of Fae royalty, I let out a sigh of relief. He led me through the grand hall, weaving through clusters of Fae engaged in animated conversations and revelry. His fingers remained lightly entwined with mine, lending me a sense of grounding amidst the swirling energies and exotic atmosphere of the Fae.

"As you can see, not everyone is as forward-thinking as we might wish," Thalion murmured, referencing my recent interactions with the royalty. "But there are those who are genuinely intrigued by you."

Before I could respond, a couple detached themselves from a nearby group and approached us. Thalion's eyes lit up with recognition.

"Lady Vale, may I introduce Lord Elion and Lady Seraphine?" Thalion announced, gesturing toward the couple.

Lord Elion looked me over with an appraising eye, not unkind but certainly shrewd. "Ah, the half-breed Fae. You've become something of a sensation tonight."

Lady Seraphine, however, smiled warmly. "Ignore him, he's overly analytical. It's lovely to meet you, Lady Vale."

"Likewise," I replied, relieved by her kindness.

Thalion subtly directed me onward. "If you'll excuse us," he said to the couple, "we have more introductions to make."

Next, we approached a group of younger Fae who seemed lost in their own world, laughing and sharing a decanter of shimmering liquid. Thalion cleared his throat to gain their attention.

"May I present Lady Vale," Thalion said, drawing me closer to him. "This is Lady Mirelle, Lord Caelum, and Lady Thalassa."

Lady Mirelle barely glanced at me, her eyes flicking back to her friends as she murmured a half-hearted, "Charmed."

Lord Caelum, however, stepped forward and took my hand, looking into my eyes as if trying to glean some hidden truth. "Fascinating," he said softly before returning to his original position.

Lady Thalassa grinned mischievously. "She's got something, doesn't she? A certain allure."

Thalion chuckled. "Indeed, she does."

As we moved away, a Fae with silvered hair and piercing blue eyes made a beeline toward us. "Lady Vale," he said, bowing slightly, "I am Sir Idris. I couldn't help but notice you from across the room."

"Hello, Sir Idris," I said, taking note of his unabashed interest. He made no effort to hide his intrigue, and his gaze seemed to drink me in.

"You've set many tongues wagging," he continued. "And I can see why. You are a novel mystery in a realm that has seen it all."

Thalion tightened his grip on my hand subtly, perhaps wary of Sir Idris's overt attentiveness. "Thank you for your compliment, Sir Idris. We were just on our way to—"

Another voice interjected, cutting him off. "Ah, there she is!"

I turned to find a female Fae approaching, her eyes sparkling like jewels. "I've heard so much about you, Lady Vale. They say you're a fresh wind blowing through these ancient halls."

"I'm flattered," I replied, a bit taken aback by her enthusiasm but grateful for the warmth in her eyes.

"Elowen," Thalion greeted her, "always a pleasure."

"Oh, don't sound so formal," she laughed, "You're with the guest of the evening!"

Elowen took my hand and drew me close. A faint scent of flowers and citrus emanated from her, light and refreshing.

"Lady Vale, I hope you are enjoying yourself tonight. We Fae can be a bit intimidating, but I assure you we mean well. At least most of the time anyway. Don't let the rumors get to you, they don't mean anything. They are just fascinated by you, a half-Fae. We are all so used to each other, but you are different and that intrigues us. Just look at you, the way your eyes glow like embers. You are something new and that is exciting for us. We can be so bored at times, and you are like a spark of fire in a dark forest."

Her words were spoken with genuine warmth and sincerity, and I found myself believing her.

"I'm enjoying myself, thank you," I said, my eyes darting toward Thalion.

"Oh, Thalion is such a wonderful host. And a fine-looking one, too," she said with a wink. "I'm sure you'll have no shortage of admirers."

Thalion's hand tightened around mine, a small, possessive gesture. He didn't seem bothered by Elowen's attention, but rather amused.

I smiled, my cheeks reddening a little at the compliment. "I appreciate your kind words," I said, a bit embarrassed.

"Of course, sweet girl. Enjoy the evening." Elowen squeezed my hands before letting go and turning away, disappearing into the crowd.

"Well, that was interesting," Thalion said, a hint of amusement in his voice.

"She's...friendly," I replied, still a bit dazed by the encounter.

As Thalion led me away, I felt both buoyed and slightly overwhelmed by the tapestry of reactions I had elicited. Elysian was a realm of contrasts—of fascination and skepticism, of warmth and cold scrutiny. I was the outsider who had, for a moment, become the center of a complex, glittering world.

"Are you alright?" Thalion asked, his eyes searching mine.

"I'm fine," I said, though my mind was racing. "It's just a lot to process."

He nodded understandingly. "Elysian can be a labyrinth in many ways. But you're navigating it remarkably well."

"As long as I have a good guide," I replied, looking up at him.

Thalion smiled, and for a moment, amidst the thrumming energies and watchful eyes, I felt anchored. It was a welcome break, a fleeting moment of clarity in a night that continued to unfurl in mysterious and unpredictable ways. The evening had been a whirlwind of introductions and encounters and I welcomed the brief respite.

Thalion began to speak, perhaps suggesting a course of action or a change in our plans, but he abruptly stopped mid-sentence. His gaze fixated on something behind me and I turned to see what had captured his attention.

A group of Fae had just entered the ballroom and at the forefront was a figure who immediately drew my eyes. He might have been considered handsome under different circumstances, with his regal bearing and striking presence. However, it was the malicious sneer etched onto his face that marred his appearance. He stood taller than his companions, exuding an aura of predatory danger that chilled my blood. My instincts screamed at me to run, to keep as far away from him as possible.

"That one is not to be trusted."

The voice of the First Witch rang out in my head, telling me what my gut already knew. She didn't often speak, preferring to remain silent, but when she did it was for good reason. There was something terribly sinister about this Fae.

"Who is he?" I couldn't tear my gaze away from the imposing figure.

Thalion's voice was low and serious as he answered, "That's Haldir." Of course, it was, I thought grimly. "The male beside him is Malachar, his son. Stay away from them both," he cautioned, though he didn't need to. There was zero chance I would willingly enter into a conversation with those two.

I glanced at the Fae beside Haldir, Malachar, who was just as handsome as his father but possessed the same malevolent air. His wicked grin sent a chill down my spine as he surveyed the room, his eyes gleaming with mischief. "Oh, I plan on it," I replied, my skin crawling with discomfort.

Haldir's gaze swept over the room and another chill coursed through me as he searched the room. When his eyes landed on me, a wicked smile curved his lips, filling me with a deep sense of unease.

"I think we should find Aerion," Thalion said, his arm wrapping around my waist protectively.

I could feel the tension radiating from him as he guided me through the crowd and I couldn't agree more. My heart raced as we made our way through the bustling ballroom, desperate to escape the ominous presence of Haldir and his son.

As Thalion led me towards Aerion, I felt a sense of relief knowing that we were approaching a familiar and protective presence. Thalion exchanged a significant look with Aerion, who turned to see what had prompted the unease.

Our fears were answered though as Haldir and Malachar strolled towards us, their demeanor oozing arrogance and disdain. Haldir, in particular, seemed to relish in the moment and his voice dripped with sarcasm as he addressed Aerion and Thalion.

"Well, well, the infamous Prince Aerion and the equally notorious Thalion," Haldir sneered, his words laced with mockery.

Aerion maintained his composure, responding with a calculated calmness, "Haldir. How unfortunate of you to join us."

Haldir's tone remained condescending as he continued, "I wouldn't miss an opportunity to spend time in the company of such... illustrious Fae."

Aerion's retort was delivered with a cold edge, "You flatter me."

Haldir's chuckle was unsettling, and his eyes lingered on me, making me feel exposed and vulnerable under his gaze. "And who is this beautiful creature?" he asked, his tone unsettlingly casual.

As Haldir's attention shifted towards me, I felt a strange sensation brushing against my consciousness. It was as if something was probing at the edges of my thoughts, a subtle intrusion into my mental defenses. I realized that it must be Haldir's magic, pressing against me and searching for any weaknesses it could exploit.

"She is our guest," Aerion's voice held a note of warning, but Haldir seemed undeterred by the caution in his tone.

Haldir's response was tinged with impatience and he leaned in closer, his eyes narrowing, as if challenging me. "What is your name, girl?"

His condescension and insistence made my blood boil, and I refused to let his attitude intimidate me. I didn't hesitate as I spoke, my voice clear and unyielding. "Vale, if you must know, and I'm not a girl."

Aerion's surprise was evident in the subtle widening of his eyes, and he glanced at me with a newfound appreciation for my spirit.

Haldir's laughter, in contrast, was filled with a sinister amusement as he acknowledged my defiance. "You have spirit, I like that," he purred, his intense gaze never leaving mine, as if he were trying to discern the depths of my character with a single look.

As we distanced ourselves from Haldir and his unnerving presence, Aerion's voice carried a dismissive tone as he addressed the Fae king. "If you don't mind, we have things to discuss."

Haldir, though seemingly unbothered by the encounter's conclusion, responded with a smug smirk. "Of course, I wouldn't dream of keeping you," he retorted with feigned politeness. "Perhaps I will see you again, Lady Vale." He inclined his head ever so slightly, his eyes never leaving mine.

I remained silent, locked in a wordless exchange of defiance with Haldir. His parting words hung in the air like a threat, leaving an unsettling feeling in their wake.

"Come on," Thalion urged, breaking the tension by guiding me away from the unsettling encounter.

As we walked away, I could sense Aerion's penetrating gaze fixed upon me. Unable to suppress my curiosity, I finally asked, "What is it?"

Aerion's response carried a sense of admiration. "Your ability to resist him is... impressive."

I furrowed my brow, puzzled by his comment. "Resist him? What do you mean?"

"He was trying to probe your mind, to see what secrets you held," Aerion explained, his tone laced with seriousness.

I swallowed hard, my throat feeling suddenly dry. I had guessed as much. "How did I stop him?"

Aerion's eyes held a subtle gleam as he responded, "Your power is greater than you know. But he also wasn't trying that hard."

Aerion's explanation left me bewildered and anxious. "I don't understand," I admitted.

He turned his gaze toward me, a solemn expression on his face. "Haldir is one of the most powerful Fae in the realm and yet you resisted him with ease. You have a strong will, Vale. I'm afraid you will need it."

His words left me with a rising sense of dread. "What is he planning?" I asked, my heart hammering in my chest.

Aerion's eyes darkened. "Whatever it is, it can't be good. Stay close to us and don't go anywhere alone."

I nodded, a chill creeping through my body. The encounter with Haldir had made one thing abundantly clear: he was a dangerous adversary, and I was unwittingly placed directly in his path.

CHAPTER NINETEEN

As dinner was served, Thalion and Aerion remained ever-present by my side, a reassuring shield against the unsettling gaze of Haldir, whose eyes bore into me relentlessly. I did my best to focus on my meal and engage in the lively conversation that flowed around us, attempting to drown out the unease that his scrutiny brought.

The food before us was nothing short of a feast for the senses. There were elegantly arranged platters of fruits that seemed to shimmer, their vibrant colors almost too beautiful to eat. A variety of meats seasoned with exotic herbs released an intoxicating aroma, complementing the assortment of vegetables that had been cooked to perfection. Delicate pastries and intricate desserts beckoned invitingly from another table, each a work of art. The wine was light yet robust, its flavor a complex dance of fruits and spices that seemed to pair effortlessly with every dish.

I took small bites, allowing the various flavors to unfold on my tongue. Each dish seemed to contain an ingredient or a seasoning that I couldn't quite identify, a little magic that elevated it from simply delicious to otherworldly. As I tasted a piece of fruit, its juices burst forth, releasing a cascade of flavors so exuberant and complex, that I wondered if I was experiencing a hint of Fae magic. The meats were tender and full of nuanced flavors that hinted at the skilled marination and preparation involved.

While the culinary spectacle was awe-inspiring, it also served as an excellent diversion. As the courses flowed, I found myself caught up in conversations with Fae nobility about the recent treaties between various Fae territories, the looming challenges from the darker recesses of the realm, and even lighter topics like the recent artistic pursuits that were becoming popular in Elysian.

Thalion seemed to effortlessly navigate the social labyrinth of the Fae court. Now and then, he would chime in with a particularly insightful comment or a well-timed joke, earning nods of approval or appreciative laughter from those around us.

Aerion, though quieter, held his own, adding pertinent remarks when the conversation swerved into areas of his expertise. His eyes would often meet mine, a silent communion that reassured me whenever the weight of Haldir's stare became too much to bear.

As the meal reached its climax with the arrival of the desserts—elegant creations that seemed to defy the laws of pastry engineering—I felt a tap on my shoulder. Turning around, I was greeted by a couple who introduced themselves as Lorienand Elandria.

"Ah, Lady Vale, you are as stunning as they say," Elandria cooed, her eyes a swirl of colors as if enchanted by some unseen magic.

"Indeed, you pique our interest," Lorien added, though his tone was considerably more subdued compared to his partner's effusiveness.

As the evening continued, Thalion guided me to meet more and more Fae. Among them were those who regarded me with a certain haughtiness, their faces unreadable and their words measured. Others seemed utterly disinterested, nodding politely but quickly returning to their own conversations as soon as the formalities were concluded. But there were also those who seemed genuinely captivated by my presence, asking me a myriad of questions about my lineage and my interests.

Throughout all these interactions, the variances in reactions to me were as diverse as the tapestry of dishes that had graced our table. Yet, for every disdainful glance, there was a smile of genuine interest; for every terse word, a warm greeting. It was a complex, even paradoxical evening, an encapsulating microcosm of the Fae realm itself. And at the center of it all was me.

After the feast, we escaped to a balcony that offered a breathtaking view of the city below. I had drank entirely too much wine during the meal, my head was swimming and my body felt too warm. The night air was cool and refreshing, a welcome respite from the intensity of the evening's events. I closed my eyes for a moment, relishing the sensation of the gentle breeze on my skin.

Thalion's soft voice pulled me from my reverie. "Are you enjoying yourself?"

I opened my eyes and to my surprise, I found that Aerion was nowhere to be seen; it was just Thalion and me. A genuine smile graced his face and the corners of his violet eyes crinkled in a friendly manner.

"Yes, I am," I replied with gratitude, my heart warming to his kindness. He rested his hand lightly on the small of my back, a gentle and comforting gesture that made me feel at ease.

I gazed out over the balcony, taking in the mesmerizing sight of the city's lights sparkling in the distance, the beauty of the Fae realm undeniable even amid intrigue and uncertainty.

"It's beautiful, isn't it?" he asked, following my gaze.

The city's radiant lights below created a breathtaking tableau, and Thalion's question brought my attention back to the view. I nodded in agreement, my voice hushed as I replied, "It is."

Thalion closed the distance between us, his presence drawing my focus away from the cityscape. His warm breath tickled my ear as he whispered, "It's nothing compared to you."

A rush of warmth flooded through me at his words and I turned to face him. His gaze was intense, his eyes fixed on mine, and I found myself captured by the seriousness in his expression.

"Vale," he began, his voice low and filled with sincerity, "I have to admit something. When I first met you, I thought you were nothing. I thought you were weak and insignificant."

His confession caught me off guard and I pulled back slightly, my surprise evident in my expression.

"But now," he continued, "I see that you are so much more. You are strong, and brave, and clever. You have a power within you that even you don't realize."

His words left me speechless and I stood there, staring at him, the gravity of his assessment sinking in.

Thalion's warm breath caressed my skin as he leaned in, his nose gliding along the delicate curve of my throat. His voice, filled with tenderness, continued to wash over me.

"And I want to be the one to help you discover that power," he murmured, his words soft and filled with intent.

As he moved closer, his hand found its way around my waist, his touch sending a thrill through me. Every sensation seemed to heighten as my mind swirled with a whirlwind of emotions.

"Thalion, I..." I began my thoughts in disarray.

His head lifted and our eyes locked in a captivating exchange.

"What is it, Vale? What are you thinking?" he inquired, his gaze a gentle inquiry.

"I'm not sure," I confessed, my voice wavering. "I'm feeling so many things right now."

His smile was a balm to my uncertainty, his eyes deeply searching mine.

"Good," he whispered, his voice tinged with husky desire, "because I'm feeling a lot of things too."

I couldn't help but swallow hard, my heart beating a frenetic rhythm within my chest. "What are you doing, Thalion?" I asked, my voice shaky.

Thalion's gaze bore into mine as his hand traced a tantalizing path down the side of my body, his touch sending tremors through me.

"What does it look like?" he countered, a playful smirk dancing on his lips.

"I don't know," I confessed, my voice catching in my throat as uncertainty swirled within me.

He chuckled softly, his eyes gleaming with amusement.

"I think you do," he whispered, his lips tenderly brushing against my ear. "Do you want this, Vale?"

I didn't know, I couldn't think with his hands on me and the Fae wine running through my bloodstream.

"Tell me," he said, his voice insistent.

I drew in a shaky breath. "Yes," I whispered, the word coming unhindered to my lips.

He groaned, his mouth capturing mine in a searing kiss. I gasped, my hands gripping his shoulders. His tongue slid into my mouth and I surrendered to the sensation. I knew this was a bad idea, but I couldn't help myself.

His hands roamed over my body and I clung to him, lost in the moment. He pressed me up against the balcony railing, his hips grinding into mine. I could feel his arousal and I shivered with desire.

His mouth moved down my neck, his teeth grazing my skin.

"Thalion," I breathed, my body aching for his touch.

"Shhh, don't worry," he whispered.

I shuddered as his hand cupped my breast, his thumb brushing over my nipple. I gasped, arching into his touch.

He kissed me again, his mouth hot and hungry. "I've wanted you since the moment I laid eyes on you," he growled.

I could feel the heat of his body, the tension in his muscles. He was holding himself back, and I wanted nothing more than for him to let go.

But he finally pulled back and straightened himself, stepping back from me. I was left confused and wanting as I looked at him, my mind reeling and clouded.

"Remember what I said about what happens after the feast, Vale?" Thalion asked, his voice low and slightly breathless.

Oh Gods, how could I have forgotten?

Aerion stepped onto the balcony and looked between us, his expression unreadable. "Haldir has left," was all that he said. My cheeks flushed at the sight of him, my head still spinning from the Fae wine.

"Are you alright, Vale?" he asked, his tone concerned. I nodded, swallowing hard. Panic was starting to bubble up at the prospect of taking my clothes off with the two Fae males. "How much have you had to drink?"

Thalion's concern was evident as he gently spoke to me, his soothing voice cutting through the haze of wine that clouded my senses. "Let's get you back to my palace," he suggested, his tone filled with care.

I brought a hand to my head, trying to clear the fog that had settled there. Confusion reigned as I tried to make sense of our situation.

"Are we not staying here?" I questioned, my voice wavering.

Thalion regarded me for a moment, his eyes searching my face for any signs of distress before responding, "No, you've had too much to drink; we should get you back."

I nodded in reluctant agreement, acknowledging the wisdom in his words.

With a surprising gentleness, Aerion, whose presence had been a comforting constant throughout the evening, wrapped his arm around my waist. The world around us seemed to warp and shift, dissolving into a whirlwind of light and colors as he used his Fae magic to transport us.

When the swirling sensations finally subsided, we found ourselves in the front courtyard of Thalion's palace. My head swam and I instinctively leaned into Aerion's supportive grasp.

"Are you okay?" he asked, his voice laced with concern.

Struggling to regain my bearings, I blinked rapidly and replied, "Yes, I'm just a bit dizzy." The sensation of shifting with Aerion had been made worse by my already swimming head.

Without hesitation, he scooped me up into his strong arms and I gasped in surprise, instinctively clinging to him for stability. His laughter filled the air, his eyes gleaming with amusement as he reassured me. "Relax, Vale. I'm not going to drop you."

He carried me through the regal halls of the palace, his steps purposeful and sure as we ascended the grand staircase. It didn't take long to reach my room. He walked through the doors and set me down gently next to the bed. I steadied myself, clutching onto the bedpost for support, my mind still reeling from the whirlwind of emotions and events that had defined the evening.

"Are you sure you're okay?" Aerion's concern was evident in his searching gaze, his eyes locking onto mine.

I offered a small, albeit tired, smile. "I'm fine," I replied softly, trying to downplay the effects of the Fae wine. "I think I just need to sleep it off."

Aerion nodded, his voice gentle as he acknowledged, "Of course."

He swiftly checked my room for any intruders and turned back to face me. There was a lingering moment where he continued to study me, his emotions concealed behind an unreadable expression. Then, with a faint smile, he turned away and quietly left the room, the door clicking shut behind him.

I removed my dress and sprawled out on the luxurious bed, my mind a swirling confusion of thoughts and emotions.

Every inch of my body seemed to tingle, the memory of both males' lips on mine still vivid and electrifying. The pull between the three of us was undeniable, a force that drew us together. Yet, deep within, I knew the risks of this dangerous game we were playing. If I wasn't careful, I could lose more than just my heart.

With a sigh, I closed my eyes, hoping that sleep would offer respite from the torrent of confusing emotions that swirled within me. It was the only way to temporarily escape the turmoil of the night, even if I couldn't escape my own desires.

Chapter Twenty

A relentless throbbing in my head greeted me as I awoke, a painful reminder of the revelry that had unfolded the previous night. With a low groan, I reached for the bedcovers, pulling them over my eyes in a futile attempt to block out the glaring brightness. The Fae wine, a misjudged indulgence, had proven far more potent than I'd ever imagined and now I was left to pay the steep price.

As the memories of the enchanting night resurfaced, I couldn't help but blush profusely. The words and actions of Thalionand Aerion danced vividly through my mind, making me bury my heated face into the softness of my pillow.

Their intentions were unmistakable, an allure that beckoned me to yield to their desires. Yet, I knew I had to resist. I couldn't afford to fall prey to their seduction, not again. The pain of heartbreak still lingered within me and I questioned my ability to endure another emotional ordeal.

Summoning all the willpower I could muster, I slowly rose from the bed, my surroundings swirling and shifting as if conspiring to maintain my disorientation. Fresh air and clarity were needed desperately.

After a splash of cool water on my face and a change into a simpler, less extravagant dress, I descended the palace's grand staircase. The familiar surroundings offered a sense of stability, grounding me as I sought solace outdoors.

Stepping out into the palace gardens, I took a deep breath, the crisp air filling my lungs. The peaceful morning was a stark contrast to the tumultuous night. The sun shone brilliantly, casting a golden glow over the meticulously manicured flora, while the azure sky stretched endlessly above.

My steps were unhurried as I wandered through the lush garden, relishing the solitude that enveloped me. The palace seemed to have embraced a tranquil hush, leaving only the melodic trill of birdsong to accompany my thoughts.

A deep inhalation of the crisp, autumn-scented air served as a balm for my cluttered mind. It was time to regain my focus, to concentrate on the reason I had come to the Fae Realm — preventing a disaster. The enticing distractions of Thalionand Aerion, though tempting, were counterproductive to my purpose.

As I meandered deeper into the garden, the faint murmur of voices drifted toward me. My brows furrowed in curiosity and I followed the sound, my steps guiding me toward its source.

Around a gentle curve in the winding path, I stumbled upon a small, secluded clearing. There, bathed in dappled sunlight, I discovered Aerion and Thalion. They sat together on a weathered wooden bench, their voices hushed and their attention fixed on a shared conversation. They looked up at me as I approached, their eyes widening in surprise.

"Vale, what are you doing out here?" Aerion's voice held genuine curiosity as he rose gracefully from the bench, his movements fluid and captivating.

I swallowed the nervous lump in my throat, my heart pounding in my chest. "I just came out for a walk," I replied, attempting to sound casual even as my insides churned.

Thalion, too, stood from the bench, his tall frame exuding an alluring presence. His eyes bore into mine. "How are you feeling?" His voice, like liquid silk, flowed with concern.

"Better, thanks," I replied, my voice slightly uneven as I fought to maintain composure in his unwavering gaze.

"That's good," Thalion murmured, his proximity close enough to catch the enticing scent of his skin—a blend of pine and leather. My heart skipped a beat at the smell.

"Well, we should get started with your training," Aerion's words broke the spell that had ensnared us at that moment.

"Training?" I asked, looking between the two of them, my brows furrowing with a mix of confusion and curiosity. I had thought we weren't training today after the long night we had.

"Yes, training," Aerion reiterated, a glint of amusement in his eyes. "You didn't think you'd get a day off again, did you?"

A nervous laugh escaped me. "Oh, of course not," I replied, shaking my head.

Thalion spoke up. "Why don't I walk you back to your rooms so you can change? We'll begin your training shortly."

"That would be great," I said, relieved for a short reprieve from their captivating presence.

As we made our way back to the palace, I couldn't help but sense Thalion's eyes on me, his silent scrutiny unnerving yet oddly thrilling.

"Can I say something, Vale?" he inquired, his voice a velvety whisper that stirred curiosity within me.

"What is it?" I asked, my anticipation making my heart race as I braced myself for whatever he was about to say.

"I want to apologize for my behavior last night," Thalion said, his gaze earnest and sincere as he locked his eyes onto mine. "I shouldn't have kissed you, I did not realize how drunk you were."

His unexpected apology left me momentarily stunned, unsure of how to respond to this unexpected turn of events. My lips parted, but I couldn't seem to find my words.

"Thank you," I finally managed to say, offering him a small, grateful smile.

Thalion returned my smile with one of his own, his eyes retaining that mischievous twinkle that had drawn me in from the start. "But I'm not sorry for kissing you," he added, his voice taking on a huskier tone.

My breath caught and I instinctively looked away, unable to meet his intense gaze. I struggled to maintain composure as a torrent of emotions and sensations washed over me.

The rest of our walk was filled with an electrifying silence, our unspoken desires settling between us. As we approached my rooms, I couldn't help but feel grateful for the chance to escape and I hurried inside, attempting to regain control of my racing heart. This was going to be harder than I thought.

I quickly dressed in a pair of snug grey pants that allowed for ease of movement and a loose-fitting green tunic. I fastened my daggers securely to my belt and gave it a final check to ensure everything was in place. Running a brush through my hair, I tried to regain a sense of control over my racing thoughts and emotions.

The events of the previous night still lingered in my mind but I couldn't afford the distraction, especially with Haldir'sominous presence lurking in the shadows.

Taking a deep breath, I made my way out of my room, resolving to focus on the task at hand. To my surprise, Aerion was waiting for me in the corridor.

"Ready?" he asked, his expression a mask of neutrality.

"Yes," I replied, forcing a smile.

We ventured outside, greeted by the pleasant warmth of the day. I needed to regain my composure and keep my thoughts from wandering back to the events of last night.

"What are we doing today?" I asked, determined to shift my focus to the training that lay ahead.

"Hand-to-hand combat," Aerion replied, his tone casual.

"Hand-to-hand combat?" I echoed, trying to hide the traces of nervousness in my voice. The prospect of physical combat was daunting for me, as I knew I wasn't the strongest fighter, and this would be a significant challenge. Aerion grinned in response to my question.

We entered the training field and I caught sight of Thalion in a sparring match with one of the guards. I couldn't help but stand back and observe, appreciating the fluidity and strength of his movements.

"He's a good fighter," Aerion remarked, catching my attention as he followed my gaze.

"I can see that," I replied. The thought of facing someone as skilled as Thalion, or even Aerion, in combat was undeniably daunting.

Aerion, sensing my unease, offered some reassurance with a touch of humor. "Don't worry, I'll take it easy on you," he said, his voice laced with amusement.

I gave him a skeptical look, clearly not convinced by his words and he responded with a sarcastic laugh. "We'll see," I muttered under my breath, my eyes never leaving Thalion as he continued to spar.

I knew that if I had any chance of besting Aerion or even holding my own in training, I would need to be at the top of my game. As we started our training session, the Fae male proved relentless, pushing me to my limits with each move and technique.

During our training session, his harsh coaching pushed me to my limits. I tried my best to keep up with his instructions and replicate his movements, though it was clear that my skills were nowhere near as honed as his.

At one point, Aerion executed a particularly skillful move that resulted in me pinned to the training mat, his muscular body pressing down on top of mine. My breath caught in my throat as I found myself in this compromising position.

"Do you yield?" he asked, a confident smirk playing on his lips.

I refused to give in easily, my determination shining through. "Never," I growled, squirming and struggling against his hold, desperate to free myself.

Aerion chuckled, clearly enjoying the challenge I presented. His eyes sparkled with amusement as he continued to maintain his dominance. "You're a feisty one," he remarked, his voice low and husky.

He held me in that position for a moment longer, his gaze intense and his body tantalizingly close to mine. "Yield," he commanded firmly, the pressure of his grip tightening. I hesitated, my heart racing as I weighed my options. "Say it, princess," he urged, his voice coaxing, his grip unwavering.

The words caught in my throat, but I knew I couldn't deny the truth any longer. "I yield," I whispered, surrendering to him with frustration.

Aerion's smirk grew and he released his hold on me, helping me to my feet. I tried to push aside the thoughts of how his body had felt pressed against mine, but it was an impossible task. The undeniable attraction between us was something I couldn't ignore, no matter how hard I tried.

The relentless day of training had left me feeling utterly drained, every muscle in my body aching from the rigorous exercises. I took a towel and wiped the sweat from my brow as I tried to regain my breath and composure.

Aerion, his own body glistening with sweat, prowled over to me. His presence was impossible to ignore and I couldn't help but steal glances at his well-defined muscles.

"Not bad for today," he purred, his eyes grazing over me in a way that left me blushing slightly.

I cleared my throat, trying to keep my voice steady. "Thanks," I managed to croak out, my voice hoarse from exertion.

It was difficult not to ogle him; he was undeniably attractive. His chiseled physique and the way sweat clung to his skin only added to his allure.

"Come, I'll walk you back," he offered, a mischievous twinkle in his eyes.

The guards, who had seen Thalion return earlier, had all retired to their barracks, leaving Aerion and me in a solitary moment of silence. I fell in step beside him as we made our way back to the palace, the silence between us stretching on.

We climbed the grand staircase of the palace, my mind still whirling from the day's events.

"Thank you for the training. I'm sure there are better things for you to be doing," I said, offering him a small smile.

"It's no trouble," he replied, his own smile warm and genuine.

I was just about to turn away when he surprised me by reaching out and gently taking my hand. His touch sent a shiver of electricity racing through me and my heart raced in response.

"Vale," he murmured, his gaze locked onto mine with a depth of intensity that made my breath catch.

"Yes?" I whispered, my voice barely audible over the pounding of my heart.

He hesitated on the verge of saying something. But then, he faltered, his uncertainty briefly clouding his features.

"What is it, Aerion?" I asked, leaning in slightly, my eyes searching his for any hint of what he wanted to say.

He swallowed hard, his gaze never leaving mine as he seemed to wrestle with his words.

"Nothing," he finally said, his voice husky.

A pang of disappointment shot through me, but I managed a tight-lipped nod. "Alright, I'll see you tomorrow," I replied, turning to leave, my heart heavy with unanswered questions.

But before I could take a step, his grip on my hand tightened, halting me in my tracks.

He pulled me closer, his strong arms enveloping me, and before I could react, his mouth captured mine in a desperate kiss. I gasped in surprise, my body trembling as if a bolt of lightning had just struck me.

The world around us seemed to fade into insignificance as he deepened the kiss, his tongue sliding into my mouth. I melted against him, every fiber of my being focused on the intoxicating sensation of his lips and tongue exploring mine.

My hands, seemingly of their own accord, found their way to his hair, threading through the silky strands as I pulled him closer, desperate for more. It was as if we were caught in a whirlwind of desire and I couldn't resist the intoxicating pull drawing me closer to him.

With a reluctant sigh, he eventually pulled away, though the blazing desire in his eyes left me breathless. "You smell like fire and ancient things I've long forgotten," he whispered against my throat.

I was left speechless, my mind a swirling maelstrom of emotions in the wake of that intense kiss. He'd left me breathless and I could hardly find my voice.

"Goodnight, Vale," he finally said, a seductive smile curving his lips. Then, with one last smoldering look, he turned and disappeared down the dimly lit hallway, leaving me standing there, my heart still racing.

I could still feel the ghostly imprint of his lips on mine, his touch setting my body aflame with a desire that was as forbidden as it was irresistible. With a heavy heart and a whirlwind of thoughts, I eventually walked into my room, knowing that this was becoming far more complicated than I had ever imagined. But one undeniable truth remained: I was undeniably and dangerously attracted to him. To both of them. But I knew it was a dangerous game, and I had to be careful. I could not afford to lose my heart again.

CHAPTER TWENTY-ONE

I lay awake in bed, my mind refusing to grant me even a moment of rest. The images of Thalion and Aerion swirled through my thoughts like a storm, an intoxicating mix of their words, their touches. It was all so overwhelming, like a tidal wave crashing over my senses, threatening to consume me.

As much as I knew I should resist, the temptation was overpowering, like a siren's call that I couldn't ignore. The pull of desire was undeniable, drawing me deeper into its seductive embrace. I was teetering on the precipice of surrender, torn between the aching in me and the rational voice of caution.

With a heavy sigh, I reached out and grabbed a pillow, burying my face in it, as if it could smother the torrent of emotions threatening to engulf me. And the turmoil of emotions regarding Kaelan only added to the chaos in my mind. I was entangled in a web of complicated feelings and desires and it was difficult to see a way out. Especially since if I focused enough I swore I could still feel him, like he was lurking at the edge of my awareness. Almost as if I could turn my head fast enough and see him behind me.

I tossed the pillow aside and turned my gaze upward to the ceiling, my thoughts still in disarray. Heat and desire coursed through me, intensifying with each passing moment. I pressed my legs together under the blankets, trying to quell the burning ache that had taken hold of me. My body felt too hot, too sensitive, and I yearned for release.

I couldn't believe how profoundly Thalion and Aerion had affected me. I was supposed to be focusing on my training, on learning magic and honing my skills. Instead, I found myself lost in vivid fantasies of the two Fae males, my hands trailing down my stomach as I imagined Aerion's piercing grey eyes and Thalion's striking violet eyes watching me with an undeniable hunger in their eyes. In my mind's eye, I felt their muscular bodies pressing against mine, their hands exploring every inch of my body.

The room seemed to pulse with the mounting intensity of my desires and I could no longer resist the overwhelming urge that coursed through me. The ache had grown to an unbearable level, stirring a primal longing within me that demanded satisfaction.

My fingers slipped beneath the waistband of my leggings, seeking the searing heat aching between my legs. As they made contact, I gasped, my body already primed for the sensations that would soon follow. The mere touch sent shivers of pleasure racing through me, electrifying every nerve.

With a heated urgency, I began to touch myself, each deliberate movement left me breathless. My panting breaths filled the room as pleasure built within me, a relentless tide threatening to consume my senses.

In the vivid depths of my imagination, I conjured the image of Thalion, his tongue trailing down my neck as he lay over me. Aerion watched with an intensity that mirrored my own desire, his hungry eyes feasting upon the scene before him. Their hands roamed over my skin, caressing and teasing me in ways that left me quivering.

My fingers moved faster, pleasure pulsing through my body. I could almost feel them, their presence tantalizingly close in the next room over. Every touch, every stroke, brought me closer to the precipice of release, a sensation that was maddening in its intensity.

"Fuck," I moaned, my voice muffled by the pillow as I bit down on it, unable to contain the sounds of pleasure that spilled from my lips. I could almost hear their voices, their words of encouragement and hunger, urging me on.

I slipped a finger inside of my wet entrance, the slickness of my desire guiding my movements. I curled it up and down, searching for that perfect spot deep inside me that would send me hurtling over the edge into ecstasy. My world narrowed down to that singular feeling, the intoxicating dance of pleasure that threatened to consume me whole.

Just as I was about to reach my peak, I heard the creak of the door, and at that moment, I didn't even think to stop. My hips rocked against my hand, a moan escaping my lips as I reached the crest. I cried out, my entire body tensing with the force of my orgasm, my mind going blank as the sensations washed over me.

Slowly, I came back to myself, the room coming back into focus as my breathing returned to normal.

I looked toward the door to find it surprisingly closed, I could have sworn I had heard it creak open. I wondered if I had simply imagined it, the rush of hormones making me think there was a watcher in the room.

With a sigh, I sat up and wiped the sweat from my brow, the cool air in the room feeling refreshing on my skin.

As I looked around the room, the lingering afterglow of pleasure ebbed away, replaced by a creeping sense of embarrassment. I had just been caught touching myself by some mysterious shadow, and I couldn't help but wonder who was watching me, and what they had thought of the scene.

No matter how satisfying that moment of ecstasy had been, it had done little to quell the burning desire that seemed to have taken root deep within me. I still longed for their touch, their kisses, and the feel of their bodies pressed intimately against mine.

The situation was an impossible one, and I was acutely aware of the dangers it posed. If I couldn't find a way to resist the torturous pull they exerted on me, I risked losing myself entirely to the sea of desire that threatened to engulf me.

With a heavy sigh, I rolled over in my bed, closing my eyes in the hope that sleep would come to claim me and temporarily relieve me from the overwhelming and deafening desires that swirled within my body and mind. It was only as I was slipping off into the depths of sleep that I remembered I hadn't looked toward the door between Thalion's room and mine.

The next morning, I was seated at the breakfast table, sipping on a cup of tea, when a knock on the door between Thalion's room and mine sounded through the otherwise quiet space. It brought back the last thought I had last night. Before I could react, Thalion opened the door, his usual charming smile lighting up his face.

"Aerion's away on business today, so I'm taking over your training," he announced, his fangs glinting in the early morning light. I couldn't help but remember my daydreams of the previous night, thinking about the two of them writhing above me, and tried to push those thoughts aside. "We'll be practicing your magic today, so you don't need any of your weapons."

"Okay," I said, setting my teacup down.

"Ready?" he asked.

"Yes," I replied, rising from my chair and brushing away the crumbs from my clothes.

He led the way as we exited my room and we walked side by side down the quiet palace corridor.

"What are we going to be working on today?" I asked curiously.

"It'll be easy today, I just want to see what you can manage," Thalion explained.

"What do you mean?" I asked, intrigued.

"I want to see how heavy of an object you might be able to move," he elaborated.

"Where will we do that?" I questioned, eager to begin our training.

"There's an old courtyard behind the palace. We'll use that," he answered.

We continued walking, eventually arriving at a secluded stone courtyard hidden away in the palace gardens. Thalionmotioned for me to stand in the center while he positioned himself off to the side.

The sun beat down on us as I stood in the courtyard. It was unseasonably warm today and sweat began beading along my forehead. Thalion's patient eyes watched my every move.

"We'll start simple. I want you to create a small flame, about the size of a candle," he instructed, his voice calm and reassuring.

I nodded, eager to show him what I could do. I closed my eyes and focused on the inner well of energy within me, letting it surge and pool in my hand. The sensation was akin to drawing power from a hidden reservoir deep within my being. It was exhilarating and terrifying all at once. I constantly had to keep it leashed, or it threatened to consume me.

With a careful release of my breath, I extended my hand, palm up, and summoned the essence of fire. It was easier now than it once was. A small, flickering flame danced above my open palm.

"Good. Now, move it around," Thalion instructed.

I obeyed, my gaze locked onto the fire as I manipulated it into a controlled circle. The warmth radiated against my skin, but I was under no threat of being burned.

"Now, try and make it bigger," Thalion urged.

That was easy enough, I focused my intent and willed the flame to grow. It responded, stretching and expanding until it resembled a small ball of fire, flickering with newfound strength.

"Very good. Now, put it out," Thalion directed.

I hesitated for a moment, then closed my hand, extinguishing the flame. It vanished with a soft hiss, leaving only a wisp of dissipating smoke.

"Perfect. Let's try something different. Try and move this rock," he said, pointing to a massive boulder nearby.

My heart skipped a beat at the challenge. This was the true test, the measure of my ability to control and manipulate the very earth itself, which I had not done as much as I probably should have. I took a deep breath, steeling my resolve. The energy surged within me as I focused on the boulder, visualizing it shifting.

I extended my hand toward the rock, straining every muscle and fiber of my being. But despite my efforts, the boulder remained immovable, a testament to the gap in my abilities.

"It's okay. Just keep trying," Thalion encouraged, his eyes filled with understanding and patience.

I attempted again and then once more, but the boulder remained resolute, refusing to budge. My frustration mounted, but I was determined to persevere.

"Try and feel the boulder, get a sense for it." He instructed.

Thalion's guidance was invaluable as I took a deep breath and centered myself. I closed my eyes and reached out with my senses, as he had instructed. The world around me faded to darkness, leaving only the presence of the massive boulder before me.

I concentrated on visualizing the boulder, trying to get a sense of its essence. I focused on its weight, the texture of its rough surface, and the coolness of the stone. It was as though I was trying to establish a connection with the massive rock, to understand its very nature.

"Good. Now, guide it, don't push it," Thalion's voice came to me, a gentle reminder.

With my eyes still closed, I extended my hand slowly, like a conductor leading an orchestra. The boulder shifted beneath my command. It moved with surprising grace.

"Yes! You're doing it!" Thalion's excitement was infectious. I couldn't help but smile, opening my eyes. The boulder continued to roll, guided by the invisible force I commanded.

"Excellent. Now, try and move something bigger," Thalion suggested, pushing me to reach further.

I nodded, determined to embrace this challenge. I closed my eyes and focused on a larger boulder nearby. I could feel the magnitude of this endeavor, but I was undeterred.

With a deep breath, I concentrated once more. The massive boulder began to respond to my will, its sheer size and weight making the task more daunting. Slowly, it started to shift, a testament to my growing mastery over earth manipulation.

"Good. Now, let's see if you can lift it," Thalion encouraged.

With newfound confidence, I directed my will toward the larger boulder. I concentrated, willing it to rise from the ground. At first, it shifted only slightly, like a colossal beast awakening from slumber. But gradually, it obeyed my command and began to hover above the courtyard's surface.

"Very good. Now, hold it there," Thalion's words of encouragement spurred me on. I clung to my focus, my mind and body working in unison to maintain the boulder's position in the air.

The boulder remained suspended. "Excellent, you're a natural." Thalion's pride was evident in his voice. This power filled me with a sense of accomplishment, the possibilities of what I could achieve seemed endless.

"Now let's give you a real challenge," Thalion suggested with a mischievous grin. "Try and lift that statue."

Following his gaze, I spotted a stone statue of a Fae warrior standing not too far away. I turned my attention to it, determined. The energy flowed through me as I focused.

Raising my hands, I directed my magic toward the statue, determination pulsing through me. It began to tremble, responding to my command. The muscles in my arms and back burned with the effort as I strained to move the heavy stone figure as if I were physically trying to lift it.

"That's it. Keep going," Thalion's encouraging words urged me forward.

I fiercely wanted to prove myself further. Gritting my teeth, I exerted all my willpower, pushing harder against the statue. It responded, slowly but surely, starting to rise from its pedestal.

"You're doing it, don't stop," he yelled.

Thalion's words of motivation spurred me on and I ignored the burning sensation in my muscles. The statue trembled in response to my efforts and the ground beneath it showed signs of strain as cracks began to form.

I could feel the energy surging within me, like a storm brewing in my chest, ready to unleash its power. The statue shook even more violently and my resolve became a desperate struggle. I had to let go, but the magic coursing through me seemed uncontrollable.

The power continued to build, the sensation overwhelming. It was as if the very earth itself was resisting my command. Panic seized me as the pressure inside me intensified, my skin prickling with the strain. I couldn't hold it back any longer.

I heard a cry and it took me a moment to realize it was my own. And then, the inevitable happened. The statue exploded with a deafening roar, sending chunks of stone hurtling in all directions. I was thrown backward, unable to stop it.

I hit the ground with a painful thud, my ears ringing from the explosion. My vision blurred for a moment and I struggled to catch my breath. Everything felt disorienting and I was vaguely aware of Thalion rushing to my side, his hands cradling my face.

"Are you alright?" he asked, his voice concerned as he leaned over me.

Thalion slowly helped me to my feet and I winced, feeling the aches and bruises that would undoubtedly develop from my fall. "I'm fine," I assured him, my voice hoarse from both the effort and the shock of what had just happened.

"We're done for the day," he declared gently, his voice filled with understanding as he continued to support me. I leaned into him, grateful for the warmth of his presence.

I couldn't shake the embarrassment I felt over the destruction I had unintentionally caused. Broken stones and rumble were strewn all about, the statue now destroyed. My cheeks flushed, but what troubled me more was my lack of control.

"Oops," I said, unable to keep the regret out of my voice.

"Don't worry," he said, letting out a soft chuckle. "We have plenty of statues."

I managed a weak smile in response to his kind words, but deep down, I still felt disheartened by my lack of mastery over my own abilities.

"Come on," Thalion urged, wrapping an arm around my waist. "Let's get you cleaned up." I reached up to my throbbing head and it came back sticky with blood. I must have been struck by a flying chunk of stone.

We made our way back to the palace and Thalion led me into his room. The room was spacious, with high ceilings adorned with intricate carvings. The walls were painted a shade of lavender, and tapestries depicting scenes of Fae lore hung at intervals. A large window allowed the sunlight to filter in, casting a warm glow over the room.

"Sit down, I'll get a healer," Thalion insisted, motioning toward his bed, his concern evident in his eyes.

"No, I'm fine. It's just a little blood," I protested, trying to assure him.

"Please, Vale. Let me take care of you," he implored, his voice gentle but firm.

Reluctantly, I nodded and took a seat on the edge of the ornate bed. Thalion left the room, and within a few minutes, he returned with a healer, a figure in white robes adorned with intricate symbols of their craft.

The healer immediately went to work, examining me for any other injuries and cleaning me up. "You got lucky. You didn't hit your head too hard," the healer commented.

"Thank you," Thalion said sincerely to the healer.

The healer offered a final piece of advice before departing. "Be more careful next time."

"I will," I promised.

As the healer left, Thalion sat down next to me, his gaze filled with worry. "How do you feel?"

"Fine," I replied, but I was still upset I had lost control.

Thalion's strong arms enveloped me, offering a comforting embrace. I nestled into him, feeling a sense of safety and warmth wash over me. The room's soothing atmosphere and his presence made it easier to let go of the tension that had built up.

"I'm sorry. I shouldn't have pushed you so hard," Thalion apologized, his voice filled with genuine regret.

I sighed, my guilt nagging at me. "It's not your fault. I should have been more careful."

Thalion's voice was soothing as he reassured me, "It's okay. You're still new to this."

We remained in that embrace for a while, the silence providing a sense of solace against the turmoil of the day. Eventually, he gently pulled away, his concern still evident in his eyes.

"You should rest. I'll bring you some lunch," he suggested.

"I'm not that hungry," I protested.

"Vale, you need to eat," he insisted, his tone leaving no room for argument. "Especially after using your magic."

With a reluctant nod, I conceded, "Alright, but only if you stay with me."

"Of course," Thalion replied, his promise offering a sense of comfort as he moved to attend to my needs.

The room had a cozy ambiance, with sunlight streaming in through the window, casting a warm glow across the wooden floors. The soft rustling of leaves from the garden outside added to the tranquil atmosphere as we shared our meal. We spent the afternoon like that, eating and talking. Thalion's presence was calming, making it easier for me to open up.

"Tell me about yourself," he said, his eyes filled with genuine curiosity.

I considered his question as I took a bite of the delicious meal he had brought up, mixed nuts and berries with a steaming bowl of stew. "What do you want to know?"

He smiled, his expression inviting. "Anything. What's your favorite color? What's your favorite food? What's your favorite flower?"

I thought for a moment before answering, "Purple, chocolate chip cookies, and moonflowers."

"Good to know," he chuckled, his eyes sparkling with amusement.

"Now, tell me something about yourself," I urged.

"Anything?" he asked, raising an eyebrow in a playful challenge.

"Yes," I confirmed.

Thalion leaned back, his thoughtful gaze meeting mine. "Well, I'm a fan of dark chocolate and red wine. My favorite color is blue. And my favorite flower is the forget-me-not."

I couldn't help but smile, intrigued by his choices. "Why those things?"

"Dark chocolate is rich and decadent like life should be," he began, his voice soft and contemplative. "Red wine is strong and full-bodied like love should be. Blue is the color of the sky and the sea. And the forget-me-not reminds us that love can be fleeting, so we should cherish it while we can."

I found myself appreciating the depth of his thoughts. The afternoon passed in a pleasant haze of conversation, laughter, and shared moments, bringing us closer together in a way I hadn't anticipated.

I knew I was stepping into dangerous territory, but I couldn't help myself.

Thalion stood up, his muscles stretching slightly as he extended his hand towards me. I accepted his hand with gratitude, allowing him to help me to my feet. But as I stood, his grip on my hand tightened and he gently pulled me closer, our bodies now pressed intimately against each other.

His voice was a soft, husky whisper as he spoke, "You are very distracting, princess."

A chill ran through me as I met his gaze, my heart racing. "Am I?" I asked, my voice barely above a murmur.

"Yes," he purred, his eyes locked onto mine, a smoldering intensity in their depths.

Without further hesitation, he leaned down, capturing my lips in a kiss that was soft and warm, heat curled low in my belly. I relaxed into the kiss, unable to resist the pull of his mouth, my body tingling with longing and passion.

"We should stop," I whispered breathlessly as I pulled away, my lips still tingling from his touch.

He looked at me, his eyes filled with a hunger that mirrored my own. "Why?" he asked, his voice heavy with desire.

"Because it's not right," I replied, though my words came out weak and unconvincing.

"What isn't?" he pressed, his lips brushing against mine as he spoke.

"This. Us," I murmured, trying to make sense of the turmoil within me.

"And why is that?" he asked, his voice gentle as he continued to hold me close.

"Because you're perfect, and Aerion...," I began, my voice trailing off as I started to come clean.

"Shhh, princess," he interrupted, his thumb gently caressing my cheek. "No need to explain. But can't we just have this moment, without any strings or consequences?"

I hesitated for a moment, my mind racing with conflicting thoughts and desires. But the intoxicating allure of the moment, the passion that surged between us, proved too irresistible to deny. With a trembling breath, I gave in to the yearning that consumed me.

"Yes," I said, my voice barely more than a whisper as I pulled him back against me with an urgency that mirrored his own.

He kissed me deeply, his lips searing against mine as his hands roamed with an eagerness that had my toes curling in my boots. His touch was claiming, igniting every nerve in my body as I surrendered completely to the moment. The world around us faded, leaving only the two of us entwined in this fiery embrace.

His intoxicating presence overwhelmed me and I found myself drawn further into the whirlwind of passion. Soon, we were lying on his bed, our bodies intertwined, with no room for hesitation or doubt.

His lips traced a scorching path down my neck and chest, each tender kiss and delicate touch setting my skin ablaze. His tongue darted out, tasting me with a hunger that left me breathless.

My body was on fire, every inch of me aching for his touch, for the tantalizing connection that bound us together.

"Do you want me to stop?" he murmured, his voice a soft, sensuous caress against my ear.

"No," I whispered, my voice filled with longing.

He chuckled, a low, sultry sound that sent waves of desire coursing through me.

"Good," he purred, as he bit my neck delicately, his fangs leaving a small scratch.

I gasped sharply, the intensity of his touch left me breathless. My body responded, arching instinctively towards him, a silent plea for more.

He continued his exploration, his fingers tracing a scorching path along my skin, leaving a trail of molten desire in their wake. Lower and lower they ventured, their journey sending electrifying sensations coursing through my every nerve.

I couldn't help but moan, the pleasure building with each tantalizing caress. His hand slipped between my legs, fingers dancing with a maddening gentleness over the fabric of my pants. The fabric offered a barrier, but it was a feeble one against the storm of pleasure he stirred within me.

"Do you want me, Vale?" he whispered, his voice thick with desire, the words hanging in the air like an irresistible invitation.

My voice trembled as I responded, unable to deny the truth any longer. "Yes," I breathed, my yearning evident in the quiver of my voice.

"Say it," he urged, his own desire evident in the smoldering depths of his eyes.

"I want you," I said huskily, the words escaping in a passionate confession.

His hunger grew, his voice demanding in a way that left me aching. "Beg me."

"Please, Thalion," I whispered, my eyes closed in surrender.

That was all he needed to hear. His mouth crashed against mine, a fierce and possessive kiss, his tongue demanding entrance. I opened to him eagerly, my body aching for his touch, consumed by an overwhelming need that had become impossible to resist.

Thalion's hands moved with practiced grace, deftly removing my shirt, revealing my exposed breasts to his predatory gaze. The air in the room seemed to sizzle as he leaned down, his mouth claiming one peaked nipple, his tongue swirling and teasing, sending waves of pleasure cascading through my body. My head tilted back, a soft gasp escaping my lips, as my fingers tangled in his hair, urging him closer.

My own hands roamed with an almost desperate hunger over his chiseled body, tracing the contours of his well-defined muscles. His mouth grew hungrier, more urgent, as the desire between us threatened to consume us completely.

Then, as the room seemed to pulse with passion, there was a sudden, unexpected knock at the door. We froze, our eyes locking in wide-eyed surprise, our breaths coming fast.

"I'm a bit busy at the moment," Thalion called out, his hand trailing down my stomach, his voice laced with frustration.

"This can't wait," came the response and it was unmistakably Aerion's voice.

"What is it?" Thalion demanded, his frustration mounting.

"We have a problem," Aerion's voice came through the door, his tone urgent.

Thalion sighed in exasperation. "Alright, give me a minute," he conceded reluctantly, his hand lingering on my skin, his eyes never leaving mine as we both grappled with the interruption of our heated moment.

"You should probably go, princess," Thalion said, his hand cupping my cheek and caressing my jaw, his touch sending a final spark of longing through me.

I nodded, reluctantly slipping on the shirt and pulling it over my head. With a sigh, I got up from Thalion's bed and walked to the door that separated our rooms, my gaze lingering on him one last time before I left. The intensity in his eyes as he watched me added another layer of desire to the already electric atmosphere between us.

The door shut behind me with a soft click, and I leaned against it, trying to calm my racing heart. A soft, warm breeze flowed in from the open door leading to the balcony. I couldn't resist the allure of the night air. Stepping onto the balcony, I took a deep breath, filling my lungs with the freshness of the outside world.

Below, the city stretched out before me, a sea of twinkling lights against the dark backdrop of the night. Lost in thought, I stood there for what felt like an eternity, contemplating the emotions that had swept over me.

Then, without warning, I felt a presence behind me. My breath caught in my throat as I turned and saw Aerion leaning casually against the doorway, his gaze fixed on me.

"How are you feeling?" he asked, his voice gentle.

"Fine. What's wrong?" I replied, turning my full attention to him, wondering what he had said to Thalion after interrupting us.

"Nothing. Thalion was just filling me in," Aerion explained calmly, though his eyes seemed to search for something more in my reaction. "He told me about your accident today."

"Oh, that," I responded, relieved but also somewhat embarrassed by the misunderstanding. My thoughts had immediately jumped to the intimate encounter between Thalion and me, not the conversation about my magical training. "Yeah, I kind of blew up a statue."

"Sounds impressive," Aerion replied with a small smile.

We lingered there in silence for a while, neither of us quite sure what to say or how to navigate the complex web of emotions that seemed to entangle us.

"Well, I should let you get some rest. Tomorrow will be another long day," Aerion said gently.

"Okay," I replied, grateful for his understanding and the offer of a reprieve from our complicated feelings.

He turned to leave but then hesitated as if there was something more he wanted to say. "Vale, I know things have been... strange lately. But I want you to know that you can always come to me if you need anything."

His words hung in the air, and I couldn't help but appreciate his sincerity. "Thank you," I replied softly.

He nodded and then left, the door clicking shut behind him. I remained standing there for a while, his words echoing in my head. Perhaps it was time to let go of some of my fears and reservations and trust him. Only time would tell how this would play out.

CHAPTER TWENTY-TWO

The next few days slipped away like sand through my fingers, marked by the relentless rhythm of our training. Each morning brought a new challenge, a new test of my abilities, and a fresh opportunity to learn from the two Fae males who were shaping me into something more than I had ever been.

Aerion, with his unparalleled combat skills, was a force to be reckoned with. His movements were fluid and precise, a deadly dance that left me in awe. He pushed me relentlessly, his determination to make me better evident in the sweat that soaked through my training clothes. His mind games were equally formidable; he was a master at testing my resolve and pushing me to the brink.

Thalion, on the other hand, delved into the mystical arts with a grace that left me breathless. His magical abilities were nothing short of impressive. His lessons were a captivating blend of theory and practice, as he showed me how to harness the arcane forces that flowed through my body. The complexity of magic was daunting, but Thalion's patient guidance made it accessible.

Despite the physical and mental exhaustion that often accompanied our training, I found myself growing stronger with each passing day. Aerion, though a relentless taskmaster, was fair in his methods. He taught me discipline and the value of pushing beyond my comfort zone.

During our sparring sessions, I marveled at Aerion's strength and speed. His strikes were like lightning and his defenses were impenetrable. I knew that if I didn't constantly strive to improve, I would never be able to keep up with him. The training was grueling, but I was determined to rise to the challenge.

Aerion's mentorship was a constant source of guidance and encouragement. He possessed the rare combination of patience and determination that made him an exceptional teacher. Even during the most grueling sessions, he maintained an unwavering belief in my potential. His mentorship wasn't just about imparting knowledge; it was about fostering growth and nurturing my capabilities. I counted myself fortunate to have him as my teacher.

As the days melted into the following week, my confidence in my abilities swelled. With every lesson, every spar, and every shared moment, the bond between Aerion and me deepened. We operated as a well-coordinated team, working in sync towards our shared objective. Our connection transcended mere student and teacher; it was a partnership built on trust and mutual respect.

Yet, alongside the growth of our partnership, something else was taking root. An intangible, unspoken connection that pulsed between us, growing stronger with each passing day. Aerion's proximity, his touches, and the subtle but undeniable tension that simmered beneath the surface began to demand my attention.

He was always close as if drawn to me by an invisible force. His touches, once purely instructional, were now laden with a charged undercurrent that I couldn't possibly ignore. He was pushing the boundaries of our relationship, and I found myself yearning for his touch, for the warmth of his presence. The lines between mentor and something more blurred and I couldn't help but wonder if Aerion felt the same way.

The nights were long and lonely as I lay in my bed, tormented by fantasies of Thalion and Aerion. I couldn't escape the vivid images that played out in my mind, both of them taking me to heights of ecstasy I had never known. It was maddening, the way my body ached for their touch, and yet, I was no closer to making a decision.

The days were equally challenging. Training had intensified and the constant proximity to both males was both a blessing and a curse. Thalion's enchanting charisma and Aerion's alluring presence were like a constant pull. I was drawn to them, intoxicated by their charm, and it was slowly wearing me thin.

I knew I had to make a decision about my feelings, but the uncertainty gnawed at me. Did I want to explore this undeniable attraction to them, or did I want to maintain the distance that had been my shield against heartbreak? The answer eluded me and the turmoil inside me only grew.

Desperate to find some clarity, I resolved to focus on my training. I had convinced myself that if I threw myself into it completely, the turmoil of my heart would be silenced, if only temporarily. But it seemed that Aerion had other ideas.

One chilly afternoon, we were engaged in intense sparring. The sweat dripped from our bodies as we moved, each strike and parry pushing me to my limits. It was during one particularly fierce exchange that Aerion managed to pin me to the ground once again, his powerful body pressing down on mine.

I gasped as his warm breath ghosted over my ear. "You need to stop letting your emotions cloud your judgment."

"I'm trying," I managed to reply, my voice trembling slightly with both fear and desire.

Aerion's grip on me tightened, his gaze locked onto mine, smoldering with intensity. "Try harder, your enemies will not go as easy on you as I have," he growled, his voice dripping with a dangerous allure that left me utterly breathless.

The tension in the air was thick and my body responded to Aerion's closeness as if drawn by an irresistible force. His powerful frame pressed against mine and I could feel the undeniable evidence of his arousal. My breath hitched in my throat as I gazed into his eyes, finding them smoldering with raw hunger that mirrored my own desires.

"Aerion," I breathed, my voice barely more than a whisper, but he offered no verbal response. Instead, he continued to hold me captive with his intense, heated gaze. Our faces were mere inches apart, his lips hovering tantalizingly close to mine, his breath heavy and ragged.

The anticipation was nearly unbearable, the electrifying charge between us sending heat pulsing through me. It felt as if the world had narrowed down to this moment, this connection that defied all logic and restraint.

But then, as abruptly as it had begun, Aerion pulled away, leaving me both relieved and strangely bereft at the loss of his body against mine. He extended his hand toward me and I took it, allowing him to help me to my feet.

"Let's take a break," he said, his voice gruff, breaking the charged silence that had enveloped us.

I nodded, my voice still shaky as I replied, "Okay."

As the setting sun painted the sky in a riot of warm hues, casting long shadows across Aerion's chiseled features, he turned to me with an inviting smile that set my heart racing.

"Would you like to take a walk with me?" he asked. I couldn't help but nod in response, and as I did, he seized my hand in his, his fingers enveloping mine with a confident yet gentle grip that sent a thrill coursing through me.

Together, we strolled through the palace grounds toward the lush gardens, the air heavy with the fragrance of lavender and roses. It was a serene and peaceful atmosphere, and for the first time in a while, I felt a sense of relaxation wash over me, like a balm for my weary soul.

The winding path eventually led us to a picturesque scene—a small pond where the graceful branches of a willow tree dipped into the glistening water. Aerion released my hand and I watched him as he moved toward the water's edge, his gaze contemplative as he surveyed the tranquil surroundings.

"This is my favorite spot in the palace," he revealed, his voice a low and intimate murmur. "It's always been a place where I can find solitude and peace."

"It's beautiful," I replied, my eyes tracing the gentle ripples on the pond's surface as I took in the enchanting view.

As I turned to face him, our eyes locked and I sensed a depth of emotion in his gaze that left me breathless. His hand reached out to tenderly cup my cheek, his touch remarkably soft and gentle, a stark contrast to the usual roughness I had grown accustomed to during our rigorous training sessions.

In an instant, his demeanor shifted and he pushed me roughly against the sturdy trunk of the willow tree. Its leaves, while providing a flimsy veil of concealment, left us exposed to any wandering eyes that might chance upon us. The exhilarating thrill of the moment coursed through me, leaving me breathless as anticipation hung in the air, charged and potent.

In the shadowy embrace of the willow tree, Aerion's kiss was nothing short of commanding, his lips demanding and insistent. The sky darkened with the setting sun as my body responded to his passionate ardor, a scorching wave of heat surging through me. His hands, strong and unyielding, roamed with a possessive fervor, leaving no inch of my skin untouched.

"You have no idea the power you hold over me, princess," he murmured against my lips, his words vibrating through me and igniting a shiver of desire.

His lips traced a burning trail down my neck, the sensation both exquisite and tormenting. Pressing me harder against the tree trunk, his hand boldly cupped my ass, sending a jolt through me. "You are driving me crazy. I can't get you out of my head," he growled, his voice heavy with longing, his eyes reflecting an almost overwhelming intensity.

"Then don't stop," I responded with a whisper, a plea that hung in the air like an irresistible temptation.

His eyes, dark and dangerous, locked onto mine, filled with a primal hunger that sent a shiver down my spine. He crushed his lips to mine with bruising intensity, marking me as his own in a possessive kiss that left me breathless and yearning for more.

My own hands roamed hungrily over his sculpted body, each touch and caress an offering of my desire. Aerion's hand slipped beneath the fabric of my shirt, his fingers squeezing my breast with an unrelenting grip that drew a fervent cry from my lips.

"You like that, don't you?" he whispered, his voice dripping with satisfaction. I could only moan in response, my body yielding to the pleasure I could no longer deny.

"Good," he purred, his hand trailing down my body, fingers reaching for the waistband of my pants. The boundaries between desire and surrender blurred in the heated moment.

Aerion's hand ventured between my legs, finding the undeniable wetness that had pooled there as a testament to my body's urgent response. A low, primal growl emanated from his chest as he discovered how thoroughly my desire had been stoked by his touch.

"I want to taste you," he rasped, his voice heavy with the raw, unbridled desire that mirrored my own.

"Yes," I gasped, surrendering completely to the intoxicating sensations coursing through me. Nothing else mattered in that electrifying moment except the pleasure that consumed my senses.

He knelt before me, his hands deftly pushing my pants down to my knees, revealing my throbbing core, which ached for his touch. The air was thick with anticipation as he leaned in closer.

Aerion's tongue darted out, moving slowly and sensuously, igniting a shiver of ecstasy that rippled through me as I braced myself against the willow tree. His hand gripped my thighs firmly, steadying me as he explored my body, his tongue dancing with expert precision over my swollen, sensitive clit.

My fingers curled instinctively in his hair as he devoured me, every flick and stroke of his tongue pushing me relentlessly closer to the precipice of ecstasy.

"You taste as good as I imagine every night in my bed," he growled against my flesh, the sheer intensity of his desire evident in every word.

"Don't stop," I pleaded, my need for release consuming me completely.

He obeyed without hesitation, his tongue continuing to flick and circle my clit, each tantalizing movement causing me to writhe and moan in helpless surrender.

"Fuck, Aerion," I cried out, my hips bucking uncontrollably against his skillful ministrations.

"That's right, princess. Fall apart for me," he commanded, his words driving me relentlessly toward the edge.

In that ecstatic moment, I unraveled, my body trembling as waves of pleasure washed over me. Aerion held me close as I quivered in the throes of release, his touch grounding me in the aftermath of a breathtaking climax.

In the hushed aftermath of my ecstasy, Aerion's eyes bore into mine, his satisfaction evident in the devilish curve of his lips. His voice, a velvet purr, disrupted the fragile quietude.

"Delicious," he purred, his words igniting a new wave of warmth within me, leaving me breathless and intoxicated by his allure. My body still tingled from his touch, a potent reminder of the fiery passion that had just consumed us.

Aerion's demeanor shifted as he stood. With a sudden, assertive move, he turned me around, pressing my body firmly against the unyielding trunk of the willow tree. The rough bark beneath my darkened hands served as a grounding sensation, contrasting starkly with the fervent desire coursing through my veins.

My breath hitched as I felt the undeniable hardness of his arousal pressed against the small of my back. He lowered his lips to the sensitive skin of my neck, teasing and tempting me with each kiss. Meanwhile, his skillful hand ventured around my hip, caressing my clit in a deliberate dance of pleasure, sending another electrifying shockwave through me. His other hand traveled down my stomach, fingers slipping inside me with an undeniable urgency.

"I need to be inside you, princess," he growled, his voice vibrating with an overwhelming craving that mirrored my own. A needy whimper escaped my lips, my body aching for the fulfillment that only he could provide.

With a practiced hand, he removed his fingers from their intoxicating dance within me, and my anticipation grew as he unbuckled his belt, the metallic clink of the buckle breaking the spell of the moonlit garden's silence.

His hands caressed my body as I waited with anticipation for what came next.

As Aerion's primal desire surged forth, he thrust into me with an intensity that left me gasping, his cock stretching and filling me to the brim. The initial shock of pleasure was mixed with a tantalizing edge of pain, creating an intoxicating whirlwind of sensations that had me crying out, my voice a symphony of raw ecstasy.

"You're so wet for me," he groaned, his body pressed against mine. His fingers dug into my hips, a firm grip that anchored me as he relentlessly pulled me back into his every thrust, the sheer force of his movements sending jolts of electric pleasure through my quivering form.

My head turned, and to my astonishment, I found Thalion across the garden, his gaze riveted on us, a hunger evident in his eyes. As if drawn by some unspoken magnetism, Aerion's eyes followed mine, and he leaned closer, his lips brushing against the shell of my ear.

"Do you like his hungry gaze on you, princess?" he murmured, his voice dripping with arousal and mischief. My response was a wordless moan, my voice stolen by the intense sensations coursing through me. This was unlike anything I had ever experienced before and I reveled in it. The thrill of being watched was almost too much.

Aerion's pace quickened, his thrusts growing more forceful, each one causing my body to jerk against the sturdy willow tree. Thalion's gaze remained locked with mine, his eyes smoldering with an insatiable desire. I was overwhelmed by the onslaught of sensations, the pleasure and pain blending into a torment that left me teetering on the precipice of bliss.

Unable to break free from the mesmerizing connection with Thalion, our eyes remained locked as he slid his hand down into his pants, freeing his large cock. The garden's shadows seemed to dance around us, heightening the illicit thrill of our forbidden encounter beneath the moonlight.

Thalion's hand, expertly stroking his throbbing length, was a hypnotic sight as he maintained his unwavering gaze on us, his eyes never leaving me.

Aerion's movements inside me grew increasingly frantic, his grip on my hips tightening to the point of bruising. The pleasure coursing through my body was overwhelming, and I found myself nearing my release once again.

"Tell me how much you want this, princess," Aerion growled, his voice a husky demand, "beg for me to please you."

My voice, heavy with desire and desperation, erupted in a pleading cry. "Yes," I cried out, unable to hold back, "please, please."

Aerion's thrusts became more erratic, his pace quickening as he approached his climax. Thalion's gaze remained locked onto us, his strokes growing increasingly frenzied as he watched our intimate connection unfold.

I was on the verge, my body throbbing with an impending climax that promised to be glorious. Aerion's fingers moved to wrap around my throat, his thrusts unrelenting, his heated breath caressing my neck with every passionate motion.

Finally, I shattered, my body trembling as the orgasm tore through me, leaving me trembling and breathless. Aerionfollowed suit, his body tensing as he came inside me, the sensation deep and fulfilling.

The night was consumed by our unrestrained passion, the moon a silent witness to our secret desires.

As the intoxicating climax subsided, Aerion's weight shifted, and his body slumped against mine, the heat from his skin still pressed intimately against me. The garden remained shrouded in the moon's gentle glow, casting long, sensual shadows that seemed to accentuate every gasp and sigh.

Thalion, his eyes locked on me, continued his sensual self-pleasure, each stroke of his throbbing length captivating me further. Aerion, his voice laced with desire, demanded my attention. "Look at him, Vale, watch him pleasure himself," he said as he gripped my chin, forcing me to lock eyes once again with Thalion.

I found myself unable to tear my gaze away from his sensual display. His hand moved rhythmically over his hardened length, his movements becoming more erratic with each passing moment.

Thalion's intense gaze bore into me as he approached us, Aerion releasing me from his hold. "Get on your knees," Thalion commanded, his voice firm and demanding. I hastened to obey, the anticipation of his touch sending shivers down my spine.

Still stroking himself, his eyes locked on mine, Thalion moved closer, the moonlight casting an erotic glow over his muscular frame. He seized a handful of my hair, pulling my head back with a rough, possessive grip, and his throbbing cock slid between my parted lips. The night was filled with a potent blend of desire and submission as Thalion claimed his place of dominance and I surrendered to his passionate demands.

Thalion's voice grew deeper and more commanding as he issued his potent instructions. "Take all of it," he growled, his fingers tightening their grip on my hair.

As he thrust deeper, my body reacted, and I gagged, a surge of discomfort mingling with the pleasure. Tears welled up in my eyes, the sensation both overwhelming and intoxicating.

His cock twitched within me, and I struggled to accommodate the forceful invasion. "Yes, just like that, princess," he praised, his voice filled with desire and dominance.

A moan escaped my lips, the pleasure of pleasing him surging through me like a wild current. His words, possessive and commanding, stoked the fire within me.

"I love seeing those pretty lips wrapped around my cock," he growled, his control slipping.

Moments later, I felt the powerful release, the pulsating waves of his climax sending torrents of warmth into my mouth. I swallowed eagerly, savoring every drop, my own moans of pleasure escaping as I fulfilled his desires.

"That's a good girl," he praised, the possessive hold on my hair loosening. With care, he pulled his cock out of my mouth and tucked himself back into his pants.

"Did you enjoy the show, Thalion?" Aerion's voice was teasing, laced with an undercurrent of satisfaction.

"Immensely," Thalion replied, his eyes never leaving mine as he spoke.

Aerion reached for my hand, his fingers entwining with mine as he helped me to my feet. The three of us stood in the hushed stillness of the garden, the aftermath of our passionate encounter hanging in the air like a shared secret.

"Well, I suppose we should return," Aerion said, his gaze drifting toward the palace, a hint of reluctance in his eyes.

Thalion nodded in agreement, and I followed them back, my thoughts a whirlwind of confusion and desire. The weight of what had transpired settled on me and the reality of the situation became undeniable.

There was something growing between the three of us. But I didn't know how to navigate these uncharted waters, how to reconcile my own desires and uncertainties.

As we made our way back to the palace, the gravity of my choices began to sink in. What was I doing? Was I truly ready to surrender myself to both of them, to explore this unconventional path? There was no turning back now, no erasing the moments that had brought us here. The die had been cast, and the only thing left was to see how this intricate dance of desire and passion would ultimately unfold.

Chapter Twenty-Three

Wren couldn't help but wonder how Vale was faring in the Fae realm. It had been a few weeks since her departure and not a word had reached his ears since. While he hadn't expected frequent visits from her, he had anticipated at least some form of communication.

As the days turned into weeks, he had grown acutely aware of her absence. The bustling activity of the camp, where construction for their new community center was well underway, provided some distraction, but there was a lingering unease in his heart. The past encounters with the Academy thugs had faded into distant memory and for now, the camp was enjoying a welcome respite from the external threats.

Yet, Wren couldn't shake the feeling that something unforeseen was lurking on the horizon, something he hadn't prepared for. He found himself preoccupied with thoughts of Vale and her well-being. He often felt like he could almost feel her standing just behind him.

"What's wrong?" Startled by the unexpected voice, Wren looked up from the blueprints that had consumed his attention. He hadn't heard Venna enter his tent, her presence catching him off guard.

"You've been staring at those blueprints for hours," Venna remarked, her gaze focused intently on him. "Is everything okay?"

Wren hesitated for a moment, debating whether to share his concerns, but then he replied, "I'm fine."

Venna didn't seem entirely convinced by his response, her eyes betraying a hint of doubt. However, she chose not to press the matter further.

"Alright," she conceded, though he could tell she was still concerned. "But if you need to talk, I'm here."

A faint smile tugged at Wren's lips as he acknowledged her offer. "I know."

"Anyway," Venna continued, her tone brightening, "I was just coming by to let you know that dinner is almost ready."

"Thanks, I'll be there soon," Wren replied, appreciating her gesture.

With a nod, Venna turned to leave, her gaze lingering on him for a moment before she exited the tent. Wren was left alone with his thoughts once more, the uncertainty of Vale's situation pressing heavily on his mind as he reluctantly returned his attention to the blueprints.

As Wren sighed, his thoughts once again gravitated toward Vale. He couldn't help but wonder about her well-being, whether she was safe and content in the Fae realm. She had expressed her desire to venture there and he had supported her decision, yet an inexplicable sense of responsibility gnawed at him. It was as though he had let her down in some way, failed to protect her.

He had been protecting her ever since that night in the woods when he had saved her and she told him her secret. It was an odd change that she was now more powerful than him, able to protect herself better than he was.

Amid the relative tranquility of their camp, a growing unease festered within him. He feared that the current calm was merely a deceptive lull before a storm of unforeseen challenges. As much as he wished to shield Vale from any harm, he had to trust in her strength and resilience to navigate whatever obstacles she faced.

With a resigned sigh, he decided to put his faith in her abilities. While Vale was away, he would continue his efforts to fortify their camp and ensure the safety of his pack. The blueprints before him represented the progress they were making, a testament to their collective determination.

Rolling the blueprints back up and placing them neatly on the table, he left the confines of his tent, craving the solace of the outdoors. The fresh air enveloped him as he stepped outside and he welcomed the relief it brought. Maybe he would go for a refreshing run in the forest later. The tension that had settled in his shoulders began to dissipate and he hoped that dinner would provide a welcome diversion.

As he made his way to join the others, a sense of longing for Vale lingered in his heart. He knew he had to be patient, for now, his role was here, protecting their newfound community. With that thought, he pushed aside his worries and focused on dinner, hoping that Vale would soon return to his side.

The campfire's warm glow illuminated the faces of those gathered around it, casting a sense of camaraderie among the people who had become Wren's family. As he surveyed the faces of the refugees, a wave of determination washed over him, and he silently reaffirmed his commitment to protect them at all costs.

As the evening wore on, Wren gradually found himself loosening up, the burdens of the day slowly melting away like the embers of the fire. Laughter and playful banter filled the air as he shared light-hearted moments with his pack. For a while, the weight of his worries were suspended in the pleasant distraction of the campfire's warmth and the company of those he had come to care for deeply.

However, the atmosphere shifted abruptly when the camp's sentries raised the alarm with haunting howls that cut through the night. Wren's heart sank as he felt a foreboding, fearing that the unsettling feeling he had experienced earlier was a prelude to whatever threat now loomed.

Rising to his feet, Wren was quick to respond as one of the sentries approached him. He was currently in his human form like the rest of them and he bore a grave expression.

"What is it, Holden?" Wren inquired, his voice laced with concern.

"It's Donovan, sir," Holden replied, his tone filled with trepidation. "He's at the edge of camp with some others, asking for you."

Donovan was a rogue wolf who had been banished from his pack after Wren defeated the previous alpha, Rafe. Wren's thoughts raced as he contemplated the possible reasons for Donovan's unexpected visit. Could it be that they sought to reconcile, to mend the rift, or did they harbor ulterior motives that could jeopardize the newfound sanctuary they had painstakingly built?

Wren's heart pounded fiercely in his chest. The news of Donovan's arrival was far from welcome and he dreaded having to confront the rogue wolf and his sycophants.

"Let's go, Venna," Wren ordered his beta, his voice carrying a steely resolve that betrayed his unease.

Venna, equally determined, nodded solemnly, her features etched with a grim determination. Together, they briskly made their way toward the camp's edge. The moon hung high, casting an eerie pallor over the tense situation that awaited them.

As they approached the edge of camp, Wren's eyes locked on Donovan and his group, who stood just outside of the gate with an air of smug arrogance. The tension in the air was uneasy and Wren wasted no time addressing the unwelcome visitors.

"What are you doing here, Donovan?" Wren demanded, his voice sharp and steady, betraying none of the anxiety that churned within him.

Donovan, a wicked glint in his eyes, responded with a venomous tone, "We've come to claim what's rightfully ours."

Wren's brow furrowed, his patience waning. "And what's that?" he asked, his voice barely concealing the seething anger that simmered beneath the surface.

Donovan's sneer only grew more pronounced as he replied, "This camp, this land. It all belongs to the alpha. That's me."

A surge of rage coursed through Wren, his control teetering on the precipice. "You are no alpha. You are a coward and a bully," he growled, the accusation vehement and unrelenting.

Donovan, seemingly unfazed, offered a twisted smile as he retorted, "That may be so, but I'm the only alpha who matters."

Wren clenched his fists, his jaw set with determination. "You're not welcome here," he declared, his voice resolute and unwavering in the face of Donovan's arrogance.

"I don't think you understand, Wren. I'm not asking." The air grew thick with tension as Donovan's menacing words hung in the night air, a dark cloud of impending conflict. His tone dripped with a chilling certainty as if he believed his claim to the camp and its territory was unquestionable.

Wren's response was swift and unwavering, his voice a low growl that resonated with a predatory intensity. "Neither am I. You're not welcome here. If you try to take what's mine, I'll kill you."

Donovan's retort was laced with arrogance, a twisted smirk gracing his bloodied face. "I'd like to see you try."

In the blink of an eye, Wren moved with a speed that left the onlookers awestruck. His fist connected with Donovan's face, a thunderous impact that sent the rogue wolf sprawling backward. There was no need to shift; Wren knew that his mortal form would be more than capable of dealing with Donovan and his henchmen.

Donovan's face was smeared with crimson. Anguish and humiliation contorted his features as he struggled to regain his bearings. Wren could feel the seething rage bubbling within him, his wolf clamoring for release, yearning to confront this threat head-on.

"This isn't over," Donovan hissed, his words muffled by the blood pooling in his mouth.

Wren's response was cold and unyielding, his voice dripping with venom. "Oh, I think it is, unless you plan on challenging me here and now."

Donovan, grasping at straws, attempted to regain some semblance of control. "We've got strong friends now, Wren, ones you shouldn't be so quick to dismiss," he taunted.

With a snarl of pure contempt, Wren's patience wore thin. "Get out of here before I tear you apart," he seethed.

Donovan, his bravado faltering, spat a final, ominous declaration. "This isn't the end of our conversation, mutt." As his battered group retreated, the threat lingered in the air.

The night air was fraught with unease as Wren and Venna made their way back to camp, shadows cast by the flickering firelight dancing across their troubled expressions.

"Who do you think they were talking about?" Venna's voice was hushed and laden with concern.

Wren's brow furrowed in deep contemplation, his gaze cast downward as if searching for clues in the dirt beneath his feet. "I have no idea, but whoever it is, they must be powerful to make Donovan feel so confident."

Venna's unease deepened at his words and she bit her lip in contemplation. "What are we going to do?"

Wren's jaw tightened, a testament to the responsibility resting upon his shoulders. "I don't know, Venna, but we're going to have to be prepared for whatever they bring to our doorstep."

As they reentered the camp, the sense of disquiet lingered, casting a shadow over the makeshift community. Wren knew that Donovan was a threat, but the true extent of that threat remained shrouded in uncertainty. The identity and capabilities of Donovan's newfound allies were a riddle that demanded solving, and it demanded it quickly.

As Wren watched over his pack, a foreboding sense of impending danger settled in his heart. He only hoped that the strength of their unity and their unwavering determination would be enough to face the storm that was brewing on the horizon.

Chapter Twenty-Four

I had just stepped out of the warm bath, the scent of lilac and vanilla still lingering in the air. The cozy flicker of candlelight danced across the walls of my room as I wrapped myself in a soft robe, its fabric caressing my skin as I tied the sash. My hair, wet from the bath, hung in tangles and I knew it was going to be a long process to brush it out.

Sitting down in front of the vanity, I picked up the ornate brush and started to work on my unruly locks. As I pulled the bristles through the knots, I began to think about the events of the past night. What had I gotten myself into? My heart raced as I replayed the memory of my intimate encounter with both Aerion and Thalion. They had orchestrated the whole thing and it was clear they had shared women before. I was in over my head and the situation was far more complicated than I had anticipated.

Lost in my thoughts, I didn't notice the room growing darker until the shadows converged, coalescing into a solid form. Startled,

I jumped in my seat, dropping the brush. My heart pounded as I recognized Kaelan, his figure now fully emerged from the shadows. Outrage overtook my initial shock.

"What are you doing here?" I demanded, my voice trembling with anger.

Kaelan didn't immediately respond, his gaze fixed on me. His expression was inscrutable, and the silence stretched uncomfortably.

"Well?" I insisted, my voice sharper this time, my hand reaching for anything that I could throw at his head.

His eyes finally met mine and there was something unsettling in their depths. "I came to make sure you were alright," he said, his voice low.

"I'm fine, now leave," I said, the words clipped.

Kaelan, however, remained unmoved, his intense gaze never leaving me. He seemed different, a shadow of the person I had known before. Dark circles marred the skin beneath his eyes and the depths of his irises held something I couldn't quite place.

Frustrated by his persistence, I grabbed a book from the nearby shelf and hurled it in his direction, but he moved with supernatural speed, effortlessly dodging the projectile.

"I said leave!" I yelled, anger coursing through me.

Despite my protests, Kaelan ignored my demands, and in the blink of an eye, he was by my side. He pressed his body close to mine, trailing his fingers along the exposed skin at the collar of my robe.

"Do you enjoy making me angry?" I growled, trying to push him away, but his presence was overwhelming.

"Maybe," Kaelan responded, his voice devoid of any amusement. His intensity unnerved me.

"Why are you really here?" I asked, my voice softer this time, the curiosity outweighing my anger.

Kaelan hesitated, the silence between us stretching. Finally, he let out a sigh, and his shoulders sagged with a hint of vulnerability.

"I told you, I'm here to make sure you're alright," he said, his voice heavy with unspoken emotions.

"I don't need you to check on me, Kaelan. I'm perfectly capable of taking care of myself," I asserted, trying to maintain a stern demeanor.

"I know you are," he replied, his voice low and filled with sincerity. "I just..." He trailed off and I watched as his gaze dropped to the floor, his thoughts seemingly scattered.

"Just what?" I prompted, a hint of curiosity breaking through my resolve.

"I can't help but worry about you, it's been weeks. Things have been complicated lately and I wanted to make sure you're okay," Kaelan admitted, his vulnerability showing through.

I sighed, my anger and frustration waning as empathy welled up within me. His concern was genuine, after all.

"I'm fine, Kaelan, really. There's nothing to worry about," I reassured him, my voice softer this time.

Kaelan's eyes met mine again, the intensity behind them chilling.

"Come back with me," he implored, a slight plea lacing his voice. "You'll be safer with me in the mortal realm than here."

I shook my head firmly. "No. I'm not going anywhere."

Kaelan's hand gently came up, his fingers caressed my cheek and his gaze bore into mine with an unyielding determination.

"You don't belong here, Vale. This place isn't for you. It'll ruin you," he insisted, his voice edged with urgency.

"This place has already changed me, Kaelan," I countered, my tone resolute. "I can't go back, not now. I can't just ignore this threat."

"You can and you should," he argued, his grip on my cheek tightening slightly. "I can protect you from the Fae king."

"I don't need your protection, Kaelan," I declared firmly, my stubbornness rising to the surface. "I can take care of myself."

The tension in the room thickened as it became evident that neither of us was willing to yield.

He released me and the silence stretched between us as he began to pace the room, his fingers raking through his disheveled dark hair.

"That's just it, Vale, you can't truly take care of yourself, you're too reckless. Not from any of this. This world is seductive, it's made to lure mortals in," he argued, his voice tinged with desperation.

"You forget I'm not a mortal and I'm not weak-minded either," I retorted, crossing my arms defensively.

"I don't think you're weak-minded, Vale. But you have no idea what these creatures are capable of. And the fact you've let yourself be taken in by them—" He cut himself off, his words heavy with frustration.

"Don't tell me what I have and haven't let myself be taken in by," I shot back, my own patience wearing thin.

"They're not your friends, Vale," he persisted, his tone filled with concern.

"How would you know? You've barely spoken to either of them!" I countered, my anger rising.

"I don't need to speak to them to know they're dangerous," he replied firmly.

"Then maybe you should leave, because I'm not going to stand here and listen to you badmouth people who have done nothing but help me," I said, my voice unwavering.

His dark eyes bore into mine. "What must I do, Vale? What extreme lengths must I go to, to earn your belief in me? Shall I rip my very heart out of my chest and lay it at your feet? Shatter my soul into pieces just to fashion a monument to you? Give me the command, any command, and consider it done. There is no boundary to what I'd do for you." We stared at each other for a moment, the silence echoing in the room.

The doors to my room flew open with a bang, causing me to startle, and in stormed Thalion and Aerion. Their eyes darted around the room, confusion clouding Thalion's features while Aerion's expression turned as stormy as a tempest at sea.

"Demon," Aerion spat through gritted teeth, his anger simmering beneath the surface like a volatile brew.

Thalion's gaze moved from Kaelan to me and then back to Kaelan, his brow furrowed in perplexity. "What's going on?" he demanded, his voice edged with suspicion.

Kaelan's jaw clenched, his stance firm and unwavering. "This doesn't concern you, prince," he replied tersely.

"It concerns me when a demon enters the palace uninvited," Thalion retorted, his tone growing more resolute.

"I wasn't aware that we needed an invitation to check on the safety of Vale in the Fae realm," Kaelan snapped, his irritation palpable.

"She's safe here, demon. We would never hurt her, unlike you," Aerion declared, his anger barely contained beneath the surface.

Thalion took a step closer to me, his concern etched deeply on his features, and wrapped a protective arm around my waist. Kaelan's eyes narrowed as he noticed the display and his anger flared like wildfire.

"Well, you seem to have gotten pretty cozy," he sneered, his words dripping with ice.

"That's none of your business," Aerion snarled, his voice dripping with venom.

"The hell it's not!" Kaelan roared, his rage now boiling over. "She's mine, we're bonded."

"Enough!" I shouted, my voice cutting through the turmoil, but it seemed to fall on deaf ears as the room exploded into chaos.

"Bonded?" Aerion yelled incredulously.

"She's yours?" Thalion scoffed, his disbelief echoing Aerion's.

Kaelan and Aerion were now standing toe to toe, their bodies tense with barely contained violence. Kaelan's fists were clenched at his sides and Aerion's narrowed eyes promised impending brutality.

"You've no claim over her, demon," Aerion growled menacingly.

"I have more of a claim than either of you," Kaelan sneered, his own anger unabated.

"Not according to her," Thalion chimed in, his voice carrying a note of finality.

"Shut up, all of you!" I tried again, desperation lacing my voice, but my pleas were once again ignored.

"You're a fool if you think she wants to be with you," Kaelan spat, his voice laden with contempt.

"You know nothing of what she wants," Aerion growled, his voice low and dangerous.

"You're damn right, I know nothing," Kaelan yelled, frustration evident in every word. "Because she won't fucking talk to me!"

"Shut the fuck up or I'll burn all your asses!" I yelled with all the authority I could muster, finally drawing their attention as flames danced across my open hands. The three of them turned their gazes toward me, but the growing danger in the room was far from dispelled.

"You're bonded to him?" Thalion asked, his expression unreadable as he sought to make sense of the chaotic situation.

"Not by choice," I replied, extinguishing the flames and crossing my arms defensively.

"I never forced you to take my blood, you did so willingly," Kaelan interjected, his frustration evident in his voice.

"You knew I had no idea what it would mean and yet you did it anyway," I told him, my tone icy as I confronted him about his actions.

"You tricked her into a blood bond?" Aerion's anger swelled again and beside me, Thalion emitted a low, menacing snarl.

"I did not trick her. She knew exactly what she was doing," Kaelan defended himself, his voice growing louder and more confrontational.

"I didn't know, Kaelan. You didn't tell me!" I shot back, my frustration and anger mirroring his.

"Would it have made a difference if I had?" Kaelan challenged.

"Yes, maybe I wouldn't have done it," I countered, my voice filled with regret and anger.

"Liar," he accused. "You would have still done it. You're drawn to me, just as I'm drawn to you. Don't try to deny it."

"We are not discussing this now, or ever, for that matter," I declared firmly. "The fact remains that you are the one who tricked me into a blood bond. If you were any kind of a friend, you would have told me."

"Friend?" he scoffed, disbelief lacing his voice. "Is that what we are, Vale? Last time I checked, friends don't fuck like we do."

"Like we DID," I emphasized pointedly, reminding him it was in our past.

"Are you sure about that? Because the last time I was inside you, you were begging for more," Kaelan retorted.

"And now I'm asking you to leave," I stated resolutely, my patience wearing thin.

"Is that what you think? Since you've tasted her, you have a right to her? Well, I've tasted her too, demon," Aerion taunted with a wicked grin, trying to provoke Kaelan.

Kaelan stared at him for a moment, disbelief clouding his eyes, before he turned to look at me. Shame surged through me, but I kept my expression neutral, unwilling to give him the satisfaction of knowing how much his words affected me.

"Is this true?" Kaelan asked, his voice filled with anger and hurt.

"That's none of your concern," I told him, avoiding his gaze.

"Vale," he said, his voice so filled with pain that my heart sank.

"She didn't just let me. She begged for it," Aerion added with a smug smirk.

"You son of a bitch!" Kaelan roared, his anger getting the best of him. He lunged at Aerion, but Thalion swiftly intervened, his hands up and glowing with magic.

"Enough," Thalion commanded, his voice echoing in the room, serving as a barrier between the two enraged males.

"I've had enough of this shit," Kaelan said, his voice seething with frustration.

"Good. Then leave," I stated coldly, my resolve unwavering.

Kaelan's eyes burned with a volatile mix of rage and regret.

"Vale—"

"I don't want to hear it, Kaelan," I interrupted firmly.

"So, this is how it's going to be then?" Kaelan's voice held a hint of desperation.

"Yes."

Kaelan fell silent for a moment, his jaw clenched and his fists tightly balled at his sides. The room felt charged with anger and I knew it wouldn't take much for him to snap.

"Fine," he said through gritted teeth, his voice a low growl. "If that's the way you want it, then fine."

He took a step forward and Thalion readied himself for a fight, but Kaelan surprised us all by merely reaching out and brushing his fingers across my cheek, a gesture that held an unusual tenderness given the circumstances.

"Remember, Vale," he said softly, his voice full of longing. "I was there first. I will always be a part of you."

And then, as quickly as he had appeared, he was gone, the shadows swallowing him up. The three of us were left in an uncomfortable silence, the tension in the room now a tangible entity.

I turned away, unable to bear the weight of their gazes, and walked toward the window, my eyes fixated on the darkness beyond.

Aerion cleared his throat, breaking the silence that had settled upon us like a heavy fog.

"So, how long has there been a blood bond between you and the demon?" he asked, his tone tinged with curiosity.

"A while," I admitted, my voice barely above a whisper.

"And you didn't think to tell us?" Thalion's questioned.

"Why should it matter?" I retorted, my frustration with the situation making my tone sharper than I had intended.

"Because he has a claim on you, Vale," Thalion replied, his voice softer but still firm.

"He doesn't have a claim over me. He may have a blood bond with me, but I am not his."

Thalion exchanged a meaningful look with Aerion and I could tell that this revelation had shifted something in their understanding of our relationship.

"He thinks you are," Aerion said, his voice gentle yet filled with concern.

"Well, he's wrong," I stated firmly, unwilling to accept the idea that my choices were somehow predetermined by a blood bond.

Aerion let out a sigh and his expression softened.

"I think it's best if we all get some rest," he suggested, looking at Thalion as if seeking his agreement. "We can talk about this tomorrow."

"I don't need sleep," Thalion declared, his gaze locked onto mine, an emotion in his eyes that I couldn't quite place. "Tell me how this blood bond came about."

I sighed heavily and sat down on the edge of the bed, suddenly feeling the weight of exhaustion bearing down on me. "I gave him my heart, my trust," I began, my voice a mix of frustration and vulnerability. "And when he told me he wanted to claim me as his, I agreed. But I didn't know what I was agreeing to, not the full extent."

Thalion clenched his jaw, his fists tightening in an evident display of anger. "He basically forced it on you," he growled, his protective instincts flaring.

"No," I corrected, feeling the need to clarify. "I had a choice, but he didn't tell me all the facts. If he had, I probably wouldn't have agreed to it."

"It doesn't matter, Vale," Thalion responded, his voice softer but still filled with concern. "He has a claim on you, a magical one that cannot be ignored."

"I don't care about his claim," I said, frustration seeping into my tone. "I am my own person. I make my own decisions."

Thalion sighed, his gaze filled with worry. "But the blood bond, Vale. It's not something to be taken lightly. It's a connection between two people, a link that cannot be broken easily."

"Easily?" I questioned, my head shooting up, a glimmer of hope igniting within me. "So there is a way?"

"Yes, there's a way," Aerion replied, his tone serious and his expression grave. "But it's dangerous and not something to be done lightly."

"What is it?" I inquired, my curiosity overshadowing my fear.

"You would have to sever the bond," Aerion explained, his words hanging heavily in the air.

"How do I do that?" I pressed further.

"You would have to sacrifice something of equal value," Aerion said, his gaze unwavering.

"Sacrifice?" I echoed, trying to wrap my head around the concept. "Like, give up something in exchange for the bond being severed?"

"Yes," Aerion confirmed.

"What kind of sacrifice?" I asked, my mind racing with possibilities.

"I don't know," Aerion admitted. "That's for you to find out."

"I see," I replied, my hope gradually fading as I absorbed this new information.

"But the point is, the bond is a connection that goes beyond the physical. It's a bond that's spiritual and emotional," Thalion continued.

"Meaning?" I asked, my curiosity urging him to explain further.

"Meaning that he can feel you, and find you, from almost anywhere," Aerion interjected. "Whether you want to admit it or not, he will always have a claim on you."

I sighed, a mix of frustration and resignation bubbling within me. "So, what? Am I supposed to spend the rest of my life tethered to a man who tricked me into a blood bond unless I can figure out how to sever it?"

"I'm sorry, Vale," Thalion said, his voice filled with genuine sympathy. "I wish there was another way."

"I understand," I replied, my tone heavy with resignation. I needed a moment to gather my thoughts.

"I need to take a walk and clear my head," I announced, pushing myself up from the bed and making my way to the door, leaving them both standing there.

"Vale," Thalion called out after me, but I ignored him. I needed solitude to process everything.

My thoughts were a whirlwind as I walked through the palace corridors and soon I found my way to the gardens. Stepping outside into the cool night air, I took a deep breath, letting the refreshing breeze soothe my nerves. As I inhaled the scent of the surrounding flowers, I felt the tension in my body slowly start to dissipate.

Alone with my thoughts, I contemplated the situation. There had to be a way to sever the bond without making a sacrifice. I didn't know if I could bear the thought of being tethered to Kaelan for the rest of my life, especially after the deception he'd used to forge the bond.

The moon hung low in the night sky, casting a silver glow over the palace gardens. Stars twinkled overhead and a gentle breeze rustled the leaves of the ancient trees surrounding me. It was a tranquil scene that brought me a sense of peace.

I strolled along the stone path, my bare feet making almost no sound on the ground. The coolness of the stone beneath my feet was soothing and I relished the opportunity to clear my mind.

Suddenly, a faint rustling broke the peaceful atmosphere, like the soft whisper of a breeze through the leaves. I halted, my senses on high alert as I strained to discern the source of the noise. An eerie sensation washed over me as if I were being watched.

"Vale," a voice whispered, barely audible but unmistakable.

My heart raced and I spun around, scanning the moonlit shadows for any sign of movement. The gardens appeared empty, the only movement coming from the occasional firefly dancing in the night.

"Who's there?" I called out.

The rustling grew louder and then I saw it, a fleeting figure, dark as the night, weaving silently through the trees. Panic surged through me, and I felt like prey in the presence of a predator.

"Run," the voice hissed once more, this time with greater urgency.

Without another thought, I obeyed the command, my instincts taking over as I sprinted through the moonlit gardens. The shadowy figure pursued, an ominous presence that seemed to hover just behind me, its silent pursuit making my skin crawl.

My breath came in ragged gasps as I pushed myself harder, my feet pounding against the stone path. The path guided me back to the palace and I rushed toward the massive doors, their ancient wood looming ahead.

"Nyxen!" I yell frantically, my familiar instantly appearing at my side. "Go get help!" Nyxen wasted no time in vanishing back into the shadows. I could feel the panic radiating from him through our bond.

An abrupt, excruciating pain jolted through my skull. A sudden blow to the back of my head sent me stumbling and for a brief, disorienting moment, my world spun in a dizzying whirl.

A strong hand clamped onto my arm, its grip unyielding and painful as it pulled me backward. A startled cry escaped my lips as I tried to regain my balance.

"Vale," the voice rasped again, carrying a menacing edge that sent shivers down my spine.

Frantically, I fought against the figure's hold, struggling to break free. Panic and confusion swirled within me as my magical instincts flared to life. I reached for the magic that dwelled within me, but it remained elusive, slipping through my grasp like water through my fingers.

The figure inched closer, its breath brushing against my ear, a sinister whisper in the darkness.

"You're mine now," it hissed, its words dripping with chilling finality.

A scream tore from my throat, echoing through the quiet gardens—a desperate plea for aid, a cry for anyone who might hear and come to my rescue. My struggles intensified, but the grip on my arm tightened, cruel claws digging into my flesh, drawing blood.

"You're coming with me," the voice declared, devoid of emotion, its words sending a shiver down my spine.

"Get the fuck off me," I growled fiercely.

Summoning every ounce of strength and determination I possessed, I continued to fight, desperation lending me a surge of power. Finally, I managed to gain a semblance of control over my magic. Flames erupted into existence in my outstretched hands, bathing the immediate area in a sudden, searing light.

The flames revealed my assailant, dispelling the darkness that had cloaked them. Before me loomed a monstrosity that could only be birthed from the darkest corners of a nightmare. Its skin was an abominable tapestry of charred flesh, resembling burnt parchment stretched taut over a twisted frame. From its hollow eye sockets emanated an eerie void, as if it were a soulless chasm into the abyss. Malformed limbs ended in razor-sharp claws that seemed capable of rending the very fabric of reality. Its mouth, a jagged tear in its face, dripped with an unidentifiable, viscous substance. It was the embodiment of unspeakable horrors, a creature that defied both logic and nature.

The sight of the abomination sent a wave of terror through me, but I held my ground, fire and determination burning within me as I faced the monstrous intruder. Desperation clawed at me as I continued to struggle against the creature's iron grip. Despite the fiery blaze that engulfed its form, it appeared impervious to the searing flames, its hold on me unwavering. Frustration and fear mingled within me as I cried out in defiance.

"Struggle all you like, your fear is delicioussss," the creature hissed, its voice dripping with a sinister edge.

As the flames intensified, I grew more desperate, my strength waning. It felt as though the battle was slipping from my grasp. But just as hope threatened to abandon me, a familiar presence entered my mind like a lifeline.

"Vale, flame will not harm it, you must reach deeper within yourself."

The First Witch's words sounded within me, and I searched within the depths of my being for something I hadn't known existed—a wellspring of inner strength.

"The creature is strong, but you are stronger. Call on the power that lies dormant within you."

With my eyes squeezed shut, I focused my thoughts, determined to unearth the hidden reservoir of power that had eluded me until now. Fueled by my desperation it came rushing forth. My magic pulsed and expanded, the raw energy coursing through me, making me feel invincible.

The flames that had once surrounded the creature flickered, then vanished, leaving behind a smoldering sense of dread in its wide, fear-filled eyes. As I opened my own eyes, a wicked grin crept onto my face and I allowed the newfound power to surge through me, filling every fiber of my being.

With a sense of grim satisfaction, I raised my free hand and brought it up to the creature's grotesque face. A bone-chilling scream tore through the night as I entered its mind, my consciousness coursing through its dark memories. Panic and agony danced in its eyes, but my magic held it fast, refusing to release it.

"This is for thinking I would be easy prey," I hissed, my voice laced with vengeance.

I channeled the newfound strength within me, releasing a torrent of power that tore apart the creature's mind, shattering its skull and causing its body to disintegrate into a cloud of fine ash. As the remnants of the malevolent being dissipated into the night, I stood there, my chest heaving from the intensity of the encounter, my heart racing with adrenaline.

The night air suddenly felt too cold as Aerion, Thalion, and a dozen guards finally burst through the grand palace doors, Nyxen close on their heels. Their eyes darted around wildly, scanning the garden for any sign of danger.

"Vale!" Aerion's voice, filled with both relief and concern, rang out as he sprinted towards me. His strong arms enveloped me in a protective embrace. "Are you okay?"

I nodded, my voice trembling slightly as I responded, "I'm fine."

Thalion, his features etched with worry, joined us. "What happened?" he asked, his deep voice heavy with concern.

I took a deep breath to steady my nerves before recounting, "I was attacked by some sort of monster."

Their expressions grew grimmer as they exchanged concerned glances. Aerion's stormy grey eyes scanned the darkness surrounding us, searching for any lingering threats.

"What kind of monster?" Thalion pressed for details.

I shook my head, the memory of the grotesque being still fresh in my mind. "I don't know, I've never seen anything like it."

Aerion's voice took on a tenser tone as he continued probing, "Did you kill it?"

"Yes," I replied firmly, my fear giving way to a sense of accomplishment. "It's gone."

Thalion's concern deepened as he questioned, "What was it doing here? This isn't normal."

"It came for me," I admitted, the chill in my spine refusing to dissipate. "My flames did nothing to stop it."

Aerion's brows furrowed deeply, a dark cloud of concern crossing his face. "Haldir must have learned how your magic manifests," he growled, his frustration evident.

"So, he sent this thing, whatever it was, to take me?" I questioned, my voice trembling as I considered the implications.

"That's our best guess for now," Thalion replied, his eyes searching my face.

A sense of dread settled over me as the reality sank in. "He's not going to stop," I said, fear clutching at my heart.

Aerion's expression remained grim as he affirmed, "No, he's not. And we need to be prepared."

I swallowed hard, knowing that the danger was far from over. Aerion offered me some comfort, wrapping an arm around my shoulders. "Come," he said, his voice gentle but determined. "Let's get you back inside."

I nodded, letting him lead me back into the palace, our steps echoing through the hallways as the chilling silence of the night followed us.

Chapter Twenty-Five

The library lay quiet, a sanctuary of silence amidst the hustle and bustle of the Fae palace. After the unsettling encounter with the strange creature the previous night, I had come here in search of answers. Nyxen nestled comfortably within the depths of my shadow keeping a watchful eye on the surroundings. He was on high alert for any signs of trouble this morning, clearly worried for me after last night.

I skimmed through dusty tomes and ancient scrolls, searching for any information about blood bonds, a concept I had been thrust into without warning or consent. However, despite my efforts, the library's offerings seemed insufficient compared to the wealth of knowledge I had at my disposal back in my own magical haven. I missed the comfort of home.

A sigh escaped my lips as I realized that this venture would bear little fruit. It was time to go back and visit my own realm, check up on everything, and perhaps find some answers there. With that thought my decision was made and a small weight lifted off my shoulders.

Setting aside my research on blood bonds, I instead began scouring the texts for any information on the creature that had attacked me the previous night. What had Haldir sent after me?

As I delved into my new research, a familiar presence passed by. It was the librarian, a Fae male with a wealth of knowledge at his fingertips. Gathering my courage, I approached him and asked, "Excuse me, do you have any books on dangerous magical creatures? I'm interested in learning more about them."

He regarded me with an intrigued expression and nodded. "Of course, Lady Vale. Follow me and I'll guide you to the relevant section."

The aisles stretched on until we reached a section in the far back of the library. The librarian pointed toward the shelves with a flourish.

"Everything we have on these topics is here," he informed me. "Take your time and enjoy the reading."

"Thank you," I replied with gratitude, watching as he departed, leaving me to explore the troves of knowledge before me. Nyxen appeared beside me, his eyes bright and inquisitive as they darted between the countless tomes and scrolls.

"Lots," his voice echoed in my mind, a recent development in our communication that I had come to appreciate.

"Yes, there is quite a bit, isn't there?" I mused aloud, glancing around at the extensive collection. "It's so much easier when you can simply ask the library for assistance."

Nyxen cocked his head, his gaze shifting from me to the books, as though he expected them to respond to my words. When they remained silent, he exhaled softly in what seemed like disappointment.

I chuckled at his confusion. "I guess we'll have to do this the old-fashioned way."

"Why?" Nyxen inquired, his curiosity evident in his eyes as he observed the volumes around us.

"Because the creature is long dead but the books aren't. I need to know more about what came after me," I explained, trying to convey the concept.

Nyxen gave me a dubious look, then finally acquiesced and turned his attention to the books.

Smiling at his inquisitive nature, I began to sift through the various volumes, searching for any tidbit of information that might offer a clue as to the identity and nature of the creature that had attacked me.

As I perused the shelves, Nyxen suddenly drew my attention. *"Here,"* He nudged a scroll off the shelf with his nose, a gesture that continued to perplex me – how could part of him seem so tangible at times when he was made of shadows?

"What is it?" I asked, picking up the scroll and unfurling it carefully, my eyes swiftly scanning the contents.

"Creatures," was his simple reply, his thoughts brushing against my mind like a fleeting whisper.

The parchment before me was filled with a comprehensive list of creatures from the Fae realm. Each entry provided a detailed account of a creature's abilities and vulnerabilities, offering a treasure trove of information about the denizens of the realm I had found myself entwined within.

As I continued to read, my eyes widened in amazement and intrigue. The list was extensive and diverse, featuring many species I had never even heard of before. I glanced at Nyxen, who observed me with a curious look.

"How did you know this was here?" I asked, my curiosity getting the best of me.

"Smelled," Nyxen replied, his thoughts once again brushing against my mind, his words concise.

"Smelled?" I repeated, still somewhat baffled.

"Yes, smell," he said.

"But I didn't smell anything," I admitted, my confusion deepening.

"You not," Nyxen clarified.

"I'm not what?" I asked, feeling a bit lost in our cryptic exchange.

"Not smell," he concluded, his shadowy form shifting and swirling in the light.

"Right," I responded, shaking my head in a futile attempt to make sense of it all. Turning my attention back to the scroll, I resumed my reading, determined to decipher the mysteries contained within.

I came to a halt upon encountering one particular creature in my research, a Fae being known as a darach. The entry depicted them as powerful, cunning, and exceptionally perilous. Most notably, they were described as being impervious to fire. A chill coursed down my spine as I considered the possibility that this darach was the creature that had assaulted me the previous night. I wondered if there might be an image of it within the library's collection.

"Nyxen," I began, my curiosity getting the best of me, "can you locate a book containing illustrations of these creatures?"

Nyxen nodded in response and with a determined swish of his tail, he embarked on a quest through the nearby bookshelves, diligently searching for what I needed.

"Found," he announced, indicating a substantial tome with a nudge of his nose.

Taking the book from the shelf, I gingerly flipped through its pages, my gaze scanning for any depiction of the darach.

"Ah, here we go," I exclaimed with relief, as I came across the corresponding page.

The entry on darach featured an eerie illustration, showcasing their charred skin and eerie, hollow eyes. There was no doubt; this was the creature that had ambushed me last night.

"So, darach are immune to fire, but how did I manage to defeat it?" I pondered aloud, voicing the perplexing question that gnawed at my thoughts.

"Other powers," Nyxen responded, his eyes lifting to meet mine.

"Yes, you're right," I replied, remembering the overwhelming sensation I had felt and the power that had flowed through me. Thalion's magic lessons seemed to be paying off.

"Vale," a voice called out, and I was automatically reminded of the creature calling out to me in the darkness last night. My shoulders stiffened and I turned around. Relief flooded through me when I saw it was Thalion walking toward me.

"Hey," I responded, smiling at him.

"How are you today?" he inquired, his voice gentle.

"I'm doing better," I assured him.

"Are you sure? No one would fault you for being shaken up," he pressed, his worry for me evident.

"I know," I admitted, offering him a reassuring smile, "but I'm okay, really."

A look of relief washed over him and I could tell he had genuinely been concerned about my well-being.

"So, what are you doing here in the library?" Thalion inquired, deftly changing the subject.

"Researching," I replied, holding up the book and scroll for him to see. "I found information about the creature that attacked me last night, or rather, Nyxen did," I added, gesturing toward my familiar, who lifted his head with a sense of pride.

"Really?" Thalion's eyes widened with interest.

"Yeah," I confirmed, excitement creeping into my voice, "apparently, the darach is immune to fire. That's how it was able to withstand my magic."

Thalion leaned in closer, his curiosity piqued. "What happened then?"

I hesitated for a moment, trying to find the right words to explain what had happened during my encounter with the darach.

"I'm not entirely sure," I began slowly, furrowing my brow in thought. "I'm not even sure what I did."

Thalion looked at me intently, his eyes searching mine for answers. "What do you mean?"

"Well, in a moment of panic," I recounted, my voice carrying a sense of wonder, "I somehow entered into the creature's mind. He didn't die, though, until I shattered his skull." The vivid memories of the gruesome battle flashed before my eyes.

"Interesting," Thalion mused, his intrigue evident.

"Yes, very," I agreed, my curiosity mingling with a sense of uncertainty about where this newfound power had come from. I would have to ask Rowena if she knew more, though her answers were usually cryptic.

Thalion's next question was probing. "Have you ever experienced anything like this before?"

I shook my head slowly. "Never. It was all new to me."

"Well, we'll have to explore this new side of your magic," he declared, determination in his voice.

I couldn't help but feel a bit apprehensive. "Do you think it's safe?"

Thalion's eyes held a reassuring glint as he replied, "I think so. We'll just have to be careful."

His words brought me comfort, and I nodded. "Okay, I trust you," I said, offering him a warm smile.

"So, what are your plans for today?" he asked genuine curiosity in his eyes.

"Oh, I was planning on visiting the human realm," I replied. "I've been neglecting my duties there."

His expression shifted to seriousness and he voiced his concerns. "You know, it might not be safe for you to leave the palace right now."

I sighed, realizing the truth in his words. "I'm aware, but I can't stay cooped up here forever. I need to check on things, make sure everything is okay."

Thalion's worry for my safety was evident in his next question. "Would you like me to come with you?"

I appreciated his offer but declined with a smile. "No, I'll be fine."

He still seemed uneasy, his worry not easily abated. "Okay, but promise me you'll be careful."

I nodded, giving him my word. "I promise."

He finally relented, though the concern still lingered in his eyes. "All right, if you're sure," he conceded.

"I am, don't worry about me. I can handle myself," I assured Thalion, a surge of confidence in my abilities washing over me.

"I'm sure you can," he replied, offering a playful grin that momentarily lightened the mood.

"What are your plans for today?" I asked him, my curiosity getting the better of me.

His expression shifted to one of relative mundanity. "Oh, nothing too exciting. Just paperwork and meetings."

However, there was something I had been wondering about since my arrival. "Where is your father, Thalion?"

His jovial attitude shifted, replaced by a melancholy that tugged at my heartstrings. Thalion hesitated before responding. "He's currently with my mother in the court she grew up, in Aurumport. She's been very sick for a while now. I've been fulfilling his duties while he's gone."

I expressed my condolences. "I'm sorry to hear that about your mother." It occurred to me that I might be able to help. "Is there anything I can do to help her? I'm rather good at healing incantations."

"You are?" Thalion asked, a mixture of surprise and hope flickering across his features.

"Of course," I replied, my tone teasing. "I'm not just a pretty face." I gave him a playful look, hoping to lighten the heavy topic at hand.

"I would appreciate that more than you could imagine," Thalion responded, his voice carrying the weight of his concern. "She's been suffering for a while now. The healers have tried everything, but nothing seems to work."

"I can't guarantee I can help," I cautioned, not wanting to raise false hopes, "but I'm willing to try."

Thalion's gratitude was evident. "I can't thank you enough," he said, sincerity ringing in his voice.

"Don't thank me yet," I cautioned once more, not wanting him to expect miracles.

"Even if you can't help, just offering is a kindness." His words warmed my heart and I responded with a smile.

"Come, let's go see her. She would love to meet you," he said, eager to help his mother.

Surprised, I asked, "She knows about me?"

"Oh yes," Thalion confirmed with a nod. "I communicate with both of them regularly. Aerion delivers our letters; his powers come in handy quite often."

"That makes sense," I said, following him out of the library. As we walked through the palace's grand halls, I couldn't help but ask, "What is she like, your mother?"

Thalion's voice held a note of pride as he spoke of her. "She's a fierce warrior. She raised me and taught me everything I know. But she's also gentle and kind, I aspire to be just like her. I think she'd love you." He mused.

"I can't wait to meet her," I said, genuinely touched by Thalion's invitation to meet his mother.

Thalion led me through the corridors of the palace, guiding me to a worn wooden door. With a single knock, he opened it without waiting for a response, and I followed him inside.

Aerion, shirtless and with a surprised expression on his face, stood in the middle of the room. I couldn't help but appreciate his strong, chiseled physique, my gaze lingering for a moment.

"I didn't expect you," he remarked, grabbing his shirt and putting it on.

"I didn't expect you either," I replied, my voice laced with amusement.

"We came to see my mother," Thalion interjected, giving Aerion a knowing look.

"Well, she's most certainly not here." His joke elicited a soft chuckle from me.

"Yes, well, Vale here has offered to try and heal her," Thalion explained.

Aerion's eyes widened as he looked at me, his voice lowering as he asked, "You can heal?"

I nodded, surprised by his reaction. "Yes, I have some proficiency in healing magic."

"We haven't seen a magical healer since your mother," Aerion said with awe in his voice. "It used to be a common but revered ability. You'd be doing a great and honorable service for all of us."

"Well, we'll see how it goes," I replied, still trying not to raise their expectations too high.

"We can all go now if you two are ready," Aerion suggested, busying himself with tucking his shirt into his pants.

"Just give me a moment to look over some incantations in my book," I replied, suddenly remembering the small grimoireHarker had given me. While I knew a few healing incantations, I wanted to be sure there wasn't a more effective one in the notebook.

"Of course, we can both take you back to your rooms," Thalion agreed.

The three of us left Aerion's rooms and walked the hallways to mine in companionable silence. As we reached my door, Thalion said, "I'll let my advisors know where we are going. Take your time and we'll meet you in the front entrance when you are ready."

"Okay, sounds good," I said, entering my chambers. I headed to my forgotten pack in the corner of the room and found the small leather-bound notebook. As I began rifling through it, I noticed there were a lot of very helpful spells and rituals that Harker had included, I felt a bit of shame at not looking through this earlier. Finally, I came upon a section on healing magic. It had just what I needed—an incantation specifically for sickness rather than injuries. I memorized it quickly before hastily leaving my room.

The guards nodded to me as I passed and made my way towards the main entrance. The palace was a maze of winding corridors and twisting passages, and it took me several minutes to navigate it. When I finally reached the entrance, Thalion and Aerion were waiting for me.

"Are you ready?" Thalion asked, his face a mask of hope.

"I think so," I replied, taking a deep breath.

"I have faith in you," he said, giving me a warm smile.

"I've got the right incantation, I hope," I told Thalion.

"I'm sure you do," he replied, his voice oozing confidence.

"Okay, let's do this," I said, feeling determined.

Thalion moved to one side of Aerion and I positioned myself on the other, grabbing Aerion's arm as we prepared to leave. I felt a small surge of energy from Aerion as the world around us shifted in a dizzying array of light and color. When the world came back into focus, I rubbed my eyes.

"I definitely prefer shadow-shifting with Nyxen; it's not as blinding," I commented, amusement lacing my tone.

As I looked around, I realized we were in a small courtyard, much cozier and more intimate than the grand one attached to the palace we had just come from. The courtyard was surrounded by stone walls covered in ivy, giving it a charming and rustic feel. In the center, a bubbling fountain sent sparkling water droplets into the air, catching the sunlight. A stone path led to a weathered wooden bench beneath a gnarled old tree, casting dappled shade across the ground. Colorful flowers bloomed in well-tended beds, their scent filling the air with sweetness. It was a peaceful and serene place and it filled me with a sense of calm.

"This is where she lives?" I asked, taking in the simple surroundings.

"It's where she grew up," Thalion replied, a look of nostalgia passing fleetingly over his face.

"It's very nice," I said, not wanting to insult him.

"Yes, I used to come here most summers growing up," he respond-ed, leading me up the weathered stone stairs and through the front entrance.

We stepped inside and my eyes fell upon a woman with long, dark hair and a jovial look in her eyes.

"Hello, boys. We weren't expecting you," she greeted us, her voice carrying a cheerful tone.

"Hello, Marla," Aerion said warmly.

Marla's eyes shifted toward me, her curiosity apparent in her gaze. "And who is this?" she asked.

"Marla, meet Vale. We've come so she can try and heal Moth-er," Aerion explained.

Marla's eyes widened in shock. "She's a healer?"

"Something like that," Aerion replied.

"I don't know how to thank you," Marla said, tears brimming in her eyes.

"Don't worry, let's just see if I can actually help first," I said, once again worried about raising anyone's hopes. Unfortunately, hopes ap-peared to be already raised.

"I will take you to her straight away," Marla said before turning and heading down the corridor at a brisk pace. We followed her to a small room at the end of a winding hallway. She knocked before opening the door and stepping inside, motioning for us to follow.

"Here she is," she said, her voice hushed. "King Celeborn? Your son is here to see the queen and he's brought someone with him."

King Celeborn, a man of regal presence with a striking resemblance to his son, looked up from where he sat. His troubled green eyes shift-ed from his son to me, curiosity flickering in their depths. A fleeting look of recognition crossed his face. "Lyra?" he whispered.

"No, father, not Lyra, but her daughter," Thalion answered him.

"My name is Vale, and if it's alright with you, I would like to try and heal your wife," I told him, my voice gentle and soothing.

He looked at Thalion briefly, who nodded, before turning his gaze back to me. "You're a healer?" he asked incredulously.

"I'm a witch," I told him firmly, choosing not to keep my true nature a secret, given the trust I had in him as Thalion'sfather.

"A witch? Thalion, what is going on?" King Celeborn asked his son.

"She's the one I've been writing to you about. We'll tell you everything you need to know afterward, Father. Just trust her."

King Celeborn contemplated this for a moment, his expression thoughtful. "Yes, of course. If she believes she can help, then she has my permission. She's been asleep for a few days now."

My eyes moved to the woman lying in bed, her light brown hair limp against her pillow, her skin ghostly pale. She appeared weak and fragile, her breathing shallow and labored.

"Do you have any idea what is causing her sickness?" I asked the king, genuine concern in my voice.

"We've been told it is a sickness of the heart," he replied, his voice heavy with pain.

I closed my eyes, centering myself, and focused my mind on seeking out the sickness within her, I had never done this before. It didn't take long to locate it—a thick, dark tendril coiled around her heart, slowly suffocating her and draining the life from her. Kneeling beside the bed, I gently took her cold hand in mine.

"It's going to be okay; I've got you," I reassured her softly.

I began reciting the incantation, my voice filled with conviction as I concentrated on the sickness within her. The words flowed easily from my lips as if they were meant to be spoken.

"By ancient winds and forest deep,
Let sickness from this soul now sweep.
With whispered words and magic's grace,
May health and vigor swiftly embrace.
As I speak this charm, let healing flow,
Banishing ailment, bringing warmth and glow."

As I uttered the final words of the incantation, I could feel my magic coursing into her, suffusing her body. Everyone in the room seemed to be holding their breath as we waited. Then, slowly at first, but gaining speed, the darkness around her heart began to retreat. Her breathing evened out and her complexion transformed from pallid to rosy.

I could sense my own power waning, my energy plummeting as the spell took its toll on me.

The queen slowly began to rouse, her eyes blinking tiredly. I couldn't help but notice that her eyes were the same captivating shade of violet as Thalion's. She gazed at me with curiosity for a brief moment.

"Mother," Thalion said, relief washing over his face. Marla, standing at the doorway, audibly gasped and the king appeared on the verge of tears of joy.

"Thalion?" the queen rasped, her voice weak, her gaze shifting toward her son.

"It's me," he replied, moving closer to her.

Her eyes wandered back to me and she looked at me with a mixture of confusion and curiosity. "What are you doing here? And who is this?" she asked, her voice gaining strength as she inquired about my presence.

"My name is Vale," I introduced myself with a gentle smile. "I am the reason Thalion is here."

She seemed to consider my response for a moment, her violet eyes locked onto mine.

"Are you the one he's been writing to us about?" she inquired, her voice growing stronger as she spoke.

"I believe so," I answered, offering her a shy smile.

"It's a miracle," the king exclaimed, moving to his wife's side and tenderly taking her hand in his.

"It's a pleasure to meet you, Vale," the queen said, her gaze shifting to her husband.

I remained humble in the presence of their gratitude. "I can't thank you enough for healing my wife. Whatever you need, we'll provide," the king said, his eyes filled with tears.

"Oh no, it was no trouble at all," I replied modestly.

"How can we ever repay you?" he asked, his eyes pleading with sincerity.

"You don't need to repay me," I insisted, my voice gentle but firm. "Just knowing that she's better is enough for me."

"We are forever in your debt," he said.

Thalion crossed the room to his mother and knelt beside her as well. The small family basked in each other's presence for a moment, their relief palpable. I discreetly looked away, granting them a bit of privacy in that intimate reunion. Aerion, having also given them their space, came to stand beside me.

"What you've done is nothing short of remarkable," he said, his gaze fixed on me with genuine admiration.

I remained humble, despite the praise. "I'm just glad I could help," I told him, giving him a warm smile.

"I think the king and queen are going to want to hear the full story," Aerion remarked, his eyes shifting to Thalion and his mother.

"I'd imagine so," I agreed, knowing that there was much to explain.

The king rose from his seat and turned to me, his expression serious. "You'd be right about that. Thalion has left out a lot of important information about you, it would seem."

I couldn't help but smile at the king's straightforwardness. "I'd love to stay and fill in the gaps, but I think I need to rest a bit first. Spirit magic tends to take quite a bit out of me."

"Of course," he said, his gaze softening as he understood my need for recuperation.

"I'll take you back, Vale," Aerion offered, stepping closer to me, his presence reassuring.

"Thank you," I told him before turning back to the king and queen. "It was a pleasure meeting you and I look forward to talking more later."

"The pleasure was ours, my lady Vale," the king said warmly, his eyes filled with gratitude and admiration as he smiled at me.

I returned his smile, giving the queen one last look before we departed. "If there's anything you need, don't hesitate to ask," she said, her voice stronger now.

I nodded to them both. "I appreciate that."

Thalion walked towards me, his hand resting warmly on my lower back. "I'll walk you out," he offered, a broad and genuine smile gracing his face.

As we left the room, Aerion joined us, his presence a comforting reassurance. "You're a hero to them now," he remarked, a hint of awe in his voice. "And to Thalion and me as well."

I waved off their praise, feeling a bit bashful. "It was nothing, really."

"To you, maybe," Thalion countered, his expression sincere. "But it meant a lot to us."

I blushed, appreciating their kind words. "I'm just glad it worked."

We continued to walk, and as we reached the front door, Thalion spoke up again. "I'll see you two soon," he said before turning and walking away.

We made our way out the front door and Aerion flanked me, taking my arm in his. Without a word from him, the world around me began to blur and I squeezed my eyes shut, trying to stave off the dizziness. When I opened my eyes again, we were back in my rooms at the palace.

Aerion turned to me, his hands cupping my face as he looked into my eyes with an intensity that sent shivers down my spine. "The king was right, that was a miracle. You are a miracle, Vale."

His gaze held mine and he leaned down, his lips meeting mine in a gentle, tender kiss. My arms instinctively wrapped around him, pulling him closer. Our lips moved together in a slow, intimate dance, each moment deepening the connection between us. I felt a warmth stir in my chest, the sensation of his body pressed against mine and my heart raced in response as the kiss continued. His tongue brushed against my bottom lip, and I eagerly allowed him entrance.

His hands left my face, trailing down my back as he held me tightly against him. After what felt like an eternity, he pulled away slightly, his forehead resting against mine. His voice was breathy as he spoke, "You should get some rest. I'll bring you some dinner soon."

"Thank you," I replied, my voice barely above a whisper.

He reluctantly left my room and I lay on the bed, the events of the day replaying in my mind. I had become a hero, a miracle in the eyes of the king and queen, and even in Aerion's eyes.

Aerion was right; I needed some rest. The healing magic I had wielded and the intensity of our kiss all swirled in my thoughts as I closed my eyes, allowing sleep to claim me.

Chapter Twenty-Six

I was awoken from my peaceful slumber by a gentle knock on my door. I sat up and rubbed the remnants of sleep from my eyes. "Come in," I called out in a soft voice.

Amris entered with a steaming tray of food in her hands. The aroma of the stew and the sight of the crusty bread, along with various cut-up fruits and a glass of juice, made my stomach rumble. "Sorry for disturbing you, my lady," she said with a respectful nod. "But Prince Aerion told me you hadn't eaten yet. He wanted you to know he's gone back to fetch Prince Thalion."

"That's quite all right, Amris. Thank you for bringing the food," I replied with gratitude, my gaze lingering on the mouthwatering stew.

"You're very welcome. Is there anything else I can get for you?" she asked politely.

"No, this is perfect, thank you," I assured her.

"In that case, I'll leave you to your meal," she said, turning to exit the room. She closed the door behind her with a soft click.

With Amris gone, I eagerly tucked into the delicious meal, savoring the hearty stew and the sweet and juicy fruits. The exotic flavors of this realm's fruits always intrigued me and I couldn't resist trying them whenever I had the chance. I quickly polished off the stew and most of the fruits, my hunger finally sated.

After clearing the tray, I decided a hot bath would be an excellent way to relax and rejuvenate. I filled the large bathtub with warm water and carefully sank into it, allowing the soothing heat to envelop my aching muscles. The tension from the day seemed to melt away as I closed my eyes, letting the tranquility of the moment wash over me.

As I luxuriated in the warm bath, the door to the bathroom creaked open, startling me but a voice I recognized immediately broke the peaceful ambiance. "Hello, gorgeous."

I opened my eyes, water droplets clinging to my skin, to find Aerion strolling into the bathroom, Thalion following closely behind him. Surprise danced in my eyes as they entered so brazenly. "You guys are back already?"

Aerion offered a lopsided smile as he settled on the edge of the bathtub, his eyes wandering over my naked form. "You've been asleep a long time."

I blinked in mild disbelief. "Really? It only felt like a few minutes."

"Well, you needed the rest," he replied, his gaze still hungrily drinking me in.

Thalion, holding a book, chimed in, "I brought something for you to read. It's the one that talks about the First Witch creating new witches."

I had almost forgotten about that intriguing tidbit of information amidst all the happenings in the Fae realm. "Oh, perfect, thank you," I said as he carefully placed the book next to the tub.

"There's a lot about witches in there," he said, looking me over as well with an appreciative glance.

I nodded, dipping my hand into the water to retrieve a bar of soap. "I'll have to go through it when I have more time," I said, my fingers lathering soap onto my body.

The silence stretched between us as they watched me. A playful glint danced in my eyes as I looked up at them. "Are you two going to join me?" I asked, arching an eyebrow suggestively.

The two males exchanged a knowing look, a hint of mischief dancing in their eyes. Aerion spoke first, his voice laced with playful humor. "As nice as that sounds, princess, I doubt we'd both be able to fit into that tub with you. Maybe we should all give Thalion's private bath a try sometime."

Thalion nodded in agreement, a smirk tugging at his lips. "Oh, I agree."

Their decision was practical, but the lingering looks they cast at my naked body sent a subtle thrill through me. I couldn't resist teasing them a bit more. "I was just wondering since the two of you are watching me with such interest."

Aerion chuckled, his gaze not quite leaving me. "I think we'll leave you to finish your bath alone," he said.

With that, they both exited the bathroom, leaving me to enjoy the rest of my bath in peace.

After finishing my bath and drying off, I slipped into a simple purple robe. Once dressed, I joined the two males in the bedroom, where they were engrossed in conversation while seated on the couch.

Aerion's eyes traveled over me as I entered, "Feeling better?"

I nodded with a smile. "Yes, much. A lot of the weariness is gone."

Thalion chimed in, acknowledging the strain I had endured. "I'm sure that was a taxing spell."

"It was," I agreed, my gaze shifting between them. "But it was worth it."

Thalion's voice softened with admiration. "You are amazing."

I appreciated the compliment and shifted the conversation to more practical matters. "How are things back in Aurumport?"

Thalion's face lit up. "Better than ever. My mother has also taken quite a liking to you, as has my father. They are planning a celebration in your honor soon."

"Really?" I asked, genuine surprise coloring my tone.

Thalion nodded with a warm smile. "Yes. They wish to celebrate the miraculous healer who saved the queen's life."

I couldn't help but feel touched by their gratitude. "Wow, that's very nice of them. But they don't have to go through all that trouble for me."

Thalion's expression turned earnest. "Well, you're the one that made it possible. My mother was near death and now she is better than ever. You've given us a second chance at a happy life."

"I'm just glad I could help," I replied modestly, still overwhelmed by the magnitude of what had happened.

Thalion continued with the news. "So, the queen wants you to come visit. She wants to thank you in person. The celebration will be in a couple of days. Until then, she would like to get to know you better if there is time."

"Really? That's wonderful," I said, feeling excitement and anticipation at the thought. I didn't have much experience with mothers, but Thalion's seemed lovely, and the prospect of getting to know her was appealing.

"Great, she'll be delighted to hear it," Thalion said before standing and walking over to me. He wrapped an arm around my waist and pulled me close, our bodies now touching intimately. "I would also like to thank you personally," he said, his tone taking on a sensual quality.

My heart rate quickened at his proximity and his suggestive words. "What did you have in mind?" I replied, a hint of nervousness in my voice.

He answered me not with words, but by trailing his lips along the sensitive skin of my throat. His warm breath sent shivers coursing through me and I couldn't deny the growing desire that flooded my senses.

"Oh," I gasped as Thalion's lips continued their sensual exploration of my neck.

Aerion moved behind me, his body pressing against my back, and his hands slid up my torso, stopping just below my breasts. His warm breath caressed my ear as he whispered, "Why don't you relax and let both of us thank you properly," his voice thick and husky.

I struggled to find my voice, my body tingling with anticipation. "You two are going to be the death of me," I managed to say, my voice shaky and breathless.

"That would be most unfortunate," Thalion murmured, his warm breath ghosting over the nape of my neck.

I tilted my head back, baring my throat to them. Aerion seized the opportunity and pressed a kiss to the underside of my jaw, his lips moving sensuously against my skin.

I could feel the evidence of Thalion's arousal growing beneath his pants, the hard length pressing against me. My body trembled slightly with excitement and nervousness. Apart from that one night days ago, I had never been with two men at once and the prospect was undeniably intimidating.

"Relax and let us worship you," Aerion whispered seductively in my ear, his words sending shivers down my spine.

My heart raced as Aerion's hands gripped my hips and his lips began to explore the other side of my neck. Waves of desire washed over me, making my knees grow weak. Thankfully, the two of them were holding me up, their strong arms keeping me steady. Thalion's skilled hands cupped my breasts and his thumbs teased my nipples through the fabric of my dress.

"I've wanted you for so long, Vale," Thalion whispered against my ear, his breath heating my flushed skin.

"And I," Aerion rasped, his teeth nipping at the delicate skin at the crook of my neck.

"We've been waiting for you to be ready," Thalion explained, his tongue trailing down my collarbone. His fingers tugged the edges of my robe down, revealing more of my shoulders and cleavage, while Aerion's hands moved from my hips to my thighs, his fingers clutching the material of the robe and slowly inching it upward.

I gasped as their mouths and hands sent electric pulses of pleasure through my body. The sensation of them surrounding me was intoxicating, and I found myself giving in to the moment.

"I've never done this before," I admitted, my voice trembling with desire and uncertainty.

"You're perfect," Thalion growled, his lips moving down to my collarbone.

"Absolutely perfect," Aerion agreed, his fingers trailing down to the hem of my dress, inching it ever higher, revealing more of my legs.

Darkness covered my vision suddenly as a silk blindfold was lowered over my eyes. Aerion tied it securely behind my head, his lips brushing against the shell of my ear as he did. I was surprised but not scared, and the thrill of being at their mercy added a new dimension to the already overwhelming sensations.

"What do you want, princess?" Aerion murmured, his lips moving lower, his fingers tracing sensual patterns on the bare skin of my thighs.

"Touch me," I breathed, the intensity of my desire overwhelming, and I ached for their touch.

Aerion's hands gently lifted my arms over my head, and with Thalion's swift assistance, my robe was swiftly removed. I stood there, completely naked and exposed, my skin flushed with arousal.

"Gorgeous," I heard Thalion whisper.

"Stunning," Aerion rasped in agreement. Their gazes felt like a caress, causing my nipples to harden and goosebumps to form all over my skin.

Hands glided down my arms and across my stomach, his fingers lightly tracing the curves of my hips and the sensitive crease between my leg and torso. His mouth continued to lavish attention on my skin, never breaking contact.

Fingers trailed sensuously down my back, following the curve of my spine and caressing the swell of my ass with a feather-light touch. Every featherlight touch sent shivers of pleasure coursing through me.

My breathing quickened as someone's hands moved between my thighs, their fingers slipping into my wetness, eliciting a soft gasp from my lips.

"So responsive," Thalion whispered, his lips brushing over my shoulder.

I moaned softly as their thumb circled my clit, sending a delightful shockwave of pleasure coursing through me.

"You are so deliciously wet," Aerion growled into my ear.

Another set of hands ventured lower, their fingers tracing the cleft between my cheeks, creating an entirely new sensation that left me gasping in surprise and delight.

"Oh, Gods," I moaned, the overwhelming sensations making it hard to stand.

"Do you want us, princess?" Aerion asked, while what I guessed were his fingers maintained their rhythmic dance against my throbbing center.

"Yes," I cried out, the pleasure building inside me like a gathering storm.

"Good," Thalion murmured, his voice a husky rasp. With a sudden, unexpected move, he swept me up into his arms, my legs instinctively wrapping around his waist as he gently placed me on the bed.

I lay there in complete darkness, the blindfold securely fastened over my eyes, plunging me into a world of sensory deprivation. Every nerve in my body tingled with anticipation, like an electric current coursing through me. In the hushed silence, the only sound that reached my ears was the soft rustle of clothing being slowly, deliberately removed.

A moment later, the sensation of the bed dipping on either side of me signaled their approach. My heart raced in response to their nearness. As their warm bodies pressed against mine, I couldn't help but shiver at the contrast between their smooth, bare skin and the coolness of the sheets beneath us.

A gasp escaped my lips as one of them took my nipple into his mouth, his tongue swirling with an expert touch around the hardened nub. Simultaneously, the other lowered his mouth to my other breast, his tongue teasing the sensitive tip with an irresistible mixture of gentle caresses and bites. My body responded with fervor, arching into their touch as their hands roamed my form, exploring every contour and curve.

Their attentions were nothing short of maddening, and before long, I found myself writhing and moaning beneath their skillful ministrations. Waves of pleasure coursed through me, steadily building like an inferno threatening to consume my very soul. It was as if they possessed an innate knowledge of my desires, knowing precisely where and how to touch me to elicit the most exquisite sensations.

One of their mouths began to trail lower, a tantalizing path of warmth and wetness as their tongue teased and licked their way down to my throbbing core. The sensation of their warm breath against my aching body nearly sent me hurtling over the edge into ecstasy. But they held back, savoring the sweet torture they were subjecting me to, taking their time to explore every inch of my desire, prolonging the inevitable climax that hung tantalizingly just out of reach.

The attention stopped as someone moved to the edge of the bed. His strong hands grasped my ankles, tugging me closer to the edge and spreading my legs wide, hooking them over his broad shoulders. The other slid behind me, his legs on either side of my body, cradling me in his lap. I could tell by the contours of his body that it was Aerion who now sat behind me, kneading my breasts in his calloused hands.

With a deliberate, sensual motion, Thalion's tongue darted out and flicked against my sensitive clit. My back arched involuntarily, and a moan escaped my lips as ecstasy washed over me.

"Fuck," Aerion groaned, his voice strained with desire as he continued touching me. My body quivered and trembled as Thalion's expert tongue continued to explore every inch of my sensitive flesh, licking and sucking.

"Do you like this, princess?" Thalion rasped, his voice rough with longing.

"Gods, yes," I panted, unable to hold back my fervent response.

"Good girl," he rumbled, his mouth descending once more upon my slick, pulsating core, his hunger for me evident in every fervent kiss and tantalizing caress.

Aerion got out from under me and I felt him positioning himself near my head, sinking to his knees in front of me. He cupped the back of my head, lifting me slightly.

"Let me fuck your mouth, princess," Aerion demanded with a husky tone that sent a thrill through me.

Without hesitation, I parted my lips and welcomed him inside, the taste of his desire flooding my senses. My tongue swirled sensually around his head, savoring the rich, masculine flavor of him.

"Oh, that's my girl," he moaned, his fingers gripping the back of my head, guiding me with an irresistible urgency.

As I pleasured Aerion with my mouth, Thalion's skilled tongue continued its seductive exploration of my dripping core. Each flick, each caress, sent shockwaves of pleasure coursing through me and I moaned, the sound vibrating around Aerion's hardness and causing him to groan in response.

With my eyes still covered, I surrendered to the overwhelming sensations—hands, lips, and tongues working together in perfect harmony to bring me to the brink of ecstasy. They took me higher and higher, pushing me relentlessly toward the pinnacle of pleasure.

The mounting sensations had me teetering on the precipice, my toes curling and my back arching as I desperately sought to draw closer to Thalion's wickedly talented tongue.

"You taste so sweet, princess," Thalion murmured, his heated breath fanning over me, further stoking the flames of desire that roared within me.

I couldn't contain my escalating desire any longer, and I trembled uncontrollably. My hips bucked in response to Thalion's tantalizing ministrations, desperate for more.

Aerion, sensing my impending climax, thrust his cock deeper into my mouth, his grip on my hair tightening as he took control. His commanding words sent a delicious thrill through me.

"Come for us, Vale," he ordered, his tone laced with undeniable authority.

I could feel the irresistible pull of my orgasm, like a tidal wave crashing over me. The pleasure surged in powerful waves, making my legs shake and my body shudder as I surrendered to the intense ecstasy, coming undone in their arms.

Even as I soared to the peak of bliss, Thalion's mouth never ceased its intoxicating dance, his tongue eagerly lapping at my clit.

When the intensity of the moment finally subsided, I collapsed onto the bed, feeling utterly sated, sweating beading down my back.

"That was incredible," I whispered, my voice hoarse from the passion that had consumed me.

Aerion's husky voice broke the momentary silence. "We're not finished with you yet."

Thalion shifted on the edge of the bed and gently pulled me into his lap, cradling me with care. He gently removed my blindfold and I looked into his violet eyes, a hunger shining there.

"I'm not sure I can move," I admitted, my body feeling boneless and content in their embrace.

"Don't worry, I'll do the work," Thalion's words reassured me as he positioned me over his throbbing erection. My anticipation grew with each passing second, my body tingling with excitement and desire.

I sank down onto him, the exquisite sensation of his hard length stretching and filling me making me gasp with pleasure.

"Gods, you feel amazing," Thalion rasped, his strong hands gripping my hips, steadying me as I settled onto him.

Aerion, his hungry eyes locked onto the point where Thalion and I were intimately connected, couldn't help but voice his own appreciation. "She's tight," he murmured, the desire evident in his voice.

"Very tight," Thalion agreed, his voice filled with longing and strain as he began to move, guiding me up and down on his rigid shaft with a deliberate and controlled pace.

"Ride me, Vale," he grunted, his hips rocking in rhythm with our joined bodies, creating delicious friction that set my senses ablaze.

"Yes," I breathed, the overwhelming sensations and the profound connection with the two men sending me into a whirlwind of pleasure.

Aerion knelt before us, his presence commanding attention. His hand moved rhythmically, pumping his hard cock, while his eyes remained fixated on our intimate dance. They blazed with an undeniable combination of lust and longing, casting an intoxicating spell upon the room.

In response to the electrifying atmosphere, I threw my head back, surrendering myself to the intoxicating sensations that coursed through my body. My hair spilled down my back in a wild, tangled cascade, framing my face in a sensual disarray.

The sight of Aerion, his arousal and desire laid bare for all to see, was almost overwhelming. The tension that contorted his handsome face, the yearning in his eyes—it was nothing short of mesmerizing.

Unable to resist the magnetic pull any longer, Thalion reached out his hand, inviting Aerion to join us in this intoxicating tryst. Aerion accepted the invitation eagerly, moving closer until his body was mere inches from ours.

With a sudden and decisive movement, Thalion shifted, turning me around so I was on my hands and knees. I moaned softly, the exquisite position allowing Thalion to penetrate me deeper than ever before. There was an undeniable urgency in his movements, and he wasted no time, his body surging forward and filling me once again with an irresistible force. Each thrust pushed the boundaries of ecstasy further and I surrendered to the overwhelming pleasure that washed over me.

Through a veil of messy hair, I glanced up, my gaze meeting Aerion's, whose eyes were fixed on the point where our bodies were joined. His expression was one of pure hunger, an unquenchable desire etched on his face, reflecting the intensity of the moment.

Thalion, driven by the passion of the moment, seized a fistful of my hair, using the grip to tug my head back. The sensation sent a jolt through my body, a sharp pain that mingled with the intense pleasure coursing through me, creating a potent cocktail of ecstasy that had my entire being trembling with desire.

Aerion drew closer, his body hovering mere inches from mine. As if in response to some unspoken command, Thalionreleased his grip on my hair, and my head fell forward, my lips coming into tantalizing contact with the velvety softness of Aerion's thick cock.

My tongue darted out and swiped along his shaft, eliciting a throaty groan from Aerion, a guttural sound that echoed through the room and fueled my own desire. "Don't stop," he growled, his fingers tangling possessively in my hair, taking control of the intimate rhythm that was unfolding.

I opened my mouth, inviting him to thrust inside, the salty taste of his desire flooding my senses as he rocked his hips with a primal urgency that mirrored the passion of the moment. Aerion's intensity added a new dimension to the pleasure, and I eagerly succumbed to the rhythm of his movements, a willing participant.

Meanwhile, Thalion continued his relentless assault on my body, his strong hands gripping my hips with an unyielding force, his fingers pressing hard into the soft flesh with each thrust. Every touch, every stroke, was an embodiment of unbridled desire, and I surrendered to the intense pleasure that cascaded through me.

The room was filled with the sounds of our passionate coupling—the rhythmic slapping of flesh, the ragged cadence of our breathing, and the unrestrained moans and cries of pleasure that escaped our lips. The air itself seemed heavy with the heady scent of our shared lust, adding to the intoxicating mix of desire and craving that enveloped us.

The exquisite sensations of having both their bodies moving in unison, each in its own intimate way, threatened to overwhelm my senses. They filled every fiber of my being, leaving no room for anything else, as I became lost in the depths of passion and longing.

Thalion's fingers, seemingly guided by instinct, moved from my hips and slid to my backside, where he spread my cheeks and boldly delved a finger into my ass, introducing a new sensation that sent shockwaves of pleasure coursing through my body. I gasped, my mouth still full of Aerion's cock, but he didn't pause or relent. He continued the sensual invasion, driving wave after wave of intense pleasure through me, pushing the boundaries of ecstasy even further.

I was utterly consumed by the sensation, enveloped and filled by their presence in a way I had never before experienced. In that moment, I reveled in the intoxicating power of our connection, lost in the depths of our shared desire.

Aerion's fingers tugged at my hair, urging me to take him deeper onto his pulsating hardness. Each pull, each inch of him that I accepted, intensified the sensation, and I willingly surrendered to the exquisite torment he imposed upon me. The sensations were overwhelming, and my world narrowed down to the rhythm of my own breath and the relentless pull of his fingers.

Simultaneously, Thalion's skilled fingers penetrated deeper, their insistent presence filling both of my most intimate openings. The overwhelming feeling of him stretching and claiming me in such a primal way sent shockwaves of pleasure through my body. The intensity of it all was enough to make my eyes roll back into my head, leaving me blissfully lost in the sea of ecstasy that washed over me.

It was an overpowering, raw, and carnal pleasure that gripped me, obliterating all thought and reason. My senses were saturated with the heady mix of desire, and I surrendered to it completely, allowing the waves of sensation to crash over me and pull me deeper into the abyss of passion.

The pleasure inside me built once more, my body responding eagerly to Thalion's skillful movements. My muscles clenched around him, and I could feel the delicious tension growing.

"That's it," Thalion groaned, his movements becoming faster and more frantic, his thrusts conveying the urgency of our shared passion.

"Oh, Gods," I cried out, my voice a passionate melody in the room, my head falling back as pleasure coursed through me in electrifying waves.

"You look so fucking beautiful right now," Aerion rasped, his eyes fixed on my trembling form, desire evident in every inch of his being.

The pressure inside me continued to mount, my body on the precipice of ecstasy. With a sudden, intense rush, I finally let go, and an explosion of pleasure tore through me. My entire body shuddered and shook as the orgasm rippled through my core, leaving me gasping for breath.

"Yes, fuck yes," Thalion growled, his hips thrusting harder and faster, his grip on my hips becoming almost bruising in its intensity.

"Come for me," I cried, my voice laced with urgency, my body quivering from the intensity of the experience.

"Vale!" Thalion roared, his hips stalling for a moment as he reached his own climax, his cock pulsing deep inside me with every throbbing beat of his heart.

His thrusts gradually slowed, his breathing ragged as he held me close, our bodies now slick with sweat and the remnants of our shared passion.

"Fuck," he breathed against my skin, his lips pressing against my neck, his warmth enveloping me.

I could feel the heat radiating from his skin and the rapid tempo of his heart beneath my hands.

"I can't wait to see what else you can do, princess," Aerion said, his gaze hungry and his hand still wrapped around his hard cock, a promise of more pleasures to come.

I gave him a mischievous smile, feeling a newfound confidence coursing through my veins.

"Get on the bed," I commanded, my tone assertive.

"As you wish," he replied, a wolfish grin spreading across his face.

"Lay down," I told Aerion, my voice low and sultry.

He did as I asked, stretching out on his back, his muscular arms folded behind his head, his gaze locked onto mine, a smirk playing on his lips.

"Now, what?" he asked, his voice a blend of anticipation and desire.

I straddled him, a slow, tantalizing slide of my body down his, feeling his hard length press against my entrance as I settled into position.

"I want you inside me," I whispered, my voice filled with longing.

"I can arrange that," he growled, his hands immediately gripping my hips and lifting me up slightly, ready to accommodate my desires.

I reached between us, my fingers deftly guiding him to my entrance. With a deliberate and teasing pace, I sank down on him, feeling his thick, pulsing shaft fill me completely, a pleasurable shiver coursing through my body as we connected.

"Fuck, princess," he grunted, his grip on my hips tightening reflexively, his eyes locking onto mine.

"You like that?" I asked, leaning forward, my breasts brushing against his chest, my lips dangerously close to his.

"Gods, yes," he moaned, the word escaping his lips in a husky breath. His hips began to move, thrusting upwards with a controlled urgency, pushing him deeper inside me as our passions ignited. Thalion watched us from the end of the bed, a satisfied look in his eyes.

I rocked my hips, savoring the sensation as Aerion's hands tightened on my hips. His eyes were shut, his face contorted in pleasure. Aerion's head tipped back lost in the sensation. "You feel so fucking good," he groaned, his hands moving to grip my hips tightly as I continued to move. "Don't stop."

I kept moving, finding a rhythm that had us gasping and moaning. The intensity of our connection was electric, and the room seemed to fade away as we focused solely on each other.

"You're driving me crazy," he grunted, his breathing becoming more erratic. His hands on my ass grew more demanding, pulling me closer to him.

My body responded eagerly, and I reveled in the intoxicating pleasure that surged through me. Aerion's moans grew louder, and I knew we were both on the edge.

"Fuck," he growled suddenly, his voice strained with desire. With a quick and powerful motion, he lifted me off of him, flipping me face down on the bed. I eagerly lifted my ass in the air, inviting him to take me from behind.

In one swift, powerful thrust, he entered me, and I gasped, burying my face in the blankets as the intense pleasure washed over me. "Fuck, you're perfect," he panted, his hips pounding into me with relentless urgency. I moaned loudly, the pleasure becoming almost overwhelming.

"Harder," I pleaded, my voice filled with desire and need.

Aerion responded with a primal intensity, increasing the force and speed of his thrusts. "Aerion," I breathed.

"Yes," Aerion groaned, his own rhythm unyielding and fervent. His gaze was locked on the erotic scene before him, the intensity of our connection undeniable.

Aerion reached around me, his skilled fingers finding my sensitive clit. He began circling it with a purpose, every touch igniting a spark of pleasure that coursed through my body.

The tension was building relentlessly inside of me, my moans becoming more urgent as I neared the precipice of pleasure.

"That's it, princess," Aerion whispered huskily, his finger never relenting in its ministrations.

I could feel myself teetering on the edge, the pleasure an intoxicating torrent threatening to consume me.

"Gods, Vale, I'm going to come," Aerion growled, his hips jerking erratically as he neared the brink.

I cried out, the orgasm ripping through me with unparalleled intensity, my body convulsing with ecstasy as I shook and shuddered.

"Fucking hell," Aerion cried out, his cock pulsing rhythmically inside of me. He continued to thrust, each stroke eliciting a new wave of pleasure, the blissful intensity of it leaving me panting and breathless.

We all collapsed in a sweaty, sticky heap, our breaths ragged and the air heavy with the intoxicating scent of our passionate encounter. The sensations still rippled through our exhausted bodies, leaving us in a state of blissful euphoria.

"That was…" Aerion started, his voice a husky whisper, his words trailing off as if language itself couldn't adequately describe what we had just experienced.

"Perfect," Thalion finished, his voice equally raspy, his eyes fixed on me with a tender, satisfied gaze.

"Absolutely perfect," I agreed, my voice barely more than a breathy murmur. My body felt like liquid, and I couldn't remember the last time I had felt so relaxed and sated.

With a contented sigh, I rolled onto my back, my chest heaving as I stared up at the ceiling. Beads of perspiration glistened on my skin, and I reveled in the warmth radiating from the two men who had brought me to this euphoric state.

"So, is that how you thank everyone who helps you?" I asked playfully, a teasing smile playing on my lips.

"Just you, princess," Aerion murmured, his fingers tracing aimless patterns on my thigh, his gaze soft and affectionate.

"We'll always take care of you," Thalion said, his lips pressing a tender kiss against my shoulder, his voice filled with devotion.

"I think I'm starting to see that," I replied, my smile growing wider as I basked in the warmth of their affection.

"Good," they said in almost perfect unison, their voices like a soothing lullaby.

We lay there for a while, our heartbeats gradually slowing, and the serenity of the moment washing over us. I could feel myself growing increasingly tired, the events of the day finally catching up to me. The weariness settled in, and I let out a soft yawn.

"Sleep," Aerion whispered his thumb gently rubbing my hip in a soothing rhythm. "We'll keep you safe," he assured me, his warm breath tickling my neck.

With their comforting words and the sensation of their protective embrace, I let sleep claim me. The warmth of their presence banished the lingering shadows of the day, and I drifted off into a peaceful slumber, the nightmares held at bay by the steadfast guardians by my side.

Chapter Twenty-Seven

I stood in my room within the palace, the familiar surroundings imbued with a sense of bittersweet nostalgia. Thalion and Aerion were here with me, their presence providing both comfort and a pang of sadness. I was returning to the mortal realm, where my responsibilities and friends awaited.

Aerion's voice broke through the momentary silence, his eyes filled with concern as he asked, "Are you ready, Vale?"

I met his gaze, feeling the weight of his worry and care. "Yes," I replied with a determined nod. I couldn't let my hesitation show. Duty called and I had to answer.

With shared nods, we moved closer, forming a tight circle as we prepared for the journey back to the portal to the mortal realm. Aerion took the lead. His fingers found mine and Thalion's large hand enveloped both of ours.

Aerion began concentrating and the magic surged around us. It was a sensation like no other, an exhilarating rush that pulled at me. The world blurred and I closed my eyes as the palace faded into the distance.

When we emerged on the other side, it was as if reality was reassembling itself around us. I found myself standing in a lush forest, the scent of earth and foliage filling my senses.

I turned to Aerion and Thalion, offering them a smile filled with gratitude. "Thank you for coming with me," I said, my voice carrying the depth of my emotions.

Thalion's eyes held a protective warmth as he spoke, "Be careful, Vale."

Aerion's gaze, intense yet tender, bore into mine. "We'll be waiting for your return," he promised.

With a final glance at the two men I stepped away, moving towards the threshold that led back to the mortal realm. Their concern for me lingered as I plunged into the icy embrace of the portal.

Emerging on the other side, I found myself in a vastly different world, the familiar sights and sounds of the mortal realm enveloping me once more. I took a deep breath, adjusting to the shift in atmosphere.

"Come on, Nyxen," I called to my familiar who stepped out of the shadow of a tree.

"*Vale,*" he greeted me, his eyes dancing with warmth.

I smiled at the fox-like creature, a sense of relief filling me as it always did at being reunited with him. "Let's go home, buddy," I told him. He slid closer to me and his shadows enveloped me as we shifted to my apartment.

Nyxen's ebony form blended effortlessly into the shadows as he bounded ahead, eager to explore the surroundings of our cozy home. His presence always gave me a sense of reassurance, a reminder of the mystical world I had come to know so intimately. The mortal realm, with its simplicity and familiarity, was a welcome change of pace, and I couldn't help but appreciate the comfort it provided.

As I made my way down the hallway toward my bedroom, a peculiar sensation nagged at the edges of my consciousness. It was as though an invisible thread connected my very soul to an unknown source, gently pulling at me. I tried to dismiss the feeling, thinking perhaps it was the blood bond with Kaelan that I was feeling since I was back in the same realm as he was.

However, the persistent tug continued to gnaw at the back of my mind, refusing to be ignored. It was an odd sensation I couldn't quite shake and my steps faltered as I hesitated, my hand resting on the doorknob of my bedroom.

A sudden noise from the living room snapped me out of my reverie and I spun around, my heart pounding in my chest. Nyxen materialized at the end of the hallway, his luminous eyes filled with concern as they bore into mine.

I let out a shaky breath, relief washing over me as I realized the source of my anxiety was nothing more than my familiar. I chided myself for allowing nerves to get the better of me, especially in my own home.

"I'm fine, just jumpy," I assured Nyxen, offering him a weak smile.

The shadowkin tilted his head, a hint of understanding in his gaze as if he sensed that something was amiss beyond my momentary panic.

"Yeah, you're right," I mused, lowering my hand and taking a step closer to Nyxen. "The past few days have been pretty crazy, haven't they?"

With Nyxen beside me, I made my way to the library, passing through the wards with ease. There, at one of the well-worn tables, sat Harker, engrossed in her usual array of tomes and scrolls. She glanced up, her eyes keen and observant, as I entered the room.

"Vale!" she said, "I didn't know you were coming back today." She seemed genuinely surprised by my unexpected return, her expression filled with curiosity. I couldn't blame her for being taken aback; my return had indeed been hasty.

"It was a bit of a last-minute decision," I admitted as I settled into the chair beside her, offering a small smile in response to her questioning gaze.

She leaned in slightly, her eyes still fixed on mine. "So, are you back for good?" she inquired, her voice laced with both hope and uncertainty.

I couldn't help but let out a heavy sigh, my thoughts weighing on me. "No," I replied, my tone tinged with regret, "There are still things I need to take care of before I can fully return."

Her brow furrowed in response, and I could sense the concern emanating from her as she processed my words.

"How are things going here?" I asked her.

Before Harker could answer, a voice pierced the library's otherwise tranquil atmosphere. It was Elara, as spectral as ever, manifesting in front of our table with her ethereal presence.

"Things here are not good at all," she declared, her translucent form shimmering with vexation. Harker's eye-roll was not lost on me, nor was the pointed look she directed my way.

"She's upset because one of the older books fell apart in my hands," Harker explained, her tone suggesting that this wasn't an uncommon occurrence. "She thinks I did it on purpose and it took two days of me arguing with her to convince her to finally let me get back in here."

"I'm still not fully convinced," Elara chimed in, her arms crossed defiantly.

I sensed the impending argument but I intervened before it could escalate further. "Listen," I interjected, trying to sound soothing, "I'm sure the book will be fine."

Elara responded with an indignant "Hmph," clearly unimpressed with my reassurances.

Seeing that the situation was far from resolved, I decided to pivot the conversation.

"Do either of you feel anything...odd?" I asked, looking from Elara to Harker.

Elara, with her skepticism evident, responded with a question of her own. "Like what?" she asked, her tone laced with wariness.

"I'm not really sure," I admitted, "I've just been feeling a bit strange since I got back."

Harker's eyes narrowed and her voice carried a sense of worry as she probed further, "What do you mean by strange?"

Struggling to articulate the nebulous sensation, I explained, "Just like something isn't quite right."

Elara's expression grew grim and she spoke, her voice solemn. "Precognition is quite common among witches and you are no ordinary witch. I would not be surprised if your magical instincts are trying to tell you something."

Her words hung in the air, casting a shadow over our small gathering and an uneasy silence settled in the room.

Harker broke the silence, her voice strained with concern. "Is there anything we can do?"

"I'm not sure," I replied, feeling helpless.

The tugging sensation in the back of my mind grew more insistent, causing a shiver of unease to wash over me. I tried to push it aside, unwilling to let it consume my thoughts.

"Just keep an eye out for anything unusual," I finally told the two women.

"Of course," Harker replied, her gaze determined.

"You can count on me," Elara added, her ghostly form flickering slightly as if she could keep an eye on things while being bound to the library.

In an attempt to shift the conversation away from the ominous undertone, I turned to Harker. "So, Harker, found anything interesting in any of these books recently?" I asked, reaching for a random tome from her pile and flipping through its pages with feigned casualness.

Harker's lips quirked into a bemused smile as she responded, "Not unless you count a ritual to combine a cow with a boar. The Gods only know why that spell was created."

A genuine laugh escaped my lips and the tension that had settled among us began to dissipate. "Okay, I have to make sure to read that ritual," I said, handing the book I held back to her.

She chuckled in response before adding, "There was also this one..."

As Harker launched into another story, her eyes lit up with excitement, and the gloomy thoughts from earlier were pushed aside.

A few hours passed, filled with discussions ranging from magical theories to mundane topics. The presence of my friend was a balm to my soul.

But despite the comforting atmosphere, the unsettling sensation persisted, a constant reminder of something lurking beyond our immediate awareness. As we eventually parted ways, the thought of it continued to haunt me, lingering like a shadow in the back of my mind.

Nyxen's shadows surrounded me and in an instant, we shifted right into the heart of the werewolf camp. The sight that greeted me was nothing short of surprising: a mostly completed pack house stood proudly in the center of the camp, its formidable structure constructed from lightweight but sturdy metal. Flanking the pack house were two smaller buildings, one of which appeared to be finished already.

As I approached the large pack house I took in the bustling scene around me. Various pack members were engaged in their tasks, some diligently working to put the finishing touches on the buildings while others carried out different duties.

Among the bustling werewolves, a familiar face caught my eye. Joelene, someone I had met during a previous visit, looked up from her work as I passed by. Her friendly smile and warm greeting welcomed me back to the camp.

"Vale, welcome back," she said, her voice tinged with genuine warmth. I offered her a nod and returned her smile as I continued on my way, feeling a sense of belonging in this vibrant community.

As I stepped through the entrance of the pack house, I found myself in a vast, open room that immediately exuded a sense of warmth and community. It was clear that this space had been designed to serve as a central hub for the pack, a place where they could come together to celebrate and share meals.

My gaze was drawn to a set of stairs on one side of the room, leading up to an upper level. The faint sounds of construction echoed from above, indicating that there was still work to be done, but the progress was evident.

To my right, a wide doorway opened into a spacious kitchen, complete with all the modern amenities one would expect.

"Vale!" a familiar voice called out, pulling my attention away from my surroundings. Turning, I saw Venna approaching with a bright smile on her face.

I couldn't help but be impressed. "This place is amazing," I remarked, my eyes still taking in the surroundings. "How did all of this happen so fast?"

Venna's smile remained, and she replied, "We had a lot of help."

I shook my head in amazement. "I can see that," I said, appreciating the unity and hard work that had gone into building this place.

"The pack has really come together," Venna continued, her eyes shimmering with pride.

Regret gnawed at me, knowing that I hadn't been here to witness the pack's transformation and growth.

"Where's Wren?" I asked her.

"He's upstairs helping with the bedrooms," she replied.

I thanked Venna and made my way towards the stairs, eager to find Wren and catch up with him. As I ascended the staircase, the hallway revealed itself, lined with doors on either side. The scent of fresh sawdust permeated the air and the rhythmic sounds of hammers and drills echoed in the background.

I ventured further into the hallway, where the activity seemed to be concentrated. Each door represented a future bedroom and the sight was a testament to the pack's dedication to their new home. Not everyone would fit in here but it was a start.

Finally, I found Wren inside one of the rooms, working alongside others to hang a door in place. His face lit up with a broad smile as he noticed my approach.

"Vale, you're back," he exclaimed, setting down his tools and moving to embrace me in a warm hug.

"I am," I replied, returning his smile. "And it looks like you've been busy."

Wren nodded, his gaze briefly drifting to the others in the room who were also busy with their tasks. "We've had a lot of help," he said, echoing what Venna had told me earlier.

I couldn't help but be amused by how in sync those two had become. "That's what Venna said too," I chuckled.

"How was the Fae realm?" He asked, his expression turning serious.

"It was...interesting," I replied, choosing my words carefully to convey the complexity of my experience.

His curiosity piqued, he leaned in slightly, his gaze unwavering. "And those guys? Are they as bad as the Fae were rumored to be?"

A soft laugh escaped me at his question. "They are certainly not good," I admitted with a grin. "But I think we can trust them."

A mischievous smirk tugged at the corner of Wren's lips as he teased, "As long as you can handle them."

I couldn't resist poking his chest playfully. "Hey, I can handle anything," I retorted, a playful glint in my eyes.

He chuckled. "Well, I'm glad you're back," he said warmly, pulling me into another warm hug.

"I'm glad to be back," I murmured, leaning into the embrace, savoring the sense of homecoming.

"Now, tell me everything that happened in the Fae realm," he requested, his hand finding mine as he led me out of the room.

The rest of the afternoon was spent in lively conversation, sharing tales and catching up on everything that had transpired during my time away.

As we talked, I felt that peculiar sensation still in the back of my mind that tugged on me. I had been so focused on ignoring it that I was shocked when the sensation intensified, refusing to be ignored any longer.

"Wren, something is wrong," I whispered, my eyes locking onto his.

His brow furrowed, his eyes searching mine as he leaned forward slightly, his demeanor shifting from casual to attentive. "What do you mean?" he asked, his voice curious.

I took a moment to find the words to describe the sensation that had been haunting me since my return. "I've been feeling strange ever since I got back," I began, my voice trembling slightly with unease. "There's this feeling in the back of my mind, and I can't shake it. It's like an impending sense of...I don't know danger, maybe."

He leaned back in his chair, his expression thoughtful. "And you haven't experienced this feeling before now?" he asked, concerned.

I shook my head, my mind racing to find any similar experiences in my past, but there were none. "No, not like this," I admitted, the unease knotting in my stomach.

For a moment, silence hung heavy between us as Wren processed my words, his gaze never leaving mine. It was clear that he was taking my concerns seriously and his response was deliberate.

"We could go check the perimeter," he suggested after a contemplative pause. "Maybe if we walk the grounds, we'll notice something unusual or out of place."

His suggestion was met with a surge of relief from my end and I nodded vigorously, grateful for his willingness to investigate the matter. "Yes, that sounds like a good idea," I agreed.

The sun was beginning to dip below the horizon as Wren and I ventured out toward the outskirts of the werewolf camp. Shadows grew longer and the forest seemed to take on a different character in the fading light.

As we walked side by side, I couldn't shake the uneasy feeling gnawing at me. My senses were on high alert, every rustle in the leaves and hoot of an owl making me jump.

"Wren, this feeling is getting stronger," I admitted, glancing up at him. His expression was serious, clearly concerned.

"I believe you, Vale," he said, his voice steady. "Trust your instincts. They've served you well before."

I nodded, appreciating his support, even as a shiver of anxiety coursed through me. The woods around us felt unusually still, as though they were holding their breath.

We reached the edge of the camp and began our patrol, moving silently among the trees. The tension in the air was undeniable, and I couldn't help but feel as though we were being watched.

"Wren," I whispered, my voice barely audible. "Do you hear that?"

He paused, his ears perking up. "Voices," he confirmed, his gaze scanning the forest. "But they're distant."

The indistinct murmurs seemed to come from deeper in the woods and I felt a sense of foreboding wash over me.

"We should investigate," Wren said, determination in his eyes.

"Wait, Nyxen can go and see for us, they won't be able to see him."

"Good idea," he said as I called to Nyxen, silently asking him to go and check things out. My familiar slipped into the shadows and I could feel him moving away.

The atmosphere in the forest grew tenser with each passing moment as Wren and I waited for Nyxen to return with information. The dappled moonlight filtered through the thick canopy of leaves above, casting eerie shadows on the forest floor.

In the stillness, Nyxen's presence in my mind was a comforting thread of connection. He melted into the darkness, his form indistinguishable from the shadows themselves, and I could sense his stealthy movements as he ventured deeper into the woods.

We waited with bated breath, our senses attuned to any signs of danger. Minutes stretched into an agonizing silence, amplifying our unease. But soon enough, Nyxen's reassuring presence returned, a mental image painting a vivid picture of what he had observed.

In my mind's eye, I saw a group of figures moving through the dense undergrowth, their movements deliberate and calculated to minimize sound. Donovan led the way, his demeanor betraying his intent. Behind him were approximately two dozen individuals, their faces obscured by the shadows, making identification difficult.

"Wren, it's Donovan, he's accompanied by a bunch of others," I conveyed, my voice barely more than a breath of air. "But there are probably more coming from a different direction since there are only about three dozen of them."

The revelation sent a jolt of alarm through us both and Wren's reaction was swift and decisive. His anger was evident as he clenched his fists, his eyes flashing with an intensity I had rarely witnessed.

"Donovan is here?" he snarled, his voice a low, dangerous growl.

"Yes," I replied, my own apprehension echoing his. "And he's attempting to approach the camp undetected."

A surge of determination filled Wren and he wasted no time. "Not on my watch," he declared with fierce resolve. "We need to go and warn everyone."

I nodded in agreement, the urgency of the situation propelling us into action. With our hearts pounding in unison, we turned as one and raced back through the forest, each step carrying the weight of impending danger.

Chapter Twenty-Eight

As we approached the camp, I couldn't help but feel the gravity of the situation intensify. The camp, once a haven of safety, now stood on the precipice of a potential confrontation.

Without hesitation, I sought out Venna, my voice quick and decisive as I delivered the dire news. "Donovan and some others are attempting to sneak up on the camp."

Venna's eyes widened in shock at the revelation. "What?" she gasped, her voice trembling.

Wren's authoritative command cut through the chaos. "You need to gather everyone who can't fight and get them inside the pack house. The rest of you, head to the edges of the camp immediately."

She nodded, the urgency reflected in her eyes, and without wasting another moment, she began issuing orders to the pack members, their responses swift and coordinated.

As the werewolves dispersed, the camp became a hive of activity, each member moving with a sense of urgency fueled by the impending threat. I felt the enormity of the situation bearing down on me. Donovan and his followers were on their way and it was up to us to defend the camp.

I watched with trepidation as the pack members transformed into their wolf forms. The transformation was swift, a blur of fur, muscle, and bone shifting to adapt to their more primal selves. The camp seemed to hold its breath as everyone prepared for the confrontation.

Standing with Wren and Venna, I could feel the adrenaline coursing through my veins, my senses attuned to every sound and movement in the forest. The tension was thick in the air and a hush settled over the camp, broken only by the occasional rustle of leaves and the soft growls of the wolves preparing for battle.

In the distance, the sounds of approaching footsteps grew louder, a steady rhythm that seemed to echo the racing of my heart. I held my breath, my muscles tense and my fingers itching for the power at my disposal. But I raised my weapons instead, not willing to use such brutal force on these intruders unless absolutely necessary. The amount of devastation I could cause would be catastrophic.

They emerged from the shadows as a formidable force, their figures etched with determination and a cold resolve in their eyes. The moonlight cast eerie shadows on their faces, making them appear even more menacing. Donovan, in particular, bore a steely expression, his presence commanding and unwavering.

The moment had come and our camp stood ready to defend against this impending threat. The clash between our pack and Donovan's group was inevitable, and the air crackled with the promise of battle. The fate of our home hung in the balance and I knew that the coming moments would determine the course of our future.

As my anxiety reached its peak, a series of haunting howls pierced the night air, reverberating through the camp. The eerie cries signaled the arrival of more and more intruders, closing in on us from all sides. The hair on the back of my neck stood on end and a chill ran through me as the situation escalated.

In response to the looming threat, Wren gave a sharp and commanding growl that echoed across the camp. It was a signal for the werewolves to spring into action, a call to arms that couldn't be ignored. Without hesitation, the pack members and Otherworlders surged forward, meeting the attackers head-on.

The clearing erupted into a chaotic symphony of sound. Growls and snarls filled the air, blending together in a cacophony of ferocity. The night came alive with the frenetic energy of the clash and the atmosphere was charged with adrenaline and fear.

Bodies collided in a brutal ballet of combat, the wolves clashing with the intruders. Teeth gnashed and claws tore through flesh, leaving behind a trail of agony and fury. It was a harrowing and gruesome scene as the battle raged on under the moonlit canopy.

At that moment, there was no room for hesitation or doubt. Our pack fought with unwavering resolve, determined to protect their home and loved ones at any cost. The fate of the camp hung in the balance and the struggle for survival unfolded in a chilling and relentless crescendo of violence.

I jumped into the fray, my weapons flashing in the moonlight as they met fur and fangs.

Some of the intruders stood on two legs instead of four, where had these Otherworlders that fought with them come from? It was just as I came face to face with one that I noticed the grey Academy uniforms. My heart quickened with dread. The Academy had finally located us after five long years of eluding their grasp. The implications of their arrival were not lost on me.

Would this be the end of their pursuit, or were they planning to send even more officers our way? The Academy had an insidious way of holding onto its assets, especially those who were highly trained and at the top of their class, like Wren and me.

Turning my attention back to the battle, I rejoined Wren's side. Together, we moved in perfect harmony, our combat skills honed through years of training. Our strength and agility made us a formidable duo and it didn't take long for the intruders closest to us to recognize the threat we posed. Their tactics shifted and they began targeting us specifically, diverting their attention away from the werewolves.

Donovan, the apparent leader of the invaders, seemed to understand this shift in strategy. He closed the distance between us, his predatory gaze locked onto Wren and me. With a primal roar, he signaled his followers to converge on us and the battlefield became a maelstrom of chaos.

The ensuing struggle was brutal, a relentless clash of wills and physical prowess. Our forces fought valiantly, but the sheer number of attackers threatened to overwhelm us. Out of the corner of my eye, I glimpsed Donovan locked in a fierce duel with Wren, both warriors displaying their formidable skills.

The air reverberated with the guttural growls of combatants and the acrid scent of blood and sweat hung heavy in the night air. The ground beneath us became slick with crimson, a stark testament to the ferocity of the battle. Exhaustion gnawed at my muscles and every movement felt like a herculean effort, but there was no room for surrender. With grim determination, I pushed through the pain and continued to fight, knowing that the fate of our camp and its inhabitants hung in the balance.

Amidst the frenzied clash of combatants, a sudden convergence of shadows caught my eye and to my astonishment, Kaelan emerged from the darkness. He materialized with a fluid grace, his sword already drawn and poised for battle.

"What are you doing here?" I gasped, sweat and exertion coating my skin as I parried the relentless assault of a grey and white wolf, its teeth narrowly missing my arm.

Kaelan's grin was infuriatingly cocky as he replied, "I felt your presence when you returned to the mortal realm and I sensed your fear not long ago. I figured something must be happening. I couldn't just ignore that, now could I?" His tone was laced with amusement. "I thought a bit of fun was in order."

I couldn't help but roll my eyes, the absurdity of the situation not lost on me. "Right, fun. Just what we need."

Turning my attention back to the fight, I observed Kaelan's movements with a mix of awe and gratitude. He flowed through the battlefield with an otherworldly grace, his sword an extension of his will. Each strike he executed was a symphony of precision, a lethal dance that dispatched attacker after attacker.

As I continued to fend off my own adversaries, a sense of relief washed over me. Kaelan's presence was a welcomed boon amid chaos. With him on our side, this fight might be over a lot more quickly. I pushed the thought of him out of my head and refocused my attention on a massive black wolf that threatened to breach my defenses.

Time seemed to warp and the battle unfolded in slow motion. The werewolves around Kaelan and I held their ground, despite the mounting exhaustion and the evidence of their injuries. The air was filled with the sounds of snarls, growls, and clashing weapons. The battlefield was a gruesome tableau of carnage.

Amidst the brutality, I couldn't shake the somber realization of the lives lost on both sides. It all felt like such a senseless waste, a tragic consequence of the relentless conflict that had ensnared us.

A sharp yelp of pain caught my attention, drawing my gaze to the sound. Donovan loomed menacingly over the russet form of Wren, who lay momentarily knocked unconscious. My heart clenched and a fierce cry of anger and determination escaped my lips.

Without hesitation, I rushed toward them, my every instinct screaming to protect Wren from his imminent demise. Donovan's intent was clear and I refused to allow it to become a grim reality.

As I made my way through the fray, my magic surged within me, its newfound potency coursing through my veins. I wielded it with confidence, channeling the energy into a focused strike that hit Donovan squarely in the side. The force of my attack sent him hurtling backward, a yelp of pain tearing from his lips.

A wicked, triumphant smile spread across my face as I finally reached Wren, standing over him protectively, my weapons at the ready. The stakes were high, and I was determined not to let Donovan harm him.

"I don't think so, asshole," I growled, my voice low and charged with defiance. My eyes bore into Donovan's, my resolve unwavering.

Donovan snarled in response, his anger and frustration etched in the fury that danced in his eyes. We faced each other with the tension between us, the world around us seemingly shrinking until it felt as if we were the only two beings in existence.

"This ends here, Donovan," I declared, my voice unwavering, the tension in the air thick.

He growled in response, his body tensing like a coiled spring, his predatory instincts taking over. I stood ready, fully aware that this was a fight that would go on until one of us was dead.

Donovan lunged forward, his powerful jaws snapping, but I was prepared. My weapons flashed with deadly intent, the resounding clang of steel meeting fur and bone echoing through the battlefield.

He snarled, undeterred, and attacked once more, but this time, I was faster. With a swift, precise motion, my blade cut a deep gash across his flank, eliciting a pained howl.

"That's right," I hissed through clenched teeth, adrenaline coursing through my veins. "You picked a fight with the wrong bitch."

Donovan's eyes burned with a volatile mix of fury and fear. He began to circle me, calculating, searching for an opening, but I remained vigilant. My senses were finely tuned to his every move and I was resolute in not letting him gain an advantage.

My latent magic surged within me, a powerful force begging to be unleashed. Yet, the risk of harming our own allies nearby held me back.

"You might as well give up," I taunted him, unwavering in my determination. "You're not going to win this."

A low growl escaped Donovan's throat, but it was evident that his confidence was waning. The fight pressed on, Donovan pouring all of his remaining strength into his attacks, but desperation tainted each move.

I countered his every assault with skill and precision, my blades finding their mark, each strike taking a toll on him.

Behind me, Wren began to rouse, still dazed and struggling to regain his senses.

"Wren, I've got this," I shouted over the tumultuous battle, aware of the urgency but also wanting to reassure him. "You focus on recovering."

His groggy acknowledgment was a barely audible whine as I swiftly ducked under a massive paw, rolling to evade the lethal strike. My blade found its mark, slicing deeply across Donovan's chest.

"You're losing, Donovan," I taunted.

Donovan snarled in response, his lips curling back, revealing blood-stained fangs. He lunged at me with relentless force and I braced myself for the inevitable impact.

As his massive form collided with mine, we tumbled to the ground, a frenzied tangle of fur and limbs. Our desperate grapple left me at a disadvantage; his size and strength overwhelmed me. His heavy paws pinned me down, his hot breath and drool dripping onto me. I fought against the crushing weight, struggling for even a glimmer of leverage.

"Get. Off. Me," I snarled, my voice fraught with determination and rage.

Donovan chuffed in response, a deep rumble emanating from his chest, a cruel enjoyment in his nearing victory.

But I had reached my breaking point. My magic surged within me, an uncontrollable torrent of power that I no longer needed to rein in. It was as if a dam had burst and the magic flowed through me unchecked.

With a roar, I unleashed it upon Donovan, a violent tempest of energy that engulfed him. He was torn from me and thrown backward with brutal force, his body slamming into a nearby tree.

I rose to my feet, my magic still coursing through me, its exhilarating energy surging in my veins. My hands, now glowing with the raw power, curled into fists as I approached the fallen foe.

"This ends now," I declared, my voice ringing with a potent blend of conviction and unleashed might.

Donovan struggled to get up, but the impact had clearly stunned him, rendering him unable to rise to his feet. His once-mighty presence was now reduced to a pathetic, wounded creature.

I approached him cautiously, my gaze unwavering and filled with a complex blend of anger, pity, and a hint of sorrow. My heart ached at the sight of him, fallen and broken, even though he had brought this violence upon himself.

I stood over him, my emotions churning inside me. It would have been so easy to end it all right then and there, to end him, and bring this nightmarish battle to a close. But as I looked at the lifeless bodies scattered around us, the aftermath of the relentless bloodshed, I couldn't bring myself to deliver the final blow.

"It's over, Donovan," I declared, my voice firm and resolute, tinged with a measure of sympathy.

He whimpered, his eyes a tumultuous mixture of fear and seething hatred, his pride shattered.

"This is your last chance," I warned, my voice edged with an underlying threat. "If you ever come near the werewolves again, if you ever attempt to harm them, I will not hesitate to end you in the most gruesome way I can imagine."

In his eyes, I could see the lingering defiance, but he remained stubbornly silent.

Turning away from him, I began to walk away, the weight of what had transpired bearing down on me. My heart felt heavy, burdened by the choices I had made and the lives that had been lost.

But then, as I ventured further from Donovan's prone form, a deafening snarl pierced the air from behind me. I whirled around just in time to witness him lunging once again, his body propelled toward me, jaws agape, claws outstretched.

Before I could react, a massive, dark figure intercepted him in mid-air. Kaelan materialized with an incredible swiftness, his sword held firmly in his grasp. With unerring precision, he impaled Donovan, driving the blade through his heart.

"Never turn your back on a threat, Vale," Kaelan admonished, a smirk playing at the corners of his lips, his eyes gleaming with a mixture of amusement despite the fact that he had just ended a life.

I stared down at Donovan's lifeless corpse, his once-defiant eyes now dull and vacant, the light extinguished forever.

The tension that had gripped me just moments before began to dissipate, replaced by a profound sense of gratitude. I muttered a heartfelt, "Thanks," under my breath, my voice trembling with relief as I glanced at Kaelan.

His eyes softened, his features displaying a rare moment of tenderness. With a gentle gesture, he reached out, tucking a stray strand of hair behind my ear. His touch was delicate, a stark contrast to the fierce battle that had raged around us. "Anytime, little witch," he whispered.

Sensing that our victory was inevitable, the remaining intruders began running back toward to the woods, a few wolves giving chase. With their diminished numbers they wouldn't be returning anytime soon.

The fragile tranquility of the moment was abruptly shattered by a deafening howl that echoed through the forest. We turned as one, our eyes locking onto the approaching figure of Venna as she shifted back into her human form, her expression twisted with wild worry.

"Wren!" she cried out, her voice carrying an edge of desperation that pierced the air.

We followed her gaze and saw Wren, battered and bloodied but mercifully conscious. He lay amidst the aftermath of the fierce battle, a testament to the brutality of the conflict.

"He'll be okay, Venna," I assured her, my voice carrying a soothing tone that I hoped would provide her with some comfort.

Her eyes met mine and she nodded in acknowledgment before hurrying toward Wren. The fellowship of the pack was evident as they rallied together to care for the injured and pay their respects to the fallen.

With the adrenaline of battle fading, the heavy weight of exhaustion began to settle over me. I couldn't fight it any longer and I allowed myself to sink to the clearing floor. The earth beneath me was cool and solid, a welcome respite after the tumultuous events of the night.

Closing my eyes, I attempted to regain my composure, seeking a moment of respite from the chaos that had engulfed us. But the tranquility was short-lived.

"Vale," Kaelan's voice called softly, pulling me from my momentary reverie. "You're hurt."

Reluctantly, I looked down at my own body, taking stock of the injuries I had sustained during the brutal fight. The once adrenaline-fueled determination that had kept me going was now replaced by a sense of vulnerability.

"Oh, it's nothing, I'm fine," I replied, my voice carrying a strained note as I attempted to downplay my condition.

Kaelan disregarded my attempt at stoicism, moving closer with a grace that seemed out of place amid the chaos. His touch was gentle as he began to assess the extent of my injuries, his fingers brushing against my skin with care and concern.

"You're not fine," he said, concern evident in his tone. I couldn't help but appreciate the worry for my well-being, even as I tried to downplay the severity of my injuries.

"It's not that bad, Kaelan. Besides, I've had worse," I insisted, offering him a feeble smile in an attempt to reassure him.

His frown deepened, and it was clear that he wasn't convinced by my words. "Let me help you, Vale," he implored, his voice barely rising above a whisper. His sincerity tugged at my heartstrings, making it difficult to resist his offer. "Please," he added, his gaze locking firmly onto mine, his eyes searching mine.

A wave of emotion washed over me, my defenses crumbling under the weight of his presence. The closeness we shared in that moment felt almost overwhelming.

"Okay," I breathed, my voice a soft whisper. "But I've got to check on Wren first." Kaelan nodded in understanding, his expression relieved.

I approached Wren, my heart still racing from the battle, and knelt beside him to check on his injuries. His eyes were open now and while he looked battered and bruised, there was a reassuring strength in his gaze.

"He's fine," I reported, my voice infused with relief as I gave Wren's shoulder a reassuring pat. "Can't believe you missed some of the action, buddy." I teased him.

Venna, who had been anxiously watching our interaction, offered me a grateful smile. Her voice was barely audible as she expressed her gratitude. "Thank you, Vale."

I returned her small smile with a nod, understanding the depth of emotion that passed between us at that moment. The bond among us had grown stronger through the trials we had faced together.

I turned my attention back to Kaelan. "Let's go, little witch," he said, his voice steady.

I nodded in agreement, falling into step beside him as we made our way through the camp. The aftermath of the battle was evident everywhere we looked, but the worst of the fight was indeed over. Now, it was time to tend to the wounded, honor the fallen, and rebuild what had been damaged.

As we walked through the camp, I couldn't help but steal glances at Kaelan, his features a mix of rugged handsomeness and genuine concern. It was impossible to ignore the complexity of emotions that surged within me. The initial anger and resentment that had fueled our interactions were now giving way to a more complicated understanding. He had come here to help, to make amends, and I had to grudgingly admit that his presence had been a significant factor in our victory.

My gaze swept across the camp, taking in the aftermath of the battle. The sight of blood-splattered earth and the fallen bodies of both our enemies and our own kind left me shaken. We had been fortunate and I couldn't deny that without Kaelan's unexpected aid, the outcome could have been far worse. He had faced numerous attackers single-handedly, risking his life to protect us.

Reaching Wren's tent, I stepped inside, feeling the weight of exhaustion and pain settle upon me. It was a relief to finally lower my guard, even if only for a moment. Kaelan's soft voice broke through my thoughts. "Vale."

I turned to look at him, his eyes filled with tenderness and genuine concern. It was a gaze that left me feeling exposed, my conflicted emotions bubbling beneath the surface.

"Why don't you sit down," he whispered, his words carrying a gentle sincerity.

A wave of emotions surged within me, my inner turmoil battling with the past and the undeniable connection we once shared. I couldn't deny the complexity of my feelings for him any longer.

"Okay," I said, my voice wavering slightly as I moved to sit on Wren's worn couch.

Kaelan nodded, his hands moving with gentle precision as he began to remove my bloodied shirt. The touch of his fingers against my skin caused a sharp sting as they brushed over my wounds.

"Sorry," he murmured, his eyes filled with sympathy, the sincerity of his apology hitting me like a bittersweet reminder of our shared past.

I braced myself as Kaelan began to carefully peel the fabric of my shirt away from the lacerations, gritting my teeth to stave off the sharp surge of pain that accompanied the movement. His touch was surprisingly gentle, his fingers tracing over my skin with a feather-light touch that sent a shiver down my spine.

"Just relax, Vale," he whispered, his voice soothing, as if he knew just how to calm the turmoil within me.

I took a deep breath, exhaled slowly, and closed my eyes, allowing myself to surrender to the sensation of his fingers tending to my wounds. The pain ebbed into the background, overshadowed by the delicate touch of his hands.

He moved away for a moment, crossing the large space to retrieve the first aid kit from a corner. As he returned and resumed cleaning and bandaging my wounds, the warmth of his body seemed to radiate around me, and his scent of woodsmoke and whiskey filled my senses.

Amid the pain and the chaos of the camp, a sudden memory flashed through my mind—the first time he had kissed me. The intensity of that moment, the raw passion we had shared, it all rushed back to me in a dizzying whirlwind of emotions. I swallowed hard, forcing the memories back into the recesses of my mind, where they belonged.

Finally, Kaelan spoke, his voice low and close to my ear as he declared, "There, all done."

I opened my eyes to find his face mere inches from mine, the intensity of his gaze locking with mine. The atmosphere was charged with unspoken emotions, and the tension between us seemed to grow with each passing second.

"Thank you, Kaelan," I whispered, my voice barely audible over the backdrop of the camp's commotion.

His eyes held mine, their depths filled with a complex mix of emotions. He leaned in slowly, his lips brushing ever so lightly against mine. The touch was fleeting, a mere prelude to what could have been. But before he could deepen the kiss, I pulled back, a pang of guilt and confusion gripping my heart.

The hurt that flashed across his eyes as I retreated felt like a fissure in my soul. "Vale," he said, his voice raw and filled with longing, his eyes searching mine as if trying to decipher the turmoil within.

I shook my head, my inner struggle mirrored in the quiver of my voice. "Kaelan, we can't do this," I managed to say, my voice trembling with restraint.

"Why not?" he pleaded, desperation lacing his voice. His proximity was maddening, the magnetic pull between us threatening to break down the last of my defenses. Was that just the blood bond?

"Because we just can't," I replied, my voice cracking with the weight of our shared history and the consequences that hung in the balance.

He moved even closer, closing the gap until his body was a mere breath away from mine. His hand rose to cup my cheek, his touch tender yet searing in its intensity.

"We can, Vale," he said, his gaze penetrating, his eyes filled with a plea that tugged at my heart.

"No, we can't, not after everything," I whispered, my resolve waning as his proximity became increasingly unbearable.

"Please, Vale," he whispered again, his lips hovering tantalizingly close to mine.

A tumultuous wave of emotions surged within me, my heart racing in response to his proximity and the magnetic pull we had always shared.

"Kaelan, no," I said, my voice breaking as I tried to maintain the crumbling barrier between us.

But his hand slipped around my waist, pulling me closer, his touch setting my desire ablaze like a flickering ember. The proximity between us was a volatile mixture of longing and regret, and I found myself surrendering, unable to resist any longer.

"Vale," he murmured, his voice a low, husky plea, "please, let me show you how sorry I am."

His words were a siren's call, my resistance crumbling like a fragile dam. With a surge of desire and longing, I pulled him closer, our lips crashing together in a fierce, passionate kiss that left us both breathless and lost in each other's embrace.

Chapter Twenty-Nine

Kaelan pulled back, his eyes smoldering with desire, his breaths ragged and uneven. His whispered plea, "Stay with me," hung in the air like a seductive melody, beckoning me to surrender to the undeniable pull we shared.

For a moment, I stood there, locked in his heated gaze, my resolve teetering on the precipice of temptation. But then, as if awakened from a trance, I took a step back. What the hell was I doing? I couldn't allow myself to go down this road again.

"Kaelan, no, I can't," I said, my voice trembling with the inner turmoil that raged within me.

The anguish that flickered across his face pierced my heart like a dagger, but I knew deep down that succumbing to our desires would only lead to more pain and confusion.

"I have to go," I said, standing and turning away from him, my footsteps hurried.

"Vale," he called after me but I didn't dare look back. I had made my decision, right?

As I rushed out of the tent, the cool night air hit me like a cleansing wave, helping to clear my jumbled emotions. I took a deep breath, trying to regain my composure.

"Vale," a soft voice sounded nearby, startling me. I whirled around to find Wren standing there, his eyes filled with concern.

"Hey, how are you feeling?" I asked, my gaze scanning him for any wounds or injuries.

"I'm fine, Vale," he replied, his expression still marked by worry, "but are you?"

I shook my head, my emotions still a tangled mess that I couldn't easily unravel.

"I'm okay," I said, attempting to downplay the storm of emotions within me. "I'm just... a bit overwhelmed."

Wren nodded understandingly, his sympathetic gaze never wavering.

"Yeah, me too," he admitted, "but we made it, thanks to you, I'm told."

A small, genuine smile tugged at my lips, his words offering a measure of solace amidst the chaos that had enveloped us.

"That's what friends are for, right?" I said, forcing a smile despite the exhaustion that clung to me. "To have your back in the darkest times."

Wren's smile in response was warm, but it didn't quite reach his tired eyes.

"Wren you should go get some rest. I'm sure Venna could handle things for a little while," I suggested, concern for his well-being evident in my voice.

"She could, and she would. You should get some rest yourself," he replied, his voice equally concerned.

I nodded in reluctant agreement, knowing he was right. We were both in desperate need of rest, physically and emotionally, but I knew he wouldn't be going to rest, not with so much to do now that the fighting was over. He pulled me into a quick, reassuring hug before turning to leave.

"Stay safe, Vale. Come back more often," he said, his voice a quiet plea.

Watching him walk away, a sense of responsibility weighed heavily on my shoulders. "I'll try, Wren," I whispered, more to myself than anyone else.

I called Nyxen to my side and he emerged gracefully from beneath the shadow of a nearby tent.

"Are you okay?" he asked his words echoing directly into my mind. It was the first time I had heard him form a complete sentence.

"Maybe," I replied, not bothering to hide my feelings from him. He sensed my turmoil through our bond. "I could just really use some rest though. Take me home?"

"Of course," he replied, his tone filled with understanding.

The cool embrace of darkness enveloped me as Nyxen transported us, the familiar shadows comforting and reassuring. I closed my eyes, allowing myself to be carried away, the weight of the day slowly fading into the obscurity of the night.

The next day in the Fae realm, as the golden sunlight filtered through the intricate patterns of leaves above, Thalion and Aerion had a determined air about them. They'd been eager to share their news with me, and as we gathered in the courtyard beneath towering trees, I couldn't help but feel curious.

"We have made a decision," Thalion announced, his voice somewhat excited. We had gathered in a small clearing near one of the lush gardens and I sat on a moss-covered stone, waiting for them to reveal their plan. "We're going to introduce you to the Fae of my court and we're going to be doing it today."

I blinked, momentarily taken aback by the suddenness of their decision. "Introduce me?" I asked, my brow furrowing as I processed his words.

Aerion, who stood beside Thalion, his features serene, nodded and added, "As a witch."

My heart raced at the idea and I had to voice my concerns. "Are you sure about this?" I said as my gaze shifted from Aerion to Thalion, lingering on the silver-haired Fae prince.

Thalion met my gaze with unwavering determination. "Yes," he replied, his voice firm and resolute. "We've thought it through, Vale."

I knew this was a significant step, one that couldn't be undone. "It's a big step, Thalion, and there's no going back. Word will spread about me," I cautioned.

"That's exactly what we're planning on," Thalion said with conviction. "Just trust us."

His unwavering faith in me was both reassuring and daunting. After a moment of contemplation, I reluctantly nodded in agreement. "Okay, if you're sure, let's do it."

Aerion gave me an encouraging smile. "We'll start gathering everyone, you go and get ready. Make sure whatever you wear makes an impression."

After Thalion and Aerion had shared their decision with me, they escorted me back to my room. The air was thick with anticipation as they left, heading off to start spreading the word about the impending meeting. They had mentioned it would take a few hours for everyone to gather.

Once alone, I took a moment to collect myself, fully aware that today marked a momentous change. The fate of our plans rested on the reactions of the Fae to my introduction as a witch. I could only hope that Thalion's faith in their acceptance was well-placed.

After a brief pause to calm my nerves, I began to prepare for the meeting. I knew that first impressions were crucial and I wanted to present myself in the best possible way.

The first order of business was a relaxing bath, washing away the grime and fatigue from the previous day's events. The warm water and scented oils eased my tension, and I emerged feeling refreshed. The superficial wounds I had incurred during the battle at the camp were already mostly healed.

I turned to my closet, contemplating various outfit options. I selected a few dresses that could work for the occasion, each one carefully chosen. However, my eyes kept returning to a particular dress – a long, flowing black gown with intricate silver embroidery adorning the sleeves and bodice. It reminded me somewhat of the attire the First Witch had worn during her visit in my dreams.

In a short while, Amris, Kelli, and Joelene arrived, ready to assist me in getting ready for the occasion. Amris helped me step into the elegant black dress, its fabric cascading around me. Kelli and Joelene, with their nimble fingers and expertise, crafted a beautiful arrangement of braids in my hair.

As they finished their work, I turned to gaze at my reflection in the mirror. A stranger looked back at me – tall, regal, and exuding a confidence that I didn't entirely feel. But in this moment, appearances mattered. I may not have felt entirely comfortable in this new role, but I was determined to carry myself with the grace and confidence the situation demanded. Today, I had to be someone I never imagined I could become, at least for the sake of our plans and the Fae realm.

Several hours had passed since Thalion and Aerion had initially shared their decision with me. While waiting, I had taken refuge in the grimoire Harker had provided, its pages filled with ancient knowledge and enchanting spells. My heart fluttered with anxiety when Aerion's gentle knock broke my concentration. I marked my place in the grimoire and set it aside.

"Everyone is waiting," Aerion informed me, his grey eyes carrying a sense of seriousness.

"Let's do this," I replied, rising from my seat.

Aerion offered me his arm, which I gratefully accepted. He led the way through the intricate corridors of the palace, guiding me towards the throne room. It was a part of the palace I had yet to explore.

As we entered the throne room, my eyes were met with a sight I hadn't fully prepared for. The grand chamber was filled with Fae, their expectant gazes fixed upon me. My palms grew sweaty and I took a deep breath to steady myself.

Aerion escorted me to the front of the room, and the crowd parted respectfully to allow us passage. Whispers followed in our wake as I took my place beside Thalion, the imposing thrones looming behind us. Thalion gently took my hand in his, offering a reassuring squeeze before he turned to address the assembly of Fae from his court.

"My friends, my kin, lend me your ears, for today marks the dawning of a new era! Unbeknownst to you, our revered Queen Elariel has been battling an ailment so grave it defies comprehension. A condition of the heart so grim, it brought us to our knees, desperate for answers."

A collective gasp rippled through the room, revealing the deep affection the Fae held for their queen.

Thalion paused, his gaze sweeping over the assembled Fae, his voice weighted with significance. "For a while now, things appeared dire. No healer within our realm possessed the knowledge to cure the sickness of the heart afflicting my mother. Until now," he continued, casting a meaningful glance in my direction.

"We find ourselves incredibly fortunate that this individual standing beside me possesses the gift to heal her. Beside me is not just a savior, but a living miracle—the reincarnation of the First Witch herself!" Thalion's words hung in the air and all eyes in the room shifted to me. The collective stares of the Fae bore down upon me and I felt my skin flush hot under their scrutiny. Whispers began to stir among the audience, filled with curiosity and wonder.

Thalion's voice remained firm as he addressed the assembly, "The Fae and the witches share a long and tumultuous history." He scanned the room, locking eyes with those present. "King Haldir, the insatiable conqueror, aims to imprison or obliterate this divine being before me. Driven by a dread of her unbridled might, he continues his unholy quest for dominion over us all. But we say, "No more!" For since the downfall of King Cael's court, his reign has spread like a plague, unchecked and unstopped—until today."

Nods of agreement rippled through the gathered Fae, their expressions etched with anger and determination. I knew there were many members of Aerion's court among them; they had suffered the most from Haldir's actions.

Thalion's voice carried a sense of pride as he continued, "Now, prepare yourselves for a revelation that will shake the very pillars of our realm. This force beside me is none other than the offspring of our lost princess Lyra—returned to us, like a phoenix from the ashes, to reclaim her destiny!" The throne room erupted into a cacophony of gasps, cheers, and joyous exclamations. I couldn't help but be surprised by their reaction. My eyes darted around the room and I saw expressions filled with happiness and wonder.

Thalion's gaze swept over the crowd before he continued, "So, as we stand on the precipice of history, I implore you: Pledge your unwavering loyalty to her. Shield her from the dangers that lurk in the shadows. Open your hearts and welcome her into our hallowed court. Will you rise? Will you join us to herald the genesis of a renaissance that will echo for generations to come? Stand by her side—now and forever!"

The Fae watched me in silence as I stood beside Thalion and then, one by one, they began to kneel. It was my turn to gasp, deeply moved by their show of allegiance.

The movement spread like a gentle wave through the room, Fae after Fae gracefully sinking to their knees, their heads bowed in a unanimous show of allegiance. The sight was overwhelming, and I could feel tears welling up in my eyes at the profound gesture of acceptance.

"Long live the First Witch and the future king!" someone cried out, their voice filled with fervor.

"Long live the First Witch!" The chant resonated through the room as the Fae echoed their support for me.

Thalion turned, his hand resting warmly on my shoulder. "They have accepted you, Vale. You are their people and they are your court."

"Thank you," I managed to say to the crowd, my voice trembling with emotion. This kind of reception was something I had never anticipated or imagined.

"Rise, everyone," Thalion proclaimed to the room. Slowly, the Fae began to stand once more. "The Queen wishes to commemorate this momentous occasion with a celebration to be held in two days' time. You are all cordially invited. Now, go and spread the word that our princess has returned. Let the world know of the First Witch, risen again."

The Fae in attendance began to disperse, their voices filled with excitement and anticipation as they eagerly discussed the news of my return and our upcoming celebration.

Aerion approached with an expression that was serene and pleased. "They accepted you, Vale," he remarked, the relief evident in his voice.

I could only nod in response, still dumbfounded by the unexpected turn of events. "I guess it worked," I replied.

Thalion chimed in, his gaze reflecting his contentment. "Yes, better than we could have ever hoped for."

The joy in my heart was barely containable. "It's incredible," I said, shaking my head, "and I honestly can't believe it."

Aerion and Thalion exchanged glances and then Thalion spoke, his tone becoming more serious. "You are the embodiment of the First Witch. You are a formidable ally to have."

However, Aerion offered a cautionary note, his tone thoughtful. "Your powers, however, are only half the battle. You are the daughter of a lost princess, which means more to the Fae of my court than words can express. The loss of our princess when my court was destroyed hurt more than the loss of the king. She was deeply beloved by all."

Thalion's gaze turned to the crowd of Fae as they dispersed from the throne room, his expression carrying a hint of melancholy. "It was devastating for all of us. For centuries, we've wondered what happened to Lyra and we've mourned her loss. But now, you're here. It's an unexpected gift, a ray of hope and happiness amid darkness. The news will spread across the realm and more will join our cause. They will be eager to lend their support."

Touched by their words and deeply moved by the sentiment behind them, I knew that in that moment, I would fight for their court, their home, and their future, just as fiercely as I would defend my own.

Chapter Thirty

As we left the throne room, a sense of accomplishment filled the air. The introduction to the Fae court had gone better than I could have ever imagined. Aerion, Thalion, and I walked down the corridor, engaged in a lively conversation about the reception and the fae's enthusiastic acceptance of me.

Aerion's eyes sparkled with pride as he spoke, "They accepted you, Vale. More than accepted, they embraced you as their own."

Thalion nodded in agreement, a smile playing at the corner of his lips. "It went perfectly and soon I'm sure they'll come to love you."

Their words filled me with warmth, and I couldn't help but smile in response. The weight of my role as the First Witch was lightened by their support and the adoration of the Fae of Thalion's court.

But just as I was basking in the afterglow of our success, Thalion's demeanor shifted. With a suddenness that caught me off guard, he pushed me against Aerion, who baked up against the cool stone wall, holding me there.

My heart raced as Thalion's hands slid down to my waist and his lips found their way to my neck. His breath was hot against my skin and his voice was a soft murmur in my ear, "I can't take the sight of you in that dress any longer."

My thoughts scattered as his lips moved down to my collarbone. His nuzzling and the sensation of his warm breath on my skin made heat curl low in my stomach.

"Thalion," I managed to breathe out, my voice trembling.

His eyes met mine and there was a spark of desire in them that mirrored my own. He didn't speak, but the longing in his gaze spoke volumes. Caught between the two of them, my mind raced with conflicting emotions. The corridor was empty but we were in plain sight, the threat of being caught heightening the moment.

Thalion's hands roamed down my sides, his fingers tracing patterns over the fabric of my dress. His lips moved to meet mine and I was lost in the whirlwind of sensations.

Desire coursed through me, I couldn't deny the pull they had over me, the overwhelming force that drew me closer to them. My hands moved up Thalion's chest, fingers trailing over the intricate patterns of his tunic. His lips pressed against mine with a deliberate slowness and I responded eagerly, parting my lips to allow his tongue to explore my mouth. A soft moan escaped my throat, muffled by the intensity of our kiss.

Thalion pulled away every so slightly, his hands shifting to cup my face, his eyes searching mine for any sign of hesitation. His uncharacteristic uncertainty was a stark contrast to his usual self-assured demeanor. It was as though he wanted to ensure I was fully comfortable with this unexpected turn of events.

But I had no intention of backing away. Instead, I pulled him toward me, my lips crashing against his with a fierce determination.

I lost myself in the taste of him, the urgency of his kiss, and the way his hands continued to explore my body.

In that passionate moment, all my worries and fears dissolved into the heat of our shared desire. There was no room for doubts or second thoughts. The only reality that mattered was the three of us, intertwined in a whirlwind of emotions and lust.

Aerion's lips found my neck, his teeth grazing my skin with a tantalizing touch as he held me in place. He kissed his way up my ear, nibbling on it, his breathing turning heavy as his arousal grew. His hands traced a path down my body, leaving a trail of fiery need in their wake.

Pausing at the bodice of my dress, Aerion's skilled fingers made quick work of the fabric, allowing it to fall away and reveal my bare skin beneath. His touch was electric, sending sparks of pleasure coursing through me as he cupped my breast, his thumb drawing slow, teasing circles around my sensitive nipple.

I was breathless, my senses overwhelmed by the intensity of desire that pulsed through me as the two males explored my body. With a deft, yet deliberate motion, Thalion hiked up the fabric of my dress, his fingers tracing a searing path along the sensitive skin of my inner thighs. I couldn't help but moan softly at the electrifying contact, a shiver of anticipation coursing down my spine as I yearned for what was to come.

In a swift maneuver, Aerion turned me around. His mouth claimed mine with an urgency that left me gasping for air, our lips locked in a passionate embrace that threatened to consume us both.

Thalion knelt behind me, his hands firmly gripping my thighs, fingers pressing into my flesh as he began a slow, deliberate ascent with a trail of kisses along my leg. Every brush of his lips sent waves of desire crashing through me and my legs trembled in response.

Aerion, sensing my weakening knees, caught me with ease, his lips brushing against my cheek as he whispered in a husky, sensual voice, "Hold onto me."

His strong arms encircled my waist, providing support as Thalion's mouth continued his thorough exploration of my body. His skilled fingers hooked around the hem of my undergarments, pulling them down and carelessly discarding them aside.

The abrupt exposure of my bare skin to the cool corridor air sent an exhilarating shiver racing down my spine. I was left entirely vulnerable, at the mercy of the two males whose desires and attentions were all-consuming. The thrill of the situation heightened the pleasure coursing through my body.

Thalion's hands roamed over the curves of my hips. His lips maintained their tortuously slow climb, inching dangerously close to the very point where I ached for his touch.

My breaths came in ragged, uneven gasps as he teased me relentlessly, the mounting anticipation reaching an almost unbearable level. Then, in one breathtaking moment, his fingers slipped inside me and an uncontrollable cry of pleasure escaped my lips. My body writhed against Aerion's and he responded by tightening his hold on me, his mouth urgently devouring mine as desire enveloped us completely.

Thalion's movements remained steady and expert, his fingers navigating my trembling body with an almost supernatural finesse. With each deliberate stroke, I felt myself succumbing to the tidal waves of pleasure that pulsed through me, rendering me utterly powerless and entirely at the mercy of the relentless electricity that threatened to consume my senses.

Thalion's rhythm quickened, his every touch and kiss becoming a blazing ember that fueled the inferno burning deep within me, propelling me ever closer to the edge.

In an exquisite moment of torment, Thalion's tongue joined the sensual dance of his fingers, and he lapped hungrily at my aching heat. My body reacted with an uncontrollable shudder and I was powerless to contain the uninhibited cries that escaped my lips, echoing through the otherwise empty corridor. The unrestrained passion of the two men as they ravished my body urged me on.

The pleasure was almost too much to bear. Overwhelmed and unable to resist, I teetered on the edge of an impending, powerful climax. With a final flick of Thalion's tongue and a deep, penetrating thrust, it happened. An electrifying surge of ecstasy engulfed me, sending shockwaves of bliss rippling through my entire being. I cried out shamelessly, the sound reverberating through the desolate hallway as I surrendered to the overwhelming feeling.

Aerion held me securely as I trembled with the aftershocks, his hands moving soothingly over my quivering form. Gradually, as my senses began to return, I became aware of Thalion's voice, low and entrancing, as he whispered to me, "That was beautiful." His hands tenderly caressed my trembling thighs. "But I'm not finished with you yet."

His promise sent a fresh wave of eager anticipation coursing through me, a renewed hunger for the pleasures yet to come. Without hesitation, Aerion's strong fingers intertwined in my hair, gripping it firmly yet tenderly as he tilted my head backward. His mouth claimed mine once again and our lips collided with an undeniable urgency.

Aerion lifted me up and I wrapped my legs around his waist, surrendering to the heady rush of emotions as the world around us exploded into a dazzling array of colors. In an instant, he had transported us to Thalion's rooms. The transition was seamless and though Thalion was conspicuously absent, I couldn't deny the thrilling anticipation that coursed through me.

"He'll catch up," Aerion murmured, his warm breath teasing my lips as he held me close.

He carried me to the grand bed, tossing me roughly onto the plush mattress as his intense gaze drank in every inch of my body. Desire smoldered in his eyes and I could feel the heat of his regard like a physical caress.

With a graceful motion, Aerion discarded his tunic, revealing the chiseled contours of his strong shoulders and the sculpted lines of his abdomen. My eyes greedily devoured the sight of his muscular form, the unmistakable bulge of his erection only intensifying the pulsing ache between my thighs.

His pants soon joined the pile on the floor and he stood before me, gloriously naked. His cock strained toward me, the sight alone igniting a fresh wave of longing within me.

Aerion's lithe form descended over mine and his skilled hands traced a sensuous path down my body, electrifying my senses with every caress.

"I can't wait any longer," he breathed, his voice husky with need.

"Neither can I," I responded, my voice a desperate plea as I pulled him closer.

A primal growl rumbled from deep within him as he covered my body with his own. His throbbing erection pressed insistently against me and even through the fabric of my dress, the scorching heat of his desire was unbearable.

His fingers found the hem of my dress, and with one swift motion, he yanked it over my head. The feel of his skin on mine was maddening.

Aerion's lips were everywhere, leaving fiery kisses, sensuous licks, and tantalizing bites in their wake as his hands roamed hungrily over my quaking form. Each touch was a searing blaze and I arched into him, desperate for more.

He poised himself between my legs, his arousal pressed tantalizingly against my eager entrance, hard and demanding. I was more than ready for him, and when he thrust into me, I nearly came undone.

A gasp escaped my lips as he filled me, my nails digging into his shoulders, anchoring myself to him. Aerion groaned in response. His grip on my hips was almost painful as he began to move, a rhythmic, primal dance that sent waves of ecstasy crashing over us both.

I matched Aerion's every powerful thrust, our bodies moving in rhythm. The room filled with the intoxicating sounds of our passion, punctuated by his primal growls and my fervent moans. Desire surged within me, reaching its precipice and I moaned loudly.

"I love the sounds you make when I'm inside you," Aerion groaned, his grip on my hips tightening as his fingers dug into my flesh. His thrusts grew more urgent, driving into me with a fierce intensity.

Just then, the door to the room swung wide open. Thalion stood in the doorway, an unabashed hunger in his eyes as he watched us. Without a word, he closed the door behind him and began to cross the room.

I couldn't tear my eyes away from Thalion as he moved closer, his hand starting to stroke himself, his unwavering gaze locked on the passionate tableau before him. The sheer intensity of his desire was evident and it sent a new wave of arousal coursing through me.

"Aerion, wait," I gasped, my voice strained with the urgent need for something more.

Aerion's thrusts stilled and he withdrew from me, his cock still hard and glistening. Confusion and concern mingled in his eyes as he looked at me. "I want to try something," I whispered, my gaze darting between Aerion and Thalion, my body aching for what I was about to propose.

Understanding flickered across Aerion's features and he nodded in anticipation. Thalion's expression remained inscrutable, but the unbridled lust in his violet eyes betrayed his desire.

Crawling across the bed, I moved closer to Thalion, taking a moment to admire every perfect line of his body. His strong jawline and sharp features accentuated his masculine beauty. The muscles in his arms rippled as he continued to stroke himself.

"Thalion," I breathed, my voice husky with need, "I want you, both of you."

"Vale," he replied, his voice a barely audible whisper. "Are you sure?" I nodded.

"I'm going to make you forget your own name by the time I'm done with you," Thalion remarked. "You are all ours."

Thalion's words sent a delicious thrill through me and the anticipation grew as the reality of the moment sunk in. Ours. The word held a promise of shared desire and pleasure and it fueled the fire within me.

Taking a confident step closer to Thalion, I reached out to place my hand on his chest. His skin was warm and taut beneath my touch and I could feel the rapid cadence of his heart, matching the quickening pace of our desires.

Thalion's readiness mirrored my own and I could see the primal hunger in his eyes. I moved closer, my fingers wrapping around his throbbing shaft. A shuddering breath escaped his lips as I began to stroke him, the velvety skin of his cock gliding smoothly through my grasp.

"Just like that," Thalion said, his voice a seductive growl. His response only ignited my own desire, knowing that I held the power to bring him pleasure and satisfaction.

His hand found its place on my hip, his grip firm and commanding as his arousal continued to build. Without hesitation, he shed his clothes, revealing every inch of his chiseled body.

"Come here," he directed, his tone demanding yet tinged with a raw need as he laid down on the bed. I obeyed, crawling over him as he swiftly turned me around to face Aerion. The hunger in Aerion's eyes mirrored Thalion's and he watched with rapt attention as Thalion's hands moved to grip my hips, his fingers trailing sensuously over the curves of my backside.

Thalion lifted me slightly, adjusting my position to allow him easy access. Aerion reached over to the bedside table, retrieving a small clear bottle and handing it to Thalion. I felt a warm liquid cascade down my ass as Thalion poured the oil onto my skin, adding an enticing slickness to our impending intimacy.

"We'll go slow," Thalion's voice was reassuring, "if it hurts, we can stop."

Thalion's words were reassuring as my anticipation and excitement continued to mount. I nodded, my heart pounding in my chest, ready to explore this uncharted territory with them.

His finger, coated in the slick oil, began to circle my tight opening, sending electrifying shivers down my spine. I couldn't help but moan, the sensation entirely new and unlike anything I'd ever experienced.

As Thalion's finger eased into me, I gasped at the incredible feeling. He moved with deliberate slowness, allowing me to adjust to the unfamiliar sensation. His free hand roamed sensuously over the curve of my ass, sending tingles of pleasure racing through me.

A second finger joined the first and the intensity of sensation multiplied. Thalion's fingers glided in and out of me, igniting waves of pleasure that surged through my body.

Glancing up at Aerion, I was met with a sight of desire and admiration on his face. He leaned down, capturing my lips in a fierce kiss that left me breathless, the intensity of it setting my senses ablaze.

Thalion's strained voice broke through the haze of desire. "Are you ready?"

With a gasp, I managed to respond, "Yes."

I felt the head of Thalion's cock press against me and he began to push inside. The sensation was nothing short of mind-blowing, the fullness and pressure, unlike anything I'd ever felt.

Aerion's hand found its way between my legs, his fingers skillfully circling my clit as Thalion continued to slide deeper within me. The combined sensations were overwhelming and I couldn't contain the loud cry of pleasure that tore from my lips as my body shuddered in ecstasy.

Thalion's grip on my hips tightened as he thrust deeper, each powerful motion filling me entirely. "Gods, you're so fucking tight." His husky words, soaked in desire, elicited another moan from me, my body responding to the intoxicating mix of sensations.

Aerion continued to tease my clit with expert fingers, drawing me into a whirlwind of pleasure. He moved forward on the bed, positioning himself over Thalion and me, his eyes locked onto mine as he watched us move.

Thalion's pace quickened, his thrusts growing deeper and harder with each passing moment. The mounting pressure within me had me writhing beneath their touch, craving more of their intense desire.

"Thalion," I moaned, the name escaping my lips in a breathy plea. My gaze flicked up to Aerion, who met my eyes with an intensity that sent shivers of pleasure racing down my spine.

With deliberate slowness, Aerion positioned himself over me, the head of his cock pushing gently against my entrance. As he entered me inch by inch, I gasped, the sensation of being stretched open by both Thalion's and Aerion's hard cocks nearly overwhelming.

Aerion's rhythmic thrusts began, his hips rocking against mine, while Thalion maintained his relentless pace beneath me. The two of them moved with exquisite precision and synchrony, their combined efforts working me into a state of pleasure unlike anything I had ever known.

As my body responded to their skillful touch, I closed my eyes, surrendering to the overwhelming moment. Their powerful movements, their fervent desire, all came together to bring me the most exquisite pleasure I'd ever experienced.

My skin was on fire from the heat of their bodies pressed against mine, their breath hot on my neck. The intense connection we shared was pushing us all to the brink of ecstasy, and the unbearable heat building between the three of us threatened to consume me whole.

"Yes, fuck me deeper," I whimpered, my voice barely more than a breathy plea, my body aching for release.

Thalion's thrusts grew faster, more urgent, his cock driving into me with a powerful force that left me gasping for breath. His hand reached up and wrapped around my neck, squeezing gently. Aerion's hips bucked wildly, his own hardness plunging deep within me, and the relentless pleasure threatened to push me over the edge.

"That's right, princess. Take it like a good girl," Thalion whispered, his breath dancing across my skin, his movements becoming erratic as he approached his climax.

"Scream for us, baby." Aerion groaned, biting my neck.

I couldn't hold back any longer. The sensation was too intense, the pressure too overwhelming, and I surrendered to the irresistible force of pleasure.

I cried out loudly, the sound echoing through the room, as the most powerful orgasm of my life coursed through me. It was all-encompassing, my entire body shaking as waves of ecstasy washed over me, leaving me trembling in its wake.

Thalion gasped in response, his cock throbbing inside me as he too reached his peak, his release spilling deep within.

Aerion, unable to hold back any longer, followed suit, his thrusts becoming frantic as he found his release, his cock twitching inside me with each blissful pulse.

The three of us collapsed in a tangle of limbs, our breaths coming in ragged gasps as we attempted to recover from the overwhelming intensity of the experience. The silence was broken only by the sound of our labored breathing.

I turned my gaze to Aerion, his brown hair damp with sweat, his grey eyes shining with satisfaction and tenderness.

"That was..." I began, struggling to find the right words to describe what we had just shared.

"Intense," Thalion finished for me, his voice a low, husky rumble that sent a shiver down my spine.

"Indeed," Aerion agreed, his expression mirroring the wonder and satisfaction on both of our faces. His grey eyes bore into mine, filled with a depth of emotion that left me breathless.

I couldn't help but smile as I basked in the afterglow, the warmth of the two males beside me comforting and reassuring. The room was filled with a sense of contentment and for a moment, all worries and doubts seemed to melt away.

My thoughts wandered to what lay ahead for the three of us, the possibilities and challenges that awaited. It was uncharted territory, a path we were forging together, but the prospect was undeniably thrilling.

The future was uncertain, but as I lay there, entangled with Thalion and Aerion, I couldn't help but feel that whatever came our way, we would face it together. The thought was a welcome one.

Chapter Thirty-One

The next few days passed by in a whirlwind of preparations as everyone got ready for the celebration the king and queen were throwing in my honor. Thalion was having a new dress made for me, stating that the ones I had weren't adequate enough for the occasion.

Our training continued in earnest. Thalion's dedicated effort to refine my abilities was both challenging and exhilarating. Each day, I could feel myself growing more attuned to the strange power that coursed within me. Thalion was a patient and skilled teacher, guiding me with a combination of encouragement and constructive criticism.

We practiced in the lush gardens of the Fae court, the vibrant flora serving as a backdrop to our training sessions as I practiced breaking through his mental defenses. The enchanting melodies of birdsong filled the air as I focused on harnessing the mental powers that had awakened within me. In the back of my mind, I couldn't help but compare this new power to the one my demon father had possessed.

Thalion watched me closely, his violet eyes never leaving my form. "Remember, Vale, it's not just about control; it's about connecting with the power. Imaging a wall you need to knock down, accessing the mind behind it."

I nodded, determination in my gaze. With each attempt, I grew more proficient, my power responding more readily to my intentions. Though Thalion's mental defenses were formidable.

Thalion's voice cut through the tranquility of the garden. "Your control is improving, but there's still a long way to go. We need to push your limits."

Aerion, who had been observing our training, chimed in with his usual dry humor. "Yes, because nothing says 'pushing limits' like having a magical mishap."

I couldn't help but laugh, my bond with the two Fae males growing stronger with each passing day. Despite the looming threat of Haldir and the impending celebration in my honor, we managed to find moments of light-heartedness and companionship.

Thalion walked toward me. "You're doing well, Vale," he said softly, his fingers brushing a strand of hair from my face. "I'm proud of your progress."

His praise sent a flush of warmth through me, and I met his gaze, my heart skipping a beat. "Thank you. I couldn't have asked for better mentors."

Aerion, leaning casually against a tree, added, "Don't let it go to his head, Vale. He's insufferable enough as it is."

Thalion's laughter cut through the serene atmosphere, echoing softly in the tranquil garden. His laugh was a testament to the joyous connection we shared, a stark contrast to the terrors that lurked on the horizon. I couldn't help but smile at the lighthearted exchange between the two Fae males. Their camaraderie was infectious.

The garden had transformed into a magical realm with the fading light of the sun. Twilight hues painted the sky above, casting a warm, golden glow over the lush foliage and vibrant flowers. The faint scent of night-blooming jasmine wafted through the air, adding to the enchantment of the moment. The garden seemed to come alive with an otherworldly charm as the first stars began to twinkle overhead. Fireflies danced in the gathering darkness, casting a soft, ethereal glow around us.

With a deep breath, Thalion began to broach the topic that had been looming over us. "There's something else we need to discuss," he said, his voice measured and serious. "It's about the celebration tomorrow night."

My heart sank at the mention of the upcoming event and I could feel the unease building within me. The celebration was meant to be a moment of triumph, a public acknowledgment of my identity as the First Witch and the daughter of a lost princess.

I swallowed hard and asked, "What about it?"

Thalion's gaze remained steady, his eyes revealing the depth of his concern. "There may be some in attendance who may not be... pleased with your arrival."

Aerion, ever direct, added, "They won't accept you. At least not yet. These are Fae from other courts. We knew this was a possibility. The king and queen will protect you, but you need to be cautious."

The significance of their words echoed in the silence, casting a shadow over the tranquil garden. My mind raced with the implications of what they were saying. The celebration that had held such promise now felt like a potential battlefield.

"I'll be careful," I assured them.

Thalion's intense gaze bore into mine, his eyes holding a mixture of worry and sincerity. "Promise me, Vale. Promise me you'll stay close to us tomorrow. We can't afford to lose you now."

His words struck a chord deep within me and I understood the depth of his concern. It was a moment of vulnerability, a glimpse into the genuine care he held for my safety.

"I promise," I replied softly, my voice filled with gratitude for their protection and the friendship we shared.

As the last vestiges of light faded from the sky, we began our journey back to the castle. The depth of our conversation lingered, a reminder of the challenges that lay ahead and the need for vigilance in the face of uncertainty.

The pressure of the impending celebration pressed down on me, its significance and potential challenges looming large in my mind. Each step I took toward the castle filled me with a growing sense of unease, a knot of anxiety coiling within my stomach.

Despite the growing trepidation, I drew strength from the presence of Aerion and Thalion, the two constants in this ever-changing world. Their steadfast support reassured me that I was not alone on this daunting journey.

As we traversed the moonlit garden, the fireflies' delicate lights flickering like a path of stars, I made a silent vow to myself. I was the First Witch and I would not let the shadows of the past or the unpredictability of the future dim the inner fire that burned within me.

The towering castle, its imposing stone structure rising before us, seemed like a sentinel guarding the Fae realm. Its presence spoke of the fae's enduring strength and the history that shaped their civilization.

I craned my neck to gaze at the intricate carvings and architectural details illuminated by the moon's gentle glow. The castle stood as a testament to the generations of Fae who had called it home, each carving and stone placed with purpose and reverence.

The grandeur of the surroundings, however, paled in comparison to the companionship of Thalion and Aerion. The ornate corridors we walked through exuded an air of culture and refinement, but it was the bond we shared that truly enriched my experience in this unfamiliar world.

Delicate tapestries adorned the walls, depicting scenes of Fae history and myth, while finely crafted furniture and paintings showcased their artistic prowess. Yet, these luxuries could not rival the value of the connections that had blossomed amidst this opulent backdrop.

I glanced at Thalion and Aerion, my heart swelling with gratitude for their unwavering support. It was the presence of these two Fae males that provided me with a sense of belonging and security.

Our footsteps echoed softly on the marble floor as we reached my door, the hush of the moment settling upon us like a heavy, comforting blanket. Each of us seemed wrapped up in our own thoughts, I was the first to break the silence.

"So, you two never told me how your friendship came about," I said, pausing in the corridor outside my chamber and turning to face the two Fae males. Their expressions shifted, exchanging glances that hinted at shared memories and a touch of amusement.

"It's not a particularly exciting story," Thalion admitted with a chuckle, his voice warm and lighthearted.

"It's not," Aerion agreed, his lips curling into a faint smile.

I folded my arms, determined to hear their tale. "I still want to hear it," I insisted, reaching for the doorknob and inviting them into my chamber. They hesitated for only a moment before entering and I followed suit, closing the door behind us.

Seated on the edge of the bed, Aerion began to recount their history. "Well," he started, "we grew up together. Our courts were peaceful neighbors, and we spent our summers together in Aurumport, just like normal Fae children, despite both being princes."

Thalion picked up the narrative, his voice tinged with nostalgia. "As we got older, we became inseparable, spending most of our time together. It was during one of those summers that Haldir finally struck. He launched a campaign against Aerion's court, Terralux, a campaign that brought nothing but death and destruction."

Thalion continued, his gaze distant as he recalled those dark times. "In the end, all that remained of Aerion's court were himself and a few hundred refugees. It was then that I convinced my father to give them refuge."

"In the aftermath, I bound myself to Thalion in gratitude," Aerion said.

I stood in my chamber, absorbing the weight of their shared history. "You bound yourself to him?" I inquired, my curiosity piqued. "What does that entail?"

Thalion and Aerion exchanged yet another meaningful glance as if silently acknowledging the significance of what had transpired between them.

"It's somewhat akin to the blood bond you've formed with the demon," Aerion began to explain, his voice laced with a hint of hesitation. "But instead of blood, it's a magical oath, a solemn vow made between two Fae."

"You can't break the bond, and it's not something one does lightly," Thalion explained.

Aerion's expression was serious. "It means that our loyalty is to each other, that we have each other's backs. We will fight together or die together. Brothers in more than blood."

Their words lingered between us and the depth of their explanation overwhelmed me. I saw the bond between them in a new light, not just as a friendship but as a testament to their unwavering loyalty, forged in the heat of battle and tempered by the shared grief of loss.

The silence stretched on, heavy with the significance of the moment, before I took a deep breath to steady myself. "I think I understand," I finally said, looking into their eyes for confirmation.

"Do you?" Thalion asked, his gaze searching for any signs of uncertainty.

"I think so," I replied thoughtfully. "You two have a connection that goes deeper than just friends, closer than family even."

"Yes," Aerion agreed with a nod.

Thalion's agreement was expressed with a simple nod, but the understanding that passed between them spoke volumes.

I met both their gazes, my voice filled with sincerity. "You two are important to me. I hope you know that."

They exchanged a glance before nodding in unison, genuine smiles gracing their faces.

"You are important to us too, Vale," Thalion said, his voice gentle.

"You can't imagine how important," Aerion added, his grey eyes holding a spark of desire.

"You know," I said, my voice dropping to a whisper. "We're alone now. We have all night. What do you two say to showing me exactly how important I am?"

Aerion and Thalion's faces lit up with matching grins.

"That," Aerion said, taking a step toward me. "Sounds like a wonderful idea."

The next morning arrived with an atmosphere of excitement and activity that permeated the entire palace. Servants bustled about, transforming the grand halls into a spectacle of enchantment and opulence, adorning the walls and ceilings with decorations that sparkled in the soft, early light. I did my best to avoid getting in their way as I navigated the increasingly busy corridors. My presence seemed to elicit a mix of curiosity and reverence among the palace staff. My identity was no longer a secret to them.

Aerion dedicated the morning and much of the afternoon to training with me, helping to ensure that I was adequately prepared for the challenges that lay ahead. As the sun arched across the sky, casting its warm glow upon the palace gardens, Aerion finally called a halt to our training, signaling that it was time for me to begin getting ready.

A few hours later, I emerged from a luxurious bath, my body invigorated by the soothing waters. My skin was pampered and pristine, my hair had been meticulously brushed until it shone like silk, and it had been artfully styled into an intricate braided updo adorned with delicate white flowers. My nails gleamed with a polished sheen and the fragrance of jasmine and honeysuckle enveloped me, a testament to the meticulous care of Amris, Kelli, and Joelene.

Armis, with her usual sense of flair, unveiled the gown that Thalion had designed for the celebration and I couldn't help but gasp in awe as I laid eyes on it for the first time. The fabric was a breathtaking, shimmery black, with a voluminous skirt that exuded elegance. The corseted bodice was adorned with tiny crystals that caught the light, creating a mesmerizing play of shimmering brilliance. Delicate, billowing lace sleeves completed the look, and a black choker with a silver chain that gracefully cascaded from it served as the finishing touch.

"It's beautiful," I breathed, my eyes wide with admiration.

Armis chuckled. "Wait until you see the shoes," she teased with a mischievous grin.

Slipping into the gown was a sensory delight. The fabric felt like a gentle whisper against my skin and Armis deftly laced up the corset, which, to my surprise, was astonishingly comfortable.

With the gown in place, Armis guided me to a stool in front of an ornate mirror. I hesitated for a moment, my excitement building as I considered the final transformation that awaited me.

"Oh, no," I protested, a playful smile tugging at my lips. "I want to save seeing myself until we're ready to go."

Armis raised an eyebrow, her amusement evident. "I have to do your makeup, Princess Vale," she reminded me, her tone both indulgent and firm.

"And we'll be late if we don't hurry," Kelli chimed in, her tone filled with a sense of urgency.

"Right," I said. I took a seat, feeling excited but nervous as the three talented Fae worked their magic. They moved around me with an effortless grace, their hands working in unison to enhance my natural beauty.

Joelene's fingers were delicate as they brushed my eyelashes with black paint. Her breath, sweet and warm, brushed against my face, adding to the intimate atmosphere of the moment. Armis's touch was equally gentle as she expertly applied makeup to my cheeks and lips, leaving behind a subtle tingling sensation.

As the minutes ticked by, I could feel myself transforming, both physically and emotionally. The anticipation for the celebration and the enchanting atmosphere in the room combined to create a sense of wonder and exhilaration.

Finally, Joelene stepped back, her expression one of satisfaction. "There," she said, a warm smile gracing her lips. "All done."

Armis and Kelli joined her, standing back to admire their handiwork. "What do you think?" she asked, clearly eager for my reaction.

I turned to face the full-length mirror, my eyes widening as I took in my reflection. The image that stared back at me was a woman I barely recognized, transformed into a vision of elegance and grace. My eyes were larger and more luminous, my skin had a radiant glow, and my lips were a startling shade of red.

"Wow," I breathed, my hand instinctively flying to my mouth.

Staring at myself in awe, I couldn't help but be amazed by the skilled work of my Fae friends. I looked and felt like a completely different person, a sensation that filled me with a newfound confidence.

"You look stunning," Kelli praised, her voice filled with admiration.

"She does," Joelene agreed, nodding in agreement with her fellow Fae.

Armis beamed with pride, clearly pleased with the result of their efforts. "It's all you," she said, giving me a gentle nudge.

I shook my head. "No, it's not. It's because of the three of you. Thank you. Truly."

Armis waved a hand dismissively. "You humble us," she said.

Joelene and Kelli shared warm smiles, clearly pleased with their work, which only added to my growing confidence.

"We'd better get going," Kelli chimed in, her voice carrying a sense of urgency. "The celebration will start soon."

"Are you ready, princess?" Joelene asked, her eyes filled with excitement.

Drawing in a deep breath, I did my best to muster the confidence I needed for the night ahead. "I'm ready," I replied, hoping my words matched my feelings.

With our preparations complete, we left the room, entering a palace that was abuzz with activity. Fae were bustling in every direction, their excitement tangible in the air, mingling with the sounds of animated conversations and the strains of music.

Armis, Kelli, and Joelene exchanged their goodbyes, leaving me to face the next part of the evening. Just as I was beginning to feel a surge of anxiety, Thalion appeared, commanding attention in an outfit that was nothing short of majestic. He wore a tailored jacket of silver, embroidered with intricate patterns of gold threads that seemed to shimmer with each step he took. The jacket was cinched at the waist with a sash of obsidian, a radiant brooch at its center that caught the light in a dazzling display. His trousers were a dark shade of grey, complementing the jacket perfectly.

His attire was completed by a circlet of intertwined vines and gemstones, resting on his forehead as if a crown, its centerpiece a stunning amethyst that matched his eyes. All in all, Thalion looked every inch a royal—imposing yet graceful, powerful yet refined.

Our eyes met, and he stopped short, his gaze sweeping over me in a way that sent a delightful shiver down my spine.

"Vale," he breathed, his voice filled with admiration. "You look..."

"Yes?" I prompted him with a playful smile, my heart fluttering at his words.

He searched for the right word and when he found it, it was filled with genuine awe. "Breathtaking. Black is definitely your color."

My cheeks flushed with warmth, and I offered him a grateful smile. "Thank you," I said, genuinely appreciative of his compliment.

He extended his arm toward me, a warm smile curving his lips. "Ready?"

With his arm offered, I took a moment to collect myself, reminding myself of the strength and confidence I'd gained in the Fae realm. Nodding, I placed my hand on his arm and met his gaze with determination. "Ready."

The grand ballroom was nothing short of breathtaking. Its floor stretched out in an expanse of glistening marble, while above, the ceiling arched high, a masterpiece of intricate woodwork adorned with delicate gold leaf. Tall, elegantly framed windows punctuated the walls, casting the last rays of the setting sun into the room, creating a warm and inviting atmosphere.

The hall was teeming with Fae from all corners of the realm, their attire as opulent as the surroundings. Their laughter and animated conversations swirled through the air, forming a harmonious backdrop to the grandeur that surrounded us.

Thalion gestured subtly as he spoke, his gaze focused on a particular spot in the room. "There's my mother and father," he said, nodding toward where his parents stood, a prominent presence near the center of the ballroom.

"We should greet them," I suggested.

A warm smile crossed Thalion's face, his almond-shaped eyes crinkling at the corners. He guided me gracefully through the bustling crowd, making our way toward the royal couple.

As we approached the King and Queen their expressions radiated warmth and welcome. The king's voice, laced with affection, reached my ears as he spoke. "My dear Vale," he greeted as he stepped forward and brushed a kiss on my cheek, his eyes holding a fondness that warmed my heart. "You look lovely tonight."

"Thank you, Your Majesty," I replied with a respectful nod of my head, deeply honored by the king's kind words.

The queen, her smile gentle, turned her attention to Thalion. "I see you've taken care of her," she remarked, her gaze softening as she looked upon her son.

Thalion met his mother's gaze with warmth mirrored in his own. "Of course," he replied, the pride in his voice unmistakable as he returned her smile.

"Well," the queen said, casting a quick glance around the lavishly decorated room. "I think it's time we began the festivities. Will you join us, Vale?" she inquired, extending an invitation that carried an air of genuine warmth and inclusivity.

My gaze shifted briefly to Thalion, who offered a subtle nod of approval. With a feeling of honor and anticipation, I met the queen's gaze once more and replied, "Yes, Your Majesty. I'd be honored."

The queen's smile radiated warmth and grace as she turned her attention to the assembled crowd. Her voice, clear and commanding, carried easily through the ornate ballroom.

"Fae of the realm," she announced, her words carrying a sense of grandeur. "Welcome and be welcome! Tonight, we gather to celebrate the arrival of our long-lost princess, Valerian."

A wave of excited murmurs rippled through the gathering, a chorus of anticipation for the festivities ahead.

With a subtle raise of her hand, the queen beckoned for silence, and the room fell into hushed expectancy.

"Let us welcome her and rejoice in her return," she continued, her voice carrying a tone of unity and celebration. "Now, please join us as the king and I begin the celebration with a dance."

As the musicians tuned their instruments, the king and queen gracefully made their way to the center of the spacious ballroom.

There, they joined hands, their connection intimate even from a distance, and began a slow, elegant dance that seemed to speak of years of shared love and understanding.

I stood mesmerized, the sight of their synchronized movements and the depth of their connection captivating my attention. Their gazes remained locked on each other, a silent conversation of love and commitment that transcended mere words.

"They love each other," I couldn't help but murmur, the words escaping my lips before I could filter them.

Beside me, Thalion stood, his eyes focused on the dancing royal couple, his expression thoughtful. He nodded, his voice soft and contemplative. "Yes, they do, and you've given them a second chance at being together. I can never thank you enough for healing my mother."

I turned to look at him, gratitude reflected in his eyes. "It was my pleasure," I replied sincerely, a shared understanding passing between us. The depth of emotion in his gaze stirred something within me.

As the melody reached its final notes, Thalion extended his hand toward me, his gaze unwavering and inviting. "Would you care to dance?" he asked, his voice gentle and warm.

A smile graced my lips as I placed my hand in his. "I'd love to," I replied, my heart fluttering. Thalion led me gracefully onto the dance floor, his hand a reassuring anchor amid the elegant celebration.

Chapter Thirty-Two

As Thalion and I approached the king and queen a sense of nervous anticipation swirled within me. The opulent ballroom and the eyes of the assembled Fae nobility added to the weight of the moment.

"Follow my lead, just like before," Thalion's murmured words were a comfort, his lips brushing close to my ear.

I nodded in response, my heart racing as the music swelled around us, the enchanting melody of the dance inviting us to join its graceful rhythm.

We began to move and I focused on Thalion's lead, allowing the steps to flow naturally, guided by the music and his confident presence. The dance seemed to envelop us, and for a moment, the world beyond the ballroom ceased to exist.

We twirled and glided across the polished floor, the soft echo of our footsteps joining the symphony of the orchestra. The sensation of Thalion's arms around me was reassuring, his voice a soothing presence near my ear.

"Simply perfect, as usual," he said, beaming at me.

As the music swirled around us, I found myself losing track of time, losing myself in the dance, and the undeniable connection I shared with Thalion at that moment.

A tap on my shoulder drew my attention and I turned to find Aerion standing there, resplendently dressed in a manner that left me momentarily breathless.

"May I cut in?" he asked, his gaze fixed on me.

"Of course," Thalion's response was accompanied by a knowing smile that hinted at a deeper understanding between the two of them.

Aerion took Thalion's place and his strong arms enveloped me, drawing me into a dance that felt somehow even more intimate than the one I'd just shared with Thalion. The shift in dynamics was undeniable.

"You look enchanting," Aerion's whispered compliment, delivered with a rough and low voice, sent a warm blush to my cheeks.

"Thank you," I replied, my own voice soft.

He pulled me closer, his breath warm against my cheek, the proximity intensifying the intimacy of the moment.

"I'm sorry I was late," Aerion confessed, his eyes locked on mine.

"I was wondering where you ran off to," I teased him, unable to conceal the smile that tugged at my lips as I looked up at him.

"I'll make it up to you," he promised, his eyes glittering with desire. Aerion's promise was laden with unspoken implications.

As the song's final notes faded away, the atmosphere in the grand ballroom shifted. The lights dimmed and a quiet, anticipatory hush fell over the room, each guest's curiosity piqued.

The queen's commanding voice rang out, clear and strong, breaking the silence that had settled upon the assembly. "Please join us outside," she beckoned, her words laced with an air of mystery. "There's something you all need to see."

Aerion and I exchanged glances, our mutual curiosity fueling our shared anticipation. We followed the crowd as it began to make its way outside to a large balcony that offered a commanding view of the city below.

"What's going on?" I wondered aloud, glancing around at the expectant faces of the gathered Fae. Aerion shook his head, his gaze fixed on the night sky above as if searching for answers among the stars. The murmurs of the Fae on the balcony blended into a collective hum of curiosity and we all awaited the revelation that the queen had promised.

Suddenly, a flash of brilliant light caught my eye and I instinctively turned my gaze upward.

"Look!" someone cried out, pointing at the sky.

A celestial wonder unfolded before our eyes—a trail of fire streaked across the vast canvas of the night, leaving behind a glowing, golden trail in its wake. The initial gasps of awe quickly gave way to excited exclamations as the luminous spectacle continued.

"It's a shooting star," I breathed in wonder, my eyes wide as I watched the display. But it wasn't just one shooting star; another flash of light caught my eye and then another until the entire night sky was ablaze with falling stars. Each one painted the heavens with its fiery tail, leaving shimmering streaks of vibrant colors in their wake.

Overwhelmed by the beauty of the moment, I turned to Aerion, my eyes welling with tears of astonishment.

"It's amazing," I whispered, my voice filled with a sense of reverence.

Aerion nodded, his gaze never straying from mine as he pulled me closer, his presence offering both warmth and comfort amid the spectacle.

"You're amazing," he murmured, his words soft and tender.

The night sky continued to rain down its enchanting display, the falling stars leaving a trail of sparkling brilliance in their wake. The balcony, once filled with hushed whispers, now buzzed with excitement and wonder.

"Some are whispering that it's a sign," Thalion's voice cut through the crowd as he pushed his way toward us, his eyes aglow with the reflected light of the falling stars.

"A sign of what?" I inquired, my curiosity piqued.

"That you've returned," he answered, his words tinged with a profound sense of hope. "That the First Witch has indeed come again."

A collective hush fell over the balcony, the Fae around us turning their attention toward me, their expressions filled with anticipation.

"What are you going to do, Vale?" Thalion asked, his voice filled with a quiet urgency.

Aerion and Thalion exchanged a meaningful glance, their unspoken communication evident. All eyes were on me, awaiting my response.

My thoughts raced, my heart pounding in my chest. The significance of the moment was not lost on me, the world holding its breath for my decision.

Then, a familiar voice rang out in my head, the gentle yet authoritative tone of Rowena.

"Hold out your hand, daughter."

Without hesitation, I extended my hand, palm upturned, and a shooting star descended from the heavens, landing gracefully in my outstretched hand. Its light shimmered and dazzled, casting an ethereal glow.

Gasps of astonishment rippled through the Fae who watched in awe as I held the falling star, its radiance illuminating my determined face.

I gazed down at the heavenly gift in my hand, then looked up at the expectant faces of the gathered Fae. These people were waiting for something from me, something magnificent.

With an idea forming in my head, I knew what I had to do.

"I am Valerian, First Witch come again, princess of the Fae," I declared, my voice echoing out among those gathered, "and I'm here to help you prevail against the darkness."

With that, I tossed the star back up into the air where it exploded above the Fae into a cascade of dazzling sparkles.

My words pierced the night, carried by the winds and the whispers of the stars, and a triumphant cheer erupted from the Fae who had longed for a beacon of hope in the face of impending darkness.

The celebration carried on, its vibrant energy and euphoria coursing through the night. Fae of all kinds reveled in the return of the First Witch, their spirits lifted by the newfound hope that had sprung forth with my arrival. Too long had they spent fearful of Haldir's tyrannical rule. The grandeur of the event was visible in the dancing, singing, and jubilant expressions that filled the air.

I became a part of the ceaseless festivities, losing myself in the rhythm of the music, my laughter mingling with the joyous cries of those around me. We danced until my feet ached and I laughed until my cheeks hurt from the sheer happiness of the moment.

However, as the night wore on, I retreated from the jubilation and found a moment of solitude on the balcony overlooking the sprawling city. Leaning against the ornate railing, I took a deep breath and allowed the cool night air to soothe my senses.

"Having fun?" a voice broke the silence, sending a shiver down my spine. I turned to find Malachar, Haldir's son, his sinister grin slicing through the air like a blade.

"As a matter of fact, yes," I responded, masking my unease with a touch of defiance. "Is that a problem?"

Malachar's eyes glittered cruelly as he drew closer, his malicious intent unmistakable.

"Not at all," he replied with a hint of mockery. "I was just wondering how long it will last."

My frown deepened. "What do you mean?"

Malachar moved even closer, his voice laced with venom.

"You really think you can prevail against what's coming?" he hissed, a hint of venom in his words. "The darkness is stronger than you can imagine and it will consume everything in its path."

I stood up straight, my resolve solidifying. "I know I can, you think I'm afraid of an insignificant asshole like you?" I asserted, my voice unwavering.

"You're a fool," he spat. "And a liar."

"That's enough, Malachar," a deep voice intervened, breaking the tension.

Malachar spun around to face Aerion and Thalion, who stood tall and imposing behind him, their expressions resolute and unyielding.

"If you ever talk to her again, I will end you," Aerion's voice dripped with loathing as he issued his threat. His anger was formidable now and a dangerous edge gleamed in his eyes.

Thalion, not one to be outdone in protecting me, took a menacing step forward. His face was a mask of unbridled fury, a stark contrast to the earlier lightheartedness of the celebration. "Get out of here," Thalion's voice was cold and unyielding, "or I'll throw you off this balcony myself."

Malachar, for all his arrogance, visibly faltered. His eyes darted between Aerion and Thalion and the veneer of anger crumbled in the face of their stern determination.

"You can't always protect her," he sneered, a last-ditch effort to maintain some semblance of defiance.

"She doesn't need our protection, she could burn you alive where you stand. Be glad she hasn't. Now go," Thalioncommanded, his voice a frigid directive.

Malachar hesitated for only a moment, then turned and retreated into the bustling crowd. His spiteful presence faded, absorbed by the sea of celebrating Fae.

Aerion, his anger still simmering beneath the surface, stepped to my side and gently took my hand in his.

"Are you okay?" he asked, as his eyes searched mine.

"I'm fine," I reassured him, grateful for their unwavering protection.

"That creature has no place here," Thalion muttered, his jaw clenched in lingering anger.

"I agree," Aerion added, his tone resolute.

"Me too," I chimed in. "But there's nothing we can do about him now."

"Don't worry," Aerion said, his gaze locking onto mine with un-wavering determination. "He won't bother you again."

Thalion nodded, his expression fierce. "Are you ready to go back to your rooms?"

"Yes, I'm exhausted and I need to get out of these shoes," I replied with a light-hearted jest, though the comfort of my room was a genuine longing after the night's events.

Aerion offered his arm and I accepted it graciously. Together, we began to walk away from the balcony, leaving Thalionbehind amidst the quiet splendor of the celebration's aftermath.

"I'll see you in the morning," Thalion called after us.

"Good night," I replied, my voice soft, a fond smile playing on my lips.

Aerion and I wandered through the labyrinthine passages of the palace, the once-bustling corridors now quiet and nearly deserted. The echoes of the night's merriment lingered in the air, a fading memory of the jubilant celebration.

"Tonight was incredible," I said, leaning comfortably against Aerion's arm.

"It was," he concurred, his tone sincere. "But not as incredible as you were."

His compliment made my cheeks flush with warmth, a spark of excitement igniting in the pit of my stomach.

"Do you mind if I escort you to your door?" he inquired, his eyes locking onto mine.

"Only if you promise to kiss me goodnight," I replied, teasing him with a playful grin.

Aerion chuckled, his voice laced with desire. "That's a promise I can definitely keep."

We continued our slow journey through the palace, eventually reaching my room. At the door, Aerion paused, his gaze searching mine with a tenderness.

"Goodnight, Vale," he whispered, his voice soft and filled with affection.

"Goodnight," I replied in a hushed tone, our closeness amplifying the intimacy of the moment.

With gentle finesse, he leaned in, his lips brushing against mine in a tender, lingering kiss. My heart fluttered in my chest and my head swam with dizzying sensations. When we finally parted, I felt breathless and my body tingled with anticipation.

"Sleep well," he murmured, his eyes never straying from mine.

"You too," I whispered, my voice barely above a soft sigh.

I watched as he retreated down the corridor, the dim light casting an ethereal glow around his figure. When he was out of sight, I stepped into my room and closed the door behind me, leaning against it with a contented sigh.

My heart raced, its rapid beats echoing in my chest, as I stood there, my lips tingling from the lingering warmth of Aerion's kiss. I couldn't suppress the elated smile that crept onto my face, a silent testament to the dizzying sensations coursing through my body.

With a sigh of contentment, I eventually moved away from the door and began to cross the room, my heels clicking softly on the polished floor. As I reached the bed, I kicked off my shoes, the exhaustion of the evening finally catching up with me.

With deliberate, languid movements, I started to pull back the covers, my gaze momentarily drifting to the nightstand beside the bed. There, amidst the soft candlelight, something caught my eye—a single, perfect black rose.

Curiosity piqued, I reached for the dark bloom, the tip of my finger brushing against a thorn, drawing forth a bead of crimson. I winced at the sudden prick, but my instinctual reaction was to place the small wound in my mouth, invoking my blood magic to stanch the bleeding. Yet, as I did so, I felt something unusual—something sinister that slumbered like a long-forgotten memory, lurking at the edges of my consciousness.

My vision began to blur and my head swam in a disorienting haze. Suddenly, a chilling voice hissed in my ear, causing the hairs on the back of my neck to stand on end.

"Soon," the voice promised, the sound dripping with venom.

The black rose slipped from my grasp, its petals fluttering down to scatter across the gleaming wooden floor. Panic began to claw its way into my chest, but before I could react, rough hands seized me from behind, their grip unyielding.

The room spun around me, my thoughts growing increasingly hazy. It became clear that the black rose had been poisoned and the realization struck me like a bolt of lightning. I struggled to break free from my assailant, but my efforts were futile. "Nyxen," I breathed, just as the world plunged into darkness.

As my consciousness faded, the haunting words of the sinister voice lingered, an ominous promise of what was to come.

CHAPTER THIRTY-THREE

"**S**he's awake." A faint and distant voice hissed through the fog that enveloped my senses. My head throbbed, each pulse a reminder of my disoriented state. Slowly, I fought to regain consciousness, determined to pierce through the heavy veil that shrouded my mind.

I managed to force my eyes open, but the harsh light overhead was blinding. It cut through the haze, illuminating my blurred surroundings. I attempted to focus, to make sense of the voices that swirled around me.

"Her blood magic must have burned off most of the poison. Shackle her now," a second voice said.

Suddenly, cool metal clamped around my wrists and the sensation of being restrained sent a jolt through my groggy consciousness. My vision remained obscured and the harsh light bore down on me relentlessly.

"Where am I?" I mumbled, my voice thick and sluggish, as if it were emerging from the depths of a dream.

"She's weak," someone observed, their words resonating with an eerie detachment that filled the dark void.

Roughly, a hand seized my hair, forcing me to tilt my head up. My eyes finally adjusted and before me loomed the cruel face of Malachar, his wicked grin cutting through the fog in my mind.

"You're going to be a useful pawn, witch," he whispered venomously, his breath hot and acrid against my face. "And then you're going to die."

Desperation clawed at me as I gasped, my head still swimming in a sea of confusion. "Burn in hell."

A sadistic chuckle escaped his lips. "You first."

His fingers slithered from my hair to my throat, digging into my skin like talons. Panic welled up inside me, my heart pounding like a trapped animal's.

"You're not going anywhere," he hissed with malevolent glee, his grip tightening like a vice.

I fought against the restraints, trying to summon my magic, but despair washed over me as I realized I couldn't reach it.

"Don't even think about trying anything," he sneered, his fingers biting deeper into my throat. "These cuffs are relics from the witch-burning days, designed to suppress magic. You're utterly helpless."

Reflexively, my survival instincts kicked in, and without a second thought, I reared back and slammed my head into Malachar's face with every ounce of strength I could muster. Pain exploded in my head as I connected with his nose, and for a moment, the world spun like a chaotic whirlwind.

"No so helpless then," I spat at him.

Malachar staggered backward, clutching his injured face, his furious roar piercing the air.

"Bitch!" he bellowed, his eyes blazing with rage.

Malachar drew back his fist, his face twisted into a grin as he aimed to strike me. His blow landed with brutal force, sending me sprawling to the ground, my world spinning as the impact stole the very air from my lungs.

The unforgiving surface greeted me with merciless hardness, pain radiating through my body. Blood mingled with the metallic tang of fear in my mouth as I tasted the consequences of his brutal strike. My vision blurred as I struggled to gather my shattered senses.

"Enough, Malachar," a second voice rang out, it sent icy tendrils of fear snaking down my spine, I recognized it instantly— Haldir.

Malachar growled, his fury palpable, yet he begrudgingly stepped back from his assault.

Haldir advanced, his dark cloak swirling around him in a sinister dance of shadows.

"Hello, Valerian," he purred, his eyes gleaming with malice. "How nice to see you again."

My chest heaved as I forced myself onto my unsteady feet, determination overpowering the pain that wracked my body.

"What do you want with me?" I gasped, my voice edged with defiance.

"Your death but only at the opportune moment," he replied, the words dripping with venom.

I locked my gaze onto his, refusing to reveal the fear that churned within me. My voice, though strained, bore an undertone of unwavering resolve.

"You're not the first to want that," I spat, my defiance burning like a beacon. "And you won't be the last."

Haldir's lips curled into a cold smile, a sinister edge to his demeanor. "Oh, I think you'll find that I'm quite different from your other enemies," he hissed with sinister satisfaction. "For instance, I've already won."

My anger surged within me, a protective fire that shielded my trembling heart. I met his unrelenting gaze head-on.

"You haven't won anything and I'm not afraid of you," I retorted, my voice laced with indignation, determined not to give him the satisfaction of seeing my fear.

A chilling silence hung between us and the poison in Haldir's eyes only deepened as he issued his menacing response. "You should be," he whispered, the ominous gleam in his gaze promising a darkness unlike any other.

Malachar's eerie laughter reverberated off the damp stone walls, sending shivers down my spine. The cruel, haunting sound clawed at my senses, filling the dimly lit chamber with a crushing hatred.

"There's nowhere to run, witch," he mocked, each word dripping with malice. "This is where you die."

Despite the grim circumstances, I managed a retort, "I can't wait," I replied, my words loaded with sarcasm.

"It's a shame that your spirit must be extinguished," he sneered, his cold eyes sweeping over me with a venomous glance. "But no matter. In the end, the result will be the same."

With fiery determination, I met Haldir's menacing gaze, my own eyes ablaze with unwavering defiance. "Not if I have anything to say about it," I shot back, my resolve shining through in my words.

Haldir's smile broadened, a manifestation of his arrogance and contempt. "Your words are meaningless, little girl," he taunted with a sneer. "You're at our mercy, and we have none."

His cutting words struck a deep chord within me, reigniting the fiery spirit that raged within my chest. My hands clenched into fists, my determination unwavering. "Then, let's get on with it," I snarled. "Because I won't give you the satisfaction of seeing me tremble."

Haldir's piercing gaze bore into me, an intensity that made the hairs on the back of my neck stand on end. The dank air in the chamber was almost suffocating, and the silence stretched ominously.

Finally, Haldir broke the stillness, his words laced with a sharp and cutting edge. "No, not yet," he declared, a sinister glint in his eyes. "There's no fun in ending a life without watching it slip away first. I'm going to enjoy every moment of your suffering."

I swallowed hard, my throat dry, and my heart pounding. Though fear gnawed at me from within, my resolve remained unshaken. No matter what horrors awaited, I was determined not to give them the satisfaction of witnessing my weakness.

"Bring it on," I whispered, my words echoing through the murky chamber, a silent promise to myself that I would face whatever torment they had planned with unwavering courage.

Haldir's sinister smile stretched across his face, his eyes gleaming with a dangerous edge that turned my blood to ice. "So be it," he declared with chilling intent.

As Haldir and his menacing entourage closed in around me, I remained steadfast, my resistance steadfast. Their grotesque visages twisted with hatred as they encircled me, but I refused to cower. I lifted my chin, allowing the blazing fire within my soul to shine brighter than ever before.

If this was to be the culmination of my journey, I was determined to meet it head-on, with no regrets and no hesitation. I would face the encroaching darkness, resolute and unyielding until the very last breath escaped my lips.

I was prepared.

I was Valerian, and fear had no dominion over me.

My words echoed throughout the chamber, my voice ringing out steady and strong. "Come on, then. I'm waiting."

Haldir's piercing eyes narrowed, their depths swirling with unfathomable darkness. He seemed to savor the anticipation of the torment he intended to inflict.

"Patience, witch," he whispered, his voice a venomous serpent's hiss. "You will get exactly what you deserve." In an instant, his hand shot out, closing around my throat, and he yanked me closer to him. His lips brushed against my ear, his words dripping with the promise of unrelenting pain. "And more."

Haldir sent me hurtling down to the unforgiving, cold stone floor. I landed with a thud, the impact jolting through my battered body. With a swift gesture, he signaled the nearby guards. "Take her to the dungeons."

The guards surged forward. Their unrelenting grip seized me and despite my futile struggles, their combined strength overpowered my feeble resistance. I was still weak from the residual effects of the poison. I was forcibly hauled away from the dark chamber, the icy fingers of the night air enveloping me as they callously flung me into the foreboding confines of a cell.

The door clanged shut with a finality, the harsh, metallic sound of the lock snapping into place echoing in the dimly lit chamber. I was left alone, my only company the oppressive shroud of darkness that enveloped me.

My confrontation with the enemy had been a test of my courage and resolve and I had stood my ground. Yet, I knew that this was only the beginning, for the true battle lay ahead.

The night stretched endlessly and the shadows harbored countless terrors. With each passing hour, my determination wavered, the insidious tendrils of fear inching closer to the edges of my consciousness. My body ached, bearing the painful reminders of the brutality inflicted upon me.

Nevertheless, I clung to the fragile thread of hope, believing that escape or rescue was not beyond reach. I attempted to call upon Nyxen for aid, but the oppressive cuffs that bound my wrists stifled my magical connection and doubts regarding the possibility of anyone shifting in or out of this accursed place plagued my mind.

The damp, cold cell offered no respite from my suffering, and as the first traces of dawn began to paint the horizon, I found myself yearning for the merciful oblivion of sleep. Anything to escape the torment of the unending night.

With a weary sigh, I slumped against the unforgiving stone wall, my eyes fixated on the approaching daylight.

"Hang on, Vale," I whispered to myself, the words a feeble mantra against the encroaching despair. "The dawn is coming."

Surely, it wouldn't be long before they realized I was missing. They knew I was in the clutches of Haldir and they would undoubtedly launch a search. But how could they possibly confront Haldir's formidable forces on their own? As much as I longed for rescue, I knew better than to rely solely on that glimmer of hope. If I were to escape this perilous situation, I had to find a way out on my own.

For now, my only recourse was to bide my time and hope for an opportunity to present itself. The cold, unyielding stone of the cell seemed to bear witness to my uncertainty and I couldn't help but wonder how long I could endure this torment.

As the first rays of the rising sun filtered through the narrow window, casting a faint, golden glow upon the cell's dank interior, a fragile sense of hope kindled within me. The promise of a new day beckoned and for a fleeting moment, the oppressive darkness seemed to lift.

I welcomed the warmth that caressed my skin as sunlight bathed me and I clung to the renewed sense of hope that accompanied it. The dawn's soft embrace whispered promises of possibilities, of a chance to forge my own path out of this dire predicament. With determination in my heart, I resolved to seize any opportunity that came my way and find a way to break free from the clutches of darkness.

Chapter Thirty-Four

WREN

The dark night enveloped the camp in an eerie stillness as Wren sat hunched over his makeshift table, scrutinizing the scattered plans for the rest of the camp construction. His brow furrowed in concentration as he traced his finger along the proposed strategy, mentally mapping out every detail. The moonlight, filtered through the canopy of trees, cast faint, shifting patterns of light and shadow across the tent walls.

A gust of wind rustled the tent's canvas walls, bringing with it a chill that crept beneath Wren's clothing. He ignored it though, his thoughts consumed by the status of his pack.

Then, as if summoned from the very shadows themselves, Kaelan materialized before him, his abrupt appearance startling Wren. So deeply engrossed in his silent contemplation that he nearly tumbled out of the worn chair he had been perched on.

"What the hell are you doing here?" Wren demanded, his tone a mixture of surprise and frustration.

The look on Kaelan's face was one of sheer desperation, his eyes darting around the cramped space as if searching for something unseen. His breath came in short, uneven gasps, and his voice trembled with urgency.

"We have a problem," he blurted out, his words ominous in the cold night air.

Wren could immediately tell that Kaelan was near frantic with worry. He swiftly rose from his seat, the chair scraping against the dusty floor.

"What do you mean? What's wrong?" Wren demanded, his gaze narrowing as he locked onto Kaelan's agitated expression.

Kaelan's voice quivered as he spoke, his tone laced with dread. "Vale's been hurt. I can feel it, but just barely. The bond is growing stronger and I can sense her, even though she's in a different realm. But something is wrong."

Wren's mind raced, thoughts colliding in a whirlwind of worry and fear. He leaned in closer, demanding more answers. "What? What do you mean by 'hurt'? Where is she?"

Kaelan's eyes bore into Wren's, the urgency in his voice intensifying. "I don't know. All I know is she's in pain and she's scared. We have to go after her, right now."

Wren's jaw clenched, his fists balling up at his sides. "Shit," he muttered under his breath, his thoughts racing to form a plan.

"We need to get to the Fae realm, right now," Kaelan urged.

Without wasting another moment, Wren turned and rushed from the tent, his heart pounding with a mixture of fear and determination.

The fate of his best friend hung in the balance and he was determined to bring her back safely.

Outside, Wren scanned the camp, his eyes settling on the familiar form of Venna engaged in conversation with several members of the pack.

Wren's hurried arrival disrupted the conversation within the camp and the hushed murmurs ceased as all eyes turned to him. Venna quickly took notice of his troubled expression. Her strong, brown eyes bore into Wren's with concern etched upon her face.

"Something's happened," he announced, his words slicing through the night air.

Venna turned to face him fully, her stance shifting from one of casual conversation to one of alertness. "What's wrong, Wren?" she pressed, her voice firm but laced with worry.

Wren wasted no time in delivering the dire news. "It's Vale," he replied, anxiety filling his voice. "She's in trouble."

His words hung in the air like a dark cloud and Venna's expression mirrored the unease that Wren felt. "What? How do you know?" she questioned, her voice edged with urgency.

"Kaelan can sense it," Wren explained, his words rushed. "She's been hurt, but he can't tell how bad it is. We have to go to her."

Venna's resolve solidified, her jaw set in determination. "All right, let's get going. We'll take the portal to the Fae realm. You can tell me more along the way."

Wren gave a brisk nod, acknowledging the urgency of the situation. He knew that every moment they wasted was a moment Vale could be suffering.

Together, they raced back to the tent where Kaelan anxiously awaited their return.

"Come on, we need to go now," Kaelan said, his voice insistent.

"Right," Venna agreed.

They both moved quickly to Kaelan's side. Kaelan's abilities, unleashed and unbound, now allowed him to shift multiple people with him. As they stood together, the shadows began to swirl around them, wrapping them in their embrace.

The world around them dissolved into a maelstrom of tumbling shadows, the sensation both exhilarating and disorienting. Time and space seemed to warp as they were pulled through the void, a sense of weightlessness engulfing them.

And then, as suddenly as it had begun, the disorienting journey came to an end.

They emerged in a darkened clearing nestled within a towering forest. The portal to the Fae realm loomed ominously before them. With a glance exchanged between them, Wren took the initiative and stepped through the portal first, his expression resolute. Venna followed closely behind and Kaelan didn't hesitate before slipping through the churning mists.

On the other side, the stark contrast of worlds was immediately apparent. Here, the Fae realm was a place of vivid, almost surreal beauty. The moon hung low in the night sky, casting its glow upon the landscape. Rays of moonlight filtered through the dense canopy of leaves, creating an enchanting interplay of light and shadow. The air was heavy with the intoxicating scent of wildflowers and the night was alive with the symphony of crickets and other nocturnal creatures.

"Where is she?" Venna inquired, her voice a quiet yet urgent whisper.

Kaelan closed his eyes momentarily, his brows furrowing in concentration as he tapped into his connection with Vale. "I can feel her," he murmured, his voice filled with concern. "But it's faint as if she's not in the Fae realm entirely, or... I don't know. We should make our way to the palace where she was staying. Maybe they know more."

Wren nodded, his expression etched with worry. "Let's go," he said, his words punctuated by a deep sense of determination. They had come this far and they would stop at nothing to find Vale and bring her back to safety.

They stood next to Kaelan once more as he manipulated the shadows, and this time, they emerged within Vale's room in the palace. However, they were not alone. Two figures stood at the center of the room.

As the trio stepped out of the shadows Thalion and Aerion immediately went on the defensive, their posture ready to face an attack. Thalion held a crumpled black rose. Aerion, his expression equally guarded, locked eyes on the newcomers, his stance poised for a potential confrontation.

"Calm down, faerie boys, it's us," Kaelan sneered with a hint of annoyance. The two Fae princes eased their defensive stances slightly, but the wariness didn't completely dissipate.

"What are you doing here?" Aerion asked, suspicion tainting his tone.

"Looking for Vale, what the hell do you think?" Kaelan snapped, his impatience flaring.

"Where is she?" Wren demanded, his voice urgent.

Thalion's gaze flickered between the newcomers, his brows furrowing with worry. "We've searched everywhere, but she's nowhere in the palace," he admitted, his voice frustrated. "All we found was a rose and the lingering scent of someone else we can't identify in her room."

"Fuck, so we're no closer to finding her," Wren muttered. His frustration was unmistakable, his concern etching lines on his face. Venna, however, remained determined.

"No," she said firmly, turning toward Wren, her voice filled with resolve. "But we're not going to stop until we do."

Wren glanced around the room, his gaze settling on the three Fae before him. "Who's been in this room, besides Vale and the intruder?" he asked, searching for any clues.

"Just us," Aerion answered, his voice tinged with worry.

Wren pressed on, his tone urgent. "And neither of you know where she could be?"

"We know exactly where she must be, the problem is getting to her," Thalion responded somberly.

"And where is that?" Kaelan demanded.

"In the Unseelie court," Thalion revealed, his voice heavy with concern. "In Haldir's prison."

Wren's eyes widened with alarm. "The Unseelie Court? What is that?"

"It's a kingdom," Thalion said, "But it's the worst place she could be. The king is a cruel and sadistic man. There's no telling what he's doing to her."

Kaelan took a step forward, his voice strained. "So, what's the plan?"

Thalion's jaw clenched and a worried look crossed his face as he replied, "We have no choice but to invade the court. It's the only way to get to her. But gathering our troops and allies, plus the journey there, could take a few days. We have no choice; we must prepare."

Kaelan's frustration boiled over, his words laced with anger. "Fuck that! We're not waiting days, not when Vale's life is at stake."

Wren mirrored Kaelan's sentiment, his expression fierce. "He's right; we need to get her back now. Every minute we waste she's in danger."

Thalion couldn't hide his irritation. "How exactly do you expect to get into the Unseelie court without a full army and without dying in the process?"

"I don't know," Wren admitted, his voice unwavering, "but we're not just going to stand here and do nothing while Vale suffers. We're going to do whatever it takes to save her and you're going to help us."

Thalion's response was stern, emphasizing the gravity of their situation. "There is no other option than the one we've laid before you. There's no other way to get inside to her than by storming the front gates."

Kaelan, undeterred, proposed an alternative. "I could break in. I can use the shadows to get us inside."

Thalion, however, dispelled their optimism with a dose of reality. "If it were any other castle, I'd agree, but it's the Unseelie court, and no matter your powers, you'd have a hard time. Their wards are powerful and the shadows won't help. They've got an entire army there and they're not going to just let you waltz in. The best you can do would be to shift into the courtyard where'd you be immediately swarmed by Unseelie court guards."

"You underestimate us," Kaelan argued.

"And you overestimate yourselves," Thalion retorted.

Venna, sensing the futility of the argument, intervened with authority. "Enough. We're not going to get anywhere by arguing. We need to come up with a plan and stick together. Vale needs us and we're not going to let her down."

Wren's shoulders sagged as he contemplated their dire situation. "I hate it, but I agree. We can't do this alone."

Kaelan, though still brimming with frustration, uncrossed his arms. "What's the plan, then?"

Aerion, the determination in his eyes unwavering, took the lead. "The plan is to gather our forces and take on the Unseelie court, rescue Vale, and destroy Haldir in the process."

Wren, absorbing the information, had an idea. "Kaelan, could you shift our wolves to the portal and then here?"

Kaelan nodded. "Yes, I could. Why?"

"Because if these Fae are right and the Unseelie Court's defenses are strong, we could use the pack's strength," Wren explained.

Kaelan agreed with a nod. "Fine."

Wren laid out the next steps. "I'll go back and tell them the situation. I'll have them get ready and we'll come back here."

Thalion took charge of their Fae allies. "Very well, I will start gathering our forces. We'll need to get word to our allies as well."

Aerion stepped up to help. "I can take care of that."

Thalion concluded their meeting, the urgency of the situation evident. "Good, let's get to work then."

Chapter Thirty-Five

I awoke in the dimly lit dungeon cell, the air choking me with dampness and despair. My head throbbed, a reminder of the darkness that had ensnared me. The guards entered, their heavy footsteps echoing off the stone walls, and I couldn't help but flinch as they unlocked the cell door.

My hands remained bound in the magic-suppressing shackles, rendering my powers useless, their cold iron cutting into the flesh of my wrists. The guards grabbed me roughly, their grips like vices around my arms, and hoisted me to my feet. Pain shot through my body as they dragged me along behind them, giving me no chance to walk along with them.

We entered another room in the dungeons and the sight that met my eyes absolutely terrified me. The room was small and oppressive, with rough-hewn stone walls and a low ceiling. The only source of light came from a single flickering torch, casting eerie shadows that danced across the cold, unforgiving surface of the stone.

In the center of the room, a sinister-looking table dominated the space. It was a crude and ominous contraption, made of blackened iron and adorned with restraints. My heart sank into my stomach as I realized its purpose.

Despite my violent struggling, they strapped me down onto the table, my shackled wrists and ankles secured tightly, rendering me completely immobilized. The iron cut into my skin even more, but it was nothing compared to the despair that settled over me.

I was trapped, alone in this sinister chamber, at the mercy of my captors. The darkness loomed and dread was an icy ball that settled in my very core.

A voice suddenly pierced the darkness. "Hello, witch. It's good to see you again."

As Malachar emerged from the shadows my heart began beating a thunderous crescendo in my chest. His appearance was haunting, his skin so pale it seemed almost translucent in the dim light, and his obsidian eyes seemed like voids, devoid of any humanity.

He moved closer, each step deliberate and predatory, closing the distance between us. The cruelty in his gaze was terrifyingly ominous and it sent another cold wave of fear through me, though I fought to maintain my composure.

"You've caused me a great deal of trouble, but I'm glad you're here. I'm going to enjoy this," he taunted, thoroughly enjoying himself. The sight of his baleful glee repulsed me.

I clenched my jaw, determined not to show any sign of fear. "I'm not scared of you. Always hiding behind your daddy," I retorted, my voice steady, or at least as steady as I could manage.

His smile, devoid of any warmth, sent a shiver down my spine. I knew I was in fucking trouble, but I couldn't afford to let him see my fear. My bravado was all I had left.

"Your words are empty," he hissed, his voice a cold, venomous whisper. "Soon, you will be begging for mercy, and I will show you none."

His fingers, as pale as death in the flickering light, reached out, brushing against my cheek. Revulsion coursed through me and I recoiled from his touch.

"Don't fucking touch me," I growled, spitting in his face.

Malachar's sadistic smile widened as he slowly wiped his face with the back of his hand. His eyes, gleaming with wicked amusement, seemed to pierce through my soul. His icy fingers trailed down my neck, leaving a clammy, uncomfortable sensation in their wake. I couldn't suppress the instinctive fear that welled up within me at his chilling touch. My heart raced as he continued to explore every inch of my body, his touch violating my personal boundaries. Panic surged within me and I squirmed, attempting to free myself from the restraints that held me in place.

"Stop," I hissed, my voice trembling with rage and fear, but he only responded with laughter, the sound filling the room and amplifying my terror.

"Oh, I'm just getting started," he taunted, his voice a whisper.

His hand ventured lower, sliding across my abdomen, and a wave of nausea washed over me. I desperately searched for any way to stop him, but with my magic suppressed and my body restrained, I was utterly powerless.

His hand continued its descent and his touch became more invasive with each passing moment. I clenched my jaw, determined not to give him the satisfaction of hearing me scream.

Malachar's gaze remained locked on mine and I could see the twisted delight in his eyes. I could no longer bear to meet his gaze, so I closed my eyes tightly, shutting out the horrors unfolding before me.

Then, as abruptly as it had begun, his hand stopped. The sudden halt left me trembling and uncertain of what would happen next.

"What's the matter, witch? Do you think you can escape me that easily?" Malachar's sinister words slithered through the air, pulling me out of the momentary relief his pause had provided. My eyes snapped open and a cold, sinking feeling of dread settled in the pit of my stomach as I looked up at him. Confusion mingled with the fear in my eyes, but he only smirked, relishing in my vulnerability.

From the hidden folds of his dark cloak, he produced a wicked-looking knife, its blade gleaming under the dim dungeon lights. My breath hitched as he brought it closer. The tip of the blade met the tender flesh of my stomach, and he applied pressure, the sharp edge biting into my skin. I clenched my teeth, suppressing the cry of pain that threatened to escape.

He dragged the knife across my skin and I felt the searing sting of the wound as it opened, my own blood welling up in its wake. Determined not to give him the satisfaction of witnessing my suffering, I locked my jaw and retorted, "Do you really think I'm afraid of you? That I'm scared of pain?"

A sinister smile tugged at the corners of Malachar's lips, and his voice flowed with sadistic pleasure as he replied, "You will be."

With merciless precision, he traced the blade across my skin once more, each cruel stroke drawing fresh blood and sending waves of agonizing pain coursing through my body. The warm, metallic scent of my own blood filled the air, a grim reminder of the torment I endured.

"Scream for me," he hissed, his voice a twisted melody of delight.

I refused to succumb to his cruel demands. My lips pressed into a tight line and I held onto my resolve, determined not to grant him the satisfaction of seeing me broken, no matter how brutal his torture became.

Malachar's obsession with my suffering only escalated. As he leaned closer, his dark eyes bore into mine and his mouth opened, his tongue slithering over one of the cuts he had inflicted. I shuddered as I watched him taste my blood, his twisted satisfaction evident in the way his lips curled into a sick grin.

"I can taste the magic in your blood, witch. It's intoxicating," he purred, his voice dark and husky.

The sudden tightening of his grip on my arms drew a sharp gasp from my lips as his nails dug into my tender skin. The blade, slick with my blood, resumed its merciless journey across my flesh, each stroke more agonizing than the last. This time, the searing pain was too much to bear, and I couldn't suppress the scream of torment that erupted from my throat.

"That's it," he taunted, his voice laced with cruel satisfaction. "Now you're beginning to understand."

The relentless onslaught continued, each cut driving me deeper into the abyss of suffering. His laughter echoed off the unforgiving stone walls of the dungeon, a chilling backdrop to my anguish.

My body trembled uncontrollably and the edges of my vision threatened to succumb to darkness. The pain was overwhelming, but I clung to consciousness with a tenacity borne from sheer determination. I couldn't afford to lose consciousness, not in the hands of this sadistic monster.

The relentless flow of blood from my wounds saturated the fabric of my tattered dress, creating a gruesome tableau of crimson. The sensation of warmth seeping into the wooden table beneath me only intensified the agony.

Finally, after what felt like an eternity, Malachar seemed to grow bored with his cruel game. He stepped back, his eyes admiring his handiwork as he surveyed my mutilated form. The cool, damp air against the open wounds sent waves of unbearable pain through me, and I couldn't help but whimper in agony, though my spirit remained unbroken.

"You're not done yet," he said, a cruel smile spreading across his lips.

Malachar's sinister smile persisted, a chilling omen of what was to come, and dread settled in the pit of my stomach like an unshakable weight. I knew that my torment was far from over and the realization left me feeling utterly powerless.

He advanced once more, his cold hands hovering ominously over my battered body. The first faint wisps of his dark magic began to coil around me, their presence intensifying with every passing moment. The agony was instantaneous and excruciating, surging through me with an unrelenting force that left me no room to breathe. I screamed, the sound of my suffering reverberating off the unforgiving stone walls of the chamber.

My body convulsed uncontrollably, each spasm amplifying the unbearable torment. The edges of my vision blurred, darkness encroaching upon my consciousness. I teetered on the precipice of surrender, my strength ebbing away.

But just as I felt myself succumbing to the sweet temptation of unconsciousness, a voice, a lifeline, broke through the maelstrom of agony.

"Vale, don't give in, they are coming for you," the First Witch's voice whispered in the depths of my mind.

Her words were a fragile thread of hope that I clung to desperately. They became my anchor in the tempest of torment, a reason to keep fighting. I couldn't allow myself to yield, not when I knew that my friends were on their way to rescue me.

The seductive allure of darkness beckoned, offering the peace of blissful oblivion, but I resisted its siren call. I battled against the searing pain, my grip on consciousness tenuous yet unyielding. I refused to surrender.

The torment persisted, waves of anguish crashing over me like a relentless tide, threatening to drown me in despair. Then, abruptly, the agony ceased.

A tentative semblance of relief washed over me as the torment abruptly halted, and the oppressive darkness began to recede. I blinked up at Malachar, a flicker of annoyance evident in his expression. It was a brief respite, but I knew that my ordeal was far from over.

"You're stronger than I thought. But it doesn't matter. You will break, and when you do, I will be there to witness your fall." Malachar's cruel words washed over me, but I could no longer summon the energy to care. The relentless torment had left me battered and broken, my spirit nearly shattered. All I yearned for was to escape this nightmarish place, to leave behind the echoes of suffering that clung to these cold, unforgiving walls.

I lay sprawled upon the wretched table, my body a canvas of torment, my once-fierce resolve now waning. This pain was unlike anything I had ever endured, and with every passing moment, I questioned whether I possessed the strength to withstand another session with my sadistic captor.

My eyes fluttered shut, my breathing ragged and labored. I turned my thoughts heavenward, invoking prayers to any benevolent deity who might hear my pleas, begging for salvation from this abyss of agony.

In the bleak stillness, the First Witch's voice was a soothing whisper within my mind. *"The others are coming. You must stay strong,"* she urged, a beacon of hope amid the darkness. I clung to her words, using them as a wellspring of inner strength, summoning the remnants of my willpower to endure what was to come.

Malachar, undeterred by my suffering, commenced his assault once more, and I found my voice, a relentless scream echoing into the void. Every agonized cry was a plea for deliverance, a desperate hope that the others would arrive before it was too late.

Yet, as if from the shadows themselves, Haldir's voice intruded upon the torment. "That's enough for today," his words sliced through the haze that clouded my thoughts. Malachar's cruel determination faltered as disappointment etched across his face.

"She isn't broken yet," he protested, his frustration evident.

"No, but we can't risk killing her yet. We still need her alive," Haldir replied, his tone unyielding.

Reluctantly, Malachar scowled and stepped back, allowing Haldir to approach. The transfer of tormentors was a grim reminder of my helplessness, and dread weighed heavily in the air as Malachar left the chamber, his visage dark and twisted.

Haldir's piercing gaze swept over my broken and battered form like a vulture circling its prey.

"You've proven more resilient than I expected," he mused. "But even the strongest wills can be broken and you will not escape that fate."

My parched throat barely allowed me to speak, and my voice emerged hoarse and ragged. "You underestimate me," I croaked, defiance still flickering within me.

Haldir's response was a chilling, humorless laugh that echoed off the unforgiving stone walls of the chamber. "Perhaps," he conceded. "But we'll soon find out, won't we?" He drew closer, his movements almost tender, a stark contrast to the brutality I had endured.

"There's no need for further violence today, witch," he purred, a sickening sweetness to his tone. "You will be taken back to your cell. You will heal. And then, the true suffering will begin. I'll take my time tearing apart your mind."

With those ominous words, he removed the restraints but kept me magically shackled, signaling for the guards to come forward.

"Drug her and throw her back in the cell," he ordered them with casual cruelty.

The guards complied, forcing a sickly sweet glass of water down my throat. I coughed and sputtered, choking on the liquid as it slid down my throat. They pulled me up from the wretched table, the encroaching darkness clouding my vision already.

Barely conscious, I was dragged through the dimly lit, foreboding halls and unceremoniously tossed into the cramped, suffocating cell. The impact of the cold, unyielding floor was jarring, leaving me sprawled in agony. The heavy door slammed shut behind me.

Curling into a ball, I surrendered to the pain and exhaustion that relentlessly besieged my body. It wasn't long before I fell into a deep sleep, though rest brought no solace. Even in the abyss of slumber, the nightmares haunted me, tormenting my fractured spirit with their relentless cruelty.

Chapter Thirty-Six

KAELAN

For seventy-two hours, an agonizing and bleak stretch of time, Kaelan had been grappling with an emotional turmoil that felt as though it had wrapped its insidious tendrils around his very soul. From the moment he sensed Vale's capture, a sensation that engulfed him like a rushing tide of dread, he had been rendered almost paralyzed, ensnared in a cocoon of worry and helplessness.

While Thalion had immediately sprung into action, his leadership abilities shining brighter than ever, Kaelan had found himself marooned in a sea of his own incapacitating thoughts. Thalion, the epitome of charisma and resolve, had instantly begun rallying troops, his voice a clarion call to arms that rekindled the spirits of their beleaguered forces. The troops had responded to him as iron is drawn to a magnet, reorganizing with newfound purpose and vigor.

In the same vein, Aerion had been the network, the lifeline that connected them to crucial allies. With a natural gift for diplomacy and an innate understanding of strategy, he had been sending missives with the urgency and precision of a master archer releasing arrows. Each message was a beacon of hope, extending the promise of support and strength through their alliance.

Wren, too, had been a whirlwind of activity, a force of nature in his own right. His werewolf pack had looked to him for guidance, and he had prepared them with military precision for the voyage to the Fae realm and the ensuing conflict. With feral eyes gleaming with fierce determination, he had imbued his pack with the fierce readiness that only a born leader could.

And then there was Kaelan—lost, ineffective, mired in a tangle of his own making. All he could do was sense Vale's fear, her torment, as if these emotions were echoing inside him, amplified a thousandfold. It was a disorienting fog that clouded his thoughts, making even the simplest decisions feel like insurmountable challenges.

Gripping the black rose he had discovered in Vale's room, its tips tainted with a poison that spoke of darker intentions, he felt as if he was holding onto the last vestige of her presence. The petals seemed almost to absorb the despair that radiated off him, becoming even darker as if wilting under his suffocating emotions.

But today, finally, there was something to be done, a purpose to be had. They were crossing the threshold, stepping through the portal to Elysian. Kaelan had been assigned the task of transporting the wolves once they were on the other side, a critical role that was imbued with its own set of challenges.

It wasn't much, but it was something—his first real opportunity to contribute, to fight back against the shadow that had stolen Vale from him. As he prepared to undertake his mission, the weight of the black rose in his hand seemed to lighten ever so slightly, as if sharing in his newfound resolve.

And so, with each step towards the portal, Kaelan felt the shackles of his own helplessness begin to loosen. The wolves sensed it too, their restless energy mirroring his own mounting determination. For the first time in three soul-crushing days, Kaelan allowed himself the luxury of hope—fragile and flickering, but infinitely precious.

The air around the portal vibrated with a low hum, its iridescent sheen reflecting in the eyes of the werewolves who had lined up in an organized formation. For Kaelan, it felt like standing on the edge of the world, peering into an abyss that could either redeem him or shatter him entirely.

Methodically, he began guiding the werewolves through the shimmering gateway, signaling to them in clusters of twos and threes. Though they numbered only around two hundred, each werewolf was a wellspring of raw power and primal fury, their collective presence more than enough to tip the scales of any battle. Their fur bristled with anticipation, eyes glowing in the semi-darkness like embers waiting for a wind to fan them into flame.

Wren stood toward the back of the formation, flanked by his beta, Venna. His posture was a mix of grim determination and subtle grace, every inch the alpha of his pack. Nearby, Harker, the lone vampire amidst the wolves, surveyed the scene through icy blue eyes. Her gaze was like a blade forged in the fires of resolve, unwavering and intense.

Finally, the last of the werewolves stepped through the portal. Wren was the last to cross, but before he did, he approached Kaelan, placing a firm and reassuring hand on his shoulder.

"Don't worry so much anymore," Wren's voice was a low rumble, infused with a conviction that seemed to pierce the haze of Kaelan's own uncertainties. "The fact that you can still feel Vale means she's alive. We'll get to her soon."

Kaelan looked into Wren's eyes and nodded. At that moment, he felt a rush of gratitude and understanding. Wren was right; the very pain that had immobilized him was also a lifeline, a sign that Vale was still clinging to existence. It was a glimmer of hope that he clung to as Wren stepped through the portal, his silhouette consumed by its faint light.

Taking a steadying breath, Kaelan followed suit. The sensation was like plunging into icy waters, momentarily disorienting but altogether exhilarating. As he emerged on the other side, he was greeted by the towering, ancient trees of Elysian's grand forests. Their branches stretched toward the sky like skeletal fingers.

The werewolves had regrouped, their eyes keen and watchful as they waited for their next move. They stood like guardians amid the forest, a formidable force ready to be unleashed.

Though they were far from their goal, and Vale's rescue was still a precarious dream, standing in that wild forest, surrounded by allies, Kaelan felt a resurgence of purpose and courage. The weight of inaction and despair that had plagued him for three long days was beginning to lift. He was no longer just a spectator to his own life, but an actor on a stage set for both tragedy and triumph. And for the first time in what seemed like an eternity, he was ready to play his part.

With a gesture from Wren, the werewolves began to form ranks once more, aligning themselves in a disciplined configuration that belied their feral nature. A few of them lifted their noses to the air as if drinking in the unique scents of this mysterious realm. The air was imbued with the heady aroma of exotic flowers and the more subtle, hidden notes of something darker, something arcane. Kaelan inhaled deeply, allowing himself a moment to appreciate the eerie beauty of Elysian even amidst the tension of their mission.

Summoning the core of his powers, Kaelan focused on the dark spaces between things—the shadows that were as much a part of the world as the light. In his mind, he felt the energies of the demon realm answer his call, swirling around him like a dark vortex. He had never attempted to shadow-shift so many beings at once, but his powers were now fully unbound, unleashed in a way that promised immense possibilities.

With a mental nudge, he extended the reach of his power to envelop the werewolves gathered around him. They felt it too, a sudden chill, and their eyes met his with awe. Wren nodded subtly as if to say, 'We're ready.'

Closing his eyes, Kaelan willed them to move. The shadows coiled like serpents, enfolding each werewolf in a cocoon of pure darkness. Then, with a sensation akin to the falling sensation one feels just before sleep, they were moving—fast, impossibly fast—through a world devoid of color or light.

When they materialized again, they were standing in the palace courtyard, a stark contrast to the towering forest they had left behind. Elegant stone masonry and lush gardens gave way to an open space, currently empty but for the presence of one figure: Aerion.

"Good, you're here," Aerion greeted them in his customary gruff, economical manner. His eyes surveyed the werewolves briefly before settling on Wren. "Get your wolves to the south field. The troops are assembling there."

Wren turned to Venna and relayed the order. "You heard him. To the south field." Venna nodded and gestured for the werewolves to follow her, leading them out of the courtyard with disciplined efficiency. Kaelan noticed that Aerion gave Harker a curious glance before watching the wolves leave.

Kaelan turned to Aerion. "Where's Thalion?"

"Inside," Aerion replied. "Strategy room, finalizing plans."

Without another word, the four of them moved in unison toward the palace. Their footsteps echoed off the ornate marble floors as they navigated through hallways adorned with artwork and tapestries that told tales of Fae history and heroism. Which was a load of bullshit if you asked Kaelan.

Upon reaching the strategy room, they found Thalion engrossed in conversation with a cadre of advisors and his father, the King, who looked every bit as regal and commanding as his son. Maps and scrolls were spread across the table, each marked with symbols and lines that depicted their planned courses of action.

Upon their entry, Thalion looked up and gave them a nod. Turning back to his advisors, he dismissed them with a curt wave of his hand. "You know your tasks. Go."

As the advisors filed out of the room, Thalion turned his full attention to the newly arrived group. His eyes met Kaelan's and for a brief moment, a silent exchange of understanding and resolve passed between them.

"We're all here," Thalion announced, his voice laced with a seriousness that filled the room. "It's time to go over the final details. Time is of the essence, and we have a battle to prepare for—and a life to save."

Thalion spread his hands over the map, his fingertips lightly brushing strategic points marked by tokens and sigils. "We will divide our forces into three groups. The first will serve as our main offensive, aimed at the enemy's front lines. The second, the werewolves among them, will flank them from the sides, to keep them distracted and unbalanced. The third group, led by me—and including all of you—will make a direct path to where Vale is being held."

Kaelan felt a sense of relief. Being in the group that would directly attempt to rescue Vale made him feel more in control, less helpless. He glanced at Wren, whose eyes were narrowed in focus, and Harker, who was taking in every detail like a hawk eyeing its prey. Aerion simply nodded, as though he had expected no less.

"We'll be heavily outnumbered," Thalion continued, "so we'll need to use every advantage we have. Kaelan, your ability to shadow-shift can give us the element of surprise. Harker, your skills in subterfuge and, well, chaos, will be invaluable. Wren, your pack will be crucial in overwhelming their defenses, and Aerion, your command over elemental magic will provide the firepower. Are we clear?"

A round of nods and affirmations circled the table. It was a daring plan, filled with uncertainties and perils, but it was fortified by the unique strengths of those who stood around it.

"We leave in thirty minutes," Thalion declared, locking eyes with each person around the table. "Use this time to prepare, both mentally and physically. Once we step out of this palace, there's no turning back."

As the group dispersed, Kaelan felt a strange concoction of emotions. Fear, undoubtedly, but also an adrenalized sort of readiness. He felt a hand on his shoulder and turned to find Wren looking at him, a mirror reflecting the same complex emotions he was grappling with.

"We've got this, Kaelan," Wren said softly, a brotherly assurance that broke through the chaos of Kaelan's thoughts. "We'll bring her back."

Kaelan nodded, his eyes meeting Wren's. "Thank you. I needed to hear that."

Taking a deep breath, Kaelan left the room, his steps purposeful. He found a quiet corner in one of the less frequented halls of the palace and closed his eyes, steadying his breathing. Shadows danced behind his eyelids, waiting for his command, pulsing with a dark energy that he now felt a master of. Taking a deep breath, he visualized Vale, her face, her laughter, her spirit, and channeled that into the power coursing through him. When he opened his eyes, they were no longer just brown but tinged with a deeper, darker hue—a sign that he was close to succumbing to something darker. At last, he exhaled, and his eyes returned to their normal shade.

As he walked back toward the strategy room, where Thalion and the others would be making their final preparations, he felt as though he was stepping through a portal of a different kind—one that separated doubt from action, hesitation from resolve. The next time he would summon the shadows to envelop him, it would be to dive headlong into a battle for the life of someone he couldn't bear to lose.

And so, with every step, Kaelan felt himself drawing closer to a destiny that was as terrifying as it was necessary. But for the first time in what felt like an eternity, he felt ready to meet it.

Chapter Thirty-Seven

WREN

Cloaked in the velvet darkness of the night, Wren stood with his companions, his senses heightened to a near fever pitch. His nostrils flared, catching scents carried on the wind, his ears twitching at every rustle of leaves or distant murmur of voices. Above them, the malevolent sky of the Unseelie Court loomed, an unsettling tapestry of colors that had never graced any sky he'd known. Terralux, once the domain of their Fae ally Aerion, now stood as a fortress under the control of the treacherous Haldir.

Venna, his trusted beta, was at the vanguard with the rest of the wolf pack. Wren had tasked her with leading the charge at the gates, creating the diversion that would allow them to infiltrate the palace and find Vale. He met the eyes of Thalion, Aerion, Harker, and finally, Kaelan.

The tension among them was thick, each knowing that the upcoming moments would decide the fate of their mission and Vale's life.

Then it came—the signal. A haunting howl, resonant and chilling, cut through the air, piercing the night like a knife through silk. As if unleashed by some unseen force, Wren's wolves surged forward, a wave of fur and fangs and ferocity aimed at Terralux's imposing gates.

Wren felt the ground tremble beneath the onslaught, but his eyes were on Kaelan. With a look of intense concentration, Kaelan reached into the shadowy depths of his power. In an instant, their surroundings shifted; the dark tendrils of shadow enveloped them, pulling them through a world devoid of light or substance. When they emerged, they found themselves in the palace courtyard, hidden behind the broad trunk of a massive, gnarled tree.

The courtyard was a flurry of activity. Fae soldiers, caught off guard by the sudden attack, scrambled to arm themselves and take their positions. The confusion provided a perfect cover, rendering them invisible in the concealing darkness of Kaelan's shadows.

Wren watched as Harker, her movements as fluid as water, melded into the shadows. Her knives gleamed ominously for a brief moment before she disappeared from sight, leaving only a whispered promise of her swift return. Wren couldn't help but marvel at her natural talent for stealth, a skill honed to perfection over years of practice, despite the fact that she preferred to remain engrossed in her research.

It wasn't long before she returned, her eyes sparkling with a sly satisfaction. "Found a way in," she reported, her voice barely above a whisper. "Soldier quarters—deserted. Everyone's out here, trying to make sense of the chaos."

Wren nodded approvingly as they moved, following Harker's lead. The adrenaline coursing through his veins was a strange mix of exhilaration and fear, but above all, it sharpened his focus to a razor's edge.

They entered the palace, navigating through dimly lit corridors that seemed to twist and turn like a labyrinth.

Wren's claws extended involuntarily, a primal reaction to the nearing danger and the promise of confrontation. His pack was fighting at the front lines, risking their lives for this mission. Failure was not an option. Every step they took was a step closer to Vale, and Wren felt his resolve harden.

The group moved cautiously, their senses alert, each aware that every corner turned could bring a fresh challenge. As they moved deeper into the labyrinthine corridors, a new scent mingled with the stale, dank air—sweat and steel, tinged with the unmistakable ozone scent of magic.

Before anyone could utter a warning, a detachment of Fae soldiers appeared, phasing in from some sort of magical concealment. Swords unsheathed with a disquieting ring, and arcane symbols swirled around the hands of Fae spellcastersat the rear.

"Stop them!" cried one, clearly an officer, as arcs of magical energy flew from the fingertips of the casters, aimed squarely at the group.

Wren shifted into his wolven form and lunged forward, his claws slashing through the air, aiming for the magic-wielding Fae, but a force field repelled him, throwing him back with staggering force. Aerion struggled against the magical restraints, his face flushed with rage and frustration.

It was Harker who broke the deadlock. Swift and relentless, she danced through the soldiers, knives spinning, cutting through the magical ropes that bound Thalion and Aerion.

"I knew these Fae-crafted knives would come in handy," she shouted behind her to the others.

But for every soldier she disabled, another seemed ready to take his place. They were outnumbered and outmatched in terms of magic.

Just as it seemed they were on the verge of being overwhelmed, a guttural growl emanated from Kaelan. His eyes, usually a calm brown, were now entirely black, matching the shadowy tendrils that began to whip around him with ferocious intensity. His features twisted, not in pain, but in utter surrender to something primal, something terrifying.

With a deafening roar, leathery wings erupted from his back, unfurling to their full span in a display of raw, nightmarish power. Twisted horns spiraled out from his temples, and the tips of his skin took on an obsidian hue.

The soldiers hesitated, their expressions twisting from determination to horror. In that moment of collective paralysis, Kaelan lunged forward. His wings created gusts of wind that knocked soldiers off balance, his newly extended claws cut through armor and flesh as if they were paper, and his horns gored through anyone unfortunate enough to be in their path.

But what was perhaps even more chilling was the precise control he exhibited. This was not a berserker's rampage, but the methodical dissection of obstacles by an unyielding force. Within moments, the soldiers were either incapacitated or had retreated, their faces pale and their spirits broken.

As quickly as it had appeared, Kaelan's monstrous form retreated, his wings folding back into his body, his horns receding, and his eyes returning to their human state—though Wren noticed they remained tinged with a residual darkness. Kaelan looked exhausted, his gaze locking onto Wren's for a brief moment as if seeking approval or perhaps forgiveness.

For Wren, there was nothing to forgive. They had been up against overwhelming odds, and Kaelan had done what was necessary. All that mattered now was pushing forward, finding Vale, and ending this nightmare once and for all.

"Let's move," said Thalion, his voice tinged with awe and a new-found respect, clearly directed at Kaelan. "We're close. I can feel it."

The team picked up their pace, their steps echoing softly through the gloomy passageways. Their senses were all heightened, each keenly aware that more challenges likely lay ahead.

As they moved, Wren felt a constant itch at the nape of his neck, like electricity coursing through his veins. He also felt something else, fear. Unbridled and all-consuming fear. The feeling confirmed something Wren had suspected for weeks, he had a blood bond forming with Vale. He could definitely feel her somewhere in this castle if he focused hard enough. It had started the second she had given him her blood after he killed Rafe.

"It's like an endless maze," Harker mused as she led the group through another winding corridor.

"Endless or not, every maze has an exit," Aerion muttered, his eyes scanning the shadows as if expecting them to lunge forward.

They reached a fork in the corridor. Aerion paused, his eyes narrowing as if trying to recall memories buried under years of exile and sorrow. "Which way?" Thalion asked.

"The left leads to the old torture chambers, the right to the main dungeons," Aerion replied after a moment's hesitation.

"Splitting up is risky," Harker observed, twirling one of her knives in her hand. "But it could save us time."

"She's right," Wren said. "Harker and I will head to the left, you three head right."

Thalion looked unconvinced, his eyes moving from Wren to Aerion, searching their faces for signs of doubt. Finally, he nodded.

"Be careful," he cautioned. "And meet back here if you find any-thing. We don't want to risk getting lost in this place."

KAELAN

Thalion, Aerion, and Kaelan took the path to the right. As they delved deeper, the atmosphere grew increasingly oppressive, the air thick and cold. Just when it seemed they were making progress, a wall of flames burst forth, blocking their way.

Aerion reached out a hand to quell the magical fire but faltered, grimacing. "This is no ordinary magic. It's laced with dark enchant-ments."

Thalion sighed, his hand resting on the hilt of his sword. "Can you break it?"

Aerion shook his head. "Not easily. It would take time we don't have."

Kaelan's gaze turned towards the wall of flames, his eyes filled with determination. "I could try."

Thalion and Aerion exchanged a glance. "You would do that?" Thalion asked.

Kaelan gave a solemn nod, his expression betraying nothing of the emotions that lay beneath.

Thalion nodded, his tone becoming firm. "Do it."

Kaelan walked slowly towards the flames, his eyes locked onto the dancing tongues of fire. He seemed to hesitate, his fists clenching and unclenching, his posture rigid. Then, in a sudden movement, he hurled himself towards the fire, his wings unfurling and wrapping around his body.

A moment later, the fire was gone, extinguished as if by an unseen force, accepting his sacrifice. Kaelan emerged from the smoke, his wings singed but still intact, his expression pained.

"It's done," he said, his voice hoarse.

Thalion nodded, his voice tinged with admiration. "Thank you."

Aerion moved towards Kaelan, his expression grave. "That was... impressive. I'm not sure many could withstand such power."

Kaelan didn't respond, his gaze distant. "Come on, we have to keep moving."

They continued down the corridor, their footsteps echoing through the dark halls. As they reached the end, a sense of unease crept over Kaelan, an instinctual feeling that something was amiss.

"Careful," he cautioned. "Keep your eyes open. This feels like a trap."

Just then, a figure emerged from the shadows, a wicked grin playing across its features. "Clever," it crooned, its voice like honey and venom. "Very clever."

The creature was grotesque and distorted, its features twisted beyond recognition. It wore the skin of a Fae male, though it was clear it was something else entirely. Its eyes were a sickly yellow, its teeth like razors, its claws as sharp as blades.

It was a harbinger of death, a thing born of nightmares and darkness, and it stood before them, blocking their path.

"What are you?" Thalion breathed, his eyes wide with horror.

The creature smiled, its voice sending a chill down Kaelan's spine. "I am a servant of my master, a loyal soldier in his army."

Kaelan didn't wait for another word. The creature was powerful, its magic evident in every breath it drew. But he could sense the fear that lurked beneath the surface, a weakness that could be exploited.

He lunged forward, his claws extended, ready to tear the monster apart. But the creature was faster, its own claws lashing out, tearing into Kaelan's flesh.

A gasp of pain escaped his lips as the monster's talons ripped through his skin.

Thalion rushed forward, his sword arcing through the air.

The creature was agile, though, and deftly evaded the strike. Its claws slashed at Thalion's arm, leaving a trail of bloody gashes.

Aerion joined the fray, his magic surging forth, crackling like lightning.

The monster was powerful, its own magic deflecting the assault. But Aerion's attack had bought Thalion an opening, and the prince didn't hesitate. His blade sliced through the air, carving a deep wound across the creature's torso.

Thalion's strike was true, and the creature howled in agony as dark ichor oozed from the gash. It staggered back, momentarily disoriented, and Kaelan seized the opportunity to regroup. Blood dripped from his injured wing, but he pushed through the pain, his resolve unbroken.

Aerion, recovering from his own failed assault, summoned a torrent of flames to engulf the creature. But it proved more resilient than expected, its twisted form somehow resisting the inferno. It retaliated with a vicious swipe, narrowly missing Aerion's face.

The creature's movements grew more erratic, its grotesque appearance contorting further with each attack. Thalion, his expression resolute, pressed the assault with relentless strikes of his sword, while Kaelan's wings unfurled like a shadowy shield, protecting them from the creature's relentless magic.

The monster roared, its fury palpable. But its rage only made it sloppy, and its next swing missed Kaelan, leaving its chest exposed. Kaelan didn't waste the opportunity. With a ferocious howl, he plunged his claws into the creature's chest, tearing its heart out. The creature let out a final, gurgling scream before collapsing to the ground, lifeless.

The trio stood over the creature's corpse, panting and covered in blood. The battle had been brutal, but they had emerged victorious.

"What was that thing?" Thalion asked, his eyes still wide with shock.

"A creature of the Unseelie Court," Aerion replied, his tone grim. "A soulless husk, an abomination created by the darkest of magics."

"Do you think the Unseelie court might be creating an army of these monsters?" Kaelan asked, his expression darkening.

Thalion sighed, his hand running through his hair. "It's possible. The Unseelie are capable of the most unspeakable horrors. If they have managed to create an army of these creatures..."

"It could spell doom for the entire realm," Aerion finished, his voice barely above a whisper.

Kaelan glanced down at the monster's corpse, his jaw clenched.

"We need to find Vale. Now."

Chapter Thirty-Eight

It had been an eternity since they had captured me, or at least it felt that way. Days bled into nights and each passing moment was marked by unrelenting torment at the hands of the sadistic Malachar. He reveled in my agony, finding pleasure in my suffering, and I became nothing more than a vessel for his cruelty.

Now I found myself in the presence of Haldir, who seemed to specialize in a different form of torment—mental torture. Seated on an ostentatious throne, his eyes glinting with a cold and calculating light, Haldir looked at me as though I were an enigma he was determined to unravel.

"Shall we continue, my dear?" His voice was smooth but dripping with a vile sweetness as he extended his hand in my direction.

I braced herself as I felt the familiar invasion of my mind, like needles piercing through the walls of my consciousness. Haldir's mental probes were incredibly painful, each one pushing deeper into my memories, violating the sanctity of my thoughts.

He sought to sift through my memories, desperate to find something—anything—that he could use to break me, to bend me to his will. With each mental thrust, it felt like a portion of myself was being torn away, leaving me raw and vulnerable. But I held on, gritting my teeth and channeling my focus into maintaining the fragile defenses I had built around herself.

I had no answer for him, but the thought of giving in, of letting him plunder my soul for his own dark purposes, fortified my defenses. It was a struggle, a painful mental tug-of-war that left me feeling drained and weary, but I could not, would not, let him win.

As the battle raged on inside my mind, I clung to fleeting thoughts of my loved ones—of Kaelan, of Wren, and of all the people who were depending on me to stay strong. Each thought became a lifeline, each memory a bastion against Haldir's incessant attack.

For now, I held on, my spirit bruised but unbroken, even as Haldir withdrew his mental needles, clearly dissatisfied but far from defeated.

"You won't win," I whispered, though I knew he could hear my thoughts.

Haldir leaned back, his eyes narrowing. "We shall see."

But even as he said it, I felt the flicker of something deep within him—a seed of doubt, a minute crack in his otherwise unyielding confidence. It was small, almost imperceptible, but it was there. And in that moment, I realized that while he might have succeeded in tormenting my body and mind, my spirit remained her own. And that was something he could never take away.

Every night, after the agony subsided, I curled into a trembling ball on the cold, unforgiving stone floor of my cell. With each passing hour, I prayed to the gods, begging them to take away the pain, to offer me some respite from this relentless torture. My resistance, my will to fight, slipped further and further from my grasp like grains of sand slipping through desperate fingers.

But even in the darkest depths of despair, there was one thing that kept the embers of my spirit flickering: the knowledge that one day soon, I would pay Malachar and Haldir back for every second of pain they had inflicted upon me. Revenge was my unwavering anchor, my only solace in this wretched existence.

I was hollow and numb, a mere shell of the person I had once been. Yet, the aching pain that plagued me, morning, noon, and night, was a cruel reminder that I was still very much alive. It was a reminder that fueled the ember of determination within me, however feeble it had become.

The First Witch had become a constant presence in my mind. Her voice whispered words of encouragement, urging me to hold on, to keep fighting, to resist the consuming darkness that threatened to claim me. Her guidance was a fragile lifeline in this abyss of despair and I clung to it with every ounce of strength I had left.

In the suffocating darkness of my cell, my only respite was the drugs they fed me. They offered a brief escape from the relentless torment, their numbing embrace temporarily shielding me from the worst of the nightmares that plagued my mind. Each dose was a temporary reprieve from the never-ending suffering that had become my existence.

But no matter how deeply I slept, no matter how many drugs they administered, the pain and anguish remained an ever-present shadow that clung to my soul. It was a constant reminder of the cruelty I endured, an unyielding presence that haunted my every waking moment.

As I lay in the cold, unforgiving confines of my cell, my battered body unable to move, the voice of the First Witch reached out to me, her words a soothing balm for my tortured spirit. Her ethereal presence filled my mind, a beacon of hope in the suffocating darkness.

"The time will come soon, Vale," she whispered, her voice a gentle caress against the chaos of my thoughts. *"Be ready. They are coming for you."*

My cracked lips formed a silent question, a desperate plea for answers. "When?" I breathed.

"Soon," she replied, her voice carrying the weight of a promise. *"You must remain strong. Resist the darkness. Hold onto the light. Only then will you prevail."*

Her words were a reminder that I was not alone in this nightmare. I clung to them like a drowning soul clinging to a raft in a stormy sea. With each passing moment, I steeled myself for the inevitable. I knew the others would come, and when they did, I would be ready.

I awoke once more in the cold and dimly lit cell, my body stiff and aching from the countless hours of torment. The scars and open wounds crisscrossing my body. It took a moment to get my bearings, my disoriented mind struggling to grasp the reality of my situation. I knew that Malachar had not yet come to visit, as the suffocating dread that accompanied his presence had not yet settled upon me.

There was no clock to mark the passage of time in this dismal place, but the gnawing hunger pangs that ate at my stomach told me that it had been a while since my captor's last visit. Each passing minute in this prison felt like an eternity.

Suddenly, the muffled sounds of a commotion reached my ears, echoing from somewhere beyond the confines of my dungeon. I strained to listen, my senses sharpening as I tried to decipher the distant noises. I turned my gaze to the lone guard stationed near my cell, hoping to glean some information from him.

"What's going on?" I asked, my voice hoarse and barely more than a whisper, but he responded with nothing more than a contemptuous sneer.

As my anxiety grew, a subtle movement in the shadowy corner of the dungeon caught my attention. I squinted through the dim light, my heart skipping a beat as I recognized the silhouette emerging from the shadows. It was Nyxen. He had found me.

Relief washed over me, but I knew better than to reveal my emotions. I maintained a neutral expression, aware of the guard's watchful eyes upon me.

"Vale," his voice whispered softly in my mind, a soothing presence amidst the turmoil.

"Nyxen! What's going on?" I inquired mentally back to him.

"Others have come," Nyxen's reply echoed in my mind.

My heart soared with newfound hope at his words and I waited with bated breath for him to continue.

The realization that I needed to escape from this torment grew stronger with each passing moment. My mind raced, desperate for a plan to break free from these infernal shackles that bound my magic. Nyxen's unexpected appearance had sparked an idea, a flicker of hope in the abyss of my despair.

"Nyxen, show yourself to the guard," I urged, my voice a whisper that carried the weight of urgency.

Nyxen moved from the shadowy confines of my cell and over toward the guard. The shadows within the cell shifted once more and the guard's eyes widened with alarm as he caught sight of the eerie, dark creature. Panic etched itself onto his features as he rushed over to where Nyxen was concealed.

"What is this? What are you doing?" The guard stammered, his voice trembling with fear.

A surge of defiance coursed through me and I couldn't help but retort, "I guess these shackles aren't as powerful as you all thought."

In a hurried frenzy, the guard reached for the key hanging from his belt and fumbled to unlock the door to my cell. As he stepped inside, Nyxen positioned himself beside me and the guard aimed his outstretched hand at the shadowy creature. A powerful blast of energy erupted from his palm, threatening to strike Nyxen.

Without hesitation, I positioned myself between the guard's attack and Nyxen, my hands rising in a protective gesture. The searing bolt of power struck the shackles encircling my wrists, the force of it sending me sprawling backward to the unforgiving stone floor. Pain coursed through me as I collided with the ground.

As the guard attempted to regain his composure, I fought through the agony, summoning every ounce of strength left within me. I staggered to my feet, drawing my hands apart with a determined force and the weakened shackles finally gave way, snapping apart with a resounding crack.

Now they would all pay.

A simmering rage burned within me, igniting a fire that danced in my eyes as I focused on the guard. With a sick satisfaction, I summoned the depths of my magic, drawing it forth like a crashing torrent of power. It surged through me, a wild and untamed force that filled every fiber of my being, a tempest within my very soul.

As the magic coursed through me, a fierce and primal roar escaped my lips. It was a sound born of pent-up fury and anguish, a scream of liberation that shattered the oppressive silence of the dungeon. The raw power I had harnessed surged outward in a cataclysmic burst, an unrelenting wave of force that I directed at the guard standing before me.

The impact of my unleashed magic struck the guard with brutal force, his body becoming a mere puppet in the merciless dance of energy. He was sent hurtling across the room, his form colliding with the unforgiving stone wall with a sickening crunch. The violence of the collision left no room for doubt; he would pose no further threat.

I stood there, victorious and unshackled, finally free from the unending torment and agony that had plagued me for what felt like an eternity. The flames of my soul still burned brightly, but there was no time to rest or savor this newfound freedom. I had to seize this opportunity and escape before Haldir and his allies realized what had transpired.

Despite the ache that permeated my body and the lingering dizziness from the impact against the floor, I steeled myself and moved forward, every step a testament to my indomitable will. The path to escape lay before me and I had no intention of faltering.

The door to the dungeon suddenly burst open, a violent intrusion that startled me. My heart raced as I beheld the figures who entered the chamber – Thalion, Aerion, and Kaelan. The shock mirrored in their eyes was a reflection of my own astonishment at their unexpected appearance.

"Vale," Kaelan whispered, his voice filled with disbelief and relief.

"Are you okay?" Thalion asked, his concern etched across his features as he examined my battered form.

"No," I replied, my voice laced with a cold determination. "But I will be when Malachar and his father are dead at my feet." My words were a vow, a promise of vengeance that burned within me like a beacon of retribution.

Kaelan approached with a grave expression, his face visibly pale as he assessed my battered state. His voice was laden with remorse as he spoke, "I am so sorry, Vale. We came as soon as we could. Tell me you're okay."

I brushed aside his words with a determined growl. There was no time for apologies or regrets. "Let's not waste any more time," I insisted, my voice resolute.

With that, I strode past them, leaving the confines of the wretched dungeon behind. Every step I took was marked by a fierce determination, a burning desire to exact revenge and reclaim my stolen freedom. As I ventured into the dimly lit hall beyond, my eyes caught sight of Nyxen. Gratitude welled up within me and I offered him a soft-spoken acknowledgment, "Thank you, Nyxen."

His response was equally tender. *"Anything for you,"* he replied, his loyalty absolute.

Kaelan and the rest of the group had converged at my side, their weapons poised for battle. A nod of readiness passed between us, an unspoken understanding that the time for retribution was upon us.

"We end this now. Where is Malachar?" I demanded, my tone laced with resolve.

"We are guessing he's in the throne room with his father," Thalion said, his face still concerned.

"Good. Let's go," I said, my voice steely and ice-cold.

Following Thalion and Kaelan, we ascended the stone stairs, ascending toward the source of our collective rage. My emotions, fueled by anger and hatred, acted as a relentless driving force, propelling me ever forward.

As we rounded a corner, we stumbled upon a group of enemy soldiers, their presence an ill-fated obstacle in our path. My command was firm and unforgiving, "Get out of our way."

The soldiers hesitated briefly, their hesitation quickly turning into a futile attempt to rush us. Yet, they proved to be no match for my fury. My magic surged to life, a potent wave of fire surging forth from my fingertips, burning the guards where they stood in a righteous crescendo of light. Their screams were drowned out by the roar of the flames, their bodies reduced to ash and embers.

The three males looked at me with wide eyes, the shock evident there. I was fully unleashed now and my rage was unbridled.

"How did you get in here?" I inquired as I turned to Kaelan.

He met my gaze with a determined glint in his eyes. "Thalion and Aerion rallied their forces and allies, Wren and his wolf pack are here too. They helped us sneak in and cause a distraction. The rest of the army is outside," he explained.

A faint, relieved smile tugged at the corners of my lips upon hearing the news. It warmed my heart to know that the wolves had not abandoned me and their presence bolstered my resolve.

Our footsteps echoed in the corridors as we pressed forward, drawing ever closer to the throne room. The once bustling halls had become eerily quiet and the silence now enveloped us like a shroud, a stark contrast to the chaos that had reigned just moments ago.

Approaching the ornate double doors that served as the gateway to the throne room, an unsettling feeling crept over me, a sense of unease that settled deep within my bones. The lack of resistance, the unnatural hush, it all made me wary.

Thalion and Aerion halted at the threshold, their expressions weighed down by the gravity of the moment. Thalion's question hung in the air, filled with concern. "Are you sure about this, Vale?"

I met their eyes with determination, my resolve unwavering. I nodded, my voice firm, "I'm sure."

Stepping forward, we entered the expansive chamber and a nause-ating stench assaulted our senses. The putrid odor of death and blood hung heavily in the air, a haunting testament to the brutality of the battle that had recently unfolded within these walls.

My gaze swept across the scene and I beheld the grim sight of several fallen soldiers, their lifeless forms strewn about the chamber. The gruesome tableau bore witness to the savagery that had transpired here.

In the heart of the room, upon his gilded throne, sat Haldir, his posture one of defiant arrogance. His presence was a chilling reminder of the evil that had tormented me for days. Malachar stood at his side. His posture exuded arrogance, but his expression was slightly fearful.

"Vale," Haldir sneered, his tone dripping with mockery. "How nice of you to join us."

I locked eyes with him, my expression devoid of fear or hesitation. "You can drop the pleasantries. We're here to kill you," I stated bluntly, my voice unwavering.

His lips curled into a sly grin. "So hasty. I think you will want to hear what I have to say."

I scoffed at his attempt to engage in conversation. "We have nothing to discuss. This ends right now," I said, my patience already wearing thin.

Haldir seemed to derive some twisted amusement from our con-frontation. "Your bravery is admirable, but it will be your downfall."

I couldn't help but laugh mirthlessly at his words. "Bravery? No, this is vengeance. You are the ones who are going to die today. Not me."

"Such arrogance," he scoffed, his arrogance mirrored in every line of his haughty posture.

My patience waned as I could feel the tension in the room mounting. "Enough talk," I spat, my frustration boiling over.

Haldir's laughter echoed through the chamber, a cold, menacing sound. "You are no match for me. You are a foolish child, playing at a game that is beyond your comprehension."

"We'll see about that," I retorted, my voice steely and unwavering.

He grinned cruelly, his amusement growing by the moment. "Yes, we will." Then, his gaze shifted to Malachar. "Malachar here is your chance to destroy her."

I locked eyes with Malachar, my hatred for him burning bright. "With pleasure."

He advanced toward me, his movements swift and calculated. Thalion and Aerion, ready to defend me, poised themselves for battle. But I halted them with a gesture, my eyes never leaving Malachar.

"No, he's mine," I hissed, my voice dripping with venom.

Thalion's begrudging acceptance was evident in his response. "As you wish."

The air in the grand chamber grew thicker with every passing moment. My entire being was consumed by a singular focus: the man before me, Malachar. His vile face contorted with a cocktail of hatred and unrestrained fury. The days of torment and agony I had endured under his merciless hands had only fueled my resolve and now, this was my moment to exact revenge.

Malachar's unrelenting stare bore into mine as he inched closer, every step calculated and predatory. My magic surged within me, a blazing ember that ignited with a fierce intensity. With a primal roar, he launched a relentless barrage of magical attacks, each one crashing against my defenses like relentless waves battering a rocky shore. The sheer force of his power was a testament to his skill and unwavering determination.

I stood my ground, every fiber of my being committed to the clash of magic that ensued. Although weakened by days of abuse, deprivation, and harsh conditions, the fury and hatred that burned within me forged my inner strength. My magic, though unsteady, surged through me, more potent than I could have ever anticipated.

"You're weak," Malachar taunted, his voice a venomous whisper. "You've always been weak. Before this is all over you'll be strapped to my table again. I'll relish your screams, witch."

A steely resolve filled my voice as I responded, "That's where you're wrong."

Malachar's sneer only grew wider as he replied, "We'll see about that."

Malachar's next magical assault surged with an even greater intensity, a veritable tidal wave of power threatening to engulf me. I held my ground resolutely, my magic forming an unyielding barrier against the relentless onslaught. His skill and potency were undeniable, but his unchecked cruelty had rendered him reckless and overconfident.

As he launched his next volley of attacks, I felt the force behind them diminish, and a glimmer of fear flickered in his eyes as he comprehended the futility of his efforts.

"This is for everything you've done to me," I hissed, my voice dripping with venom and anger.

Summoning the depths of my magical reservoir, I unleashed my full fury with a guttural cry. The full weight of my power crashed down upon him like a mighty tidal wave, and he staggered under the relentless onslaught, ultimately dropping to his knees. Thalion wordlessly handed me his sword, and I accepted it with a grim determination. Each step I took toward the Fae male was slow and deliberate, his wide eyes reflecting a mixture of fear and despair.

"Soon, you will be begging for mercy, and I will show you none," I declared, echoing his earlier sadistic words back at him.

"Bitch," he spat, moving to stand.

My magic surged anew and flames erupted from the blade, enveloping the metal in a brilliant dance of fire. His gaze remained fixated on the weapon, a blend of terror and awe etched across his face.

"This is for the pain you inflicted upon me, for every second of agony you made me endure," I declared, my voice seething with righteous fury.

With a ferocious battle cry, I swung Thalion's blade downward, its keen edge severing Malachar's right hand from his arm. An anguished scream tore from his throat, and blood gushed from the gruesome wound. Though his face contorted with pain, the look in his eyes remained one of pure, unbridled hatred.

"I will kill you for this!" he hissed.

"You won't get the chance," I retorted.

I swung the blade once more, this time severing his left hand with a clean, brutal stroke. His screams reverberated through the chamber, creating a grotesque symphony of suffering.

"This is for the nightmares you inflicted upon me, for every waking moment of horror you forced me to endure," I declared.

Malachar's face turned pale and haggard, his eyes wide with terror. His body trembled as he looked up at me, his gaze filled with pain and despair.

"I am going to end you, just as I'll end your father."

"Father, help me!" he roared desperately. But Haldir remained stoic, his gaze fixed on his son with empty, indifferent eyes. Malachar desperately flung out his magic again, feeble and inadequate.

But my words were not idle threats; they were a promise. My magic surged to life, a brilliant, scorching surge of power coursing through me, fueled by my unbridled rage and unwavering determination. I allowed it to build, the pressure within me mounting until it felt as though I might burst. Then, with a fierce cry, I channeled that pent-up energy and unleashed it upon him—a torrent of fire and fury that consumed him from the inside out.

Malachar's screams intensified, a roar of agony and torment filling the air. His writhing, contorted body bore witness to the relentless flames that ate away at him, his skin melting and charring as the inferno raged hotter and hotter.

Malachar's piercing screams continued to reverberate in the chamber. But amidst the torment, I felt no trace of remorse or pity for the man who had subjected me and numerous others to unimaginable pain.

My eyes remained locked on the gruesome spectacle as the relentless flames greedily consumed his flesh. The once formidable and cruel figure now withered away before my eyes, his body reduced to a charred husk of ash and smoldering embers. The unrelenting inferno showed no mercy and with a final, blinding burst of incandescent light, Malachar was reduced to nothing more than a fine, swirling dust.

"One down," I said, my voice steady and resolute, "one more to go."

Chapter Thirty-Nine

Haldir's expression remained utterly impassive, his demeanor an unsettling contrast to the maelstrom of emotions swirling within me. His face was a portrait of unruffled calm and unwavering composure, devoid of any visible signs of fear or concern for the lifeless form of his son that now lay scattered as ashes on the chamber floor. It was an infuriating sight and I found myself inexorably drawn towards him, the searing flames of my magic casting a fiery halo around me.

"Your son is dead," I hissed. "And you're next."

In response, Haldir remained a pillar of stoicism, his silence an infuriating provocation. His utter lack of reaction further fanned the flames of my anger, causing my clenched jaw to ache from the intensity of my fury.

"You have no idea what you're dealing with," he finally spoke, his voice as devoid of emotion as his expression.

"And neither do you," I growled.

"You are nothing but a child," he said condescendingly, his words laced with arrogance. "You have no idea what power lies within you."

"Power enough to kill you," I shot back, the flames of my magic intensifying in response.

As I advanced toward him intending to end his cruel reign, my magic erupted in a violent explosion of power. Haldir, however, seemed unimpressed. With a raised hand, he deflected the fiery onslaught effortlessly, the flames parting around him to dance harmlessly to the side.

"Is that all you've got?" he taunted, his voice dripping with arrogance. His smug expression and taunting words only fueled the rage burning within me.

The chamber was charged with an overwhelming tension, the standoff between Haldir and me reaching its climax. Behind me, Kaelan's voice broke through the silence, his words filled with determination.

"No, she's got us too," he declared.

I turned my head, a smile forming on my lips as I beheld the stalwart figures of Aerion, Thalion, and Kaelan, all poised and ready, their weapons gleaming in the flickering torchlight. Nyxen was still here too, my faithful familiar, ready to intervene for me.

Returning my attention to Haldir, I couldn't help but let a note of amusement creep into my voice. "You really think you can take on all of us?" I taunted.

Haldir's response was chillingly confident. He closed the distance between us with unhurried steps, his demeanor exuding an unsettling sense of calm and calculated intent. I refused to take a step back, standing my ground as he reached me.

"Possibly," he replied ominously, "But then again, I don't have to."

Before I could react, Haldir's hand shot out, seizing my arm with a vice-like grip. In an instant, a familiar sensation enveloped me and the world exploded into a blinding burst of brilliant light.

As my senses gradually returned, I found myself immersed in an eerie and disorienting environment. We were in a desolate, shadowy realm, a place where darkness seemed to stretch endlessly in every direction. There was no horizon, no visible landmarks, just an all-encompassing obscurity. The only source of illumination was two otherworldly moons that hung ominously in the sky, casting an eerie, bluish glow over the bleak landscape. It was unnatural and a ball of icy fear wormed its way into my stomach. The terrain beneath my feet was uneven, as though composed of shifting sands that whispered secrets of forgotten souls.

"Where are we?" I demanded, my voice filled with growing panic, as Haldir stood before me, his demeanor unsettlinglycomposed.

"In a realm far beyond our own," he replied with a twisted smile, his eyes gleaming with dark amusement.

"Daughter," The First Witch's voice suddenly echoed urgently in my mind, panicked and urgent. *"You must leave this place, and quickly. It was not meant for the living."*

"We're in the spirit realm?" I ventured, casting a wary glance around our surroundings. Haldir's grin only widened in response.

"Yes, indeed," he confirmed with chilling certainty. "Tell me, do you know what lurks in the spirit realm?" His voice took on a sinister edge and his eyes blazed into me.

"I know this place isn't meant for the living," I retorted, struggling to keep the fear from my voice.

"You are correct," he agreed, his voice growing even darker. "This is a realm where the spirits of the dead dwell, a place where souls wander aimlessly, lost in the ethereal void." He paused, his eyes gleaming with malice. "But there is another presence that hunts in this forsaken place—an entity known as the Grimgyre."

The ominous name sent shivers coursing down my spine, and I couldn't shake the foreboding feeling that accompanied it. I did not know what this creature was, but Haldir's sinister tone left no room for optimism.

"You will die here, and I will feast upon your soul," Haldir's voice dripped with malice, making my skin crawl.

In my desperate attempt to summon my magic, I found it to be unresponsive, leaving me with a sense of helplessness and dread. My hands trembled as I gazed at them in horror, the inky black tips of my fingers trembling.

"I can't use my magic here," I gasped, my voice quivering with fear.

"This realm is not yours to command. The only thing that will save you now is your own strength," Haldir replied, his words plunging me further into despair.

Desperation surged within me and I tightened my grip on Thalion's sword, ready to face Haldir, even in this dreadful place. But before I could make a move, a spine-chilling and unnatural roar echoed through the dark void, shaking me to my very core.

Haldir's gaze shifted past me and I swiftly turned to follow his line of sight. Emerging from the oppressive shadows was a monstrous figure, its massive form concealed by the darkness, rendering its features indistinguishable.

"That is the Grimgyre, it can sense the living trapped within this realm," Haldir declared, a sinister satisfaction tainting his words. "Run, or be devoured."

I heeded his warning without a second thought. Adrenaline surged through my veins as I bolted into the suffocating darkness, the pounding of my heart reverberating in my ears.

As I fled deeper into the unending abyss, Haldir's menacing laughter continued to echo through the darkness, gnawing at my fraying nerves like a relentless predator.

"You will not escape the Grimgyre," his voice taunted, his cruel words clinging to the air like a sinister omen.

Every step I took felt like a herculean effort, as if the ground beneath my feet had turned into quicksand, relentlessly pulling me downward. The world around me was shrouded in blackness, and the only sounds that reached my ears were the rapid thudding of my heart, the harsh rasp of my breath, and the ominous sounds of the Grimgrye's footfalls.

"Come to me," the creature's voice boomed, pounding through my very being. The sound was both deafening and haunting, an eerie call that sent a chill coursing through me.

As terror gripped me, I called out to Nyxen, hoping beyond hope for his aid. But my familiar remained absent, his presence eluding me in this nightmarish realm.

"He cannot find you here just yet, you must run until he can reach you. Run, Vale, run!" The voice of the First Witch sounded in my thoughts.

The echoes of Haldir's tormenting voice surrounded me, his words an unending barrage of ridicule and dread.

"You're alone. Your familiar can't hear your call. Just like your friends can't hear your cry for help. This place is for the dead and you're not meant to be here. Only the Grimgyre will find you," he said, each word a malicious taunt that chipped away at my resolve.

I struggled to regain my focus, my mind a tempest of fear and panic. The oppressive shadow of the Grimgyre's presence pressed down upon me, threatening to suffocate any semblance of hope.

"Don't give in, Vale," the First Witch's soothing voice echoed in my mind. *"You are strong, and you can overcome this."*

With her words of encouragement, I pressed on, determined to defy the stifling grip of despair that surrounded me.

The relentless pursuit of the Grimgyre was a nightmarish symphony of dread. Its labored breathing, hot and fetid, seemed to claw at my neck, urging me to run faster. My legs, already burning from the strenuous effort, ached with each stride.

"You cannot escape," the monster's thunderous proclamation reverberated through the eerie abyss. Its voice was a chilling sound, an ever-present reminder of the impending doom that lurked behind me.

"Fuck you!" I screamed back, my defiance a desperate plea to drown out the haunting echoes of despair.

I continued to sprint aimlessly through the all-consuming darkness, my desperation propelling me forward into the unknown. I had no destination, only the relentless need to evade the relentless predator pursuing me.

The darkness grew thicker, more suffocating as if it were closing in on me. The air turned colder and heavier, making each breath feel like an arduous task. My heart pounded in my chest, its rhythm a relentless drumbeat of fear. I wondered if the spirit realm was slowly draining my life force.

Then, a faint glimmer of light appeared in the distance, a beacon of hope in the abyss. It was feeble, but it was something—a chance to escape the relentless grasp of the Grimgyre.

"There is no escape, witch. You will never leave this place," Haldir's chilling voice slithered from behind me. The noxious scent of decay and rot reached my nostrils, a grim reminder of the monstrous entity closing in on me.

"You will die here," the Grimgyrew hissed, its words dripping with venom.

"Not today, you bastard," I whispered with a newfound resolve, determined to fight against the encroaching darkness and claw my way toward that distant glimmer of salvation.

Every ounce of strength within me was channeled into one final burst of speed. My muscles screamed with exhaustion and my lungs burned for oxygen, but I refused to relent. The beckoning light grew closer with each stride, my life hinging on reaching it in time.

"Fight, Vale. Don't let the darkness consume you," the reassuring voice of the First Witch whispered in my mind.

My outstretched hand strained for the light, my fingers trembling. It was almost within my grasp when an excruciating jolt of pain laced through my shoulder. The Grimgyre had ensnared me, its razor-sharp teeth biting into my flesh, violently yanking me backward and throwing me onto the ground.

I gazed up, dazed and disoriented, to find the creature looming over me—a great hulking beast on all fours with wicked black-tipped claws and serrated teeth dripping with my blood, its eyes twin blazing orbs radiating death.

"I will consume your soul," the creature snarled with a ravenous hunger that chilled my very soul.

"No!" I shrieked, a surge of sheer terror coursing through me.

As the Grimdark prepared to unleash its horrific fate upon me, a brilliant bolt of white light erupted from the surrounding darkness, striking the creature squarely in the chest. It reeled backward, releasing an anguished bellow that echoed through the spirit realm.

"Leave her be, demon," a commanding voice, undeniably familiar, rang out with unwavering authority.

The Grimgyre's guttural growl echoed through the shadowy abyss, a menacing tone that hinted at the horrors it had wrought in this eternal realm.

"I am the Guardian of the Veil and you will release the witch, or I will banish you back to the pit of hell from whence you came," the resolute voice declared, embodying an unwavering authority.

"You will not stop me, witch. I am the Grimgyre and I will have my prize," the creature hissed.

But the voice was unyielding. "You will not have this soul," it proclaimed.

As if summoned by the sheer force of will, a figure emerged from the twisting shadows. The First Witch stood before me, her presence radiating with an aura of power that imbued the darkness with a gentle, iridescent glow. Her form seemed to shimmer, a living manifestation of otherworldly might.

The First Witch extended her outstretched finger toward the Grimgyre. A bolt of pure, blinding white light shot forth, unerringly homing in on the creature's chest. The Grimgyre recoiled with a spine-chilling howl, a cacophony of agony and rage splitting the silence through the spirit realm. But the First Witch's relentless assault did not waver; she continued to assail the creature with her radiant bolts of light.

The Grimgyre, consumed by fury and desperation, retaliated with its own attacks, unleashing torrents of dark energy in a frantic bid for survival. Yet, despite the monster's ferocious onslaught, the First Witch remained standing and unaffected, effortlessly deflecting the blows with her unwavering might.

"You will not escape me," the Grimdark bellowed, its voice tinged with boundless fury and unquenchable hatred.

"You cannot win. The witch is under my protection and you will not have her," the First Witch declared, her voice imbued with a serene yet indomitable conviction. Sensing a glimmer of hope in this tumultuous abyss, she urged me to escape, her words laced with a heartfelt urgency. "Run, Vale, go!"

Every step I took felt like an eternity, each breath a battle against the looming darkness that sought to smother me. I was caught in a race against time, my very existence teetering on the precipice between life and the void as the spirit realm sapped my strength with each passing moment.

The distant light, once a beacon of hope, now seemed further away than ever, a tantalizing mirage that beckoned me forward with an alluring yet unattainable promise of escape.

Behind me, the First Witch and the Grimdark continued their otherworldly duel, their titanic clash resonating through the endless obsidian expanse. It was a clash of chaos and strife, a discordant ballet of powers beyond mortal comprehension. The First Witch's unwavering strength pierced through the abyss, serving as both a guiding light and an unyielding fortress against the encroaching darkness.

With every step I took, the light grew brighter, casting a warm and reassuring glow that pushed back the icy grasp of the spirit realm. The air itself seemed to come alive, whispering promises of salvation, of a return to the realm of the living.

Yet, just as hope began to kindle within me, Haldir materialized in my path and his demeanor transformed from cold detachment to seething fury. His very presence exuded a miasma of despair, a harbinger of doom that threatened to snuff out my flickering hope.

"You will not escape," he snarled, his voice a corrupted rasp.

"Like hell, I won't," I retorted, determination flooding my voice as I faced my tormentor.

Brandishing Thalion's sword, I held it with a white knuckle grip. The blade gleamed with a dim but defiant light, a symbol of my unyielding resolve.

"You're a fool if you think you can take me on," he sneered, his eyes ablaze.

"I may be a fool, but I'm not afraid of you," I declared.

"You should be," he warned, his voice dripping with menace.

"Not even close," I shot back. The darkness could not break me; I would defy it with every fiber of my being.

In the bleakness of the spirit realm, our deadly dance unfolded with a surreal grace. Every movement was amplified, every clash of steel resonating through the void. It was a duel between light and darkness, hope and despair.

I launched myself at Haldir, my sword cleaving through the air in a deadly arc. He moved with an eerie grace, his lithe form effortlessly sidestepping my blade, his disdain evident in every fluid motion.

"You are weak," he taunted, his voice dripping with contempt.

"You haven't seen anything yet," I retorted, the burning fire of defiance raging within me. I refused to let his words undermine my hope.

We circled one another, our blades flashing in the dim, ethereal light. The battle was fierce, the air charged with raw energy.

Haldir's movements were quick and precise, his sword a blur of calculated strikes. Yet, I matched his speed, parrying most of his attacks just before they connected.

"You think this is the end? This is only the beginning. You may be the First Witch, but do you really think you are still the only one?" he taunted, his words laced with a sinister promise.

His revelation struck me like a physical blow, momentarily catching me off guard. "What are you talking about?" I demanded, blocking another of his relentless assaults just in time.

"The coven of The Seven is rising. They will come for you and you will not be able to stop them," he declared, his voice seething with menace.

"You lie," I spat back, my heart pounding with disbelief and dread.

"It is the truth and you will not be able to deny it. Their power will surpass even yours, and you will be nothing but a footnote in history," he continued, his words cutting deep, sowing seeds of doubt in my mind.

"I will stop them," I vowed, though my voice quivered with uncertainty. The impact of the revelation jarred me, a grim reminder that even in the face of my current tormentor, an even greater threat loomed on the horizon.

The revelation of The Seven's resurgence was something I was not at all expecting. Questions swirled in my mind, a tempest of uncertainty and dread. How could this be? How could The Seven rise again? And why would they come after me?

"You are nothing but a speck in the grand scheme of things. Your magic is a pale imitation of true power and it will not save you," Haldir's words cut through the maelstrom of my thoughts, his voice oozing with disdain and hatred.

My voice wavered as I responded, disbelief and fear clawing at my throat. "You are wrong. I will stop them just as I will stop you."

But Haldir's cruel laughter rang out in the darkness, his mockery a chilling reminder of the perilous situation I found myself in. "No, you will not. Your fate is sealed. You will die here, among the dead, and no one will ever know your name."

I couldn't allow his words to become my reality. The fire of determination surged within me, a fierce resolve to defy my tormentor.

My grip on Thalion's sword tightened, newfound strength coursing through my veins. "You will not defeat me," I declared, my voice unwavering, a beacon of defiance in the shadows.

"You are nothing but a foolish girl." Haldir's retort was filled with scorn, his blade slicing through the air toward my face. I reacted with lightning reflexes, dodging his strike and countering with a fluid, practiced motion. My blade sang through the eerie void, an embodiment of my unyielding spirit.

"I am more than you can handle," I declared, determination lending power to my words.

Haldir's response was laced with venom and pride. "Are you sure about that?" he said with a cold smirk. The battle raged on, my resolve pitted against his arrogance, each clash of our swords echoing in the heart of the spirit realm.

Haldir's relentless assault continued, his blade a blur of deadly precision. Each strike was met with swift parries and calculated blocks as we danced in the heart of the spirit realm's darkness. The clash of our swords reverberated through the void, a relentless cadence that punctuated our battle.

As our blades sang with each collision, the First Witch's duel with the Grimgyre provided a haunting backdrop. Their struggle, too, sounded in the distance. Yet, amidst the cacophony, my focus remained fixed on the duel before me.

Haldir's skill was undeniable, his movements a testament to his mastery. But my determination outmatched his finesse, my resolve unbreakable in the face of his relentless assault. It was only a matter of time before I found an opening.

Finally, it came. My blade sliced across Haldir's chest and he staggered back, an expression of disbelief contorting his features. His voice trembled as he demanded, "How?"

A cold smile graced my lips as I answered him, throwing his own earlier words back in his face, "I am the First Witch, and you are nothing but a speck in the grand scheme of things."

With renewed determination, I lunged forward, thrusting my blade into his chest. "No," he managed to gasp, desperation tainting his voice. "This cannot be."

"It can, and it is," I declared, my tone cold and unyielding.

With a swift motion, I pulled my blade free from his chest, and Haldir fell to his knees, defeated and broken in the dark expanse of the spirit realm.

Haldir's defiance echoed through the darkness as he snarled, "I will not die here." With that, he shifted away, leaving me in a seething fury.

"No!" I cried out, my anger boiling over at his escape.

The Grimgyre's thunderous roar reverberated through the dark abyss, the ongoing battle between it and the First Witch still a distant tumult. I couldn't afford to linger. My priority was to return to the land of the living, and I had to do it swiftly.

I sprinted toward the ever-brightening light, my footfalls echoing in the desolate realm.

"Vale," Nyxen's voice suddenly filled in my mind as he materialized beside me.

"Nyx, I'm so glad you're here," I breathed, relief washing over me.

"Quickly," he said, an urgency in his voice that mirrored my own.

Together, we reached the radiant threshold of the living world and its comforting warmth enveloped us.

I glanced back one last time, the darkness and the relentless conflict between the First Witch and the Grimdark still engulfing that forsaken realm. Yet, I was safe now, embraced by the luminance of the living world.

The voice of the First Witch echoed within my thoughts, her words laden with a solemn warning.

"*Be careful, Vale. The Seven are rising, and their power will rival even mine. You must be prepared.*"

"I will," I said.

"*Do not forget who you are, and do not allow fear or doubt to cloud your judgment. You are strong, Vale. Stronger than you know,*" she declared, her voice brimming with conviction.

"I will not forget," I vowed, my voice resolute.

"*Good. Now go and beware the rising of The Seven,*" she concluded, her words piercing my mind as I turned away from the shadowy realm and stepped firmly back into the living world.

CHAPTER FORTY

I emerged from the portal onto a clifftop that overlooked a tumultuous, stormy sea. My surroundings were shrouded in an eerie, desolate beauty. The cliff's edge was jagged and worn, carved by the relentless assault of wind and waves. The sea stretched out as far as the eye could see, its waters dark and foreboding, like a vast, untamed beast.

The sky above was a swirling mass of heavy, gray clouds, pregnant with the promise of rain. The wind howled with an almost sentient rage, whipping my hair about and stinging my skin. The waves crashed against the rocks below with a thunderous roar, their white froth contrasting starkly with the dark depths of the sea.

The air was thick with the scent of salt, the briny tang of the ocean permeated every breath I took. It was a place of raw, elemental power, where nature's fury held dominion.

Amidst this dramatic backdrop, I turned to Nyxen, my voice carrying over the wind's wail. "Where are we, Nyxen?"

He responded with a simple, *"Do not know."*

Just then, the shifting shadows coalesced before me and Kaelan materialized, his face contorted with pure panic.

"Vale!" he cried out, crashing into me and enveloping my body with his strong, desperate embrace.

"Ow," I winced, feeling the pain from the wound on my back flare up as Kaelan clung to me, unwilling to let go.

"I thought you were dead, I thought you were dead," he repeated over and over in shock. "I thought he had killed you, Vale, that you were gone forever. I couldn't feel you anymore and then..." he paused, drawing in a deep steadying breath, "The part of my soul wrapped around yours withered away," he confessed, his voice muffled into my shoulder, his body trembling against mine.

He finally pulled back, his hands coming up to cup my face. Shock surged through me, leaving me momentarily speechless as I stared into his eyes, the emotions between us swirling like the sea below us.

"I'm fine," I said, my voice shaky as I began to process the events that had just taken place. With a deep, quivering breath, the weight of survival hit me like a stone, and the adrenaline that had fueled me started to ebb away. "At least, I'm alive, I mean."

"You're alive," Kaelan repeated, his voice still trembling. "I don't care that you hate me, I don't care that you are with those two Fae. You're alive and I love you."

I hesitated, my heart racing, and my trembling hands betraying my emotional turmoil.

Kaelan's lips descended upon mine, his kiss searing and demanding. He enveloped me in his arms, careful of my hurt shoulder, his body warm and solid against mine.

"I can't lose you, Vale," he whispered, his lips brushing mine as he spoke. "I can't live in a universe where you don't exist."

"Kaelan," I breathed, finally allowing myself to surrender to the flood of emotions that had been bottled up for so long.

I pulled him closer, my fingers clutching the edges of his jacket as our lips met in a passionate, desperate kiss. It was a kiss filled with the intensity of pent-up longing and the overwhelming relief of a reunion.

My fingers tangled in his hair, pulling him even nearer. I needed him desperately, like oxygen after being deprived for too long. The love I had tried to deny surged back to the surface, undeniable and all-consuming.

The wind howled around us and the sea churned below, mirroring the tempestuous emotions we shared.

"I thought I lost you," Kaelan said, his voice hoarse with emotion.

"I thought I was dead," I admitted, tears forming in my eyes. "Haldir took me to the spirit realm."

"How did you escape?" Kaelan asked, his eyes locked onto mine, searching for answers.

"The First Witch, she saved me," I replied, my voice catching with the lingering shock of my miraculous rescue.

"What?" Kaelan's eyes widened with incredulity.

"She came to me. She saved me," I repeated, my own disbelief mirrored in my words.

"How?" Kaelan pressed.

I shook my head, still struggling to comprehend it fully. "I don't know how, but she did. And she told me something." The memory of her words sent a shiver down my spine.

"What did she tell you?" Kaelan asked, concern etched across his features.

"She said that the coven of The Seven is rising and that their power will rival hers," I explained, my voice trembling slightly.

"That can't be true," Kaelan protested. "The Seven have been gone for centuries."

"But what if they're not? What if they're coming back and what if their power is greater than mine?" I asked him, panic threatening to overwhelm me.

"You're the strongest witch I've ever known," Kaelan stated firmly, his eyes filled with unwavering conviction.

"What if it's not enough?" I couldn't help but voice my fear, uncertainty gripping my heart.

"We'll find a way, Vale," Kaelan declared. "I promise you, we'll find a way."

His lips brushed against mine, the touch reassuring and warm, a promise sealed with a kiss.

The world shifted around us and as the shadows released their hold, we found ourselves back in the courtyard of Haldir's castle. Chaos reigned in every direction, soldiers scurrying about, taking orders, and trying to restore some semblance of order. The battle, it seemed, had reached its conclusion.

"What happened while I was gone?" I inquired, my eyes scanning the tumultuous scene before us.

Kaelan turned to me. "The Fae army and Wren's forces successfully overtook the castle. It's ours now."

I walked further into the center of the courtyard. The grounds were a macabre tableau, littered with the lifeless forms of fallen soldiers. Blood soaked the earth, staining it a deep crimson, almost black. The acrid stench of death pervaded every breath we took.

"I need to tend to the wounded," I declared, my voice barely above a whisper, but the words carried the weight of an unshakable determination.

Kaelan reached out, his hand resting gently on my unwounded shoulder. "Vale, you've been through so much. Perhaps you should rest for a moment. The healing can wait."

I turned to meet his gaze, my eyes resolute. "No, Kaelan. Every moment we waste, more lives may be lost. I'm stronger now and I understand my limits."

He studied me for a moment, the concern in his eyes giving way to a reluctant acceptance.

"Okay," he finally conceded. "Let's start by finding the others."

I gave Kaelan a determined nod and together, we stepped onto the grim battlefield. The ground was a haunting tapestry of death and destruction, with fallen soldiers strewn about like discarded pawns on a macabre chessboard. The relentless buzzing of flies was a morbid symphony that filled the air, a testament to the brutal aftermath of the battle.

As we ventured deeper into the heart of the castle, the echoes of our footsteps reverberated off the cold stone walls. The fortress bore the scars of conflict, with broken banners and shattered armor fragments scattered about.

Eventually, we reached the heart of the castle, the grand throne room where my friends, including Wren, had come together. Their hushed conversation ceased as I entered, and the expressions on their faces conveyed shock and relief.

"Vale!" Wren's voice rang out and he rushed forward to embrace me. Thalion and Aerion followed suit, their expressions a blend of emotions that I couldn't quite decipher.

"When Kaelan left, we didn't know what to think, but we held onto hope," Wren began, his voice cracking with emotion. He held my gaze for a moment before hugging me again.

"Are you alright? What happened?" Thalion inquired, concern for me etching his features.

I took a deep breath, steadying myself, and proceeded to recount the events of my journey through the spirit realm and my encounter with the First Witch. Their rapt attention did not waver as they hung on to every word and I could see the awe and disbelief in their eyes.

"So, you met the First Witch in the spirit realm?" Thalion asked, his voice tinged with amazement.

I nodded solemnly. "Yes, and she saved me. I wouldn't be standing here if it weren't for her," I admitted, my voice trembling slightly with the realization.

"That's incredible," Aerion marveled, his eyes wide with wonder.

I took another deep breath, knowing that there was more to share. "There's something else," I added, my tone growing more serious. "She said that the coven of The Seven is rising and that their power will rival hers."

The implications of the revelation about The Seven stretched in the silence surrounding us, casting a somber shadow over our group. Wren's question, filled with concern and disbelief, resonated through the grand throne room.

"How is that possible?" he asked, his voice reflecting the astonishment that we all felt.

"I don't know," I replied honestly. "But we need to be ready, whatever comes."

Wren's expression hardened, his jaw set with determination. "We will."

Aerion, ever practical and pragmatic, shifted the focus of our conversation. "Haldir is still alive then?" he asked, his tone measured.

I nodded, a hint of regret coloring my features. "I'm afraid so. He escaped the spirit realm, but I don't know where he went."

Thalion's eyes narrowed, his voice a dark promise. "We'll find him. And when we do, he'll pay for what he's done."

Aerion, equally resolute, chimed in. "He'll tear him limb from limb. Slowly. Until he's begging for death."

A low, primal growl escaped Kaelan's lips. It was a sound that promised vengeance and retribution.

Taking charge of the situation, I spoke up. "Right now, I need to focus on healing the worst of the wounded."

Wren, having processed the shock of my return, decided to leave in search of Venna and Harker. He offered me one more quick hug before striding off with purpose.

Once he was gone, I turned my attention back to Kaelan, Aerion, and Thalion. The three men stood there, their expressions expectant.

Another matter needed to be addressed before I could attend to the wounded. Drawing a deep breath, I mentally prepared myself for the conversation that was about to unfold.

"I love all three of you," I began, the words heavy with sincerity.

The silence stretched, each second feeling like an eternity. I met the eyes of each of the three men before me, conveying the depth of my feelings.

"And I want to be with all three of you," I said bluntly, not wanting to draw this out.

Kaelan appeared surprised, his features reflecting his astonishment. Thalion's eyes flickered with a myriad of emotions and Aerion remained enigmatic, arms crossed, an unreadable expression on his face.

Kaelan was the first to break the silence, his voice wavering slightly as he asked, "How would that even work?"

My throat tightened as I answered, "We would have to make it work. I can't choose."

Thalion stepped closer, his warm hand cupping my cheek. "Vale, if this is what you want, then we will make it work."

Aerion, always thoughtful and measured in his responses, nodded in agreement.

I turned my attention to Kaelan, awaiting his response. His eyes bore into mine, torn between his emotions. After a moment of contemplation, he spoke with a somber tone, recounting the anguish of my disappearance, "Today, I thought I would never see you again. You were torn from me and not even the blood bond could tell me where you were. I will do whatever you want if it means I never have to be parted from you again."

Relief surged through me, a radiant smile breaking through the uncertainty that had weighed on my heart.

"Okay, then it's settled," I said, my voice carrying a mix of resolution and reassurance. "We'll figure it out as we go."

Leaning into Aerion, I pressed my lips to his in a gentle, affectionate kiss, a tender moment shared between us. Then, I turned my attention to Thalion, repeating the gesture with him, our connection speaking volumes despite the silence. Finally, I approached Kaelan, who met me with a soft kiss, his hand gripping the back of my neck. The promise of a future worth pursuing.

For a fleeting moment, the world seemed to fall back into place, the harmony between us momentarily restoring a sense of balance.

However, the pressing need to attend to the wounded couldn't be forgotten. With reluctance, I pulled away from Kaelan, and together, the four of us made our way back out to the courtyard, ready to face the challenges that lay ahead.

EPILOGUE

As my eyes fluttered open, I found myself alone in my room at the palace. The soft, sunlit ambiance seemed to cast a surreal light on the events of the past. For a fleeting moment, I allowed myself to entertain the thought that it had all been a nightmarish dream – the kidnapping, the torture, and the harrowing battle against Haldir in the spirit realm. But reality soon pressed in, reminding me that it had been all too real, and yet, I was still alive.

A dull ache emanated from my shoulder as I gingerly sat up in bed, muscles stretching as if to reclaim their vitality. The toll of my recent trials had weighed heavily on my body and mind, and I hadn't even realized how exhausted I was. My captivity, healing the wounded, the fierce battle, and my confrontation with Haldir had left me feeling hollowed out.

Turning my attention to the window, I was greeted by a pic-turesque winter scene – a brilliant sun illuminating a clear blue sky. It felt as if life itself were beginning anew, a beacon of hope amidst the darkness that had recently engulfed us, yet I was standing still.

The door creaked open and Aerion entered the room, a tray of food balanced carefully in his hands. His relief was evident in his voice as he greeted me. "Vale, you're awake."

The sound of my stomach growling betrayed my hunger. "Please tell me all of that is for me."

Aerion chuckled, a warmth in his eyes as he set the tray down on the bed before me.

"Yes, all of it is for you," he confirmed, amused. As I eagerly began to devour the meal, Aerion couldn't help but laugh again. "Slow down," he teased. "It's not going anywhere."

With my appetite voraciously sated, I finally managed to speak, though my words came out somewhat muffled due to my mouth being full.

"Sorry, I'm starving," I said, offering a sheepish grin.

Aerion regarded me with a concerned expression, his eyes trailing over the crisscross of scars all over my body, "Do you feel alright?"

Swallowing my food, I thought carefully about my response. "I'm fine," I assured him, my voice a bit hoarse. "Just a little sore and tired."

Aerion's gaze locked onto mine. "I don't think you're being truthful," he admitted softly.

I sighed, my shoulders drooping as I set down my fork. He was right, of course. The truth was, I was still deeply shaken by everything that had happened.

Despite the victory I had achieved, I felt empty inside. The burden of all the death and destruction I had witnessed still weighed heavily on my heart and the guilt of knowing that I was partly responsible for it lingered like a shadow, always there in the back of my mind. The torture I had endured had also left an indelible mark on my psyche, a constant reminder of the fragility of life.

But perhaps more than anything, I was haunted by the knowledge that Haldir had survived. My attempt to destroy him had failed, and he was still out there, a looming threat to the safety and stability of the realm.

In a way, the uncertainty was even more unsettling than the thought of him returning. As long as his fate remained unknown, my mind would conjure up endless possibilities, each more terrifying than the last.

I couldn't bring myself to look at Aerion. The words tumbled out of my mouth in a jumbled mess. "I'm so sorry, Aerion. I know I've caused you and everyone else so much pain. I never wanted any of this to happen."

Aerion's face fell as the weight of my confession hit him. "Vale," he whispered, his voice laced with a deep, sorrowful understanding. "It wasn't your fault. None of it."

A single tear trickled down my cheek. I didn't bother wiping it away.

"Maybe not," I murmured. "But I'm still responsible."

Aerion pulled me close, wrapping his arms around me and holding me tightly.

"I'm just glad you're alive," he said, his voice catching in his throat.

I melted into his embrace, my own tears flowing freely now. "So am I," I replied.

The warmth of his touch and the sound of his beating heart grounded me, helping to temporarily repress the darkness that had settled within my soul.

"I was so worried about you," Aerion said softly, pulling back and gazing down at me with tender affection.

"I'm here now," I replied, mustering a weak smile. "And I'm not going anywhere."

"Good," Aerion replied. "Because I'm not letting you out of my sight."

I nodded. I had no desire to be apart from him, or anyone else I loved, ever again.

"What happens now?" I asked.

Aerion's response was reassuring as he reached for my hand, his fingers entwining with mine. "I don't know," he admitted honestly, "But whatever it is, we'll face it together."

"Together," I repeated, a sense of calm washing over me at his words.

The door swung open once more, and Thalion entered the room, his voice filled with relief as he addressed me. "You're awake."

"Yes, and full thanks to Aerion," I said.

Thalion settled onto the edge of the bed, his hand resting gently on my leg. "I'm glad."

With a tender affection, I leaned forward, capturing Thalion's lips in a gentle kiss. His response was immediate, his mouth warm and velvety against mine.

As our lips parted, I couldn't help but voice the question that had been haunting me, the same one I had asked Aerionearlier. "What happens now?" I questioned.

Thalion's expression shifted, becoming more serious as he considered the weight of his words. "Well, we now have a whole new court to rule," he began.

The realization of the responsibilities that lay before us dawned on me. "Oh, yeah," I murmured, my gaze drifting as I contemplated the enormity of what we faced.

Thalion's eyes held mine, his voice dropping to a low, intense register. "It's your court, Vale. You will be queen," he declared, his words leaving me stunned and wide-eyed.

"Are you serious?" I blurted out, my astonishment laid bare.

"Completely," he said, his gaze unwavering.

I found myself momentarily at a loss for words, the burden of the future settling heavily on my scarred shoulders.

"It will take some time," Thalion continued, his tone now focused and resolute, "but we will rebuild the kingdom."

With a resigned nod, I acknowledged the daunting work that lay ahead. "It will be a lot of work," I admitted, recognizing the undeniable truth of his statement.

Thalion concurred, his unwavering determination underscoring his words. "It will," he agreed.

As I sat there, I contemplated the path that lay ahead, both for me and the kingdom we were destined to rebuild.

"I guess we have a lot to do," I remarked, my gaze wandering around the room.

"You'll have help," Aerion reassured me, his voice carrying a comforting tone that eased some of the anxiety building within me.

"I'll be there too." Kaelan's voice echoed from the doorway and I turned to see him standing there.

"Thank you," I said, my gratitude genuine as I met his gaze. The past was a complicated tangle, but in this moment, it felt like we were all moving forward together.

Kaelan nodded, his actions speaking louder than words as he walked into the room and settled on the edge of the bed.

I took a deep breath, allowing the warmth of their presence to wash over me. The weight of responsibility and leadership was daunting, but I wasn't alone. I was surrounded by people who cared about me.

"So, when do we start?" I asked, a small smile curling my lips.

"As soon as you're ready," Aerion replied, his grip on my hand reassuring.

"I'm ready," I declared, the resolve settling firmly within me.

"Good," Thalion chimed in, his mouth curling into a warm smile.

"Let's go make history," Kaelan added, his eyes bright with anticipation, and the future seemed full of possibilities.

I sat alone in my room within the palace later that day, a leather-bound book resting in my hands. The tome was weathered, its pages worn by time, but it held secrets of immense importance. It was the very book that Aerion and Thalion had presented to me, containing the elusive knowledge of how the First Witch had managed to create more witches, a concept I found both fascinating and daunting.

With gentle reverence, I turned the pages until I found the passage that spoke of the creation process. The words were cryptic, filled with ancient wisdom that hinted at a power far beyond my understanding. As I read, I couldn't help but feel a connection to Rowena, the First Witch herself, whose legacy now rested within me.

"Rowena?" I called out to her, my thoughts reaching out in a gentle, hesitant summons.

Her response came as a whisper within my mind, her presence familiar and comforting. *"Yes, daughter?"*

I took a moment to gather my thoughts, my fingers tracing the words on the page. "Tell me more about how you created more witches," I asked, my voice a soft plea for guidance and understanding.

"It involves blood magic and can be a complicated ritual," she explained, emphasizing the caution in her words.

Despite the uncertainty that warred within me, my determination remained unwavering. "I'm willing to try," I replied, the prospect of acquiring this ancient knowledge both thrilling and intimidating.

A hint of apprehension tinged Rowena's mental voice as she cautioned me further. *"You must be careful. This is not something to be undertaken lightly. The ritual is powerful and the consequences if done incorrectly can be dire."*

I nodded solemnly. "I understand," I assured her, even as a surge of anxiety coursed through me.

With Rowena's guidance, she began to share the intricate details of the ritual, her presence providing clarity and insight. Her words flowed through my mind like a sacred chant, etching the steps into my consciousness.

Closing the leather-bound book with reverence, I set it aside. Rising from my seat, a newfound sense of purpose filled me. I understood the responsibility that rested on my shoulders, knowing that the fate of not only the Fae realm but also the mortal realm hung in the balance.

I reached for the grimoire that Harker had thoughtfully crafted for me. As I began to transcribe each step of the intricate ritual, I contemplated the individuals I would approach, knowing that I needed others to stand with me in this perilous endeavor. If the rumors of the Seven's resurgence were true and their intentions were evil, then unity and strength would be our greatest assets.

The knock on my door was unexpected, breaking the trance that had enveloped me. "Come in," I called out.

Kaelan's entrance was like a calming breeze on a warm day. His presence alone had the power to soothe my frayed nerves. "Hey," he greeted, his voice soft and gentle, his gaze taking in the sight of me engrossed in the ancient tome. "Are you busy?"

I glanced up, a wistful smile gracing my lips. "Just trying to learn how to create more witches," I replied casually, my hand gesturing towards the worn leather-bound book that held the secrets of Rowena's power.

Kaelan's expression shifted, a flicker of concern passing over his features. "Really? Are you sure you want to do that?" he asked.

I nodded firmly. "If we're going to stand against The Seven and stop whatever their plans are, then yes, I am sure," I affirmed, my conviction resolute.

He inhaled deeply as if bracing himself for what lay ahead, before finally nodding in agreement. "Do you have anyone in mind?" he asked.

A rush of anticipation coursed through me as I nodded, my heart beating faster with each passing second. "I do."

"Who?" he pressed, his curiosity piqued.

I met his gaze, my resolve unwavering.

"Ava, for starters, the Otherworlder currently taking care of the bookshop."

Kaelan arched an eyebrow. "Interesting choice," he remarked.

"She's strong-willed and brave. She was willing to put herself at risk to protect the bookstore and its contents."

"You have a point," Kaelan conceded, his lips curling into a knowing smirk.

"Other than her, I have no idea who else. But maybe she has some ideas."

Kaelan paused thoughtfully before responding.

"I can't imagine anyone else I would want fighting alongside us," he replied.

I sighed, running a hand through my hair. "It's just...the stakes are so high. If this fails, the realms could be plunged into chaos. There would be no stopping the Seven."

"It won't fail," he promised, his voice steady and strong.

The confidence in his words eased some of the worries that plagued me.

"Thank you, Kaelan," I said softly.

He leaned down and placed a tender kiss on my forehead.

"Get some rest," he urged, his tone gentle.

As he stepped away, I reached out, placing my hand on his arm, "Stay?" I requested, the desire to feel his presence beside me was almost overwhelming.

"Always," he agreed, a soft smile lighting up his face.

Later that night, I found myself lying in bed beside Kaelan, the dim glow of the moon casting a soft silver light upon us. We had faced countless challenges, and the weight of the world had felt unbearable at times, but now, we were here together, our souls intertwined like the stars in the night sky.

Kaelan's gentle touch brushed a stray strand of hair back from my face, his fingers warm against my skin. His eyes, deep and full of emotion, met mine, and he whispered softly, "I missed you."

His words washed over me and my heart swelled with contentment. "I missed you too," I confessed, my voice filled with honesty. The truth was, I had tried to deny it, to suppress my feelings, to fight against the tide of emotions that threatened to overwhelm me. But, in the quiet moments when I was alone with my thoughts, his absence had always lingered in the back of my mind, a constant ache that refused to fade.

Our journey had taken us to the brink of despair, and I had faced horrors I couldn't have imagined. Yet, through it all, one thing had remained steadfast—the love I held for Kaelan. Now, as I lay beside him, it felt as if we were finally home.

"I don't know if you can comprehend how much I missed you, Vale," Kaelan's voice, laced with longing and sincerity, wrapped around me like a warm embrace. I listened intently, knowing that each syllable carried a piece of his heart. "Every day my thoughts were consumed by the memory of you, of your skin on mine, your lips. I had never felt more empty, hollowed out. But now, being here with you, it was worth it. I'd wait a thousand more years for you if I had to."

His confession, so raw and heartfelt, sent my heart soaring. It was as if the universe had conspired to bring us back together, and in that moment, nothing else mattered. Leaning forward, I closed the gap between us, my lips seeking his in a gentle yet fervent kiss. Our bodies pressed together, his warmth seeping into my very being, leaving only the two of us in our private haven.

As our kiss deepened, our passion flared, reigniting a connection that had never truly dimmed. In the intimate embrace of the night, we surrendered to our desires.

We had faced trials and tribulations that had tested the limits of our strength, but through it all, Kaelan's love had remained unshaken. As we lost ourselves in each other, I felt the bond between us solidify, binding us together in an unbreakable union that transcended the realms.

In that fleeting moment, as our hearts beat in unison, I knew with absolute certainty that, regardless of the challenges that awaited us in the future, we would face them together. The depth of our love was a force that could not be reckoned with, and it would guide us through whatever lay ahead.

As the weight of the day began to pull at my eyelids, and the comforting lull of sleep beckoned me, Kaelan's words echoed in my mind, a sweet song that serenaded me into dreams. With a soft, contented smile on my lips, I whispered back, "I love you too."

Pronunciation Guide

Names

Thalion- Thal-E-on

Aerion- Air-E-on

Haldir- Hal-Dear

Malachar- Mal-a-car

Lyra- Ly-R-ah

Grimgyre- grim-Jie-er

Places

Virelium- Vi-rEE-lee-um

Caeluxa- key-LUX-ah

Aurumport- Or-um-port

Terralux- tear-ah-lux

Aquavale- ah-qua-vale

Caelistis- Kay-list-us

Serenium- sir-rEE-knee-um

Acknowledgements

This book would not have been possible without the support and encouragement of countless individuals whose contributions have been invaluable. First and foremost, I must express my heartfelt gratitude to my family for their unwavering belief in my work and their understanding during the many hours spent away from them.

A special thanks to my alpha readers, Sam and Erin, for their critical eyes and honest feedback. Your suggestions and enthusiasm were instrumental in refining the story's flow and depth. Your belief in my aspirations has often been the spark that kept the embers of my determination alight during moments of doubt.

A profound thank you to my circle of friends, who have stood by me throughout this journey. Alex and Lauren, your unwavering support and enduring faith in my dreams have been a source of strength and motivation.

I am also grateful to the members of Between the Pages, whose camaraderie and constructive critiques were always encouraging and often enlightening. Sharing this journey with you has been an inspiring experience. Crabs for all of you!

And to my readers, both new and old, thank you for joining me on this adventure. Your enthusiasm and support are the reasons I write, and I am deeply thankful for each and every one of you who picks up this book.

Last but never least, I would like to express my endless gratitude to Nathan, who has been my rock, my sounding board, and my constant source of joy. Your love and support have sustained me through the challenges and triumphs, and this book is as much yours as it is mine.

Also By Ember East

Daughter of Realms

About the Author

Ember East lives in Murfreesboro, TN, but was raised in Western KY. She spends her days reading, writing, crocheting, and taking care of her three feral children and her dog. She is AuD-HD, and wants all of her neurodivergent readers to know that following your dreams is possible with hard work. She's dreamed of seeing her name on the spines of the books that line her shelves since she was nine years old, and now she isn't even using her real name, what a schmuck. She plans to write many more books for as long as possible.

www.ingramcontent.com/pod-product-compliance
Lightning Source LLC
Chambersburg PA
CBHW031235310726
48971CB00004B/1026